Dreaming of
Mr. Darcy

VICTORIA CONNELLY

sourcebooks
landmark

Published by Sourcebooks Landmark, an imprint of Sourcebooks, Inc.
P.O. Box 4410, Naperville, Illinois 60567-4410
(630) 961-3900
FAX: (630) 961-2168
www.sourcebooks.com

Library of Congress Cataloging-in-Publication Data

Connelly, Victoria.
  Dreaming of Mr. Darcy / by Victoria Connelly.
    p. cm.
  1. Women illustrators—Fiction. 2. Motion picture producers and directors—Fiction. 3. Actors—Fiction. 4. Triangles (Interpersonal relations)—Fiction. 5. Lyme Regis (England)—Fiction. 6. Austen, Jane, 1775-1817—Fiction. I. Title.
  PR6103.O547D74 2012
  823'.92—dc22

2011040667

Printed and bound in the United States of America
VP 10 9 8 7 6 5 4 3 2 1

To my dear friend, Deborah, with love

'Is not general incivility the very essence of love?'

—Elizabeth Bennet, *Pride and Prejudice*

Prologue

Peggy Sullivan leant forward in an attempt to get the pillows behind her just right.

'It's my eyes I miss the most,' she said to the young woman sitting by the side of the bed. 'I wasn't too bothered when my legs went. I was too tired to walk around much anyways. I didn't even mind when my right ear went last month, but I do miss my eyes.'

The young woman leant forward and patted her hand.

'It's so kind that you come and read to me, Kay,' Peggy said.

'It's my pleasure.'

'It can't be easy for you, my dear. Coming here, I mean.'

Kay looked at Peggy for a moment before answering. 'It wasn't at first. I kept seeing Mum everywhere—sitting in the conservatory gazing out at the gardens or serving everyone tea in the sitting room.'

'We all miss her so much. She always loved taking care of everybody—just like you do.'

Kay nodded. 'She used to call me "Little Mother" when I was growing up.'

Peggy smiled, but then her expression changed to one of bemusement. 'How you came to work at Barnum and Mason's, I'll never understand.'

'It was the first job I was offered,' Kay said with a shrug. 'I took it thinking I'd be there only a little while. I was hoping—'

'Someone would discover your paintings,' Peggy interrupted.

'Yes.'

'They're taking their time, I must say.'

They were silent for a moment, and Kay looked out of Peggy's window. She was on the ground floor of The Pines and overlooked the communal garden, which was shivering under a layer of early snow. The poor Cyclamen were doing their best to survive, but one more fall of snow, and they'd be buried alive, Kay thought.

Buried. The word sent a shiver through her. It had been only a month since her mother had been buried in the local churchyard after a brief but devastating illness. She'd been sixty-seven—not old by today's standards—and Kay missed her more than she could say. Perhaps that was why she was spending time with Peggy. She'd met her whilst visiting her mother, and the two of them had clicked. Both had a profound love of the novels of Jane Austen, and when Kay had discovered that Peggy was blind—a fact that she'd kept marvellously hidden—Kay had offered to read to her.

Peggy never seemed to have any visitors, and Kay couldn't quite give up visiting The Pines.

'I do wish I could see your paintings,' Peggy suddenly said.

'I do too, Peggy.'

'Tell me about your new ones.'

'I've got only one new one. I'm afraid work's been a bit hectic, and—'

'That ratbag Roger still working you late?'

Kay grinned.

'I remember him when he was a lad. I knew his father. Lived

in my road. Bullies—both of them. You mustn't let him push you around, Kay.'

'I don't.'

Peggy nodded. 'Because I'll have words with him, if he's bullying you. I've got one of them portable phone jobbies. It'll only take one call.'

'It's all right. There's no need to call him.'

Peggy shifted forward, and Kay got up to rearrange her pillows. 'So, tell me about your picture.'

Kay's eyes took on a wistful look as she thought about her latest painting.

'You know the last chapter of *Persuasion* we read together? That moment when Anne Elliot and Captain Wentworth see each other for the first time since he went away?'

'I love that scene,' Peggy said, her face glowing with the pleasure of remembering it.

'I chose that moment when Jane Austen writes "a thousand feelings rushed on Anne".'

'*Wonderful!*' Peggy said with enthusiasm.

'And "a bow, a curtsey passed".'

'Yes, yes!' Peggy said. 'I can see it now. All those pent-up emotions they still have for each other. Oh, I *wish* I could see it.'

'I've always wanted to capture that moment when their eyes meet,' Kay said, tucking a strand of toffee-coloured hair behind her ear. 'It's fleeting, yet so much happens in it.'

'Which scene are you illustrating next?'

'One of the Lyme Regis ones. I want to paint that wonderful seafront with the sweep of the Cobb. I only wish I could visit it.'

'You've never been to Lyme?'

'No,' Kay said, her eyes taking on a dreamy look again. 'I've always imagined myself living by the sea one day, and I think Lyme would be just the place to be.'

'Then what are you doing in landlocked Hertfordshire?' Peggy asked. 'I mean now that you don't have any family ties.'

'My job's here. My house is here.'

'Oh, rot!' Peggy said. 'I know it's a terrible cliché, but if you don't take charge of your life, nobody's going to do it for you. Think of Anne Elliot and all those years she wasted.'

'But I've got a mortgage to pay. I'm kind of stuck here.'

Peggy's mouth narrowed. 'I don't like to hear such excuses. If you want to live near the sea then you should. It's as simple as that.'

'I wish it were,' Kay said. 'I really wish it were.'

Chapter 1

THAT NIGHT, KAY ASHTON DREAMT OF MR DARCY AGAIN. IT wasn't the first time, of course, and it wouldn't be the last. She often dreamt about her favourite fictional hero, and she often *day*dreamed about him too. How many dull afternoons in the office had been cheered up by imagining the sudden arrival of Mr Darcy? He'd come striding in across the carpeted reception, his eyes fixed on Kay.

'In vain have I struggled,' he'd say, confessing his love to her there and then and sweeping her up in his arms, telling her to leave her desk behind and run away to Pemberley with him.

If only I could, Kay thought.

It was funny that she should be dreaming about Mr Darcy, because she'd been drawing Captain Wentworth for the last few weeks now. Darcy had been the main subject of her last book—a collection of drawings in pen, and watercolour paintings of scenes from *Pride and Prejudice*.

She couldn't remember the first time she'd drawn Mr Darcy, but she'd been putting pen to paper all her life, sketching little scenes of handsome princes and fairy tale princesses which, as she'd grown older, had become heroes and heroines from the books she read. It was a world she'd loved diving into, because the real one around her had been a cold and cruel place.

Kay had been ten years old when her father had left her. She'd been upset and confused and had watched as her mother crumbled before her. The two of them clung to each other and slowly built a new life for themselves, but just as they were getting used to being just the two of them, the unthinkable happened. Her father returned.

Life had been turned upside down once again, and Kay was forgotten in the space of a moment as her parents got on with the business of fixing their marriage.

It hadn't been easy. Kay often wondered how her parents managed to stay together for so long, because they seemed to spend most of their time fighting. She could hear them shouting from her bedroom, even when she closed the door and hid her head under her pillow. They shouted at night too, when they thought she was asleep, their voices only slightly dimmed by the thin wall that separated their bedrooms.

Her mother always looked washed out and red-eyed in the morning, whilst her father would be silent and morose, his eyes avoiding hers as she ate her breakfast before school.

Then, after a year of endless fighting, he left again. This time, it was for good. There was no forwarding address, and he never rang. It was as if he forgot that he was a husband and a father.

Kay, who already spent most of the time with her head in a book, retreated in to her fictional world like never before and had never really surfaced since. For her, reality was only made bearable by the existence of novels, and her beloved stories and sketches got her through the traumas of a dozen father figures, the trials of her own string of disastrous relationships, and the boredom of her job at Barnum and Mason. It had been the one constant of her life.

The strangest thing was that Kay never let the experience of her parents' marriage affect her own views of relationships. She still believed in the possibility of love and that her soul mate was out there just waiting to be found. Maybe it was a notion she picked up from the books she read, but she truly believed it.

She looked at her collection of illustrations. It had been sitting on her desk for weeks now, and she didn't quite know what to do with it next. She supposed she should send it to publishers, but what if they rejected it? What if all her hopes and dreams of seeing it in print came to nothing? Leaving it sitting on the desk might not result in it seeing the light of day, but at least her dreams remained intact that way.

The Illustrated Darcy, she called it, because although she'd made sketches and paintings of all the main characters and major scenes, the emphasis remained on Darcy. He was a hero for all time, wasn't he? Kay often wondered if Jane Austen had known it when she created him. Had she known the power of her very special hero? Had Jane's sister, Cassandra, said, 'Wow, Jane! You've done it. There will never be another hero to match this one.'

Kay often wondered what it was about Mr Darcy that fed the female imagination so much. There was a constant need for the man. The films and TV adaptations were proof of that. The merchandise, too. One only had to take a trip to the shop at the Jane Austen House Museum in Chawton or the Jane Austen Centre in Bath to see the image of Darcy staring handsomely out from the shelves. Well, Colin Firth, really. 'The face that launched a thousand bookmarks,' Kay said to herself with a smile.

There was something so special about Austen's heroes that had never been matched in other fiction. Kay had once—very briefly—gone through a Brontë faze, but pulling your lover's hair out and then digging up her grave wasn't really the mark of a hero, was it? You wouldn't get Mr Darcy prowling around graveyards in the middle of the night.

Ah, could there ever be a hero to match Fitzwilliam? she wondered.

Getting out of bed, Kay grabbed a sheet of paper and sketched a few lines, desperately trying to recall the man from her dreams. It was always the face that eluded her. She could capture the stride, the movement of the man, and the clothes were always easy to remember, but the face always seemed to hover on the outskirts of her consciousness. What did the perfect hero look like?

She sketched on, covering sheet after sheet, her stomach rumbling in a bid to be fed, but nothing was more important than her drawing. Food could wait; drink could wait; but art could never wait.

The telephone rang. Why did the telephone always ring when one was in the middle of something very important? Kay dropped her pen and sighed.

'Hello?' she said.

She didn't recognise the voice on the other end, but as soon as the woman said where she was calling from, Kay knew that it wasn't good news.

Peggy Sullivan had died.

Denis Frobisher's face was, perhaps, the longest face Kay had ever seen. It reminded her of a basset hound, but he had a warm smile that made his eyes twinkle, and she understood why Peggy had chosen him as her solicitor.

'But I don't understand,' Kay told him. 'She left me *everything*?'

Mr Frobisher nodded. 'It's very simple. There were no siblings, no children. Nobody. Just you, Miss Ashton.'

'But I knew her only a short time.'

'Then you obviously made an impression.'

Kay shook her head. 'This is crazy.'

'Her husband left her very comfortable. Of course, the nursing home fees made their dent over the years, but she still left a sizeable chunk.'

'Yes,' Kay said. It was all she could say.

Something occurred to her: their last conversation. What was it she'd said to Peggy when they were talking about dreams for the future?

'If only it were that simple,' Kay said.

'I beg your pardon?' Mr Frobisher said.

'I made this happen,' Kay said, her voice quavering. 'I wished things were simple and that dreams could come true, and now Peggy's dead. I didn't mean to wish her dead. Oh, dear!'

'Miss Ashton!' Mr Frobisher said. 'You're upsetting yourself unnecessarily. Mrs Sullivan was an elderly woman who'd been seriously ill for many years. It was her time. You didn't bring this about, I can assure you.' He pushed a box of tissues towards her, and she took one and dabbed her eyes.

'Oh, Peggy!' she said. 'I never expected this. I never imagined…'

'Of course you didn't,' Mr Frobisher said.

They sat quietly for a moment whilst Kay recovered her composure.

'There's a letter too,' Mr Frobisher said gently. 'One of the nurses at the home wrote it for Peggy, but she managed to sign it herself.'

He handed her the white envelope, and with shaking hands, Kay opened it and took out the folded sheet of paper.

My dearest Kay. I hope this doesn't come as too much of a shock to you, but I've left you a little bit of money.

Kay stifled the urge to laugh at the understatement.

You see, I don't have anyone close to me, and unlike most elderly ladies, I don't have an affinity for cats, so I won't be leaving my worldly goods to any rescue centres.

I know your mother didn't have much to leave you, and I know you've got a whopping mortgage and an unfulfilled dream. Well, my dear, if you use my money wisely, you can fulfil that dream right now, and I will feel that I am living on through you. Is that silly of me?

I'm going to miss you, dear Kay. I always loved your visits, and thank you so much for the wonderful hours of reading. I hadn't read Jane Austen for years, but your beautiful voice brought all those stories back to life for me again, and for that I am truly grateful.

So this is your chance, isn't it? Do something amazing!
Your friend,
Peggy.

Kay looked at the scribbled signature in blue ink. It looked more like 'Piggy,' really, and Kay could imagine Peggy's arthritic hand skating over the paper, determined to leave its mark, and the image brought more tears to Kay's eyes.

'So you see,' Mr Frobisher began, 'she wanted you to have

everything. We've been in the process of sorting things out. The house was being rented for the past few years—that's what brought in most of the income to pay the nursing home, but the tenant has gone now, so the house is yours.'

Kay nodded, desperately trying to follow everything.

'Mrs Sullivan thought you'd want to sell it straightaway.' He paused, waiting for her reply. 'But you probably want to think about things for a while,' he added.

'Yes,' Kay said. 'Think.'

'And you have my number. I'm here if you have any questions.'

'Questions.' Kay nodded. 'Thank you,' she said. 'You've been very kind.'

'Not at all,' Mr Frobisher said. 'Simply doing my job and carrying out the wishes of my client.' He stood up to escort Kay to the door. 'Dear Mrs Sullivan,' he said. 'How she will be missed.'

Kay nodded as she stood up and could instantly feel her eyes vibrating with tears again. She turned back around to the desk and took another tissue from the box—just to be on the safe side.

Chapter 2

KAY SAT AT HER DESK IN THE OFFICE AT BARNUM AND MASON. It had been three months since Peggy's funeral, and Kay still couldn't believe that her dear friend was gone and that Kay could no longer visit her at the nursing home, a pile of books in her bag ready for reading.

On a February morning that was sunny but bitterly cold, Peggy's funeral had taken place in the same church as that of Kay's mother. The snow had melted, and everything seemed wonderfully green, but there had been nothing to rejoice about that day. Kay had sat shivering in the same pew that she occupied only a few sad weeks before, watching the service through a veil of tears.

Now here she was sitting in the office as if nothing had happened. How callous time was, she thought. It hadn't stopped to mourn the passing of a dear friend but had marched onwards with ceaseless optimism and dragged Kay along for the ride.

She hadn't sketched for weeks, choosing to read instead. There had been the usual diet of Jane Austen, with Kay choosing *Northanger Abbey* in the hopes that Catherine and Tilney's company would cheer her up. She'd also been trying to find out more about preparing her illustrations for publication and had raided the local library. There was one very useful book full of tips for the first-timer, and she'd sneaked it into work in the hope that she'd be able to photocopy some of the pages in a quiet moment.

'Which is possibly now,' she said to herself, looking around the office. It was a small open-plan office with four desks occupied by her colleagues. Paul and Marcus were out at lunch and Janice was on the phone laughing. It obviously wasn't a work-related call; none of the business at the solicitors was the stuff that provoked laughter.

Opening her bag, she took out the book and walked over to the communal photocopier. She hoped she could get the pages copied before the silly old machine pulled a paper-jam stunt.

She was halfway through her copying when her phone went. Janice was still laughing into her own phone, so Kay had no choice but to return to her desk to answer it.

She was just replacing the receiver when Roger Barnum walked into the office brandishing a large document that looked as if it had an appointment with the photocopier.

Kay watched in horror, unable to make a move in time to rescue her book, watching as Mr Barnum lifted the lid of the photocopier.

'Whose is this?' he barked, holding the book up and grimacing at it as if it might be infected. '*Painting for Pleasure and Profit.*'

Kay, blushing from head to foot, stood up to claim the book. 'It's mine, Mr Barnum.'

'And what's it doing on the photocopier?' he asked.

Kay wanted to groan at the ridiculous question, but she didn't. She simply took it from him and mumbled an apology.

Mr Barnum sniffed. 'I'd like to have a quiet word with you in my office, Miss Ashton,' he said.

Kay nodded and followed him through.

'Close the door and sit down,' he said.

Kay did as she was asked.

Mr Barnum walked around his desk and sat down on an expensive-looking chair. It wasn't like the threadbare office chair Kay had.

'If you don't mind my saying,' Mr Barnum began, 'your mind hasn't really been on your work lately, has it?'

'Well, no,' Kay said. 'My mother died recently, and I've just lost a dear friend too.'

'Ah, yes. Well, one has to get over these things—move on and all that.'

Kay blinked hard. Had she just heard him right?

'People come and people go. It's a sad fact of life, and we have to get on with it.'

'Right,' Kay said. 'I'll try to remember that.'

'And this drawing of yours,' he continued, 'you mustn't bring it into the office with you. I think we had an incident before, didn't we? Something concerning that Mr Darcy. For the life of me, I can't see what it is you women find so fascinating.'

Kay didn't say anything.

'It's interfering. You must keep these things separate. Quite separate. Work is work. Play is play.'

'But it isn't play, Mr Barnum. It's my passion.'

Mr Barnum's eyes widened in shock at the word 'passion,' as if it might leap across the table and do him some sort of mischief.

'In fact,' Kay said, enjoying having provoked such a response, 'I've been thinking of *playing* a bit more. You see, I've just had a phone call, and it seems I've got some money coming my way very soon. I was left a property recently and it's just sold, so I'll be moving.'

'Moving?' Mr Barnum said.

'Yes. To the sea. I've always wanted to live by the sea. It's another of my passions. So you'd better accept this as my notice. I'll put it in writing, of course, during my lunch break which is now, I believe.' She stood up and smiled at Mr Barnum. She was feeling generous with her smiles now that she knew she was leaving.

❧

Arriving home that night, Kay flopped onto her sofa, kicking off her shoes and sighing. She felt exhausted. Decision-making was a tiring business, she decided, but she felt happy tired. She'd handed in her notice! She smiled as she remembered the look on Roger Barnum's face. It was the first time he'd actually looked at Kay—*really* looked at her. Usually his eyes just swept over her as he handed her a pile of paperwork.

Perhaps, she thought, it was also the first time she'd ever really looked at herself. She was thirty-one. She knew that age wasn't exactly 'past it,' by modern standards, but she wasn't exactly a spring chicken, either. Enough years had been wasted. In Jane Austen's time, thirty-one would have been a very dangerous age for a woman. She would have been rapidly hurtling towards spinsterhood.

Life had to be grasped, and what better time than now? What was it Peggy had said? *Do something amazing!*

'I will!' Kay said. 'I owe it to you, Peggy.'

Getting up from the sofa to pour herself a glass of wine, Kay still couldn't comprehend everything that had happened to her over the past few months. It was still impossible to believe that she was a relatively wealthy woman. She'd never had so much money, and she was determined to use it to its best advantage.

She was going to move to the sea—that much was certain, and

as a Jane Austen fan who was currently reading *Persuasion* for the seventh time, it seemed only right that she should focus her search on Lyme Regis. She'd already Googled it a dozen times, gazing longingly at the images that greeted her. The picturesque fishermen's cottages, the high street that sloped down to the perfect blue sea, and the great grey mass of the Cobb all seemed to speak to her.

Hey, there, Kay! What are you waiting for? Come on down. You know you want to!

Having grown up in landlocked Hertfordshire, Kay had always wondered what it would be like to live by the sea. For a moment she remembered a family holiday in North Norfolk. Other than two glorious sun-drenched days, the weather had been dreadful, and Kay had to spend most of the time trapped in the tiny chalet with her mum and dad, who did nothing but row. Kay had done her best to shut herself away with an armful of secondhand books she found in a nearby junk shop. Reading about dashing highwaymen and handsome cavaliers helped enormously, but it was still a wonder that the whole experience hadn't put her off the idea of living by the sea for good.

What exactly was she going to do in Lyme Regis, though? Was she going to buy a tiny cottage as cheaply as possible and live off the rest of the money whilst she hid herself away with her paintings and waited for publication? She'd never been a full-time artist, and she had to admit that the thought of it panicked her. What if she wasn't good enough? What if she spent years striving for publication whilst eating into the money that Peggy had left her? She was a practical girl, and the thought of running out of money was terrifying. She might have hundreds of thousands to her name, but she also had a lot of life to lead, and she was planning to live to a ripe old age. Besides, she'd always worked. Perhaps her job at Barnum and Mason's hadn't been the best in the world, but she'd been proud to make her own way and pay her own bills. What could she do in a house by the sea in Lyme Regis?

'There's only one way to find out,' she said.

It had been decided that Kay could take the annual leave that was owed to her in lieu of her notice, which meant that she could get down to Lyme Regis this very weekend and not have to worry about being back home for work on Monday.

Finishing her glass of wine, she went upstairs to start packing her suitcase, and she felt that Peggy—wherever she might be—was smiling down at her in approval.

Chapter 3

ADAM CRAIG HAD LIVED IN LYME REGIS ALL HIS LIFE OR, TO BE more precise, in a tiny village called Marlbury in the Marshwood Vale just a few miles north of the seaside town. He'd studied English at Cambridge and worked briefly in London, but he never wanted to live anywhere else.

With its winding country lanes, tiny stone cottages, and ever-present caress of a breeze laden with the salty scent of the sea, he couldn't imagine anywhere else coming close. He loved the rolling fields filled with lambs in the spring, the hedgerows stuffed with summer flowers, the tapestry colours of the trees in autumn, and the slate-grey sea in winter. Every season had its joy, and he welcomed each one.

His parents had moved to California twelve years before. His father had taken early retirement from his antiques business in Honiton, and determined to give the wine business a go, he bought an established vineyard in the Napa Valley. Adam had been invited to join them but had declined. The Dorset coast and countryside were in his blood, and he could no more leave it than he could his old nan.

Nana Craig was eighty-four years old and lived in a tiny

thatched cottage in a hamlet not far away from Adam's own. Of all his family members, it was Nana Craig who was his closest. Whilst his parents had been building their business, Nana Craig was the one who cleaned his scraped knees as a toddler, bought his first pair of football boots as a youngster, and read each and every one of his screenplays since he'd scribbled his first attempt as a teenager—a rather embarrassing romance called *The Princess and the Pirate*. Adam sometimes wished that his nan's memory weren't *quite* so sharp.

He'd been a screenwriter and film producer for more than ten years now, and his newest project was the one he'd been planning in his head for that entire length of time, for what screenwriter who lived near Lyme Regis wouldn't—at some point in his career— turn his attention to Jane Austen's novel *Persuasion*?

He had to admit that he hadn't been a fan of Austen growing up, but what young lad was? Austen was for girls, wasn't she? All those endless assemblies and discussions about men's fortunes that went on for entire chapters weren't the stuff to stir the imagination of a young boy. As an adult, though, and as a writer, her books, particularly *Persuasion*, began to make their mark, and three years earlier, he started putting things into motion. It was all coming together wonderfully. Very early on, he managed to get highly respected director Teresa Hudson on board. She had a string of period dramas under her belt and had won a BAFTA for her recent adaptation of Thomas Hardy's *Two on a Tower*. Whilst she was filming it in Dorset, they had got together and started discussing *Persuasion*.

Now the crew and all the actors were on board, and filming had begun. They were due to descend on the unsuspecting town of Lyme Regis soon, and Adam was looking forward to it. He'd long been envisaging the scenes he'd written around the Cobb, imagining the fateful leap of Louisa Musgrove and the cautious exchanges between Anne Elliot and Captain Wentworth.

He was envisaging them as he walked into town, walking down Broad Street with great strides, shielding his eyes from the sun so that he could catch a glimpse of the wonderful sea.

He was heading to the bookshop when he saw her. Tall and slim with a tumble of toffee-coloured hair, she was gazing in the window of an estate agent and was frowning. She was wearing a floral dress that was far more summery than the weather, and her hands were busy doing up the buttons of her denim jacket in an attempt to keep the nippy little breeze at bay. She had a rosy face and intensely bright eyes which Adam wished would swivel around in his direction, but what would he do then? What exactly would he do if she swivelled? It would take a small miracle for a girl like her to notice him.

It was a sad fact that Adam had spent most of his life unattached, and it wasn't because he was unattractive—far from it—but that he was painfully shy when it came to women. He was the man who stood in the corner at a party waiting for the host to introduce him, and whilst he might have a lot more of interest to say than the party bore who didn't stop talking all night, Adam's stories would rarely get an airing, because of his shyness.

It had always been the same. At primary school, he had been the one to work behind the scenes in the school play, because he'd been too shy to put his hand up for the acting roles. At high school, he'd never dare ask a girl to dance, even when encouraged by all her friends to do so. University wasn't much better. He spent most of his time with his head in his books.

Maybe that was one of the reasons he became a writer. Writers were behind-the-scenes sort of people who could hide away for months at a time.

Oh, there had been a few relationships over the years, but they were more happy accidents where he'd been physically flung together with somebody. Like Camille. She was the co-producer on his first film a few years before, and he fell head over heels in love with her. It hadn't lasted, of course. She told him she needed someone to take control of her—to tell her what to do. Adam had given her a baffled look, and she flung her hands up to the heavens as she searched for some words to fling at him.

'You're so… so *quiet*, Adam!'

You're so quiet. The words had haunted him down the years—the long quiet years.

As he was mulling over the memory, a small miracle occurred. The toffee-haired girl swivelled her eyes in his direction, and he was met with a warm smile, but being Adam, all he could manage was a smile back before she turned and entered the estate agent's office.

Chapter 4

KAY WAS SITTING IN THE ESTATE AGENT'S OFFICE LOOKING AT the frowning face of Mr Piper.

'I'm afraid we really don't have much at all, not with your proposed budget, that is.'

Kay frowned back. She'd set aside a large portion of her inheritance to buy a seaside property, and he was telling her it wasn't enough.

'There's a little cottage out in the Marshwood Vale. It's at the top of your price range, though, and only has two bedrooms.'

'Are you sure there's nothing in Lyme itself? I'd really like to be in the town.'

Mr Piper shook his head. 'Not with the sea view that you want. As I say, properties move very quickly here. It's a very popular spot with people looking for second homes and holiday rentals. Everything's snapped up immediately.'

Kay puffed out her cheeks. She hadn't reckoned on Lyme Regis being quite so popular. For a moment, she looked around the small office, eyeing the overpriced cottages in which you'd be lucky if you could swing a catkin, let alone a cat. They were all beautiful, of course, but there was nothing actually in Lyme Regis itself.

'Perhaps if you looked farther along the coast. How about Axmouth or Seaton?'

Kay shook her head. She hadn't come all this way to end up in Seaton. Jane Austen hadn't stayed in Seaton, and Kay was fairly sure there was no Cobb there.

Her gaze fell on a property she hadn't noticed before.

Wentworth House.

Kay blinked in surprise. Wentworth—as in Captain Frederick Wentworth—the magnificent hero from *Persuasion*. Well, she thought, if that wasn't a sign, she didn't know what was. She got up from her seat so she could read the notes.

It had been a former bed and breakfast but needed 'some modernisation throughout.'

A bed and breakfast. Kay had never thought of that. It was the perfect way to make a living by the sea, wasn't it? Lyme Regis had been popular with tourists for centuries, and that wasn't likely to change in the foreseeable future. It was a surefire way to enable her to live by the sea—*right* by the sea, judging from the photos of the place.

'Can I see the details for this one?' Kay asked, pointing to Wentworth House.

'Oh, I'm afraid that's way above your budget,' Mr Piper said.

'Well,' Kay said, 'I could go a bit higher. I mean, if I can make a business out of it.'

Mr Piper opened a drawer and retrieved the details, handing them to Kay, who looked them over quickly.

'I'd love to see it,' she said. 'How about now?'

The startled look on Mr Piper's face made Kay smile. She seemed to be doing nothing but startling men lately.

Mr Piper got up from his seat and muttered something about

closing the shop. Kay just smiled. She had a feeling she was about to spend a rather obscene amount of money.

Wentworth House was only a short walk away, and Kay's eyes darted around as she and the agent made their way there. Lyme had the most wonderful shops. There were mouthwatering bakeries, pretty boutiques, a delightful bookshop, and stores selling fossils, but she was shopping for a house, and she had to keep focussed.

'This is Marine Parade,' Mr Piper told her a moment later as they walked along the pavement lined with ice cream parlours that skirted the seafront. 'Wentworth House is just up ahead.'

Kay's eyes widened. Wentworth House, Marine Parade, Lyme Regis. She liked the sound of that address and immediately visualised the headed paper she could make. She looked out across the sea and tried to imagine what it would be like waking up to that view every morning. Life in Lyme would be like a permanent holiday.

'Here we are,' Mr Piper said a moment later. They had arrived at Wentworth House.

It was a large Victorian building with bay windows at the front that would make the very best of the fine views. It was painted the palest of pinks, like the inside of a shell, and it had a brilliant blue front door. That was all that was needed, really, for Kay was in love before she even crossed the threshold.

The door opened with two determined pushes, and Mr Piper turned to look at her with a nervous smile. 'Just needs a bit of oil,' he said.

Kay nodded. She wasn't going to let a drop of oil come between her and her dream home. Nor was she going to be put off by the strange, musty smell, like a cross between a wet dog and a peed-in bus shelter.

'Just needs a good airing,' Mr Piper said.

Kay nodded again, following him inside.

'The breakfast room,' Mr Piper announced as they entered a room at the back of the house.

Kay grimaced, thinking that she wouldn't want to eat in there. The walls were covered in thick, gnarly wallpaper the colour of nicotine.

'Just a splash of paint here and there,' Mr Piper said.

Kay nodded, and he led her to the kitchen, which was a long, thin room in need of some modernisation. Still, it had everything she needed.

The rooms at the front of the house looked far more promising, with a proper dining room and a living room, both with bay windows overlooking the sea. Unfortunately, the nicotine-coloured wallpaper put in another appearance, but Kay could see beyond it to the rooms' true potential.

Upstairs was more of the same with six rooms, all en suite, that needed a bit of a makeover to bring them into the twenty-first century. There were tatty floral wallpapers with the edges peeling by the doors and window frames. There were carpets covered in dizzying swirls, and everywhere she looked, the ugliest brass light fittings she'd ever seen. It would all have to go.

One thing about the house didn't need to be changed, though, because it was absolutely perfect, and that was the view. Wentworth House was situated in the very heart of Lyme Regis, which meant it had an unrivalled view of the Cobb. Kay gasped when she caught her first glimpse of it from the first bedroom. The vista looked like a huge grey runway stretching out to sea, and people were walking along it to enjoy the views just as they would have done in Jane Austen's time.

'Isn't it wonderful?' she said to Mr Piper.

'Hmm? Oh, yes,' he said, noticing what she was seeing. 'You're in a very good position here,' he said. 'You've got the beach, the Cobb, and plenty of shops and restaurants. If you really wanted to make a go of this as a bed and breakfast, you should have no trouble at all.'

Kay nodded. A bed and breakfast would be perfect. She could make a good living without having to leave her home, which meant she could paint whenever things were quiet. And she liked working with people. Peggy had often told her how good she was with people.

'I'll take it,' she said, realising that she'd be spending every penny of her inheritance if she bought it.

Mr Piper looked astounded. 'But this is the first property you've seen.'

'It's the only one I need to see. It's perfect.'

Mr Piper didn't try to dissuade her. 'Well,' he said, 'shall we get back and make a start on the paperwork?'

Kay smiled. She'd just bought a house—a six-bedroom house *and* a business venture—on the seafront in Lyme Regis. Peggy would be proud of her.

Chapter 5

Three months later

THE REHEARSALS WERE OVER.
Gemma Reilly stood in a corner by the bar, anxiously surveying the rest of the cast. They had just checked into The Three Palms Hotel in Lyme Regis, and welcome drinks were being served in the lounge. A pair of double doors had been opened onto a terrace, and most of the cast members were enjoying the views of the sea. Most of the cast except Gemma, that was. She felt more like the new girl at school. Everyone seemed to know everyone else. The director, Teresa Hudson, obviously knew everyone, as did the assistant director, Les Brown. Not that he was talking to anyone. He was known as Les Miserable, because of his permanent scowl and lack of humour, and he wasn't known for his small talk. Right then, he was emptying a bowl of nuts into the palm of his hand and chasing them down his throat with a gulp of whisky.

Gemma let her gaze roam the room, and it rested next on actress Sophie Kerr. Gemma knew of her work—mostly an impressive stint with the Royal Shakespeare Company, wowing audiences with her varied performances from her wonderfully witty Beatrice in *Much Ado About Nothing* to the most heartbreaking Ophelia in *Hamlet*. She watched as Sophie flirted with ease with one of the guys who was always carrying cables around. Gemma wasn't quite sure what he did, but he was absolutely spellbound by Sophie, and why shouldn't he be? With her bright blond curls and bubbly personality, she was the answer to most men's dreams.

Nearby stood another well-known actress, Beth Jenkins, in a dress that was slashed to her very navel. She had striking red hair that fell to her shoulders in an immaculately straight curtain and lips painted a dangerous-looking red. She was beautiful. She was playing Louisa Musgrove, and from the rumours Gemma heard, nobody would mind too much if she really did crack her head open after flinging herself from the Cobb during the famous scene from *Persuasion*, because Beth Jenkins was a grade-one bitch.

'I heard she ran off with the producer's husband on the set of her last film,' Gemma heard somebody say behind her. She turned to see two young girls serving behind the bar. They were giggling and whispering, pointing at each actor in turn.

'Wasn't she having an affair with that pop star at the same time?' the other girl asked.

'What pop star?' her colleague asked.

'I don't know. All of them, probably.'

The both giggled again.

Best keep my distance from her, Gemma thought.

That was the problem with filming, though. Casts became like families, in that you couldn't easily escape one another. Gemma had already learned that lesson on her first production—a TV drama called *Into the Night*. Part love story, part whodunit, it had been cruelly slated by the critics, as had Gemma's performance.

'Destined to play nothing more than the blond bimbo,' the television critic from *Vive!* had said.

'Legs like runner beans,' *Star Turn* had said, 'and they were her best feature.'

Gemma had been mortified and went into hiding for months, dyeing her hair black and building her leg muscles up at the gym.

Things weren't helped by the fact that her mother was the much-loved actress Kim Reilly, who starred in the 1970s cult TV show, *Bandits.* As soon as Gemma had dared to follow in her footsteps, comparisons had been made. It was inevitable, she supposed. Her mother had been beautiful, talented, and lucky. *Bandits* had been one of the biggest shows of the time, with sky-high ratings. It had run for five series before the lead actor was tragically killed in a motorbike accident. If that hadn't happened, the show would probably still be running today, Gemma often thought, her mother dressed in her trademark skintight trousers and skimpy tops, her hair blow-dried and bouffant.

Her mother never topped her performance in *Bandits*, although she tried to top herself a couple of times. In the public's mind, she personified success; women wanted to be her, and men wanted to bed her. She was incredibly fragile, though, and although she adored attention, she also found life in the public eye difficult to cope with, and Gemma, it seemed, took after her. She was a bag of nerves just thinking about taking part in a film, yet there was something in her that compelled her to do it. At stage school, she used to get physically sick before going on stage, but then she always gave a dazzling performance—well, that's what the other students and her tutors told her. What happened with the fated TV drama, then?

'Just critics trying to get a cheap laugh,' one of her old stage school friends had told her when they met down at the pub to discuss it. 'Don't pay them any attention. You were marvellous!'

'What could you possibly do with a script like that?' another—more honest—friend had told her. 'I think you did very well, considering.'

Thank goodness Teresa Hudson had believed in her and gave her a much-needed second chance. There had obviously been something in her performance that she liked. If only Gemma had that belief in herself, she thought.

Looking around the room again, she saw a young man with dark, tousled hair. A pair of bright grey eyes sparkled from behind his glasses as he listened to Teresa talking about something or other. Gemma had seen him at rehearsals. He was the screenwriter and one of the producers, but he never said much. He had a kind face and a nice smile and seemed almost as shy as she was. There was another man just behind him, and Gemma suddenly caught his eye. He smiled, and his eyes almost disappeared into two happy creases. He had thick brown hair and looked as if he was about to cross the room to talk to her, but Gemma turned her back to him. She wasn't interested in being chatted up. She had heard plenty of stories about on-set relationships, and they never *ever* worked out.

She watched as a couple of actors came in from the terrace and approached the bar. They nodded at Gemma but didn't start a conversation. She was glad, for there was only one actor there that interested her, and that was Oli Wade Owen.

Gemma swallowed hard. Of all the actors in the world to play Captain Frederick Wentworth, why did it have to be Oli Wade Owen? She'd had a crush on him for as long as she could remember. All of her walls at stage school had been covered in posters of the young actor, and she'd gazed longingly at them, fantasising about playing Juliet to his Romeo or Cleopatra to his Antony.

He was tall and classically handsome with soft blue eyes and thick blond hair that she just wanted to reach out and touch, but it was his smile that was his best feature. 'The smile that stole a thousand hearts,' the press had called it, because Oli Wade Owen was never short of a girl or two. Frequently photographed coming out of expensive restaurants and exclusive nightclubs, he was front-page tabloid news, and there was always endless speculation as to who was accompanying him.

Gemma watched him as he chatted with Beth Jenkins. She was obviously enjoying the attention and was in full flirt mode. How could Gemma ever compete with the likes of Beth? she wondered. It was a whole other league of womanhood.

But it was you Teresa chose for the lead role, a little voice told her, and it was true. She wouldn't be surprised if she'd made a mortal enemy of Beth in the process, but nevertheless, here she was—about to act opposite Oli Wade Owen on a big-budget film.

As Oli suddenly turned and flashed her a dazzling smile that almost melted the ice in her drink, Gemma still couldn't believe it. She didn't feel ready for this. The role of Anne Elliot was her first in a film, and she had the feeling that everybody was waiting for her to fail. Even worse, she herself fully expected to fail.

Chapter 6

I T WAS LATE BY THE TIME ADAM LEFT THE THREE PALMS HOTEL and headed back to his home in the Marshwood Vale. He had to admit that the party had been fun. He usually tried to avoid social situations. He was far more of a stay-at-home-with-a-bottle-of-wine-and-a-good-film type of guy, but he had enjoyed chatting with the cast and crew. Teresa, the director, although never the life and soul of a party, had nevertheless been fascinating, telling him about the ideas she had for the film and how she hoped to use Lyme Regis to its best advantage. She was also excited about the two locations Adam had found for Kellynch Hall and Uppercross but was a little concerned about the weather reports, which were promising rain, rain, and more rain. They'd just have to keep their fingers crossed.

Adam had been delighted when he found Marlcombe Manor. He knew immediately that it would make an ideal Kellynch Hall, and he was thrilled when the owners and the film company agreed with him. Situated just five miles from Lyme Regis, the Jacobean manor house was the perfect answer to the great seat of the Elliots, and the nearby village of Ashbury was going to stand in for Uppercross, with the exterior of a fine Georgian house being used for the home of Charles and Mary Musgrove.

It was always so much easier when filming could take place in as few locations as possible. It saved time and money and cut back on hassle. It was also particularly welcome for Adam, who was able to stay at his own home instead of booking into the hotel along with the cast and crew. He valued his privacy and preferred his own company once the working day was over.

He thought again about the party. He'd done his best to make conversation with the assistant director, Les Brown, but nothing had come of it. Les had grunted and mumbled and then left to go to the Gents'.

'Take no notice of him!' Beth Jenkins had said, sidling up to him in her slinky slashed dress. 'He's a total bore. You do know his nickname, don't you? Les Miserable.'

Adam laughed, and Beth took the opportunity to link an arm through his.

She hadn't been interested in him really, though. Adam noticed how she kept glancing back at the terrace, where Oli Wade Owen was standing.

As Adam slowed down to take a bend by a church, he chuckled to himself. The only reason a beautiful actress would fling herself at him was in the hope of making another man jealous.

Then there'd been Gemma. Sweet Gemma Reilly. At last Adam had met a woman who was as shy as he. He watched her hovering around the bar, stirring her drink, and watching the action from a distance. He'd spoken to her briefly before and had immediately warmed to her.

'All ready for the big day tomorrow?' he asked as he approached her.

'As ready as I'll ever be,' she said.

He looked at her pale face and the look of uncertainty in her eyes. 'You nervous?'

'Yes!' she said, the word leaping from her mouth. She looked surprised that she'd confessed such a thing.

'But you're a great actress,' Adam told her. 'I've seen you in rehearsals, and you're fabulous. I'm really excited about this production.'

She looked up at him and smiled. 'That's really sweet of you.'

'I'm just being honest.'

'It's just—' she stopped.

'What?' he asked.

'This is my first film, and I'm terrified of letting everyone down.' Her eyes were wide and fearful.

'But you won't,' he said.

She nodded. 'I mean, what if I'm just not a very good actress?'

Adam couldn't believe what he was hearing. This was one insecure lady. There was only one thing for it—to lie. 'But everyone feels like that on a film set.'

'They do?' She didn't look convinced.

'They certainly do. I was talking to Beth Jenkins before. She was shaking with nerves. I couldn't believe it.'

'No way! Beth Jenkins is nervous?'

Adam nodded, wondering where all this was coming from and if he could keep it up. He supposed it was just an extension of his storytelling abilities. 'She said there hasn't been a single film where she's felt confident beforehand, but it's those very nerves that drive a good performance.'

Gemma nodded. 'I was the same at stage school. Every performance gave me the shakes.'

'But I bet every performance was brilliant,' Adam said.

'I'm not sure about that,' she said with a little blush.

'You wouldn't be standing here right now if anyone doubted your ability. A film's too expensive a project to cast the wrong person,' Adam said and then regretted it, as he saw her pale again. 'Which is why you've nothing to worry about. Teresa was just telling me how wonderful you are. This production's already in the can. It was, the day you were cast.'

Gemma let out a long sigh and reached out a hand to touch his arm. 'Thank you,' she said.

Driving back through the darkening country lanes, Adam thought about Gemma's beautiful young face and how genuinely scared she'd been. He hoped his words had calmed her, and he hoped he'd be around to comfort her if she had another attack of nerves.

Later that night, Gemma woke up with the strange sensation of feeling wet. She flung back the bedclothes and leapt out of bed, turning on her bedside lamp, and shrieking as she saw a huge wet patch on her pillow. She looked up to see the ceiling dripping.

'Oh, my goodness!' she exclaimed, stuffing her feet into a pair of shoes and grabbing a jumper from her suitcase. Where was it coming from? Was the ceiling about to collapse? Was she in danger of dying before she could make her mark in the world of film?

There were voices in the corridor, and Gemma opened her door.

'My room's turned into a swimming pool!' Beth squealed. Gemma noticed the woman had still managed to brush her hair and apply a coat of mascara and lipstick in her panic.

'My bed's completely soaked,' Sophie said. She was wearing a cute pair of pyjamas covered in teddy bears, and like Gemma, hadn't been anxious to apply makeup in such circumstances.

'Everyone all right?' Oli asked, coming down from the floor above them. 'There's a burst pipe. Everywhere's drenched.'

'Oh, this is dreadful!' Beth said.

'You should see our rooms,' Oli said, and Gemma noticed that his jeans were soaked and his hair was plastered to his face.

Teresa appeared on the landing, her face dark and drawn. 'Grab your things as quickly as you can,' she said.

'I'm not going back in my room,' Beth said. 'I could drown!'

Oli shook his head and dashed in for her. Gemma returned to hers and packed, grabbing her things as quickly as she could and meeting everyone out on the landing a few minutes later.

'What the hell are we going to do?' Les Miserable said, scratching his head and making his hair stick up even more than usual. 'Where are we going to sleep?'

'I don't know,' Teresa said. 'They must have more rooms available here.'

Les shook his head. 'Fully booked.'

'What are we going to do?' wailed Beth. 'I need my beauty sleep. I can't work without a good night's rest.'

Gemma tuned out as she watched Oli shaking the excess water from his hair. His T-shirt was soaked too. Gemma turned away. Now was not the time to be thinking about heroes in wet shirts.

The hotel manager appeared, his arms waving around like the blades of a windmill.

'I am so sorry, ladies and gentlemen. Is everybody okay?'

'*I'm* not okay!' Beth announced, stepping forward and looking pristine.

'Oh, my dear!' the manager said. 'I will never forgive myself if my favourite actress were hurt whilst in my establishment. Where are you hurt, my dear?'

Beth looked shifty for a moment, rearranging her dressing gown. 'My toes got a bit wet, but my suitcase is ruined. *Everything* will need replacing.'

'Oh, don't fuss,' Sophie admonished.

Teresa stepped forward to take charge. 'Are there any other rooms we can use?'

The manager pulled a face. 'I'm afraid we are completely booked.'

'Oh, this is ridiculous,' Beth said. 'Do you expect me to hang around all night on a draughty wet landing in only a thin, lacy negligee?' she said, batting her eyelashes in Oli's direction. Oli grinned and Les Miserable did too, except it was more of a leer, and Beth thought it prudent to cover up at least half of her cleavage.

'I'll tell you what we can do,' the manager said. 'We have lots of spare bedding and can make beds up in the lounge for the rest of tonight.'

Beth tutted. 'I've never heard the like!'

'There *are* only about two hours left before we're due to get up anyway,' Sophie said. 'I don't see what the big problem is.'

The two actresses glared at each other.

'We'll make proper arrangements tomorrow,' Teresa cried above the chaos. 'Let's just try to get through the rest of tonight.'

Gemma sighed and watched as Oli sauntered casually downstairs with his suitcase, and there was a sudden scramble between Beth and Sophie to follow, both, no doubt, intent on grabbing the nearest makeshift bed next to him.

Chapter 7

THE LAST FEW WEEKS HAD PASSED IN A BLUR OF ACTIVITY FOR Kay. She sold her little house in Hertfordshire and left the county that had been the home of the Bennet family in *Pride and Prejudice* and the scene of so much of her own personal sadness and moved into Wentworth House in Lyme Regis and a brand new beginning. The trouble was that her dream to be an artist by the sea hadn't materialized. She hadn't even had time to unpack her paintbrushes, let alone paint anything. There was just so much to do, such as saying good-bye to all her old friends and promising that they could come and stay at the B&B as soon as it was ready.

Mr Piper had recommended a local painter and decorator, Charlie Evans. He turned up with his seventeen-year-old son, who didn't look at all happy to be there and kept disappearing, only to be found at the nearest slot machines. Still, they'd made a start with the hallway, dining room, and the bedrooms, as they were the most visually horrific rooms and the ones that paying guests would be most likely to notice. The living room and kitchen would have to wait.

Out went the headache-inducing carpets and the pink sinks, and in came tin after tin of cream paint and an army of white sinks.

To replace the carpets, Kay chose seagrass. She'd always loved it, but had never been able to afford it before. The fun bit then arrived—choosing the accessories. There were some gorgeous shops in the area, and bedding, towels, lamps, and mirrors were chosen with love and care until all the rooms were worthy of featuring in a glossy magazine and Kay could feel just a little bit proud of the new home she created for herself and her guests.

How quickly she'd got used to her new life on the coast. She loved waking up to the sound of seagulls. Their raucous cries were the most efficient of alarm clocks, and she always tried to get a quick walk along the Cobb before breakfast, taking in the bracing sea air and watching the ever-changing moods of the sea.

She bought a map of the area and was learning all the names. To the west of the Cobb was Monmouth Beach, and farther along, Pinhay Bay, but her favourite place was still Lyme. She loved the view across Lyme Bay to the great hulk of Golden Cap, and on a very clear day, it was possible to see as far as the Isle of Portland.

There was so much she wanted to see and explore, too. All the places had magical-sounding names, such as Gabriel's Ledge and Black Ven along the coast, and inland, villages with names like Wootton Fitzpaine and Whitchurch Canonicorum.

She loved the street lamps along the front in Lyme Regis that were shaped like ammonites. She loved the shiny mud of the harbour, which reminded her of the bitterest chocolate, and she loved the evenings, when the sea and the sky turned the palest pearly blue and it was impossible to tell where one ended and the other began. In short, she loved *everything*, but her favourite thing was the Cobb. She'd looked at it and walked along it, photographed it, and worshipped it from every angle, admiring the sloping sweep of it, sketching it in her pad over and over again, determined to paint it one day soon. It seemed like a living thing to her, and she desperately wanted to capture that energy on paper.

What she loved most about the Cobb was how welcoming it seemed to be—how everyone could walk there, from toddlers with grandparents to the dozens of dogs who came to Lyme with wagging tails and lolling tongues.

At the end of a particularly long day of ripping out old shelves and painting walls, there was a knock on the door. Kay had been sitting in the living room at the front of the house. Although it hadn't been decorated yet, it looked jolly enough, with her old sofa and a couple of armchairs, and she was already beginning to feel quite at home there.

She'd just been rereading a few of the Lyme Regis pages from *Persuasion* and wondered who on earth was calling. She hadn't been in Lyme long enough to make any friends, and she hadn't yet opened Wentworth House for business. Kay walked down the hallway and unlocked the door. There was a slim woman standing on the step. She looked about forty years old with a careworn face that wasn't smiling.

'You're a bed and breakfast, aren't you?' the woman asked, desperation in her voice.

'I guess I am,' Kay said.

'Good,' the woman said. 'It's just possible that you could save my life.'

Kay didn't quite know what to say to that. She'd never saved anyone's life before, but before she could say anything, the careworn woman invited herself in and was talking ten to the dozen.

'I'm Teresa Hudson. You've probably seen some of my films. *Passion of a Lady, Two on a Tower*—that sort of thing. I'm a director. We're making *Persuasion* here in Lyme, and the whole cast and crew are with me. How many rooms do you have?' she asked, bustling about and poking her head around the door. 'It's very small, isn't it?'

'Five,' Kay said. 'I have five rooms, all en suite.'

'Five? Twins, double?'

'Three double, two twin, but the twins aren't quite ready. We've been redecorating, and I wanted to—'

'I'll take them. I'll take all of them. Doesn't matter if they're ready. We're a bit desperate, you see. We've been staying at The Three Palms up the road, but a burst pipe's made a few of us homeless, and there's absolutely nowhere left in town. I've got production assistants running up and down the streets hammering on doors. It's ridiculous. Somebody mentioned this place, except it didn't look very promising from the outside.'

'I've just moved in,' Kay said, feeling it necessary to explain but annoyed that she had to. This was, perhaps, the rudest woman she'd ever met.

'We'll want breakfast and dinner. No lunch. We'll be eating early and late, okay? Now, let me see the rooms.'

Teresa didn't bother to wait for Kay to lead her upstairs but made her own way, opening doors and peering inside.

'Nice,' she said. 'Small, but nice. Paint smells a bit strong.'

'We've just decorated,' Kay said, 'as I explained.'

Teresa nodded and got out her mobile from her jacket pocket. 'Les, it's Teresa. I've found somewhere. Parking?' she said. 'Is there parking?'

'Not far away,' Kay said, pointing in the direction.

'Yes, there's parking nearby. You know what Lyme's like.' There was a pause, and Teresa frowned. 'Hurry up and finish eating and then get yourselves down here. Marine Parade. It's a place called—' she stopped and looked at Kay with raised eyebrows.

'Wentworth House.'

'Wentworth House,' Teresa repeated with a wry smile. 'I know. It's fate,' she said, snapping her phone shut. 'Right, I'll choose myself a room.'

Kay watched in total bemusement as her first guest disappeared up the stairs.

'Extraordinary,' she said to herself.

∞

Things got a bit chaotic after that. The next time Kay opened the door, she came face to face with a droopy sort of a man who was stubbing his cigarette out in Kay's new terra-cotta pot. He didn't say anything, only nodded and pushed into the hallway, where he hollered, '*Teresa!*'

Kay jumped.

'*Les!*' Teresa shouted back, appearing on the landing. 'Everyone with you?'

'They're on their way. I've got Gemma, Sophie, Beth, and Oli. The others are okay at The Palms.'

'Their rooms okay?'

Les nodded.

Before Kay had time to hear more, there was another knock on the door.

'Is this Wentworth House?' a young woman with a pretty, heart-shaped face and blond curly hair asked.

'Yes, it is.'

'I'm Sophie,' the woman said. 'Sophie Kerr.'

Kay frowned. She'd heard the name before. Recognition suddenly dawned as she ushered her inside. 'You were in *The Solitary Neighbour*.'

Sophie nodded. 'I was. How sweet of you to remember. That was years ago.'

Kay smiled. *The Solitary Neighbour* was a Gothic Victorian

made-for-TV movie, just the sort of thing that Kay lapped up, and Sophie had played the heroine.

'So you're in this production of *Persuasion* now?' Kay asked, hoping she didn't sound too starstruck.

'Henrietta Musgrove,' Sophie said. 'The boring sister who doesn't get to jump off the Cobb and nearly break her neck in the name of flirtation.'

Kay laughed.

'To be honest, I don't mind. At least I don't have to risk an injury doing stunts like Beth will.'

'Beth?' Kay asked.

'Somebody mention my name?' a voice called, and Kay and Sophie looked around to see the red-haired actress entering the bed and breakfast.

'*Beth Jenkins!*' Kay all but screamed.

Beth batted her eyelashes. 'Oh, a fan,' she said.

'I can't believe it! I just can't believe it. I've just been reading *Persuasion*—look!' Kay ran into the sitting room and came out holding the book.

'Well, how funny!' Sophie said.

'I had no idea it was being filmed here.'

'Yes, well, one has to slum it occasionally,' Beth said, looking up and down the narrow hallway. 'My last job was filming in a villa in Marbella. Stunning views. Simply stunning. Got to top up my tan and everything.'

'Yes, but Jane Austen heroines are meant to be pale and interesting,' Sophie said, 'and not look like an old leather handbag.'

Beth glared at her, and Kay's mouth dropped open. She couldn't believe it. There were two famous actresses standing in the hallway of her bed and breakfast, and they were fighting!

'I'll show you to your rooms,' Kay said.

'I want a double,' Beth said. 'With a view.'

Kay nodded. 'Sophie?'

'Oh, just stick me in anywhere,' she said with a wave of her hand.

'Do you have any bags?' Kay asked.

'Oli's bringing them,' Beth said.

Kay wondered who Oli was. Probably some poor put-upon assistant.

'This is the best double,' Kay said. 'You can see the Cobb and the whole of the front.'

'Is there a bath? I must have a bath *and* a shower.'

Kay nodded. 'The shower's above the bath—'

'Oh, God! Not one of those pathetic pieces of work that dribbles tepid water, is it?'

'Don't pay any attention to her,' Sophie said. 'She's nothing but a spoilt brat.'

Beth turned around to face Sophie, and for one frightening moment, Kay thought Beth was going to punch Sophie.

'And there's a lovely twin next door,' Kay said, thinking it wise to move Sophie out of harm's way.

'Oh, it's lovely!' Sophie said. 'Will I be sharing it?'

'Depends how many of you there are,' Kay said.

'Hasn't Teresa told you?'

Kay shook her head.

'I think there's only Gemma and Oli, and I'd better not be sharing with Oli—no matter how divine he is.' She flopped back onto the bed and sighed. 'I wouldn't want to make Beth jealous. She's such a diva. All the attention's got to be on her twenty-four seven. I wouldn't mind, but she's not even the lead.'

'No?'

Sophie sat back up. 'Gemma's the lead, and you wouldn't find a sweeter actress anywhere, but she's as jumpy as anything. The complete antithesis of diva-face next door. God! I can't believe I'm working with her again. She haunts me!'

Kay grinned. 'What have you been in together?'

'There was that dreadful TV thriller last year, and before that, we were in that boarding-school drama that seemed to go on for decades without any of us growing any older.'

'Oh, yes!' Kay said. 'I remember that. Gosh, you've both been acting for years, then.'

Sophie grinned. 'You make me sound like an ancient dame.'

'Oh, no! I mean, you've got so much experience. You make me feel so ordinary.'

Sophie looked at Kay. 'But you've got this place. It's pretty amazing.'

'Thanks. I just bought it. I was left some money,' she said, thinking how easy it was to talk to the woman. 'I've always wanted to live by the sea.'

'I live near Waterloo Station in London. It's horrible. I've got a flat that's not too bad, I suppose, but it's so ugly there. I try and work as much as possible so I don't have to stay there.'

'But isn't it odd living in hotels all the time?' Kay asked.

'You get used to it. I don't mind living out of a suitcase, and I love acting. I love becoming someone else.'

'It must be a strange life,' Kay said. 'I can't quite imagine it.'

'Some are better suited to it than others,' Sophie said. 'Diva-face next door makes life miserable for everyone whose path she crosses. You won't have to let her get to you, but Oli, now he's brilliant.'

'Who's Oli?' Kay asked.

'*Hello?*' a male voice yelled from downstairs. 'Anyone here?'

Sophie smoothed down her hair with her hands. 'I think you're about to find out.'

Suddenly everyone was out on the landing.

'We're up here, Oli,' Teresa shouted.

'I hope you've got my bags,' Beth said, walking out from her bedroom, her lips now painted a fierce scarlet.

'There's a double left for you, Oliver,' Teresa said, and that's when Kay saw him for the first time. He was walking up the stairs, and at first, all she could see was a shock of butter-blond hair. He lifted his head, a pair of blue eyes met her own, and a huge smile broke across his face.

'Hello,' he said.

Kay's mouth dropped open. It was the actor, Oli Wade Owen, and he was the most handsome man she'd ever laid eyes on.

Chapter 8

I F SHE COULD HAVE TAKEN HER EYES AWAY FROM HIM FOR A second, Kay would surely have done a prize-winning double take. To have a director in her house had been excitement enough; to have two famous actresses had almost caused Kay to combust with delight; but to have one of Britain's most handsome actors—the man who'd played a thousand heroes, the man who'd adorned every cover of every magazine and newspaper—was almost too much to bear. And he was walking straight towards her.

'You must be the good lady of the house,' Oli said, extending a hand towards her. Kay held hers out, and he took it in his and shook it. It was a warm, melting sort of a moment, and Kay felt sure that her entire store of blood rushed to her face, because she felt as if her cheeks were on fire.

'Kay,' she managed to say. 'Welcome to Wentworth House.'

'Very apt,' Oli said. 'Seeing as I'm Wentworth.' He looked around at the group that had gathered on the landing, and everyone laughed. It was as if he were a king holding court.

'Right,' he said, breaking the spell as he retrieved his hand. 'Who's for a drink?'

'I am,' Beth declared.

Teresa stepped in, holding up her hand. 'One drink,' she said. 'We've got an early start in the morning, in case you'd forgotten.'

Oli clapped his hands together. 'The Habour Inn it is, then. For one drink,' he added.

Kay watched in bemusement as everyone bundled downstairs, and she couldn't resist following. The front door was flung open.

Oli exclaimed as he almost smashed into a young woman standing on the step, 'Gemma! What took you so long?'

'I was carrying all these,' she said, gesturing to the two suitcases and a bundle of carrier bags.

'Oh, my hats!' Beth said, nodding to the bags. 'I found this divine hat shop here in Lyme. Take them upstairs, will you, Gemma? I'm in the double at the front.'

'I bet you are,' Kay heard Gemma say under her breath as she squeezed into the hallway.

'I'll give you a hand,' Kay said, stepping forward and smiling at the pale-faced actress.

'Oh, you're not coming with us?' Sophie said. 'And Gem— you're coming, aren't you?'

'I'm a bit tired,' Gemma said.

'She's always tired,' Beth said. 'Come on, Oli.'

Kay watched as they all left. 'Hi,' she said, turning to Gemma. 'I'm Kay.'

'Gemma.'

'Gemma Reilly?' Kay asked, thinking that life couldn't get much more exciting. 'I saw that film of yours last year.'

Gemma pulled a face. 'Sorry about that.'

'But I liked it!'

'Did you?' Gemma said, sounding genuinely surprised.

The two of them made slow progress up the stairs with the suitcases.

'I did. You were great.'

'Well, you're the only person in the country who thinks so.'

'But it was one of those roles, wasn't it?' Kay said. 'I mean, it probably didn't really stretch you—acting wise—the character was just a spoilt little rich girl, wasn't she? But you were so convincing.'

'Was I?'

Kay nodded as they reached the landing. 'And by the end, I really warmed to her, you know? I began to understand her.'

'Thanks,' Gemma said. 'That means a lot to me.'

Kay smiled. 'I'm afraid you'll have to share.'

Gemma's face fell. 'Not with Beth?'

'No.' Kay laughed. 'Beth grabbed a double. With Sophie. Is that okay?'

Gemma sighed with relief. 'That's fine,' she said, and the two of them entered the room. 'Sophie's one of those people you feel like you've known forever—in a good way, I mean.'

'But not Beth?'

'Beth's an acquired taste,' Gemma said with the tiniest of smiles.

'Can I get you anything? A cup of tea?' Kay asked. 'I was just going to make a quick bite to eat. Not much, just some soup or something. You're welcome to join me—if you're not going to the pub, that is.'

'I won't be going to the pub,' Gemma said, sitting down on the edge of the bed. 'I think I'll just have an early night with a book.'

'Okay,' Kay said. 'I'll be downstairs if you need anything.'

Gemma nodded, and Kay left the room, closing the door and returning to the living room downstairs. She saw the opened paperback of *Persuasion* on the chair where she'd left it and smiled. It was as if the characters from the book had walked out of the page and right into her bed and breakfast.

She sat down heavily in her chair by the window. Sophie Kerr, Beth Jenkins, Gemma Reilly, and Oli Wade Owen.

Oli Wade Owen! Kay's eyes widened at the thought. How many daydreams had Kay had over the years about Oli Wade Owen? How many boring office hours had been enlivened by thoughts of that gorgeous smile of his and the twinkle in his blue eyes? She remembered cutting out a picture of him from *Vive!* once, because she thought he would make the perfect hero to paint. Where was the painting now? she wondered, but maybe she could get on with some new ones. Maybe he would sit for her—in costume!

She picked up her copy of *Persuasion*, but she couldn't concentrate, so put it down again. She could hear Gemma moving about upstairs and wondered whether she should make her a cup of tea anyway and take it up to her, but the actress was probably exhausted and wouldn't want to be disturbed, which was a shame, because Kay would have loved to talk to her.

'Don't rush things,' she told herself. 'They'll all be here for a while.'

For a blissful moment, she thought about what the next few days might bring. She might end up best friends with Gemma Reilly and Sophie Kerr! They'd invite her to red carpet premieres, and Kay would get a swishy new haircut and become a media darling. 'Confidante to the stars,' they'd call her. 'Former B and B owner, Kay Ashton, is now a star in her own right, with her bestselling book, *The Illustrated Darcy*.' She'd be an overnight sensation, and Oli Wade Owen would fall desperately in love with her. Teresa Hudson would also be dazzled by her talents and insist she take up the lead role in her next film, starring opposite Oli, of course. They'd have just come back from their honeymoon, and the film would be the talk of the—

A shy voice interrupted her. 'I've changed my mind about that cup of tea.'

Kay blinked her delicious daydream away and saw Gemma standing in the doorway.

'Of course,' Kay said with a smile, and she thought that her daydream wasn't quite as outrageous after all and that she and Gemma were going to be friends in no time.

She led Gemma through to the kitchen.

'You'll have to excuse the mess. I've not been here long and wanted to get the bedrooms done first.'

'They're lovely,' Gemma said.

'Thanks. This will be, too, when I get round to it.'

'So you've always run a B and B?'

'Oh, no!' Kay laughed. 'I've only just bought this place. I've just done office work up until recently.' She filled the kettle with water and switched it on. 'I—well, I came into some money,' she said. 'Unexpectedly.'

'Oh,' Gemma said, and she smiled. 'Oh,' she added, seeing Kay's face.

Kay nodded. 'I'm afraid a very sweet friend of mine died.' She sighed. 'I still can't believe it. The last few months have been strange, and I sometimes can't believe that I'm here leading this new life.'

'You mean you've not always lived here?'

'No. I moved down from Hertfordshire, but after my mother died and then my friend, I didn't have anything keeping me there. I mean, there are a few friends and some of my work colleagues I'll miss, but I didn't feel I belonged there anymore, and I thought it was the right time to make a move.'

Gemma's face softened. 'I'm so sorry,' she said. 'You've been through a lot.'

The kettle boiled, and Kay got two floral mugs out of the cupboard and made the tea, noticing that Gemma liked hers with milk and one sugar—just like her.

'It's hard, some days,' Kay said at last as they walked back through to the sitting room with their tea. 'I can't help feeling a bit lonely. I walk around with all these thoughts in my head, like I must tell Mum this, or Peggy will laugh when I show her this, but then I remember they're not here anymore.'

'Oh, Kay,' Gemma said, leaning forward in the chair she'd sat down in.

'It's all right,' she said. 'I mean, it's easier with me living here. If I were still in my old town, I'd be reminded of them everywhere I went, but it's different here. Everything's new.' She looked out the window. The sky was darkening and the lamps had come on. 'But I still find it all impossible to believe. It's horrible to think that I can't pick up a phone and talk to them. I can't ask their opinions about things anymore. All that's been taken away from me, and I wasn't ready for it.'

Gemma put down her mug of tea and leant forward to take Kay's hand in hers.

Kay blinked her tears away and then waved her hand in front of her face. 'I'm okay,' she said. 'Don't worry about me. I didn't mean to be miserable. You shouldn't be sitting here, listening to me wittering on. You should be down at the pub with the others.'

Gemma shook her head. 'I'm not into all that. They'll all be drinking too much and bitching about the business. It's not me.'

'No,' Kay said, 'it wouldn't be me either. I'd rather curl up with a good book.' She picked up her copy of *Persuasion* and showed Gemma.

'You're reading *Persuasion*?'

'It's one of my favourites. It's why I chose to move here.'

'And then the whole cast descended on you!'

They sat quietly for a moment, sipping their tea.

'Well,' Gemma said at last, 'thanks for the tea. I think I'll go and do a bit of swatting.'

Kay looked quizzical.

'It's what Beth calls learning your lines,' Gemma explained. 'She's always teasing me that I'm swatting again, but I can't help it. I need things fresh in my mind.'

Kay smiled and watched as Gemma left the room. She was one of the sweetest people Kay had ever met, and she was going to make a wonderful Anne Elliot, Kay thought.

Suddenly Kay got very excited at the thought of being able to watch some of the scenes being filmed. She had a front-row view of the Cobb for a start, and she wondered if Teresa would let her get even closer whilst they were filming. Maybe she'd be asked to be an extra! Or maybe nasty Beth would twist her ankle during the scene on the Cobb steps, and Kay would stand in for her, doing such an amazing piece of acting that Teresa would be completely bowled over and recast Kay as Louisa Musgrove. During the wonderful scene where she jumps down the steps into Captain Wentworth's arms, she'd look deep into the blue eyes of Oli Wade Owen, and he'd fall madly in love with her.

It would be a small wedding with six hundred guests, Kay thought, and a few helicopters from rival magazines flying overhead trying to get a shot of Oli's bride. They'd become media darlings, their every move photographed.

She shook her head. It was so easy to get carried away and daydream. It was one of the little quirks from her childhood that had followed her into her adult life, and she knew she had to learn how to control it, because daydreams—as harmless as they might seem—had a way of disappointing the daydreamer by not coming true. Kay was just an ordinary young woman running a bed and breakfast, and Oli Wade Owen was never going to pay her the slightest bit of attention, was he?

Chapter 9

AS PREDICTED, THE CAST AND CREW CAME HOME ONLY AFTER they'd been chucked out of the pub. Kay heard them from halfway down Marine Parade from her bedroom and was sure she could hear Beth Jenkins singing. Well, screeching really. It wasn't melodious enough to be called singing.

There was a banging and a scratching at the front door as somebody tried to get it open, and then it sounded as if everybody tried to get in all at once. Kay giggled as she opened her bedroom door and dared to peep over the stairs.

'Shussssssshhhh,' Sophie was whispering.

'You shusssshhhhh!' Beth retorted, stumbling up the first stair.

'You always have to overdo things, Beth. That's your problem.'

'Don't you tell me what my problem is,' Beth said. 'My problem is you!' she said, poking a finger into Sophie's chest.

'Yeah? Well my problem is *you*!' Sophie said in response.

'Ladies, ladies!' Oli cut in. 'We can't have the Musgrove sisters at war with each other now, can we?'

Kay watched as they all came tripping up the stairs. Beth's face was bright red, and she had a naughty gleam in her eye. Oli's blond hair was tousled as if somebody had been ruffling it—Beth, probably, Kay thought. Teresa's eyes were almost completely shut, as if her mind were already in bed and only her body had to catch up. Les brought up the rear with Sophie. He looked as morose as ever, his face sullen and sunken as if it had been sat on. Sophie was the only one who looked relatively normal. Her face looked a little flushed, but she was smiling and managing the stairs better than any of the others.

''Night,' she said when she reached the top.

Beth shoved a hand in the air by way of response and fell into her bedroom.

'Good night, my sweet princesses,' Oli said before disappearing into his own room. The others did likewise, and Kay quietly closed her own door.

For a moment, she stood perfectly still wondering, once again, if she'd imagined the whole thing.

'Where's my hair dryer?' a voice suddenly bellowed into the corridor. It was Beth Jenkins's voice.

No, Kay thought. She hadn't imagined it. There really were several film stars staying in her home.

'Sophie? Have you got my hair dryer?'

'No, I haven't got your poxy hair dryer. Keep your voice down. Gemma's trying to sleep in here.'

Beth slammed her bedroom door, and all was quiet again.

Kay giggled. This was too strange. Just a couple of doors away, Oli Wade Owen would be getting ready for bed. Kay got into her own bed. She must stop thinking about him, but it was hard to ignore somebody who had crossed her threshold with the true panache of a Jane Austen hero, and as she closed her eyes that night, Kay didn't dream about Mr Darcy but Oli Wade Owen.

Making breakfast for six people was a novelty for Kay, but not one she wasn't enjoying. Sophie had been the first one up, looking bright-eyed and eager to throw herself into the day ahead, even though it was only six in the morning, which was more than could be said for Beth, who entered the dining room with her eyes half closed.

'Good morning, bright eyes,' Sophie chirped. 'And how are you this morning?'

'Shut up, Soph!' Beth groaned as she pulled out a chair at the dining table and sat down. 'Oh, my head. Who bought me all those drinks?'

'You did,' Sophie told her with a bright laugh.

'Don't laugh. Don't say anything. It's too painful.'

'You'd better smarten yourself up before Teresa makes an appearance,' Sophie warned her. 'You know what she's like.'

'Oh, God! If she tells me to wake up and shake up, I'll scream,' Beth said.

Kay placed two pots of coffee on the table. She watched as Teresa and Les walked in together.

'Good morning,' Teresa said. 'Good God, Beth! What happened to you?'

'Nothing. I'm fine,' Beth lied, wincing at the sound of her own voice.

'You look appalling. You'd better wake up and shake up before we start filming. The makeup artists can't perform miracles, you know.'

Beth glared at her tormenter, and Sophie did her best to stifle a giggle.

Les grabbed the coffee pot and started pouring. 'Looks like

it might rain,' he said in a voice that reminded Kay of a rainy grey morning.

'Forecast isn't good,' Teresa agreed. 'We might have to do the Uppercross scenes instead.'

Gemma, who was just walking into the room, suddenly looked startled. 'The Uppercross scenes?'

'Unless the rain holds off and we can shoot some of the Cobb stuff,' Teresa said.

Kay watched as Gemma pulled out a chair and sat down. She didn't look happy.

'Good morning!' A bright voice filled the room, and Kay looked up to see Oli striding into the dining room, his smile filling his face. It was all Kay could do not to tip Sophie's juice into her lap. 'How are we all this morning?'

'God, Oli!' Beth said. 'How can you be so unrelentingly joyous? And how did you escape without a hangover? I saw the amount you put away last night.'

Oli grabbed a piece of toast from the centre of the table and started spreading it thickly with yellow butter. 'Don't know what you're talking about, my poppet,' he said, taking a big mouthful and munching happily. 'I hardly touched a drop.'

Beth shook her head and returned to her cereal in disgust.

'I did warn you all,' Teresa said. 'I said one drink, didn't I?'

Kay grinned at the conversation, but her eyes hadn't left Oli's face. As she fussed around making sure everyone had what they needed, her gaze kept flicking back to him, and she recalled the films that she'd swooned over in the past. It had been the adaptation of Charles Dickens's *A Tale of Two Cities* when he first caught her eye. He played Sydney Carton, and Kay had cried her eyes out when he sacrificed his life for the woman he loved.

There followed some rather awful romantic comedies where he played vacuous heroes who always got the girl. Still, he'd been very cute, and his audience swelled. The temptation of Hollywood then beckoned, and he was cast as the wife stealer in a film called—unsurprisingly—*The Wife Stealer*. It had been dreadful. The only redeeming thing about it had been the near-nude scene and the press that followed. Many a still from the film had been published in the tabloids, and Kay had to admit that it brightened up a few dreary lunch-hours.

Looking at him now, she tried not to think about the near-nude scene and the length of his bronzed back and his tight, firm—

'I'll get some more toast,' she blurted, causing everyone to turn and look at her.

'You all right, Kay?' Sophie asked. 'You look all flushed.'

'I'm fine,' Kay said, hurrying from the room as quickly as she could.

She must not fall in love with him. She must not fall in love with him. Handsome men were bad news. How many times had she had her heart broken? She didn't like to think about the number of handsome men who won her heart and then stepped all over it. She hadn't come to Lyme Regis just to repeat her past. She was going to throw herself into her work, make a go of her new business, and focus on her illustrations too. She did *not* need a man in her life.

But as soon as she returned to the dining room with a pot of tea and more toast, she knew it was too late, and when Oli looked up and beamed a smile at her, she knew that she was in love.

Chapter 10

Gemma couldn't believe that they might be shooting the Uppercross scenes that day. She'd thought they were doing the ones on the Cobb. She was *ready* for the Cobb.

How could film companies do that? It seemed perverse to her, like reading a book out of order. Of course, she knew what it was all about—making the most of the weather conditions and making sure the locations worked for you, but for actors, it was always difficult. Take her first job on *Into the Night* for example. She arrived on set that first day and had to shoot the final scene. It was a topsy-turvy sort of a world, and such things could easily unbalance an insecure actress.

Gemma sank onto her bed and picked up her script. She was quite sure her mother had never had such a problem learning her lines. Gemma could remember her with her scripts throughout Gemma's childhood.

'Mum,' Gemma would say, 'can you help me with my homework?'

'Darling, I have homework of my own,' her mum would say, flicking her long, dark hair over her shoulder and then sitting herself on the floor in a strange yoga position, her script in front of her and her back to her daughter.

Gemma would go upstairs to her room, and about an hour later, there'd be a knock at the door.

'Did you still want some help?' her mum would ask. Gemma would shake her head. She'd have done her homework by then.

Thinking back to those times now, Gemma knew her mother had never needed more than one read through a script, and she had it down. Maybe she had a photographic memory, or maybe her crime-caper lines had been easier to learn than a Jane Austen adaptation, but one thing was for sure: her mother never got nervous. She thrived on the adrenaline that filming produced. There was a permanent buzz about her. She oozed energy and was always the life and soul of the party—and there had been quite a few at the height of her success in *Bandits*. Gemma remembered them well. She'd be trying to sleep upstairs, when downstairs, dozens of guests were dancing and shouting in the living room. And the dining room, kitchen, and garden. Even Gemma's bedroom hadn't escaped, with one amorous couple once falling onto her bed in a lusty heap, the woman screaming to high heavens when she realised there was somebody already in it.

'Come on! It's time to go home,' Kim Reilly would yell several hours later. 'It *is* a school night, after all.' There'd be ripples of laughter, and Gemma would check the little light on her bedside clock. Her mother's idea of ending a party early would be somewhere around three o'clock. Because she didn't like to shirk her motherly duties, she'd then come into Gemma's room and squeeze her shoulder. 'I didn't wake you, darling, did I?'

'No, Mummy,' Gemma would say.

'We were nice and quiet, weren't we?'

Gemma would nod, the shrieking of the guests still ringing in her ears.

She lost count of the number of night's sleep she lost over the years and the number of tests she failed because she'd been too tired the next day in class.

Gosh, Gemma thought, is that who I'll turn into in a few years' time? The thought terrified her, because more than anything else, Gemma wanted to settle down with the perfect man and have lots of perfect babies. What if she turned into her mother, though, putting her career as an actress first and partying hard into the night? She shook her head. She was never going to allow that to happen. It just wasn't her. She was more of your sit-at-home-with-a-good-book-and-a-cup-of-tea sort of girl. And then there was the knitting. Gemma really wasn't your typical young actress courting the press by spilling out of taxis wearing the latest fashions and schmoozing with her fellow celebrities at every red carpet event. Getting drunk in the newest bar or dancing at the trendiest night-club wasn't her style. She'd rather get comfortable in the big old armchair she inherited from a maiden aunt and pick up her beloved basket of wool.

Beth had already sussed Gemma's little knitting quirk.

'Oh, it's so wonderfully mumsy!' she said, making the word *mumsy* sound like the foulest of insults, whilst also insinuating that Gemma didn't have a sexy bone in her body. Everyone in rehearsal had turned to stare at Gemma and the ball of lilac wool she was clutching, and there had been a few sniggers, which had cut her to the quick, but Gemma needed her knitting. Not only was it her passion, but it also calmed her down. The click clack of the needles was mesmeric, and her work in progress took her mind off things when she wasn't needed on set. At least she didn't spend her spare time bitching about people behind their backs, she thought, remembering the vitriol that had spilled from Beth's mouth in between takes in the studio. That woman might have a face that could grace any magazine cover in the world, but her language was as foul as a cesspit.

Gemma closed her eyes. It was people like Beth that really made working in this industry difficult. For some reason, the world of acting seemed to attract some of the nastiest examples of human-kind, and it pained Gemma that she had to spend hours of her life doing her best to dodge them.

'You ready to rock?' a voice said, startling Gemma from her thoughts. She looked up to see Sophie enter the room. At least there was one ally on this film set, she thought, thanking her lucky stars that she'd bonded so quickly with Sophie. 'Time we were out of here.'

Gemma nodded and got up off the bed, her script in her hand.

'You don't need that, do you?' Sophie said lightheartedly.

'Oh, you know,' Gemma said, 'it's just in case. I like to have it with me.' She turned around and grabbed her oversized bag, her knitting needles poking out of the opening.

'Are they yours?' Sophie asked in bemusement.

Gemma nodded.

'I didn't know Anne Elliot knitted. Can I see?'

'It's just a little something. It's not really fin—'

Sophie had already pulled it out of her bag and was inspecting it. 'Oh, it's adorable!' she said, holding up a little baby jacket in pearly pink wool.

'My sister-in-law's just had a little girl—Harriet.'

'This is gorgeous,' Sophie said. 'Really gorgeous. Could you make one in a size ten for me?'

Gemma grinned, delighted at the praise.

Sophie returned the little jacket to her. 'Into the fray,' she said, and as they closed the bedroom door behind them, Gemma wished, with all her heart, that she could stay on the other side of that door with her knitting needles.

～⌒

Kay watched as everybody congregated in the hallway. She'd never heard a small group of people make so much noise.

'We've just had the latest weather report,' Teresa announced, 'and we might be able to get a couple of shots in on the Cobb before the heavens open. Anyway, into makeup and costume first, and we'll take things from there.'

Les opened the door, and everybody spilled out into the early morning.

''Bye, Kay,' Sophie said.

Kay beamed her a smile. It was nice of at least one of them to remember her. Oli then turned around and winked at her. Kay's mouth dropped open but then clamped shut again, as Teresa glared at him and pushed him out the door. Kay turned away in embarrassment. She should be getting on with tidying up, not standing in the hallway flirting with film stars.

Flirting! He *had* been flirting with her, hadn't he? Teresa had said they'd all be wanting an evening meal that night and Kay had quite enough on her plate, preparing to fill theirs, without the distraction of flirting.

As the door finally closed, silence filled Wentworth House. It was funny. They'd only been there one night, but the bed and breakfast felt strangely empty once they left. Kay looked at the enormous pile of dirty bowls, plates, and cups, knowing she had plenty to get on with, but she had a better idea. Flinging her tea towel over a chair, she took the stairs two at a time, rushing into her bedroom and staring out the window. Her guests had reached the Cobb where several vans were already in position. It was too early yet for tourists to get in the way, but Kay could see that the area had been roped off.

She looked around her bedroom. Now, where had she put them? She hunted through her wardrobe and the drawers of her bedside table. They were there somewhere; she was quite sure of it. Ah, there they were! Tucked away at the back of the second drawer, behind a notebook featuring the face of Mr Darcy, was a pair of miniature binoculars. Kay pulled them out, grabbed a drawing pad and pencil, and ran downstairs, pulling on a pair of boots and heading along Marine Parade in the direction of the Cobb. She didn't want to make a nuisance of herself, so she found a quiet stretch of wall along the beach and sat down.

'That's better,' she said to herself as she brought the binoculars into focus and settled on the little crowd of people who had joined her guests on the Cobb. There was a lot of pointing going on, and everyone looked out to sea, where a heap of bruised clouds was looming over the horizon. Teresa nodded, and Les looked as miserable as ever. And Oli was looking handsome. He had a great profile, just the sort of profile a heroine would sketch as a silhouette. Kay smiled. What a great idea that would be! She could get him sitting for her one evening and make one of those fabulous Austenesque silhouettes, just like the one Marianne made of Willoughby in the film adaptation of *Sense and Sensibility*.

In the meantime, the artist in her got the better of her, and she opened her pad and began sketching. That beautiful slope of his forehead, that perfect nose and strong jaw, the sensual curve of his smile, and the buttery floppiness of that hair. Kay quickly sketched, her eyes focussing through the binoculars and then down on her pad, capturing the magic of the man as quickly as she could.

She was just putting the finishing touches to it when she looked through the binoculars again. Oli had turned around, and he was waving. Kay moved the binoculars to the right, trying to see at whom he was waving, and something odd happened. Oli pointed towards her, a big grin on his face.

Kay gasped. He was waving at her. She bit her lip and quickly got up to leave, but it was too late. She'd been well and truly rumbled. She closed her eyes for a moment and allowed herself a good old cringe. What on earth would Oli think of her now? He'd think she was some ogling starstruck fan. It was awful! She'd just have to try to explain what she was doing.

You were ogling him, a little voice inside her said as she quickly headed back home.

'No, I wasn't. I was sketching him as part of my work. He is playing Captain Wentworth, after all.'

You were ogling him! You know you were!

Kay groaned. She had better things to do than stand around arguing with herself. There was the dishwasher to load, for a start. She was piling in the dishes and thanking her lucky stars that she had the foresight to buy one, when there was a knock at the door. For a moment, her heart raced. Maybe it was Oli. He'd raced back to the B&B after seeing her ogling him—*watching* him. It had suddenly dawned on him that she was the girl for him. How hadn't he seen it sooner? He should have realised it when she was serving him breakfast. Oh, all the time they'd wasted!

Kay opened the door. It was a man, all right, but it wasn't Oli.

'Hello,' he said.

'Hello,' Kay said, her heartbeat returning to something approaching normality again.

'I'm Adam. Adam Craig.'

'I'm afraid we're full at the moment. If you're looking for a room,' Kay said.

'Oh, I'm not,' he said. 'I'm looking for Teresa. I believe she's staying here.'

'She's down at the Cobb,' Kay said. 'They left about ten minutes ago. You can't miss them—they've practically taken over the whole of that part of town.'

Adam turned to look in the direction of the Cobb. 'Ah, yes. I should have thought to go there first.'

'You're with the film people?' Kay asked.

He nodded. 'I'm the screenwriter and producer.'

'Oh,' Kay said.

'Don't worry,' he said. 'Nobody ever knows what a producer does, and nobody ever cares what a writer does.'

'I didn't mean—'

'It's okay.'

'Would you like to come in?' Kay asked, not quite sure what she was going to do with a screenwriter/producer but feeling it was the polite thing to ask.

'This place was empty for a while, wasn't it?' Adam stepped inside and looked around. 'It's good to see you're breathing new life into it,' he said with a smile.

'I've just had all the bedrooms redecorated and the dining room. The rest will have to wait, I'm afraid,' she said, leading him into the living room.

'Ah, yes. I see what you mean.'

Kay nodded as Adam took in the nicotine-coloured wallpaper and swirly patterned carpet.

'An acquired taste, perhaps,' Kay said. 'And one I have no intention of acquiring. Oh,' she suddenly added, 'I'm Kay.'

Adam smiled and stretched out a hand to shake hers. His sight caught the book she'd left open over the arm of a chair.

'You're reading *Persuasion*?' he asked.

'It's one of the reasons I'm here in Lyme. I was reading it when Teresa arrived and told me she was filming it right here in Lyme.' Something occurred to Kay. 'You must be staying somewhere else.'

'In a way. I've got a little place a few miles away.'

'Oh, you're local?'

'Born and bred,' he said. 'I've got a few acres of land in the Marshwood Vale.'

'What do you use the land for?' Kay asked.

'To walk on, mostly,' he said with a smile. 'Although I've been thinking of getting a horse. What do you think?'

Kay's eyebrows rose. She wasn't used to strange men asking her advice about equestrian matters.

'I used to ride, but I got out of the habit when I had to work for a living.'

'I've got nothing against horses,' Kay said. 'All the best heroes have them.'

'Heroes?'

'In books.'

'I see,' he said with a nod of recognition. 'I suppose horses were the status symbols of their day.'

'But where would you park a horse in Lyme?' Kay asked.

'That's a very good question,' Adam said. 'Still, imagine the fun of turning up to work on a horse with your briefcase in your hand.'

Kay laughed. She'd known Adam for only about five minutes, but she already liked him.

The front door opened and closed.

'Kay?' a voice called. It was Gemma. 'Oh, Adam!' she said as she came into the room, and Kay noticed that Adam's face lit up, and—in true Emma Woodhouse style—she had them matched and married off in a blink of an eye. After all, Adam wasn't bad looking, now that she came to think of it. He had dark brown hair that was a little bit tousled, as if he'd been cycling down a windswept hill, and his eyes were an intense grey behind his glasses, and his smile was very cute too.

'Everything all right?' Kay asked.

'Teresa wants to know if we can borrow your copy of *Persuasion*. She wants to check something, and nobody has a copy. Can you believe it?'

Kay picked up her copy and handed it to her.

'Thanks,' Gemma said. 'We'll bring it right back.'

'How's it going?'

'Not good. We think we might get a couple of shots in, but the wind's really picked up, and it's going to rain,' Gemma said.

Adam nodded. 'It's meant to be quite heavy.'

'Oh, dear,' Gemma said looking anxious.

'It'll be all right,' Adam said. 'You worry too much, Gemma.'

Kay observed the look that passed between Adam and Gemma and smiled. They were cute together.

What Kay didn't notice, however, was the fact that Adam's gaze soon left Gemma's face and returned to hers.

Chapter 11

OF COURSE, IT SHOULDN'T HAVE BEEN GEMMA WHO RAN BACK to Wentworth House to find a copy of *Persuasion*, but she took off before Teresa could stop her. Any excuse to get off the set for a while and postpone the inevitable.

Adam had been there. He even walked back with her, giving her loads of encouragement and being a sweetheart.

Gemma then climbed the steps into one of the vans being used as a dressing room and sat in what she had come to think of as 'the chair of doom' whilst a makeup artist turned her into a nineteenth-century heroine. It was the most bizarre of processes, Gemma thought. She didn't usually bother much with makeup, and having somebody else attacking her with sponges, brushes, and pencils was somewhat alarming.

Beth, of course, loved it. She adored any form of attention and would always be sure to complain if she thought she wasn't getting enough.

'Shouldn't I be wearing more mascara than that?' Beth asked, peering into the mirror with a horrified expression on her face.

'You're playing Louisa Musgrove in *Persuasion*,' Sophie said with a laugh. 'Not Sally Bowles in *Cabaret*.'

Gemma tried to hide her smile. Beth had already been severely reprimanded by Teresa for wearing scarlet lipstick. They'd been halfway through shooting a scene before Teresa noticed and went completely mad.

Makeup complete, it was time for the costumes, which were so beautiful that it was hard not to fall in love with them and try to smuggle them home, especially if you were an Austen fan like Gemma and Sophie were. It was a novelty to be wearing something other than jeans. How many women wore pretty, feminine dresses anymore? And the fabrics that had been chosen were exquisite. The only problem was that they did absolutely nothing to keep the cold out, and when shooting on a windblown Cobb, it could result in white limbs covered in goose bumps.

But there was more to a part than makeup and a costume, Gemma thought. You had to *be* the character. When she got the call from her agent telling her she'd got the part of Anne Elliot, she'd done a little dance in her living room and then grabbed a copy of the book and read it right through. The panic then set in. Playing Anne Elliot was a huge responsibility. For many readers, she was the perfect Jane Austen heroine: selfless, loyal, and compassionate. Some even believed she was Jane Austen herself, and it was made all the more special, for being the last novel she wrote. She'd been writing it when she was dying, and ardent fans felt it was the closest they would ever get to their beloved author. There was an honesty and a simplicity about *Persuasion*. It might not have the exuberance of *Pride and Prejudice* or the naughtiness of *Emma*, but it was all the more dear because of that, Gemma thought.

The reason Gemma loved the novel so much, though, was because of Anne. Readers couldn't fail to feel Anne's pain, because which of us hasn't experienced the pain of a lost love? We have all had our hearts broken, and we have all made mistakes, Gemma thought. Perhaps that's why it was so easy to identify with Anne.

What if the fans didn't like Gemma? What if she let them down? What if they didn't *believe* that she was Anne? Gemma knew only too well how disappointing it could be if actors in literary adaptations didn't live up to expectations. Such was one of the major worries about adapting a much-loved novel. People knew the characters well and had incredibly strong views as to how characters should be portrayed and what they should look like.

'I don't care how handsome he was,' a fan might say, 'he was not *my* idea of Mr Darcy.'

'Her hair! Did you see Fanny Price's hair? What were they thinking?'

Gemma sighed. Adapting a classic novel was a minefield, and taking on the role of its heroine was fraught with potential disasters.

As Gemma got up to leave the relative warmth of the van and was rudely accosted by the wind, which quickly whipped around her thin muslin dress, she could only hope that her performance wouldn't disappoint the legion of fans out there.

She was trying to take shelter in the curve of the Cobb until she was needed, when a dark-haired man walked past her. It was the man from the bar at The Three Palms—the one on whom she'd turned her back.

'Hello,' he said.

Gemma nodded.

'You okay?' he asked. 'You look cold.'

'I'm fine, thank you,' Gemma said politely, half expecting him to move on to wherever he had to move on to. But he didn't.

'That dress doesn't look very substantial,' he said.

'It isn't,' Gemma said and then blushed as she saw his eyes sweep over her exposed bosom.

'*Rob?*' a voice yelled from the other end of the Cobb. 'Get over here, will you?'

The man shrugged. 'No rest for the wicked,' he said, and as quickly as he'd appeared, he disappeared, leaving Gemma with the impression that he was, indeed, very wicked. Rather cute, too.

Adam always felt like a bit of a spare part when he was on set. For a start, he wasn't really needed. Nobody asked him his opinion about the way a scene should be shot, and if there were any questions about the script, they were always directed to Teresa. He didn't mind, though. He quite liked being in the background. It gave him a chance to observe everything that was going on around him. He loved the bustle of film sets; the excitement had never waned over the years. No matter how many he'd been on, there was always something different to experience. For the *Persuasion* shoot, it was the transformation of the Cobb. There were canteen trucks, trucks for the actors full of costumes and makeup, vans full of cables, dolly tracks for the camera, and ropes cordoning off several streets, with notices apologising for any inconvenience. He'd been working on a film up in Scotland when the 2006 production of *Persuasion* had been shooting in Lyme Regis, and he'd been gutted to miss it. Now he took a step back and gloried in the chaos that he caused by sitting down to write a script one day.

He'd been told about the burst pipe at The Three Palms and how Teresa had managed to find Wentworth House. Adam smiled as he thought about its new owner. It had been her, hadn't it? The girl with the toffee-coloured hair he'd seen outside the estate agents. She hadn't recognised him, but how could she have? He hadn't exactly made his presence known that day, had he? But he remembered her. There'd been something about her that captivated him immediately. She had a sweetness about her the like of which he'd never seen before, and it had been easy to talk to her. He'd been surprised at how at ease he felt in her company. Women usually had the effect of tying him up in knots, but Kay loosened him. Gemma was the same. He adored Gemma and cared enormously about her, but she didn't give him the fluttery feeling in the pit of his stomach that Kay did.

Adam took a deep breath of salty air. Now was not a good time to fall in love. He'd just started a new screenplay and was up to his eyeballs in ideas, plus there was still much to sort out with the film. His phone never stopped ringing, unless he switched it off, which he often did when he was writing. His imagination was working at full capacity at the moment, and there wasn't room to start imagining romantic scenarios in his own life. He had to write those of his characters' first, but that was easier said than done, wasn't it?

A sudden gust of wind buffeted Adam, and he buttoned his coat. It was cold for May, and the sea was a menacing grey to match the sky. He watched as the actresses left the safety of the makeup vans, the fine fabric of their dresses whipping around their legs. They were all wearing coats, and he could see strands of hair desperately trying to escape from the confines of their bonnets.

'It's impossible!' Beth shouted above the wind. 'I can hardly get my breath.'

Sophie and Gemma linked arms and struggled along behind Beth as they approached the Cobb. The sea was whipping up some alarming waves, and they hit the Cobb on the far side and sprayed over the top, soaking anyone who dared to stand nearby.

Teresa shook her head. 'It's no good,' she bellowed. 'We can't shoot in this.'

'I told you,' Beth bellowed back. 'We should have had that lie-in.'

'Best hangover cure, though,' Oli said with a laugh. He was wearing an enormous coat over his Captain Wentworth clothes, and his face was damp with sea spray. The other actors who were part of the Cobb scene were similarly attired, and most were bent double to try to cope with the ever-increasing wind.

Then the rain came. There was no buildup—no hesitant drops to warn of an impending downpour—the heavens just opened and dumped their load onto the poor unfortunates below.

Adam pulled up the hood of his coat and ran towards the nearest van for cover, as did everyone else. Bonnets and hair were flattened in an instant, and makeup rivered down each actor's face. Dampened dresses clung to the actresses' legs, and everyone's face was as glum as Les Miserable's.

Towels were quickly passed around and the makeup girls went into standby to repair the damage, but Teresa shook her head.

'Get out of those wet things,' she shouted. 'Get dried, and then we're heading out to do the Uppercross scenes.'

Adam saw Gemma's face fall, and he could guess why. She'd psyched herself up for the Cobb scene, and now the weather had put paid to that.

'Hey,' he said, sidling up to her, 'you'll be fine.'

She looked up at him with wide eyes, reminding him of a traffic-startled deer, but then she nodded.

'Come on, everyone,' Teresa suddenly bellowed. 'Get moving!'

Adam knew that they'd hired a minibus, and it wasn't long before the cast were battling their way along the windy Cobb and boarding the vehicle. Nobody asked him if he wanted to join them, but he hadn't expected that they would, and he didn't mind. He had his own wheels, and he also had an idea brewing.

'Kay,' he said quietly to himself as he left the Cobb. Kay could come with him. She was reading *Persuasion*. She was bound to want to see it being filmed, and it would be the perfect opportunity to get to know her.

Bowing his head against the wind, he walked along Marine Parade towards Wentworth House, making a couple of quick calls to the production team first, so he couldn't be accused of skiving.

This is a good idea, isn't it? a little voice inside him said as he approached Kay's. He cleared his throat and pulled down his hood, raking a hand through his hair, which he feared was even more tousled than usual, with the wind he'd been battling. Before he could change his mind, he knocked on the door.

And waited.

He knocked again, rapping the knocker as loudly as he could.

He waited some more. Lucky there was a porch, he thought; otherwise he would have been soaked to the skin by then.

Finally the door opened. 'Oh!' Kay said.

'Hello,' Adam said, noticing her face was flushed and her long toffee-coloured hair had been piled on top of her head in a funny sort of bun.

'I was under the bed,' she said.

He gave her a quizzical look.

'Vacuuming,' she explained. 'Did you forget something?'

'No. Can I come in?' he asked, knowing he was the kind of guy who girls didn't automatically invite into their homes. 'It's a bit blustery out here.'

'Oh, right,' Kay said.

'There's something I want to ask you,' he said as he walked inside, waiting for her to close the door behind them. 'They've broken off filming at the Cobb. The weather's too bad. They're going to do some of the Uppercross scenes—up in the Marshwood Vale.'

'Where you live?'

'Nearby, yes. I was going to drive up there and wondered if you wanted to come along.' He paused, his heart thudding in his chest. This isn't a date, he told himself. There's no need to get tied up into nervous knots about it.

'Right now?' she asked, her bright eyes widening.

'Yes.'

'I don't know,' Kay said. 'There's so much to do here. I've got beds to make and towels to wash and carpets to vacuum and sinks to clean. And I've got to prepare a meal for tonight.'

Adam watched as she puffed out her cheeks.

'Okay,' he said.

'Maybe another time?'

'No. I mean—okay—I'll help you,' he said. 'I'll make the beds and wash the towels and vacuum anything that needs vacuuming.'

She gave him a quizzical look. 'Why?'

'Because I think you should come and see *Persuasion* being filmed, and I want to show you the Marshwood Vale.'

Kay looked thoughtful for a moment.

'All the cast will be there. I'm sure they'd be happy to see you,' he added, and he watched as Kay's expression changed.

'You'll really help out here?' she asked.

'Of course. Just point me to the nearest sink that needs scrubbing.'

A smile broke across Kay's face, and Adam found himself mirroring it. He'd known this would be a good idea.

Chapter 12

THERE FOLLOWED A MAD FRENZY OF VACUUMING, DUSTING, AND scrubbing as Adam and Kay worked their way around the bedrooms of Wentworth House. Bed sheets were straightened and tucked, pillows and duvets were shaken and fluffed, towels were swapped and washed, and everything else was cleaned until it shone.

Finally, when Kay was quite sure everything looked perfect, she turned to Adam. He was ready with a smile for her.

'I think we deserve the rest of the day off, don't you?'

Kay nodded. 'That's certainly a job well done,' she said. 'Thanks so much for helping. If you ever give up the film world, there's a job for you right here.'

'I might take you up on that,' he said, thinking how wonderful it would be to work alongside Kay all day. How distracting it would be too. No, he decided, he probably wouldn't get any work done at all, if he knew she was just in the next room, because the temptation to down tools and take her in his arms and—well, it just wouldn't be viable, would it?

'Let's get going, shall we?'

'I'll just get changed,' Kay said.

Adam nodded and decided to take himself downstairs to the

living room. Being on the same floor as Kay getting changed was more than any sane man could bear.

It was a funny little room with its nicotine-coloured wallpaper and flowery carpet, but Kay had made it wonderfully homey. There was a glass vase of freesias on the windowsill, and two big lamps promised a warm glow once evening set in. She'd also filled the shelves in the alcoves with books, and he couldn't resist looking at them as he waited for her. He smiled to himself as he saw a row of jewel-bright Regency romances by Lorna Warwick. Hadn't the author recently been revealed to be a man? Adam was sure he'd read something somewhere.

Nestling alongside the Lorna Warwick titles were the obligatory Jane Austen novels—an impressive three copies of each title, all with different covers. Then there was the nonfiction associated with the great woman—the biographies, the histories of England in the time of the writer, collections of her letters, and new critical studies of her work. It was a collection worthy of any Janeite, he thought as he pulled out one of the collections of her letters.

'They're wonderful, aren't they?' Kay asked.

Adam spun around and saw Kay standing in the doorway. She'd untied her hair, and it cascaded around her shoulders in light waves, making Adam want to reach out and touch it. She'd changed out of her jeans too and was wearing a long pink dress with a berry-red jacket over it.

'I love Jane Austen's letters,' she said. 'Her humour is wonderful. She's so naughty—just what a younger sister should be.'

Adam nodded, realising he was staring like a mad man. 'Do you have any younger sisters?'

'No,' Kay said, and her smile instantly vanished. 'No brothers and no sisters. Just me.'

'That must have been a bit lonely growing up,' he said.

'Oh, I had my books,' she said. 'My fictional families.'

'Me too.'

'You're an only child?'

'Perhaps that's why I'm a writer. I was always creating fictional families.'

Kay smiled. 'I think onlys have a tendency to hide within their imaginations.'

'I think so too,' he said, 'but it's not a bad place to be.'

'No,' Kay said, 'especially when things get to be too much.' She bit her lip. She hadn't meant to say so much, but there was something about Adam that made it easy for her to talk. 'So are we going to Uppercross?' she added, quickly changing the subject before she inflicted her whole past on the poor man.

'Absolutely,' Adam said, grabbing his coat from the hallway.

The rain had stopped by the time they left the bed and breakfast, but the sky was still a deep bruised purple and the waves looked angry and threatening, as if they were plotting something.

'Wow,' Kay said. 'I've never seen it like this.'

'Get used to it,' Adam said. 'Winters can be pretty tough on the coast.'

'I guess we only think of these places as being filled with summer sunshine and tourists.'

'But that's one of the benefits of winter,' Adam said. 'The tourists go home, and you have it to yourself.'

'Don't you like tourists?' Kay said. They reached the end of Marine Parade and crossed the road towards the parking lot. 'Jane Austen was a tourist, and you wouldn't have a film being made of your screenplay if she hadn't visited Lyme.'

Adam grinned. 'Of course, but there are tourists and there are tourists. I object only to the ones who come to Lyme and aren't inspired to write great literature.'

They walked on, and Adam finally pointed to his car and unlocked it. It was an old Volvo that had a pair of wellingtons on the back seat that had seen better days. The Volvo had seen better days too, and Adam knew it.

'Sorry about the dog hair,' he said, getting in beside her. 'I was looking after somebody's German shepherd, and he seemed to be moulting. He was even worse than my cat.'

'You have a cat?' Kay asked.

'Sir Walter. After Anne Elliot's father, because he's a terrible snob who's forever looking down his little pink nose at me.'

Kay laughed. 'I'd like to meet him.'

Adam swallowed. Things didn't normally happen that easily for him. Women didn't usually just invite themselves to his house. If he'd known that all he had to do to get a woman to come home with him was mention his cat, he would have done it years before. Who would have thought that dear old Sir Walter would earn his keep?

'But first, Uppercross.'

It had been a pleasant enough drive from Lyme Regis into the Marshwood Vale. The film crew left the worst of the weather behind them at the coast, but Teresa was still looking anxious about things. Gemma had been watching her closely, wondering which scenes they would be filming in the course of the day. The sky was still dark, and large clouds scudded their way across it like malevolent phantoms. It was very unlikely that they'd be filming anything outdoors that day.

Gemma stole a glance at Beth and Sophie. They were both joking about something, and Sophie was laughing. Gemma adored Sophie. She was always happy. Nothing seemed to faze her. *If only I could be like that,* Gemma thought. *Why do I have to worry so much? Why can't I just look out of the window and enjoy the day or be able to tell silly jokes? Why does my stomach always have to be doing the cancan?*

For a moment she wondered whether she could get her knitting out and try to settle her nerves, but the twisting country lanes would turn her needles into instruments of danger, and she didn't want to risk injuring anyone, not even Beth.

Teresa was on her phone, barking a list of instructions to some poor soul at the other end. Gemma bit her lip. She was glad she wasn't a member of the crew. Teresa seemed to handle the actors with kid gloves in comparison to how she handled the crew, although she seemed to take exception with Oli. For some reason, he seemed to wind her up constantly. Gemma knew that they had worked together before and often wondered why they agreed to work together again, if that was the way they felt about each other. Maybe it was one of those funny relationships where their passion for the art they were creating overruled anything personal. They knew that what they were producing would be a little bit of screen magic, and they were willing to put up with all the irritation that went with it.

When she was quite sure nobody was looking, Gemma surreptitiously opened her bag and fished out her copy of the script. It was getting battered, with its curling pages and bashed-in spine, but it still served its purpose well, and Gemma soon found the scenes she needed for the day ahead. Anxiously her eyes cast over the lines that weren't completely new to her but seemed like a memory of a distant dream, and her heart beat faster. She didn't feel ready. She wanted more time, *needed* more time, but before she had time to read more than three pages, the minibus slowed down to turn into a long tree-lined driveway.

Beyond the trees, there was a field full of sheep, and then the countryside rolled away into the distance. As the bus made a final turn, the house was revealed to them.

Marlcombe Manor was a Grade I Jacobean house that sprawled across an immaculate lawn like a sleeping dragon. It was built in glorious honey-coloured stone and looked as if it housed at least three ghosts, with its enormous mullioned windows and barley-twist chimneys. Swallows swooped across the lawn, and a po-faced peacock made its sedate way up the driveway.

'Here we are,' Oli announced. 'Home sweet home.'

Adam's phone beeped as they were at a quiet junction by a village pub, and he took the opportunity to read the text.

'It's from Gemma, my spy,' he said. 'They've reached Marlcombe Manor.'

'Is it far?'

'No,' Adam said. 'Just a couple of miles.' His phone beeped again. 'Right,' he said as he read the text.

'Everything okay?'

He sighed. 'Just something else to worry about, I'm afraid.'

'The life of a producer?'

'Yes,' Adam said. 'Nobody seems to know what a producer does, but if I didn't do it, the whole film would fall apart.'

Kay nodded and then rooted around in her handbag.

'You okay?' Adam asked.

'Just checking that I've got my camera. I'm sure I put it in, and I'd hate to be without it.'

They followed a high hedgerow along a country lane that seemed to stretch for miles without any traffic on it at all.

'This is all so beautiful,' Kay said.

Adam glanced quickly at her as she gazed out of the window. 'I couldn't live anywhere else,' he said.

'Doesn't Jane Austen mention this countryside in *Persuasion*?'

'She certainly does,' Adam said. 'She says, "a very strange stranger it must be, who does not see charms in the immediate environs of Lyme, to make him wish to know it better".'

'Maybe I should take up hiking or something,' Kay said. 'You know—really get to know the area.'

'Well, it is the best way to see the countryside.'

'Maybe we could go together,' Kay said. 'You could show me around.'

Adam almost choked in surprise.

'I mean, when you're not too busy.'

'I'd be very happy to show you around,' Adam said.

Kay smiled, and her face lit up. Adam did his best to focus on the road ahead. He wasn't going to think of romantic footpaths that led far from the madding crowd. He wasn't going to think of getting Kay alone on the side of some windswept hill or in the seclusion of a glorious beech wood full of bluebells. He must keep his eyes on the road and remain in the present.

He was driving down a hill into a sweep of valley when he heard Kay gasp. Ahead of them, a little ford had turned into a swollen river.

'I didn't realise there'd been so much rain,' Kay said.

'Mostly in the night,' Adam said. 'The last few have been very wet, and it doesn't take much to flood these lanes.'

'Will we be able to get through?'

'This car's older than the Jurassic coast, but it's got me through worse than that before.' Adam slowed down and wound down his window as he approached the flood. 'It's not too bad,' he said.

'Famous last words,' Kay said as the car neared the water. Kay held her breath as they approached, anxious as to how deep it was. The last thing she wanted was to be stranded in the middle of nowhere, when she could be in Oli's company on the film set.

'Here we go,' Adam said, and the car splashed through the water. Kay closed her eyes for a moment, but she needn't have worried, because they made it safely through to the other side.

Kay smiled in relief.

'Soon be there,' Adam said. Kay nodded, and he watched as she opened her handbag and took out a lipstick, unfolding the car mirror and applying a thick slick of pink gloss. Adam sighed. He had the feeling that she wasn't doing it for his benefit.

Chapter 13

GEMMA WAS BEGINNING TO THINK THAT HER WISHING FOR A delay actually worked, because something mysterious was happening with the lighting department. It had been decided that they would shoot one of the indoor scenes with Sir Walter Elliot, and it was to take place in one of the upstairs rooms, as agreed with the owners. It was a beautiful room overlooking the gardens, but the stormy skies made it almost pitch black.

'Are they ever going to need us today?' Beth complained as she mooched about on the lawn, moaning to anyone who would listen. Gemma had done her best to avoid her, managed to fit in a bit of private time with her script, and was feeling a little bit more confident about her Uppercross scenes.

Walking across the lawn, she took some deep breaths, inhaling the sweet rain-washed air. She saw one of the technicians had set up a laptop at the back of one of the vans, and a crowd gathered around him.

'What are you watching?' Gemma asked, daring to squeeze in next to Oli to see what was going on.

'*Killer Zombies Take Manhattan,*' Sophie said. 'It's horrible blood-spurting, mind-numbing violence.'

'It's brilliant,' Oli said, obviously engrossed.

Gemma looked up at him. How could he go from zombie fan to sophisticated hero in just a few minutes? He really was a great actor, wasn't he? If only his fans could see him with his smile as wide as a child's as he watched a zombie ripping the arm off a poor taxi driver in Times Square.

'Gross!' Sophie shouted.

'There's that book out, isn't there?' Gemma said. '*Pride and Prejudice and Zombies.*'

'Cool!' Oli said.

Gemma grimaced, her romantic allusions of Oli fast disintegrating.

Kay didn't like to keep checking her reflection in Adam's mirror, but she wanted to make quite sure that her hair hadn't gone flyaway and that nothing had smudged. It was strange. She had already spent a whole night under the same roof as Oli and shared breakfast with him. Well, she *served* him breakfast, anyway, yet this trip to see him filming was beginning to feel more and more like a first date.

As Adam turned into a long driveway lined with trees, the anticipation was almost too much for Kay as she unwound her window and peered out, desperate for the first glimpse of the house and the actors.

'It's one of the loveliest houses in Dorset,' Adam said.

Kay nodded. She liked a beautiful house as much as the next Jane Austen fan, but she was far more interested in seeing Oli again. As the car drove around the final bend and came to a standstill alongside the actors' minibus, she caught sight of them all across the lawn.

Leaving Adam to lock up, she got out of the car, walked across the driveway, and stared at the group of actors. They hadn't seen her, and she took advantage to sneak a hand into her bag and find her camera.

It was thoughtful of Adam to bring her. She turned around to smile at him and saw that he was looking at Gemma, and Kay realised *that* was why he had been so keen to come out to the Uppercross shoot. He wanted to see Gemma, just as she had wanted to see Oli. They did make a lovely couple too—or rather, they *would*, once things were sorted out between them. The trouble was that they were both shy, and Kay doubted that either of them would dare to make the first move.

Maybe that's where she could help. Perhaps *she* could get them together. She smiled as her mind wandered over the possibilities. Gemma was staying at the B&B, and Adam was forever dropping by. Maybe she could make them a meal. The next time the cast went out to the pub, she could ask Gemma if she'd like to join her for dinner. She wouldn't be joining Gemma, of course—Adam would, because she would invite him too.

She'd buy some candles—pretty red ones. Flowers too. She'd transform the dining room so that it became the perfect setting for romance. It would be wonderful. She'd serve them dinner, and they'd have no choice but to talk to each other. Their shyness would fall away, and they'd discover how much they had in common and fall madly in love.

A summer wedding wouldn't be out of the question if they got a move on too, Kay thought. How beautiful Gemma would look in a frothy lace dress, and Adam would wear something smart and understated, his hair newly cut and not quite as tousled as normal. Kay would have to buy herself a new dress for the occasion, and how wonderful it would be to sit at the front of the church, knowing that the bride and groom were there because of her. They'd thank her in the speeches too, and Kay would blush at the top table, saying that it was nothing, really—that you can't stop romance.

There would be dancing—just like in Jane Austen's time. Oli would be there, of course, and he'd lead Kay onto the dance floor, telling her how beautiful she looked and how he hadn't been able to stop thinking about her since filming had stopped. He had been mad to leave her behind in Lyme. What had he been thinking? Could she forgive him?

'Of course I can, Oli,' Kay said, except she said it out loud in the here and now, and Oli heard his name and turned around. He'd been half hidden amongst the group crowding around the back of one of the vans, but suddenly the group dispersed, and there he was.

'Hey, you!' he said as he strode across the lawn towards her. Kay gulped. He did it so well. Maybe it was the boots he wore. Maybe they had the effect of making him stride like a fine pair of heels will add that extra little something to the way a woman walks.

'Hello,' she squeaked. She swallowed. What happened to her voice? He smiled. 'You come out to see us lot, then?'

'Yes,' she said, her voice seeming to return to normal. 'Adam brought me.'

'Adam?'

Kay pointed to where Adam was standing with a polystyrene mug in his hands.

'Oh!' Oli said. 'Him.'

'He's the writer and producer,' Kay explained.

'Yes, I know. Doesn't have much to say, does he?'

Kay thought that comment was a little unkind. Maybe poor Adam didn't get a chance to say much when surrounded by verbose actors.

'Coming out here was his idea,' she said. 'It was kind of him to bring me.'

'I'm glad he did,' Oli said. 'Fancy a walk?'

'Aren't you needed on set?' Kay asked.

'Nah. Not for ages. They're about to film the retrenching scene—you know the one with Sir Walter Elliot?'

Kay nodded, remembering the scene from the book.

'Come on,' he said.

They left the noise of the cast and crew behind them and skirted around the side of the house, through two tall hedgerows that led into a secluded knot garden.

'It's lovely,' Kay said, reaching out and pinching a lemon balm leaf between her fingers before sniffing it appreciatively. 'How old's the house?' she asked him.

'Marlcombe Manor?' Oli said, seeming surprised by her question. 'Oh, it's old. Very old. Stone Age or Roman or something like that.'

Kay laughed.

'And these gardens,' he continued. 'Very fine gardens, I'm led to believe. They were designed and everything.'

She laughed again. 'You don't know very much about Marlcombe, do you?'

'Nope,' he said. 'I'm just an actor. I go where they tell me, and I attach myself to the locations with great aptitude, but I rarely get to know them at all.'

'That's a shame.'

'That's the life of an actor. You can't get too attached to anything, because you're always moving on.'

Kay wondered if his comment was a veiled warning to her. *You can't get too attached to anything*, but maybe she was reading too much into it. Anyway, who was to say that he had any notion of attaching himself to her? She must stop thinking like that.

'So what's it been like for you, with us all invading?' he asked.

'Wonderful,' Kay said, the word slipping out before she had a chance to rein herself in and appear cool and aloof. 'I mean, I've just opened, so it's wonderful to have all the rooms full.'

They walked in silence for a moment, their feet crunching lightly on the gravel pathways. Kay could hardly believe it. She was walking in a beautiful English country garden with the most handsome actor in the world, and he was dressed as one of her favourite heroes from literature.

'You look happy,' Oli suddenly said.

Kay looked up, and for a moment, she really did see Frederick Wentworth standing there.

'What were you thinking of?' he asked.

She looked away, distracting herself by plucking a leaf from a peppermint plant. 'Just thinking,' she said.

'Tell me.'

'You'll laugh.'

'No, I won't.'

Kay took a deep breath and turned to look at him. 'I was just wondering what it would be like to be Anne Elliot and live in a place like this with—with Captain Wentworth.'

'Ah,' Oli said.

'What?'

'You have Captain Wentworth fever?'

'What do you mean?'

'It's like Mr Darcy fever, only slightly less acute, and that's only because poor old Wentworth's never had a wet-shirt moment. Not yet, anyway.'

'You're teasing me,' Kay said.

Oli nodded. 'I'm merely making an observation. As an actor, one has to be aware that some roles come loaded with expectation, and I think all the Austen heroes fall into that category.'

'But you weren't put off by that?'

'Are you kidding? It's a dream come true,' Oli said. 'Think about it—I'll be forever associated with one of the sexiest heroes of all time. Women will throw themselves at me, even when I'm an old man and have lost all my hair. What actor could possibly say no to such a role?'

Kay grinned.

'I mean, I know I'll never reach the heights of Colin Firth, but I like to think that I'll earn my place in the hero hall of fame. I mean, I might not have the wet shirt, but Wentworth does have the advantage of a uniform, doesn't he?'

Kay nodded, eyeing up the handsome uniform before her. 'I'm illustrating all of Austen's stories,' she told him.

Oli's eyebrows rose. 'Really? You're published?'

'Oh, no!' she said. 'Not yet. I'd like to be, but it's just something I do for myself at the moment.'

'And is that what you were doing this morning—drawing me?'

Kay nodded. She could feel a blush creeping up her cheeks. 'I didn't mean to stare. Except, well, I suppose I was, wasn't I?'

'Looking at a person through binoculars is usually construed as staring,' Oli said.

Kay hid her hands in her face for a moment. 'I'm so sorry. You must have thought I was rude.'

'Not at all,' he said. 'I'm used to being stared at. Comes with the territory.'

'Of being handsome?' she said and then bit her lip. What a thing to say!

'Of being an actor,' he said with a little smile. 'And I suppose there's a certain amount of staring to be done in your line of work.'

'Running a bed and breakfast?' Kay said.

'No,' he said with a laugh. '*Illustrating!*'

Kay laughed too. 'Yes, I suppose so. I mean, it's what I have to do—if I want to capture a face.'

Oli looked at her. It felt strange having those piercing blue eyes fixed on her. How many times had she gazed at them within the safe confines of her television set? And now here they were—just a couple of feet away—staring at her.

'I've never been drawn before,' he said. 'It must be a rather intimate experience.' He held her gaze, and Kay felt riveted to the spot, believing that a tornado wouldn't have the power to move her if it struck at that moment.

'Intimate,' she said, and the whole world seemed focussed on that one word, its three syllables vibrating on her lips.

Oli nodded and took a step towards her. 'Perhaps I could sit for you sometime.'

Kay frowned. Had she heard him right? 'Really? You would? I mean, would you?'

'I would be honoured,' he said.

She smiled and felt as if her face would break in two from the very width of it.

'Oli!' a voice suddenly called from the other side of the hedge. It was Beth, and she did not look happy as she entered the knot garden and saw them standing there. '*There* you are,' she said as she approached them, looking down her perfect nose at Kay, but speaking to Oli. 'You're wanted.'

'Already?'

'Not by Teresa—by us,' Beth said, slipping an arm through his. 'We want your opinion on a scene from the zombie film.'

Oli turned to look at Kay as he was marched away and gave her a wink. Kay blushed and smiled as Beth turned around to give her a Medusa-like glare. Kay's moment of magic was over, but she felt as if she could feed off it for decades. She had walked in a beautiful garden with Oli Wade Owen, and they talked about heroes and he promised to sit for her. And he had looked at her. He had really *looked* at her.

She wrapped her arms around her body and glanced up into the sky. The darkest of the clouds had passed, and patches of blue promised kinder weather. Kay inhaled deeply, and all seemed well with the world. Oli Wade Owen was going to sit for her.

But you mustn't think any more of it, a little voice told herself. *You know what you're like—you always get carried away.*

'I'm not going to get carried away,' she said. 'He just wants his portrait drawn—that's all. How can anyone possibly read more into it than that?'

But Kay was already imagining. She would be sitting there drawing him. He'd be wearing a white shirt, unbuttoned at the top, his blond hair flopping over his face. They'd have been sitting together in silence for a few minutes when suddenly Oli would get up and stride across the room.

'I can't stand it any longer!' he'd say.

'What?' Kay would ask, her eyes wide.

'You staring at me like that—with those huge eyes of yours and that perfect mouth that I just want to kiss.'

'Oh, Oli!' she'd say before his mouth came crashing down onto hers, her paint brushes rolling to the floor in abandon.

'Kay?'

Kay gasped, spinning around at the sound of her voice being called.

'Oh, Adam!' she said.

'Sorry. Didn't mean to shock you.'

'It's okay.'

He walked towards her. 'You looked deep in thought.'

'Did I?' Kay said, suddenly becoming engrossed in a rosemary bush.

'What have you been up to?'

'Oh, not much. Just talking to Oli.'

Adam nodded, and Kay noticed that his smile slipped away.

'You've been talking to Gemma?' she asked.

'Yes. She always gets a bit anxious before filming.'

'It's so nice that you care about her,' Kay said.

'I just try and keep everyone together, you know?'

'But Gemma's a bit special, isn't she?'

Adam frowned. 'What do you mean?'

'I mean she's such a lovely person,' Kay said.

'Yes,' Adam said, 'she is.'

'And so pretty too. I think she's one of the prettiest actresses around, don't you think?'

Adam's eyes widened. 'I've not really thought about it.'

'But she is,' Kay said enthusiastically. 'I think she's lovely. But she's a bit shy. I think she's one of these girls who has so much to give if only she could find the right man.'

Adam cleared his throat. 'And I'm sure she will, one day.'

'Are you?' Kay said, her eyes lighting up. 'I am too. In fact, I think that day might be fast approaching.'

Chapter 14

THE RETRENCHING SCENE WAS IN THE CAN, AND TERESA WAS keen to move onto the next indoor scene—the one where Anne Elliot and Captain Wentworth see each other for the first time after their years of separation. It was to be shot in one of the ground floor rooms of Marlcombe Manor, which was filled with oak panels and had a beautiful mullioned window and an impressive door through which Wentworth was going to make his entrance.

As ever, it was a problem getting the lighting just right for this scene. Teresa wanted it subdued and tender, but not so tender that you couldn't actually see the actors' faces, as had happened in the first shot.

Beth and Sophie had their hair fixed and faces made up and were looking a little more like sisters, but they were far from acting like sisters when the cameras weren't rolling. Beth seemed to be in a permanently bad mood, and Sophie took great delight in teasing her, which wasn't exactly helping things along.

Finally, everything was ready. Taking some steadying deep breaths, Gemma tried to focus. It was one of the most important scenes for Anne, and Gemma was feeling the whole weight of it. How could she convey Anne's inner turmoil, when she was a woman of few words? Her feelings of both dread and longing at seeing Wentworth again had to be portrayed subtly. Anne wasn't the kind of character to gasp aloud or clutch at her bosom.

'It's all in the eyes,' Teresa told her.

Gemma understood, but could she do it? Jane Austen had written that 'a thousand feelings rushed on Anne' when she realises that Captain Wentworth was going to call, and Gemma had only a few seconds to convey it all. She twisted the tiny gold cross hanging around her neck. She always fiddled when she was nervous, which was one of the reasons why knitting was good, because it occupied her anxious fingers. Her knitting was in one of the vans outside, though.

After an agony of waiting, they were ready, and Gemma was no longer Gemma but Anne. The twenty-first century became the nineteenth. Beth and Sophie became Louisa and Henrietta, and Oli became Captain Wentworth. It was always a strange yet wonderful moment. Gemma thought it was the deepest sort of alchemy, a moment of magic, when the script came to life and nothing else existed.

By the time Adam and Kay left the knot garden, most of the cast had disappeared.

'I don't think we're wanted here anymore,' Adam told her.

Kay sighed. 'I think you're right.'

'You ready to go?'

'Yes,' Kay said, although she would have willingly stayed all day and all night.

'They always stick to their own type,' Adam said.

'What?'

'Actors. They always stick together.'

Kay frowned. 'What do you mean?'

'I mean you're too sensible to even think about getting involved with an actor, aren't you?'

Kay's mouth dropped open at the impudence of his question. After all, wasn't he thinking about getting involved with Gemma?

'I don't know what you're talking about,' Kay said as she headed towards his car.

'I think you do,' he said, quickening his pace to keep up with her. 'I've seen the way women react when Oli Wade Owen's around, and I've seen the way he encourages it, as well.'

'What's Oli got to do with anything?' Kay said a little too defensively.

'You were talking to him just now, weren't you?'

'So?' Kay said. 'What harm is there in talking? It's not often that I meet a movie star.'

'I know,' Adam said, 'and that's my point. He plays on that. I've seen it before. I've worked with his type for years, and it always ends badly for any girl who gets involved.'

'Aren't you typecasting?'

'Typecasts are typecasts for very good reasons—they're instantly recognizable.'

Kay reached the car and was waiting for Adam to open it when she suddenly wondered if there was a bus she could catch back to Lyme Regis. She didn't like being interrogated like this. He was making assumptions about her and her feelings towards Oli. So what if he was absolutely right? She didn't need his warnings. She was a grown woman, and she could look after herself.

'Adam—please don't talk to me like a child.'

He looked hurt for a moment and then sighed. 'I'm sorry,' he said. 'I just couldn't bear to see you... to see Oli...' he paused. 'Well, it's none of my business.'

Kay hesitated for a moment, wondering what would happen next.

'I have to get back,' she said at last as Adam found his keys and opened the car.

'Listen,' he said as they both got in, 'Teresa said they're going to be hours yet on set, so you don't have to rush back and prepare dinner.'

Kay glanced at him, wondering what he was thinking.

'I mean, say no if you don't want to.'

'Want to what, Adam?'

'Go and visit my nan.'

'Your nan?'

He nodded. 'She doesn't live far from here, and she'd love to meet you. And you'd love her too. I mean, I think it would be fun—for you both.'

'I don't know,' Kay said. 'I should be getting back.'

'Please,' he said. 'Come and have some tea with my nan—as a way of showing you forgive me for making a prat of myself just now.'

Kay pursed her lips. Tea with Adam's nan. How bad could it be?

'Okay,' she said.

Adam smiled and started the car. 'You'll love Nana Craig,' he said.

Nana Craig's cottage was tucked away down a quiet country lane lined with cow parsley and red campion, and with its coffee-coloured thatched roof and its fat chimney, it looked just like the sort of cottage a child would draw. A tiny front garden was stuffed with flowers, and a herringbone brick path led to a fat wooden front door that was painted yellow.

Kay had to stop herself from gasping at it all; it was picture perfect.

Adam walked ahead and rapped the knocker on the front door.

'She's a bit hard of hearing,' he said, 'except if you're gossiping with somebody in the room next door, and then she hears everything.'

Adam knocked again. A couple of minutes later, the door opened, and a lovely round face greeted them.

'Hello, Nana,' Adam said, bending down to kiss her powdery face. 'I've brought somebody to meet you.'

'Oh, my boy!' she said. 'You're married at last!'

'Nana! You know I'm not married,' Adam said, his face flushing furiously.

Kay couldn't help smiling.

'Was I expecting you? I can't remember, but that's normal these days,' Nana Craig said.

'No, you weren't expecting us. I just thought we'd drop by. We've been up at Marlcombe. They're filming there today.'

'Oh, you and that film,' she said. 'You're obsessed.'

'Yep!' Adam said. 'Can't help it. I've waited a long time to see it all come to life.'

'I know you have, my love,' Nana Craig said with an affectionate squeeze of his arm. 'Now here we are standing and talking a lot of nonsense, when there's a lovely young lady on the doorstep.'

'Pardon my manners,' Adam said. 'Nana, this is Kay Ashton. She's just opened a terrific bed and breakfast in Lyme and is housing half the cast of the film. Kay, this is Nana Craig.'

The two women shook hands, and Kay smiled at the friendly face that greeted her.

'Come in, my dear. You're very welcome, even if Adam hasn't made an honest woman of you yet.'

'Nana! I've only just met Kay.'

'Never stopped anyone before,' she said. 'In fact, it often helps these matters along.'

'You mustn't tease Kay. She won't know you're joking.'

Nana Craig giggled, and it was the kind of giggle that belonged to a very naughty young girl.

They walked through a tiny narrow hallway painted red in

which stood a variety of wellington boots in different colours and state of disrepair. An old-fashioned coat hanger stood in the corner and was covered in bright raincoats.

'Nana likes colour,' Adam explained, and Kay saw what he meant when they entered the living room at the front of the house. It was simply awash with colour, from the pink floral wallpaper to the two squashy sofas in yellow and red. There were bright paintings of country scenes on the wall, a multitude of pretty figurines in a corner cabinet, and a coffee table covered in a shocking pink tablecloth.

'I'll make a pot of tea,' Nana Craig said, bustling out of the brilliant room.

'Wow!' Kay said. 'I've never seen anywhere like this.'

Adam shook his head. 'It can be a bit trying if you have a headache.'

'I heard that,' Nana Craig called from the kitchen.

Kay smiled.

'You should see the kitchen,' Adam said in a lowered voice. 'It's a symphony of yellows, and her bedroom's every possible shade of blue and a few more too.'

They sat on the squashy yellow sofa.

'Kay,' Adam began, 'I didn't mean to overstep the mark before. I'm sorry if you felt I did.'

Kay turned to look at him, and sure enough, he seemed sorry. 'I don't know what you were imagining,' she said. 'It's not as if I'm thinking of getting involved with anyone,' she said, trying to push back the image of herself with Oli Wade Owen in a passionate clinch in the middle of the knot garden.

'I know,' Adam said. 'I'm just a worrier.'

'Why are you worried about me?' she asked, eyes wide with surprise.

'Because I like you,' he said in a low voice—Kay imagined in case his nan might be eavesdropping and was planning the flowers for a church wedding. 'You seem like the kind of girl who's too nice to get involved with an actor.'

Kay frowned. 'I'm not going to get involved with an actor. I merely admire Oli's work. I can't help it if I'm a little bit star-struck. It's not every day that one of my favourite actors is staying in my house.'

'I know,' Adam said. 'Just be careful.'

Kay wasn't sure how to respond, so played it safe and said nothing. She wasn't sure how she felt about Adam's concern. It was nice that he cared about her, but it was none of his business, and he was treating her like a child who was likely to make silly mistakes without a bit of guidance.

Nana Craig returned to the room carrying the tea tray. Adam leapt up from the sofa and took it from her.

'You should've called through, Nana.'

'Oh, nonsense! I'm not an invalid yet, my boy.'

Adam set the tray down on the table, and Kay admired the candy-striped mugs and the polka-dotted teapot.

'Nothing matches in this house,' Adam said, shaking his head.

'Why should things match? Matching's highly overrated.'

'I agree,' Kay said. 'Who wants order, when disorder is so beautiful?'

Nana Craig smiled. 'Now here's a girl who finally makes sense. Not like that last one you brought round.'

'Nana—'

'Who was wearing that awful grey suit. Who wants to wear grey? She looked like an old dishcloth!'

'Nana!'

She waggled her finger at her grandson. 'But Kay here—look at her pretty clothes.'

'Thank you,' Kay said, fingering her pink dress. 'I think colour's so important.'

Nana Craig nodded, and it was only then that Kay noticed what she was wearing. From its shape and cut, it was a conventional sort of a cardigan, but being a cardigan owned by Nana Craig, it was a rainbow riot of colour. There were pinks and yellows and purples and blues all flowing together in a swirling spectrum. It was being worn over a lilac skirt that hovered over a pair of fluffy hot-pink slippers.

'You're not one of those actresses my grandson keeps hanging around with, are you?' Nana Craig asked.

'Oh, no,' Kay said.

'I'm very glad to hear it. No good at all, those sort of girls. Always flitting from job to job, never a moment to settle down and make a proper home for a man.'

Adam rolled his eyes. 'Kay runs a bed and breakfast in Lyme. I told you, Nana.'

'I paint too,' Kay said.

'You didn't tell me you painted,' Adam said. 'I should like to see your paintings.'

'What do you paint?' Nana Craig asked.

Kay took a sip of her tea. 'I like to paint anything, really, the sky, the sea, fields—anything. But for the last few years, I've been working on illustrating the books of Jane Austen.' She dared to look at Adam.

'Really?' he said.

Kay nodded. 'I finished *Pride and Prejudice* last year. I've called it *The Illustrated Darcy*.'

'How marvellous!' Nana Craig said. 'I should very much like to see it.'

'So should I,' Adam said. 'Are you going to try to get it published?'

'That's where I'm floundering a bit. I love the illustrating. I love getting lost in my own imagination. There's no pressure there. I do what I want when I want. But when it comes to the publishing business, I don't know where to begin.'

'Maybe I can help you,' Adam said. 'I know a few agents in London. That's where you want to start.'

'My dear boy's been doing this for more years than I can remember. I remember those early days when you were sending your first plays out into the big wide world.'

'It must be a brave thing to do,' Kay said. 'I mean, my paintings are mine at the moment. They're my private world, and although I'm desperate to see them published, I'm terrified of letting them go.'

'That's perfectly normal,' Adam said. 'But you have to send them out if you want them to find a home.'

'I know,' Kay said. 'But what if nobody else likes my drawings? What if I'm the only person in the whole world who likes them?'

'All artists think that about their work,' Adam said. 'I know I did when I was beginning. Still do.'

'He just doesn't know how talented he is,' Nana Craig said.

'Nana!'

'He's always shying away from praise, aren't you? I bet you haven't even told Kay about *The Princess and the Pirate*, have you?'

'What's that?' Kay asked with a smile.

Nana Craig's eyes lit up. 'It's the very first play Adam wrote, and I'm proud to own the only known copy in existence. I can get it for you, if you want.'

'No, Nana!' Adam protested. 'She doesn't want to hear about all that.'

'But I do!' Kay said, becoming more intrigued by the moment. 'What's it about?'

Nana Craig looked dreamy. 'It's a marvellous swashbuckling romance set on the high seas. Well, Lyme Bay.'

Kay giggled, and Adam actually blushed.

'But Adam refuses to produce it.'

'Nana, I've explained, it's not very good.'

'It *is* good!'

'It's the first thing I ever wrote. Trust me, it's not very good.'

Nana Craig shook her head in despair.

'Listen, we'd better be getting back,' Adam said.

'But you've not even had a second cup of tea,' Nana Craig said.

'Kay's got to sort things out at the bed and breakfast, and I've got a hundred calls to make.'

'Always so busy, you young ones,' Nana Craig said, getting up.

'It's been lovely to meet you,' Kay said. 'Thank you for the tea.'

'Any time,' she said. 'You know where I am now, don't you?'

They leaned forward and gave each other an affectionate hug.

'I like this one, Adam,' Nana Craig said. 'Get a ring on her finger before she's snapped up by someone else.'

Adam rolled his eyes. 'Good-bye, Nana.'

'She's a love,' Kay said once they were back in the car.

'I can't imagine life without her,' Adam told her. 'She was there for me when nobody else was. Both my parents were workaholics and didn't have much time for me when I was growing up, but Nana Craig was always there. She was the one who came to parents' evenings, and she was the one who got me through all those awful spelling tests. She even helped me pick out my first suit for a job interview.'

'She clearly adores you.'

'And you too. I think you're her new favourite person.'

'Just as well I'm not an actress,' Kay said.

'Yes, she does have a problem with actresses.'

'Why is that?'

'Maybe it's because she was once married to an actor.'

'Really?'

Adam nodded. 'Before she met my grandfather, she was married to a man we know only as Bas.'

'What happened?'

'He ran off to London with some girl who promised to get him a part in a movie. He was never heard of again.'

'Poor Nana Craig!'

'Oh, she soon got over him,' Adam said as they reached the main road back towards Lyme Regis.

'But not all actors are awful. What about Gemma? Nana Craig couldn't possibly have a problem with her, could she?'

'I don't suppose we'll ever know,' he said.

'But she's bound to meet her sooner or later,' Kay said.

Adam frowned. 'What makes you say that?'

Kay groaned. He was being tremendously dim.

'Oh, you mean if I take Nana out to see some filming?' he said. 'That's a good idea, although she's not shown any interest in seeing it so far. It might well stir up some bad memories for her.'

'I'm sure she'd like Gemma.'

'Yes,' Adam said.

'You couldn't not like Gemma, could you?' She looked directly at Adam.

'No,' he said.

Kay sighed. She supposed it was a start—the start of something she was going to nudge along in the right direction.

Chapter 15

ADAM DROPPED KAY OFF IN LYME REGIS AND FELT disappointed that she hadn't invited him back for coffee. She did have a lot to do, he supposed, watching as she walked down Marine Parade towards the bed and breakfast. She then did something unexpected—she turned around and walked right back towards him.

'Would you like to come to dinner tonight?'

'With the cast?' Adam asked.

Kay shook her head. 'I just got a text from Teresa,' she said, holding up her phone. 'They're going to be filming for goodness knows how long. She told me not to worry about feeding everyone. They'd get something at the pub later.'

'Okay,' Adam said, a huge smile crossing his face. 'What time?'

'Eight o'clock?'

'Fine,' he said. 'I look forward to it.'

He watched as she walked away, her long hair swinging about her shoulders. Nana Craig would certainly be pleased with the speed of his progress, and he was rather delighted with it himself.

Later that evening, Kay was buzzing around like a mad thing. Everything was fine in the oven. She really didn't need to keep checking things. The clock, however, was another matter. Teresa said they would be back by eight 'at the latest,' but there was still no sign of them. Adam would be turning up at any moment, and he would be expecting dinner—with her—but that wasn't really what she had planned. Oh, no.

She checked the oven one more time. The shepherd's pie was fine. The assorted vegetables were fine. Everything was ready except the guests.

There was a knock on the door, and Kay hoped against hope that it was Gemma, but Gemma would have her own key, wouldn't she?

Kay rushed to the door and opened it. It wasn't Gemma at all. It was Adam.

'Hello!' he said.

'Hi. Come in,' she said, turning her back on him and marching back down the hallway. 'You've not seen Teresa and the gang, have you?'

'They're not back yet?'

'No sign of them at all,' Kay said, puffing out her cheeks.

'Oh, well, at least it will be quiet here,' Adam said, suddenly flourishing a red rose from behind his back.

'Oh!' Kay said. 'I'll fetch a vase.' She took the rose, went back through to the kitchen, reached for a slim vase from the back of a cupboard, and filled it with water. A single red rose, she thought. He'd bought her a single red rose. She shook her head. It wasn't for her, and very soon, Adam would see it too.

'You need a hand?'

Kay spun around, vase in hand, to see Adam standing in the doorway. 'No, thank you. You're the guest, and guest rhymes with rest.' She shooed Adam out of the kitchen. 'Come and sit in the dining room,' she said, following as he made his way to the room at the front of the house.

'Oh,' Adam said. 'It's a bit dark in here, isn't it?'

'But the candles are so pretty,' Kay insisted, placing the rose in the centre of the table. 'Your eyes will adjust.'

'Is this because you're not a very good cook and don't want me to actually see the food?'

Kay's mouth dropped open.

'Only joking,' Adam quickly said.

'I'll just check on the dinner,' she said, bustling out of the room. She must calm down. He'd only been teasing her. She didn't want him to get suspicious or jumpy. She had to relax.

She leaned against the sink and took a few deep breaths. At least Adam had turned up. That was half the plan in place.

But where on earth was Gemma?

~⊙

The day had been long and tiring. The actors and crew managed to shoot most of the indoor scenes but would have to come back the next day to finish off. They even managed to film a quick scene in the garden when the clouds parted and a sudden blast of sunshine turned everything golden.

Gemma was relieved that the day was over at last. Once she was back in the comfort of her own clothes and brought the knitting out of her bag, she began to relax and felt the vestiges of Anne Elliot slipping away and Gemma Reilly returning. She was sitting in the minibus, waiting for the others to get out of makeup. Beth was the first to board the bus.

'God, I'm starving!' she said.

Gemma looked up briefly from her knitting. Her own tummy was rumbling like a volcano about to erupt, but she just wanted to retire to her room. Maybe she'd grab a bag of chips on her way back to the B&B.

'You knitting again?' Beth asked.

Gemma didn't bother answering. It would only provoke a disdainful response. Actually, *not* answering would provoke a disdainful response too.

'I don't get it,' Beth said. 'Isn't knitting for old women?'

'Not at all; all sorts of people are knitting these days: Madonna, Julia Roberts, Angelina Jolie—'

'You're kidding me.'

Gemma cleared her throat. She had tagged Angelina Jolie on at the end, but it might not be strictly true. Still, it sounded good.

'How do you think she clothes all those children of hers?' Gemma said, falling into acting mode. It was always a useful skill to have.

Beth looked dumbstruck.

Sophie, Teresa, and Oli boarded the bus.

'Come and sit here, Oli.' Beth patted the seat next to her. 'I wouldn't go anywhere near Gemma. You're likely to be stabbed by a knitting needle.'

Gemma could feel her face heating up as Oli cast a glance her way.

'What are you making?' he asked.

Gemma held up the little pink jacket for his inspection.

'Cute!' he said. 'Hey, Teresa—look what Gemma's making.'

Teresa glanced over, her tired eyes widening when she saw the baby's jacket. 'That's gorgeous!' she said. 'Let me see.' She took the seat next to Gemma, and her fingers reached out to stroke the soft wool. 'I love it! Do you make them bigger? I've got a five-year-old girl.'

'That's just what I was thinking,' Oli said.

Teresa nodded.

'I can make whatever size you want,' Gemma said, surprised at the positive attention her little knitting project was getting.

'Annabel sure would look sweet in something like that,' Oli said.

Beth glared at him. 'I would have thought wool would snag on a child.'

Nobody seemed to be listening to her. They were all watching Gemma as her needles clacked happily together.

'You really are talented,' Sophie said. 'I think you could have your own business if you wanted it.'

Gemma looked up and grinned. 'It's just a hobby. Just something I do when I'm—' she was going to say 'stressed,' but that wasn't the kind of thing she wanted Teresa or any of the others to hear. 'When I'm not doing anything else,' she said.

'I know several people who'd be willing to pay money—really good money—for that sort of handmade item,' Teresa said.

Beth huffed. 'Are we going to eat, or what?'

～

'You okay in there?' Adam called through to the kitchen.

Kay had been leaning up against the cooker, anxiously watching the clock. Poor Adam. He'd been sitting in the dining room on his own for about twenty minutes. She was being a terrible host.

'Everything's fine,' she said as she walked through to the dining room.

'My eyes seem to have adjusted now,' he said with a grin.

'Would you like some more wine?' Kay asked.

He nodded. 'Dinner ready?'

'It's taking longer than I thought,' she lied. It had been ready

111

ages ago, and she had to turn off the oven and hope it wouldn't completely dry out before Gemma got back.

'Won't you join me in the meantime?' Adam asked.

'Oh, I'd better keep an eye on things.'

Adam looked at her, and she immediately felt guilty, although she was quite sure he couldn't read her mind. He couldn't possibly know what she was planning, could he?

There was a sudden scraping of a key in the front door. Kay hurried through to the hallway, and when the door opened, she breathed a sigh of relief. It was Gemma—thank goodness! Just as Kay had predicted, she was alone.

'Hi!' Kay called. 'I was just making dinner. Do come and join us in the dining room.'

Gemma looked surprised. 'Oh, I don't want you going to any trouble on my behalf.'

'It's no trouble at all,' Kay assured her. 'In fact, it's almost ready, but I can keep it warm for you whilst you get changed. Maybe a dress would be nice.'

Gemma looked even more surprised. 'A dress?'

Kay nodded. 'Dinner's always a bit special, isn't it?'

'Erm, I guess so,' Gemma said.

'Great!' Kay clapped her hands. 'I'll see you in the dining room in five, then?'

'Right,' Gemma said, disappearing up the stairs.

Kay popped her head around the dining room door. 'Won't be long now,' she said with a big smile.

Five minutes later, Gemma came down the stairs wearing a little black dress that had been scrunched into the corner of her suitcase just in case she needed to dress up. She hadn't imagined having to dress for dinner when they booked into the bed and breakfast, but she didn't mind too much. Kay was a sweet girl, and it would be fun to get to know her better over dinner.

Entering the dining room, Gemma realised she wasn't on her own. 'Adam?'

'Hello, Gemma,' he said. 'You look lovely.'

'Thank you.'

'Come on in,' he said, getting up and pulling out a seat for her.

Gemma sat down and then frowned. 'Why isn't Kay joining us?'

'What do you mean?' Adam said. 'She is.'

'But there are only two places set at the table.'

Adam looked at the table for the first time, and it was his turn to frown. 'I'm not sure I understand.'

Gemma smiled. 'I think I do.'

'What?'

'Well,' Gemma said, nodding to the two place settings, 'there's you and me and candles and a single red rose.'

'I bought that for Kay,' Adam said. 'I thought I was Kay's special guest this evening, but I think I'm beginning to understand now.'

Kay entered the room with two plates filled with the homey—if well done—shepherd's pie.

'That looks wonderful,' Adam said politely.

'I put all the vegetables on already, but don't feel you have to eat them all,' Kay said.

Gemma looked in horror at the loaded plate before her.

'Let me know if you'd like anything else.'

'Aren't you joining us?' Adam said.

'Gracious, no! I've already eaten,' Kay said, hurriedly leaving the room.

As soon as Gemma was quite sure Kay was out of earshot, she leaned forward towards Adam. 'You're going to have to help me out,' she told him. 'I had no idea Kay had planned this, and I had a huge portion of fish and chips on the way home.'

Adam chuckled. 'Okay, pass me your plate,' he said, forking a great chunk of the shepherd's pie onto his own, together with a couple of potatoes.

'Thanks,' Gemma said. 'I'll be bulging out of my muslin if I attempt to eat all *that*.'

'What's she up to, do you think?' Adam asked.

'I think she's trying to matchmake us.'

'What?'

'Shush!'

Adam rolled his eyes. 'Oh, my God! You're right. She keeps talking about you all the time.'

'She does?'

Adam nodded. 'Keeps drawing my attention to you.'

'Oh!' Gemma said. 'Whatever gave her the impression that— that you and I—?'

'I have *absolutely* no idea.'

'I'm so sorry,' Gemma said.

'It's okay. I mean, it's not as if it's your fault, is it? Anyway, I do like you.'

'Just not like *that*?'

'I didn't mean you're not attractive,' Adam hastily added.

'It's okay! I'm just teasing,' she said with a grin.

'So what are we going to do?'

Gemma sighed. 'I don't know. I really don't know.'

∽

It was all going well, Kay thought. She wasn't one to eavesdrop— well, not unless it was absolutely necessary. She hung around quietly between the dining room and the kitchen, and although she hadn't heard anything in particular, she could hear faint murmurings. Adam and Gemma's voices were low. They were whispering together. That was a good sign, wasn't it? Lovers whispered together. It was a sign of cosiness, intimacy, and contentedness.

Kay smiled. She'd been right all along about those two. They were perfect for each other.

As she returned to the kitchen, she imagined herself as a modern-day Emma Woodhouse, except she wouldn't bungle things quite as horribly as Emma had, and nobody would tell her things were 'badly done.' No, Kay had a natural flair for this kind of thing. She could just feel it.

Chapter 16

ADAM WOULD NEVER FORGET THE EVENING FOR AS LONG AS HE lived. How could he have been so stupid? How could he have thought that Kay would have liked him enough to invite him to dinner? She had only been interested in matchmaking him. That was all that he was good for—to play some role that she defined for him. She wasn't interested in him—she was interested in what she could do with him. He was her toy, her pawn, her plaything. That was all.

It was the story of his life. He had a long history of being either overlooked or used by women who were on their way to something better. He was also very good at getting stuck in the role of the best friend or advisor.

'You're too nice,' Nana Craig once told him. 'Girls don't like the nice guys.'

It had sounded perverse to him. 'What, they want me to break their hearts?'

Nana Craig nodded with a big smile on her face.

Adam would never understand women. Just look at the Jane Austen novels and their fixation with the snobbish, insulting Mr Darcy. Okay, so he comes good in the end—big deal! Who really wants to hang around on the off chance that you've misunderstood somebody? If Adam were a woman, he'd have gone for someone like Mr Bingley—nice and uncomplicated. What you saw was what you got. No messing around.

As he drove home through the darkened Marshwood Vale, he thought about the bizarre evening. The situation was awful, and it wasn't exactly going to further his relationship with Kay, was it?

He thought back to the gorgeous tiramisu Kay brought in, her eyes flashing from him to Gemma, and he could only imagine what she was thinking.

'Having a nice evening?' she said.

'Lovely!' Gemma gushed.

Adam cringed.

'I thought it would be,' Kay said. 'I mean, I guess film sets can be busy places, and it must be difficult to really get to know people—people you care about.'

Adam's left fist balled up under the table. How on earth was he going to sort out this terrible muddle?

∾

Kay lay in bed that night with a smile of satisfaction on her face at a job well done. She had a natural talent for this matchmaking lark, didn't she? She'd been a bit nervous at first at the thought that Gemma might not turn up or that the whole cast and crew would come traipsing in with her, but it all went according to plan. If only she could shake from her mind the memory of Adam and the red rose. But it was no good. A niggling little voice kept whispering, *He bought it for you. That red rose was for you—not Gemma.* But a red rose could mean anything, couldn't it? Adam was nothing more than a gentleman, and a true gentleman bought flowers when invited to dinner, and maybe he just happened to like red roses. Or maybe the florist didn't have anything else. There could be any number of explanations.

Kay shook her head while she did her best to deny it, but Adam had turned up expecting to have dinner with her. She had invited him. She had said nothing about any third party.

'But I did it for him,' she whispered into the stillness of her bedroom. *He might not know it yet, but Gemma's so right for him,* she thought. *He's not interested in me, and if he is, he'll soon see how silly that is.*

She thought of the two of them sitting in her dining room together. They looked so cute. The candlelight made Gemma's skin glow, and Adam's eyes looked soft and adoring. And they'd chattered away like old friends. She was proud of herself.

The proof had been there too, when Adam had got up to leave. Gemma escorted him to the door, and as tempting as it was to make her presence known, Kay left them to it, hiding behind the kitchen door, where she could glimpse a thin sliver of them as they said their good-byes.

'It's been really lovely,' Gemma said.

'Yes,' Adam replied. 'I had a great evening.'

Kay scrunched up her apron in excited hands as she listened. Would it happen? Would there be a good-night kiss? She pushed her nose closer to the crack in the door and almost gave her presence away by the gasp that left her when Adam inclined his head towards Gemma and kissed her. Okay, so it was on the cheek, but it was a move in the right direction. Lips followed cheeks, didn't they?

Gemma had knocked tentatively on the kitchen door, and Kay grabbed a pot and a tea towel, to look as if she'd been preoccupied and hadn't had a moment to hang around in gooseberry mode.

'Thank you so much,' Gemma said.

Kay turned around and feigned a look of surprise. 'Did you have a nice evening?'

'It was lovely.'

'My pleasure,' Kay said. 'You got on all right?' She tried to make the question sound casual as she picked up a glass and dried it.

Gemma nodded.

'He's a very special person, isn't he?' Kay said and was answered with a look of the tenderest affection, and she knew that all her instincts had been right.

One of the things Kay hadn't thought about when she decided to open a bed and breakfast was how very early in the morning she would have to get up—especially when she had a film crew staying. The office job she held for years had been a short walk away from her home, and she never had to get up early. The early morning views out over the harbour and sea were worth it, though. The Cobb wall was in morning shadow, and the gulls hovered around the harbour, their white wings bright in the morning light.

As she stood yawning in the kitchen, cracking eggs into a bowl before scrambling them, she smiled at the thought of Oli Wade Owen sitting in her dining room. When Kay had taken the coffee through, she noticed how dishevelled his blond hair looked and how heavy his eyelids were. He looked half asleep and didn't look a bit like a hero.

She stirred the eggs around the pan, the creamy yellowness making her smile.

'Good morning!' a voice suddenly said from the doorway.

Kay jumped and spun around. It was Oli.

'Hi,' she said. 'You—erm—startled me.'

'Just wondered how you were getting on.'

'Me?'

He nodded. 'Need a hand? I'm pretty good in the kitchen,' he said. 'I can open a mean can.'

Kay grinned. 'It's all under control,' she said, her scrambling spoon in her hand.

'I was thinking about you last night,' Oli said.

Kay's mouth dropped open. 'Really?'

'Yes,' he said. 'Wondering about what you said—about the portrait.'

'Oh! The portrait.'

'I mean, I'm happy to sit for you—if you'd like that.'

'I'd *love* that,' Kay said, perhaps with a little too much enthusiasm. 'I mean, great.'

'How's about tonight, then? I'll give the pub a miss; how's that?'

Kay smiled and nodded and stared into the blue eyes that were crinkling with merriment at the edges.

'What's that smell?' he asked, his nose wrinkling.

'Oh, no!' Kay screamed, turning around. She had left the heat on, and the scrambled eggs were a shrivelled, dry mass of black at the bottom of the pan.

'I'd better leave you to it,' Oli said, holding his hands up as he sneaked out of the kitchen.

Kay turned the gas off and stared at the blackened contents, but she smiled. She was going to sketch Oli. He was going to sit for her. That meant he would be alone with her.

For absolutely ages.

'It looks like another wet day,' Teresa said at the breakfast table, 'although we should get a morning's sunshine first.'

Gemma poured herself another coffee to help her get through the day ahead.

'The light should be right for the big Cobb scene, at least.'

Beth nodded. It was going to be her big day, and she was ready for it. She had been going on about it all morning. 'If it weren't for Louisa Musgrove, the story of *Persuasion* just wouldn't exist,' she had told Gemma as they came downstairs together. 'She really is the pivotal character in the whole plot and far more appealing than dreary Anne, who never has anything remotely interesting to say. No, I think Captain Wentworth should have stayed in Lyme and married Louisa. You know he wants to. She throws herself into everything with such—such—'

'Lack of thought,' Gemma said quietly.

'Pardon?'

'Nothing.'

Beth sighed. 'Louisa is the forgotten heroine of English literature,' she went on. 'I'm really very surprised that she hasn't got more lines. I must have a word with that screenwriter person. What's his name?'

'Adam.'

'Right. I think he'll see sense when I explain things to him. I was thinking there should be a scene between Louisa and Wentworth when she's recovering in bed. It could be very romantic. I think it would work really well.'

Gemma hadn't bothered to reply. Whatever she said would have been ignored unless it fanned Beth's own opinion, but how ridiculous she was to think that she could rewrite Jane Austen to suit her selfish needs.

Beth clearly wasn't going to let the subject drop, though. At the breakfast table, Gemma watched as Beth whispered in Teresa's ear, and she couldn't stop a tiny smile from playing around her lips at Teresa's expression.

'What?' the director said, almost choking on her coffee.

'Don't you think that would make more sense?' Beth said, fluttering her eyelashes.

'That's the most ridiculous thing I've ever heard,' Teresa said, scraping her chair back and standing up. 'If you're not happy with the role as it is—' Teresa continued threateningly.

'Oh, I'm happy,' Beth said, knowing when she was defeated.

'Good,' Teresa said. 'Then I'll see everyone at the Cobb in twenty minutes.'

Once Teresa left the room, Beth tutted. 'You have to wonder with some directors,' she said. 'They really have no insight at all.'

Chapter 17

I T WAS TIME, GEMMA THOUGHT, TIME FOR, PERHAPS, THE MOST famous scene in *Persuasion*: the scene where Louisa Musgrove insists on being 'jumped' from the steps on the Cobb into the arms of Captain Wentworth but flings herself from its heights before he is ready and lands on the hard ground beneath. Everyone knew it was a key scene to get right and that the fans would be watching very carefully. All the main actors were there, and Beth Jenkins knew that the scene was all about her and was prancing around like a prima donna.

'This dress is too tight,' she complained. 'How am I meant to launch myself into Oli's arms when I can barely breathe?'

The costume girl rushed forward and disappeared behind Beth.

'And my hair?'

'What's wrong with your hair?' the girl dared to ask.

'I don't know—it feels uncomfortable. Fix it.'

The girl, when finished fiddling with Beth's dress, examined Beth's wig. 'It's the same as it's always been,' the girl said.

'Then it's always been on wrong. Do something!' Beth all but screamed. 'I can't have wrong hair, can I?'

Gemma caught Oli's eye, and he winked at her before rolling

his eyes at Beth's performance. Gemma smiled back. If only she had the courage to go up and speak to him, but what would she say? He didn't want to talk to her. No matter how tender and intimate the scenes they would share as Anne Elliot and Captain Wentworth, the two weren't at all likely to make the same connection as Gemma and Oli.

If only it were as easy with Oli as it was with Adam, Gemma thought. Why did things never work out like that? Why did we always fall for the one who wouldn't even notice if we stopped breathing?

Deciding to make the most of her surroundings, Gemma walked a little along the Cobb as everybody fussed around Beth. Lyme Regis really was a pretty town, and it was easy to see why it had been attracting tourists since Jane Austen's time. Its harbour was full of colourful boats; its rows of bay-fronted cottages and candy-coloured beach huts looked jolly and welcoming, even in the most unpromising of weather, and she loved the wooded cliff that rose up behind the town. She wished she could pack a rucksack and lose herself in the famous Undercliff.

One of the curses of filming was that you never had much time to see anything—not if you were in most of the scenes, as Gemma was. There was usually a lot of hanging around, but never quite enough time to go off and see something interesting. That's why Gemma always had her knitting nearby. She hated wasting time, and her knitting projects filled it beautifully.

Gemma stopped walking and looked out at a stretch of grey blue sea towards the hills that lined the coast. Somebody had told her the name of the big one—Golden Cap—and it was pyramidal in shape. The rest of the cliffs undulated along the coast like sleeping dinosaurs, making Gemma remember that it was known as the Jurassic Coast. She would have loved to walk along them with the sea-tossed wind in her hair and no thoughts about scripts and lines, but she wasn't being paid to take off into the hills, was she? What would her mother say if she knew how often her daughter thought about running away? She was lucky to get this role—she'd worked damned hard to get it, so why wasn't she happy now she was here? Why did she keep thinking about abandoning it all? Many of her friends from drama school would kill to get this role, yet it seemed only to fill her with dread.

'I'm in the wrong job,' she said to herself. It wasn't the first time she thought it, but it seemed to be dawning on her only now. Here she was, the lead character in an adaptation of a book she adored, starring opposite a man on whom she'd had a crush for years, and she still wasn't happy.

She leaned up against the cold Cobb wall and gazed out to sea. Her whole life had been invested in acting, from the age of three, when her mother took her to that audition for the soap commercial. She hadn't got it; she'd cried through the whole audition process. Maybe she should have taken that behavior as an omen, but her mother hadn't given up. There was a whole string of auditions after that, and Gemma had—at the age of six—been chosen as the face of Sparks Knighton, an upmarket version of Mothercare. She was photographed in denim, gingham, cords, and florals, and her image had been blown up larger than life and placed in stores and magazines and on the sides of buses. Her mother was proud, but Gemma had been mortified. People pointed at her, and she didn't like being pointed at. What on earth had propelled her towards acting? Her mother had encouraged her, of course, and she must have inherited some of her mother's acting genes, because she was accepted into drama school without any fuss at all and had done well, too. Always, however, there had been a niggling feeling that it wasn't quite right for her. She knew that stage fright and first-night nerves were the norm—they were what drove a performance and gave an actor that edge—but Gemma felt it all the time, even in the tiniest of groups, when she had nothing more to do than walk through a scene and say a couple of lines.

She asked her mother about it once.

Her mother shook her head. 'You've just got to get on with it,' she said. 'What else are you going to do?'

That was the crux of it. What else was there for Gemma to do? Acting was the only thing she ever knew, and it seemed too late to change things now.

She started walking back before Teresa sent a search party out for her, and when she neared the cast and crew again, she heard Beth's voice ringing out across the harbour.

'It's still itching me!' she cried. 'Honestly, what do you make these wigs out of, steel wool?'

Gemma rolled her eyes.

'She's a case, is that one,' a male voice suddenly said.

Gemma turned to come face to face with a man with smiling eyes and thick dark hair. It was the same man who had been eyeing up her bosom the other day.

'That Beth,' he said, nodding towards her.

'Oh, yes,' Gemma said.

'There's always one,' he said. 'In my experience.'

'One what?'

'Case. On every film set, you can guarantee you'll always get one head case.'

Gemma grinned and then wondered if she should. Surely there should be some sort of solidarity among actresses, but she didn't feel any kinship with Beth and couldn't help agreeing with the man. 'I think she just likes all the attention,' Gemma said.

'Like most actresses?' the man asked. It was a question, but his eyes glittered as if it might be a naughty statement.

'We're not all the same, you know.'

'I hope not,' he said. 'You're a quiet one, aren't you?'

Gemma's eyes narrowed, not sure how to respond to such a question.

'I mean, I've seen a lot of quiet actors too. They're perfect to work with. They come on set, do their bit—no fuss, no grief.'

'I hope I'm not the sort to cause grief,' Gemma said sincerely.

The man shook his head. 'Absolutely not. Just the opposite, I'd say.'

She smiled at him and then wondered who on earth he was.

'Oh,' he said, as if realising himself, 'I'm Rob.'

'Gemma,' she said.

'I know.' He gave a little smile. 'We keep missing each other, don't we?'

'Do we?'

He nodded. 'Our timing never seems quite right. I've been trying to speak to you.'

'You have?' She remembered the times their eyes had met across the bar and their brief encounter by the Cobb wall the other day.

'Yes. Did you know this is our second film together?'

'Really? You were on *Into the Night*?'

'Yep.'

'I didn't know. I'm sorry.'

'That's okay,' he said. 'I tend to blend into the background.'

'What is it you do?'

'I help take care of the lights. You could say that—wherever I go—I light the place up.'

Gemma smiled, and as his eyes crinkled in merriment, she thought it was exactly what he did.

〜

As Adam parked his car, he thought of what Nana Craig had told him before he left. He got up early to get her shopping done before heading into Lyme for the filming, dropping it off at her cottage. Like most retired people, Nana Craig was up at first light, even though she had nothing to get up for. When Adam arrived, she was out tending her garden, bending over her pots and plants in a manner that alarmed him.

'Should you be doing that, Nana?' Adam asked as he walked up the little path.

'I don't like the look of those black spots,' Nana Craig said. 'Look!'

Adam bent to look. 'What is it?'

'I don't know, but it looks like trouble to me. I'll have to pull them up.'

'You'll do no such thing,' he said. 'Leave them for me. I've told you before to leave the gardening to me.'

Nana Craig tutted in annoyance. 'If you stop me gardening, you might as well shoot me where I stand.'

'Come on and get this shopping inside before the ice cream melts down my leg,' Adam said, not wanting to get into the whole gardening argument so early in the morning.

'Raspberry ripple?' she asked as they walked into the kitchen.

'No. Er, mint and chocolate.'

His nana pulled a face.

'Of course raspberry ripple!'

Her smile returned. 'Time for some now?'

'It's not even nine o'clock!'

'Oh, yes,' Nana Craig said.

'Anyway, I've got to get to Lyme for today's shoot. They're trying for the Cobb scene today. Do you want to come along?'

Nana Craig shook her head. 'Not for me, dear. Lyme's always so busy these days. Besides, I wouldn't want to get in the way.'

'You won't get in the way,' Adam said.

'But you'll be with that nice girl.'

Adam frowned. 'What do you mean?'

Nana Craig flapped her hands. 'You know—that nice girl who was here.'

'Kay? She might be on the set.'

'So you should be talking to her, not looking after your old nana.'

Adam shook his head. 'She's not got eyes for me, I'm afraid. If she's on the set, there's only one person she'll be interested in.'

'Then it's your job to make her interested in you, isn't it?' Nana Craig said.

Adam helped put the shopping away, packing the raspberry ripple ice cream into the tiny freezer and placing all the jars in the cupboards, loosening all the lids first, so his nana wouldn't struggle with them when he wasn't around. 'And how am I going to do that?' Adam asked, leaping back as a bright red wave of beetroot juice flooded over a jar lid.

Nana Craig shoved her hands in the pockets of her primrose and violet cardigan. 'Do you like her?'

'Of course I like her.'

'How much?'

'What do you mean?'

'How much do you like her?'

'A lot,' Adam said. 'I like her a lot.'

'Well, then. You'll find a way. Men usually do, although you sometimes take your time about things, I have to say. Only don't take so long about it that somebody gets there before you do.'

Adam's eyes widened in surprise at her words.

'I'm just saying,' Nana Craig said.

As he parked his car in Lyme, he thought of his nana's words of warning. She was right—he knew she was right—but what could he do, when he knew that Kay was besotted with Oli? Not only that, but Kay had it in her mind that he fancied Gemma. Honestly, you couldn't invent such a muddle, could you?

Walking towards the Cobb, he saw the crowd of cast and crew and a gathering of onlookers too. Word soon got around when Oli Wade Owen was in town, Adam thought as he pushed his way through a group of girls who were all squealing, holding up their mobiles to take photos.

He saw her. She was standing up against the Cobb, her long toffee-coloured hair streaming behind her in the wind, a big smile on her face as she watched the actors coming and going.

'Don't take so long about it that somebody gets there before you do.'

The words of Nana Craig echoed in his head, and taking a deep breath, he walked up to Kay.

'Hello,' he said.

She turned to face him. 'Hi!' Her eyes darted away from him in an instant, and Adam didn't need to follow her gaze to know where she was looking.

'Gosh, this is exciting,' she said, her eyes bright. 'I can't believe this is happening. I mean, this is one of my favourite scenes.'

Adam looked at her. She was shivering. 'You're cold,' he said, noticing that she was wearing a thin dress with insubstantial sleeves.

'I'm okay. I didn't realise how chilly it was. There's a bit of a breeze about, isn't there?'

Without thinking, Adam took off his jacket. 'Here,' he said.

Kay turned to look at him. 'Oh,' she said, her face full of surprise. 'I didn't think men still did that.'

'I do.' He held her gaze with his own for a wondrous moment.

'Thank you.' She shoved her arms quickly into his jacket and then returned her gaze to Oli.

How am I doing, Nana? Adam sighed to himself.

Chapter 18

AFTER WHAT SEEMED LIKE AN AGE TO THE CAST, CREW, AND onlookers, the filming of the famous scene began. A huge blue mat had been set up under the Cobb, and it was onto it that Beth Jenkins had to leap in her portrayal of Louisa Musgrove. Teresa had ruled out the Cobb's most famous steps, known as the Granny's Teeth, for being far too dangerous, even though Beth protested that she could jump from them. The modern ones were far easier to negotiate in Regency costume and were sheltered too.

Gemma, who was on the Lower Cobb, was watching Beth and counting her blessings that she didn't have to perform the stunt.

'Do you think she'll really do it?' Sophie whispered to her.

'I don't know,' Gemma said. 'She looks nervous to me.'

Everything else had been filmed; it was just the leap that they had to cover, and all eyes were turned to Beth, who was standing on the top step with Captain Wentworth, Anne, and Henrietta watching her from below.

'Blimey! It's a lot higher up than I imagined,' Beth said with a little smile as she gazed down at the mattress that was set up to catch her.

'Oh, come on, Beth!' Sophie said. 'You said it was a piece of cake.'

'I didn't say I couldn't do it,' Beth said, hands on her hips.

'We have Kerry on standby, Beth,' Teresa said, nodding to the stuntwoman hovering in the background.

'I said I'm doing my own stunts,' Beth said, and everyone waited until she gave the nod before flinging herself from the Cobb with the words, 'I am determined I will.'

For a few seconds, time seemed suspended, and Beth seemed to be flying through the air for an age before landing in an ungainly heap on the blue mattress below. There was a huge round of applause from the rest of the cast and the crew. The onlookers, too, clapped like crazy, and a few wolf whistles drowned out Beth's initial cries.

'She's injured!' somebody shouted.

'Beth?' Gemma ran towards her. 'You okay?'

'My ankle!' she screamed. 'My ankle!'

'What's wrong? What's the matter?' Teresa asked, rushing forward.

'She twisted her ankle landing,' Les Miserable said.

'It *hurts*!' Beth cried, doing her best to stand.

'Get her back to the B and B, and we'll get a doctor.' Teresa looked around for help. 'Adam?'

Adam ran to the mattress. 'Put your arms around my neck,' he said. 'Can you stand?'

'I don't know.' Beth winced when she moved to walk.

'Which ankle is it?'

'My right one.'

Adam helped her off the mattress and onto firm ground again.

'*Ouch!*' Beth cried.

'Okay,' Adam said. 'This isn't going to work.'

'Hold on there, guys,' a voice said, and everyone turned as Oli stepped forward. 'There's only one way to get Louisa back to the

B and B.' He swooped Beth up into his arms. There was a collective gasp from the crowd of onlookers, and Beth caught her breath too.

Gemma sighed and watched as he moved with ease through the crowds hollering for his autograph, even though it was obvious that he didn't have a free hand. Photos were taken as the tall, uniformed hero strode by, and squeals of excitement filled the air like manic seagulls.

Gemma looked back at Teresa, who was pacing up and down. 'Did we get the shot?'

There was a nod from the camera operator.

'Thank goodness for that,' Teresa said. 'Right, Gemma—we'll need you for the Captain Benwick scene.'

❦

Kay ran along the side of the harbour to get ahead of Oli's arrival with Beth at the bed and breakfast. Her heart hammered. She didn't wish Beth ill, but this was the most exciting thing to have happened. Oli looked like the perfect hero with Beth in his arms, and she seemed to have cheered up the minute he swooped her up. There was a definite rosy tint in her cheeks, and she somehow managed to position herself in such a way that her bosom was right under Oli's nose.

Why couldn't I have twisted my ankle? Kay thought, quite sure that she wasn't the only female in Lyme Regis that morning to have wished herself harm in order to be in Beth's position right now.

Kay hurried towards the front door, jamming the key in the lock and opening it just as Oli and Beth arrived.

'Through here,' Kay said, leading the way. 'We'll make a bed up for you in the living room. We don't want you attempting those stairs.'

'But I want Oli to take me to my bedroom,' Beth said.

'Kay's right,' Oli said. 'You're better off down here,' he said, depositing her on the sofa.

'Careful!' Beth said. 'I'm not a sack of spuds.' Her face crumpled up in resentment. 'Take off my shoes, Oli, baby,' she said.

Kay rolled her eyes. Beth was making the very most of her predicament—as any woman would.

Dreading what would happen next, Kay left the scene in the living room and rooted around in the freezer for the ice cube tray, tipping the cubes out into a thick plastic bag and bashing them with a rolling pin.

'I must not think of Beth as I do this,' Kay said to herself. 'She's my patient, and I must be compassionate.'

Ice suitably crushed, Kay fastened the bag and found a clean tea towel to wrap it in.

'Here we are,' she said a moment later, placing the ice pack against Beth's ankle.

'Ouch!' she screamed. 'That's cold.'

'Of course it's cold—it's ice!' Oli laughed as he stood back to enjoy the proceedings.

'Ice will bring the swelling down,' Kay said.

'Can't I have a hot water bottle instead? Or some vodka?'

'I think ice is probably better for you,' Kay said.

Beth clutched the ice pack and flung her head back against the cushions in dramatic resignation. 'What I suffer for my art!' she groaned.

'It was one hell of a performance, though,' Oli said. 'It'll go down in movie history.'

'I'd better win a bloody BAFTA; that's all I'm saying,' Beth said, and Oli and Kay grinned at each other.

There was a knock at the door and a voice in the hallway.

'Hello? Everyone okay?' It was Adam.

'We're in the living room,' Kay called back.

Adam came through. 'Anything I can do to help?'

'I think it's all been taken care of,' Oli said, and Beth smiled up at him from her position on the sofa.

'Oli has been an absolute darling,' Beth said. 'You will stay with me, won't you?'

'I think I'm probably wanted back on the set,' he said.

'Oh!'

'But I'll be back later. I've promised to sit for Kay.'

'What do you mean, *sit*?'

'She's going to paint my portrait,' Oli said, flashing a smile at Kay.

'Really?' Beth said, her voice sounding dark and threatening. 'Why?'

'Because our Kay is an artist,' Oli said.

Kay loved the way he said 'our Kay.' It was as if she were part of the acting family, although she would have preferred 'my Kay.'

'Perhaps you'd prefer to paint my portrait,' Beth said. 'I've been told I have very good cheekbones, and it looks like I'll be sitting around here doing nothing.'

Kay bit her lip. 'That's very kind of you. Perhaps I could. After I've drawn Oli.'

Beth looked put out, punching her fist into one of the cushions and then yelling at the ice pack again.

'Poor darling,' Oli said, walking towards the sofa and bending down to kiss her on the forehead.

'Don't go, Oli!'

'Gotta go, babes.'

Oli left the room, and Kay followed him down the hallway.

'You were wonderful,' she said, her voice sounding horribly breathy, even to her own ears. 'The way you carried her all that way.'

Oli shrugged and smiled that boyish smile of his. 'You do what you have to do,' he said. 'Maybe it's these clothes I'm wearing. Perhaps the spirit of Captain Wentworth entered me, and I couldn't help but be a hero.'

Kay beamed a smile at him. It was the most magnificent of thoughts.

'I'll see you tonight,' he said, winking at her before leaving the bed and breakfast.

For a few moments, Kay stood in the hallway completely dumbstruck. He'd winked at her again. That had to mean something, didn't it? Once might be just a tick, but more than once had to mean that she was somebody special, and that night couldn't come fast enough.

Turning around, she almost crashed into Adam. 'I've just put the kettle on for Beth. She keeps on about a vodka, but I thought a cup of tea might be better.'

'Oh, that's kind of you, Adam.'

'Perhaps I could stay for one too?' he said, eyebrows raising.

'If you like,' Kay said, dreamily walking towards the kitchen. 'Shouldn't you be doing something on the set?'

'No, I've sorted things out there for the moment,' he said. 'In fact, I was wondering—if you're not too busy—'

'I'm afraid I'm terribly busy,' Kay said, grabbing her hair and tying it up with a pink ponytail ring. 'I've got so much to do before Oli comes back, I can't think.'

'Oh,' Adam said.

'Why?'

Adam shook his head. 'It's nothing. Don't worry.'

Kay took a couple of mugs out of the cupboard and then remembered that Beth didn't like mugs. She liked only cups in saucers.

'And now I'm Beth-sitting too,' she said. 'Who would have thought that I'd have Beth Jenkins on my sofa?'

'I don't think many people would envy you that,' Adam said.

'Oh, she's not so bad,' Kay said. 'As long as you give her lots of attention. How do you take your tea?'

'Milk, no sugar, please.'

'Sweet enough?'

Adam grinned. 'You've noticed?'

'I have, and I think Gemma has too,' Kay said with a naughty smile. She couldn't resist pushing things. 'Have you seen her today?'

'No,' Adam said. 'I mean not to talk to. I'd just arrived on the set when Beth fell.'

'Of course,' Kay said. 'Then you must go and talk to her.'

'Why?' Adam asked.

Kay looked up from pouring the milk into his mug. His was a strange response, she thought. Surely he couldn't wait to see Gemma after their wonderful dinner.

'She said she couldn't wait to see you again,' Kay said.

'Did she?' Adam said.

Kay swallowed. Actually, Gemma had said no such thing, but a little fabrication here and there didn't harm, did it? It would probably help things along nicely.

'She did,' Kay said. 'She told me what a perfect gentleman you were and that she was hoping to spend more time with you. Isn't that nice?'

Adam's eyebrows rose, and there was a funny look in his eyes that seemed to suggest that he didn't believe her. Kay decided to ignore it.

'You know what your problem is, Adam?' she continued.

'No,' he said, 'but I have a feeling you're going to tell me.'

'You don't realise how sweet you are,' Kay said. 'And genuinely sweet men are in short supply.'

'Right.'

'Yes.' Kay thought about the men in her past and how every single one of them had ended up letting her down. Things always started well, and Kay—being a romantic—always believed that she'd found 'the one,' only to be nursing a broken heart a few weeks later. 'There are plenty of charming men out there. I've been charmed by most of them, but that doesn't last. Charm is temporary. It's like a fancy suit you put on to wow your date with, but it soon gets taken off, and then you're left with—'

'What?' Adam said, a little smile beginning at the corner of his mouth.

Kay cast her eyes to the ceiling. 'You're left with a hollow egg.'

Adam's eyes narrowed. 'A hollow egg?'

Kay nodded. 'Like an Easter egg. It's a wonderfully sweet concoction, but it's perfectly hollow inside.'

'With a suit on?'

Kay looked flustered for a moment. 'Oh, you know what I mean. Anyway, you're not a fancy suit—or a hollow egg.'

'I'm glad to hear it.'

'You're very sweet, and you deserve to be happy,' Kay said, pausing whilst she stirred the tea, wondering if she dared to say more, but she handed him his mug of tea and quickly focussed on making Beth's instead.

'You seem to think you know me so well,' Adam said. 'But there's one important thing you've overlooked. Something you're forgetting.'

'What's that?' Kay asked.

'You're still wearing my jacket.'

'Oh!' Kay gasped. 'I am!' She laughed, taking off the jacket quickly and returning it to him. 'You're so sweet, Adam. Have I told you that?'

'You have,' he said.

'Owwwwwwwch!' came a cry from the living room.

'Ah, your patient calls,' Adam said. 'I'll leave you to it.'

Kay smiled and grabbed the pretty china cup and saucer and headed towards her patient in double quick time.

Chapter 19

OTHER THAN BETH'S TOPPLE FROM THE COBB, EVERYTHING seemed to be going well that morning, and Teresa was pleased with the scenes they shot. The crew were going to take a break for lunch and then move on to some interiors at Marlcombe Manor.

Even Gemma was happy with the way the morning's shoot had gone. She had been the only one not to fluff her lines, and her new friend, Rob, had told her how brilliant she'd been. She turned to look at him as he helped pack up the equipment, his broad shoulders and strong arms straining under the weight.

'Gemma!' a voice shouted over to her, and Gemma saw a girl with a pretty face running along the Lower Cobb towards her, a notepad and pen in her hands. 'Will you sign this for me?'

Gemma smiled. She hadn't signed many autographs yet and was always surprised that anyone would value her loopy scrawl.

'What's your name?' she asked the young girl.

'Emily—but don't put my name on it,' she hurriedly added. 'I'm going to sell it on eBay.'

'Oh,' Gemma said, disappointed by this bit of news.

'Where's Oli?'

'I think he went off for lunch,' Gemma said.

'Will he be coming back?' Emily asked, her face eager for information.

'Are you hoping for his autograph to sell?' Gemma asked, knowing it was mean, but unable to resist.

'Oh, no,' Emily said. 'I'll keep his autograph. What about Beth Jenkins? Is she around?'

'I'm afraid she twisted her ankle and won't be filming again today.'

'Oh,' Emily said. 'I really wanted her autograph too. She's really famous, isn't she?' She turned and left, making Gemma feel like a very poor substitute indeed.

As Gemma stood, trying not to feel too sorry for herself, she felt a hand land on her shoulder, and she spun around.

'Nice work, Gemma,' Les Miserable said with something that almost approached a smile but wasn't quite.

'Thank you. I thought it w—' she didn't get a chance to finish her sentence, because he was walking away in search of lunch, but she was grateful for having had anything remotely approaching a compliment from Les Miserable.

'You want some lunch, then?' Sophie asked, coming out of the costume trailer wearing a duffle coat over her Regency dress.

'I'd love some,' Gemma said, and the two of them walked along the Lower Cobb together.

'Poor old Beth,' Sophie said. 'I mean, she's not my favourite person in the world, but I hope she's not done anything too nasty.'

Gemma nodded. 'She really threw herself from those steps, didn't she?'

'I think she only did it to impress Oli.'

'I think it worked.'

'Do you?' Sophie said.

'He swooped her up, didn't he?'

'But he would have done that for anyone. Even if Les Miserable had taken a tumble.'

Gemma laughed. 'But the way they looked at each other,' she said, 'there's got to be something going on.'

'It's only Beth who gives the looks,' Sophie said. 'I've not seen Oli show any interest in her.'

'Haven't you?'

Sophie shook her head. 'I think he's got his eye on somebody else.'

'Who?'

Sophie pursed her lips. 'I think—' she stopped.

'What?'

'Oh, my God!' Sophie suddenly exclaimed. 'Is that who I think it is?'

'Who?'

'Wow!' Sophie's eyes went wide with excitement. 'I mean— blimey!'

'Who are you looking at?' Gemma asked. She had taken out her contact lenses for filming, and her long-distance vision wasn't good.

'And she's still so stunning. Not that she's old or anything,' Sophie said, grabbing Gemma's arm. 'But she doesn't look a day over forty, does she?'

Gemma looked around, and her sight landed on a figure she hadn't expected to be there. Even without her contact lenses, there was no mistaking her or the work she'd had done to keep the ageing process at bay.

'Gemma!' the woman with the sleek black bob called, a manicured hand waving in the air.

Gemma walked towards her and was instantly enclosed in a heavily perfumed embrace.

'Hello, Mum,' she said.

Kay watched Beth being examined by Dr Floyd, a portly gentleman whose fat hands were holding Beth's ankle oh, so gently.

'There are no bones broken,' he said with a smile. 'But it's a very nasty sprain.'

'Nothing broken?' Beth groaned. 'Then why does it hurt so much?'

'You put the entire weight of your body on this little ankle,' Dr Floyd said, using the excuse to stroke it again. 'You're very lucky it's only a sprain.'

Beth grimaced, and Kay bet she wished it was Oli's hands that were touching her and not an overweight GP's.

'I'm glad to see you're already doing all the right things. Plenty of rest, try to keep the foot elevated, and ice is an excellent idea to prevent swelling.'

'Have you got any painkillers?' Beth asked in a girly voice, her eyes suddenly looking twice their normal size.

'I really wouldn't recommend them,' Dr Floyd said. 'Pain is nature's way of reminding us to take things easy, and my guess is, if you think the pain's gone, you'll be up and around, jumping off Cobbs again. Am I right?' He smiled, but Beth didn't smile back at him.

'Sadist!' she said as he left the bed and breakfast.

'Can I get you anything?' Kay asked. 'Another cup of tea?'

'God! I've got more tea swirling around my system than blood.'

'Any magazines to read? Or a book? I've got all the Jane Austens,' Kay said.

'A sprained ankle *and* Jane Austen—could the day get any worse?'

Kay frowned. She always made the mistake of assuming that everyone loved Jane Austen as much as she did. 'I'll leave you to have a little rest, then.'

'*Kay!*' Beth called. 'Don't leave me, will you?'

'I'll only be upstairs or in the kitchen.'

Beth pouted. 'Nobody cares! Everyone's forgotten about me.'

'No we haven't,' Kay said. 'But I've got baths and sinks to scrub, that's all.'

'Will you come and talk to me later?'

'Of course I will.'

Beth nodded. 'Maybe I'd better have a book—just for company.'

Kay smiled. 'I know just the remedy,' she said. 'Wait here.' She returned seconds later with an old paperback copy of *Pride and Prejudice*. 'It's the best medicine there is.'

Beth gave a little smile, not looking totally convinced. 'Seeing as there isn't a single glossy magazine in this establishment, I'll give it a go.'

⁓◯

Kim Reilly's arrival in Lyme caused no end of excitement, and Gemma was soon forgotten in the general scrum to get close to the famous actress. Hot dogs by the harbour were abandoned, and a sit-down meal in The Harbour Inn was demanded by the cast and crew as Kim regaled them with stories of her career.

'Take after take in that jumpsuit,' Kim said, sipping a lunch-time martini. 'I tell you, I lost a stone in weight that day.'

'You didn't need to,' Oli said. 'You were always the perfect shape. If you don't mind my saying so.'

'Honey, I don't mind your saying so,' Kim said, batting enormous eyelashes at Oli.

'Do you still have the jumpsuit?' Sophie asked. Gemma rolled her eyes. Her mother's famous jumpsuit had been regularly wheeled out at parties over the years as guests harangued her until she put it on, posing and pouting for photographs in the iconic outfit.

Kim waved a hand in the air as if batting the question away in embarrassment. 'I think I may still have it somewhere.'

'And I bet it still fits you like a glove,' Oli said.

Gemma groaned. She wished Oli wouldn't encourage her mother, not that she needed any encouragement. She always had the knack of steering the conversation around to whatever she wanted to talk about, and sooner or later, the famous black jumpsuit would be the topic of conversation.

'I'm just going to make a call,' Gemma said, getting up from the table in the corner of the pub.

Gemma wasn't going to make a call. She needed to get away for a moment. Goodness, her mother had been in Lyme Regis for less than half an hour, and she was already driving Gemma nuts.

What is it about Mother that upsets you so much? she asked herself, looking in the mirror of the ladies' toilets, where she'd taken refuge.

'She always—always upstages me,' she said to her reflection.

But doesn't everyone? That's one of the downsides of being shy.

It was also, perhaps, one of the reasons Gemma had become an actress. A part of her wanted to shine as brightly as her mother. She wanted people to see that she counted too. She wasn't just Kim Reilly's daughter; she was a person in her own right, and she didn't need a black jumpsuit, either. She had as much talent as her mother ever had.

Competing with your mother was exhausting sometimes, and Gemma wondered why she even tried to bother, because it was always going to be a losing battle that she didn't really want to win anyway.

'Not *really*,' she said to herself. Because she knew she wouldn't be happy being the centre of attention. As much as she'd love Oli to look at her the way he was looking at her mother and pay her that sort of attention, she knew it wasn't in her to command such interest.

She'd rather be sitting in a nice comfy room somewhere with a cup of tea and her knitting. She laughed at the image. She sounded ancient before her time, didn't she?

She fished in her handbag for her lip gloss, covering her lips with a nice red coat. It looked funny, with her Anne Elliot hair and her Regency costume, but it made her feel a little less invisible.

The door to the ladies' opened and her mother stepped inside.

'There you are!'

'Mum!'

'I thought you were making a call. Where've you been?' She looked annoyed, and Gemma guessed that she'd missed her mother recounting some scintillating anecdote that Gemma had heard a hundred times. 'And why aren't you out there flirting with that gorgeous man?'

'Oli?'

'Of course Oli. Who else?'

For a moment, the face of Rob floated before Gemma's eyes.

'Because if you don't make a move on him, I will!' her mother said with a lascivious wink.

'Oh, Mother!'

'Don't *oh, Mother* me!' she said, nudging her daughter out of the way so she could get to the mirror. Gemma watched as Kim brought out her own lipstick. It was called Red Vamp, and her mother had been wearing it for about twenty years longer than she should. Next came the powder—a dab here and a dab there. Gemma knew the routine so well. Then the perfume. Three liberal squirts of Lady of the Night. Gemma grimaced. She'd never liked the perfume, finding it heavy and cloying, but her mother never travelled anywhere without it.

'Will I do?' she asked, her fingers pulling her dark hair until it was just right.

'You'll do,' Gemma said, and they left the ladies' room together.

'Just one thing, darling,' her mother said, stopping before they got back to their table.

'What?'

'Try and make an effort with everyone. You were sitting at the table like a stuffed doll before. You can be quite the sparkling personality when you want to, except I get the feeling you never want to.'

Gemma sighed. At least her mother understood one thing about her.

Chapter 20

A<small>FTER A LUNCH FILLED WITH EVEN MORE ANECDOTES FROM</small> K<small>IM</small> Reilly's days as a TV sex goddess, it was time to resume filming.

'It was lovely to see you,' Gemma said, leaning forward to kiss her mother's cheek with the generosity of spirit available to one who knew her guest was leaving.

'You say that as if I'm going somewhere,' Kim said.

'You're not going home?'

'I've only just arrived!' She laughed.

'You mean you're staying?'

'I've booked a couple of nights at some bed and breakfast down the road. Charmouth?'

Gemma nodded. 'I didn't know.'

'Of course you didn't. I wanted to surprise you. I thought I'd better come and see if my daughter really could act.'

Gemma swallowed hard, knowing that her mother wasn't exaggerating. She'd want to know if all the drama school fees she'd paid over the years had been worth it.

'Is that a good idea?' Gemma said lamely. 'I mean, I don't know if Teresa will—'

'Oh, I've sorted all that out. She said I can stay as long as I like.

In fact, she said she'd value my opinion. I could maybe give her some direction, what with all my experience.'

'But you've never directed.'

'My darling girl, you don't need experience in this business. You just need opportunity and a bit of cheek.'

Gemma watched her mother waltz over towards Teresa and then closed her eyes. This was a nightmare.

Sophie tapped her shoulder. 'Wow!' she said. 'I wish I had a mum like yours.'

Gemma was tempted to say, *take mine*, but resisted, thinking that it might sound ungrateful.

'I can't believe she came down to see you.'

Gemma shook her head. 'She's not here to see me. She's here so people can see her.' She watched in horror as her mother joined Teresa. Oli was deep in conversation with her, but the two of them broke off when Kim approached. Gemma looked on as her mother batted her long eyelashes at him again.

'Angela Tyrrel was one of the defining roles of seventies' cult television,' she heard Oli say to her mother.

'Oh, you're too sweet.' She was lapping up praise like a kitten would cream.

No, Gemma thought, her mother wasn't here to see her at all.

⁓

'It's so unfair!' Beth complained from the sofa. 'Everyone's at the pub having fun with Kim Reilly, and I'm stuck here with a sore ankle.'

It was ten o'clock in the evening, and word of Kim Reilly's arrival had reached the bed and breakfast.

'I'm stuck here too,' Kay said.

'Yes, but you don't count,' Beth said with a sigh.

Kay looked across at Beth, shocked by her comment.

Beth turned to see her expression. 'You know what I mean. You're not an actress—it couldn't possibly mean as much to you to meet Kim Reilly as it would to me.'

Kay supposed she was right in her own rude way, but she would still have liked to have seen the famous actress. Not that she didn't have famous actresses coming out of her ears, and Beth was more than enough for any sane person to cope with.

'God, I'm bored,' Beth said with an enormous sigh. 'I could never have lived in Jane Austen's time and just hung around the house all day.'

Kay looked across at her. 'How are you getting on with *Pride and Prejudice?*'

'Oh, I got fed up with it,' Beth said. 'I read as far as that ball where Elizabeth gets in a tizz with Darcy for not dancing with her and gave up.'

Kay's mouth dropped open. That was one of her favourite bits. How could somebody give up there? she wondered 'You really should read some more.'

'*Please* don't make me!' Beth said dramatically. 'It would be like doing homework, and I never bothered with that, even when I was at school.'

Kay shook her head in miscomprehension, wondering what on earth they were going to talk about if Beth wasn't an Austen fan.

'What made you want to become an actress?' Kay asked at last.

Beth—who had slumped since the *Pride and Prejudice* conversation—seemed to perk up a little. 'You get to wear nice things,' she said. 'Did you ever have a dressing-up box at school?'

'No,' Kay said, thinking back to the school she attended. Actually, she attended three different schools, because her mother moved house a fair few times in an attempt to make 'a fresh start' after Kay's father left them, but it had always been disappointing, with Kay's mother still unable to find the perfect relationship and Kay feeling displaced in her role as the new girl at school. 'I would have loved a dressing-up box,' she said, thinking of how one might have helped her to feel more at home at her new schools. She had always loved dressing up and pretending she was a fictional character.

'We had one,' Beth said, 'and there'd always be an almighty scrum for the best clothes. I remember there was this emerald gown with sequins along the top. All the girls would make for that, and whoever got it would be instantly transformed into a princess. It was glorious,' Beth said, smiling. 'I thought acting was like that too. You got to wear glamorous clothes that transformed you into somebody else. But it doesn't always work out like that. My first job was as a walk-on in one of those dreadful kitchen-sink dramas, and my costume was hideous. I looked like a dishcloth.'

'I suppose that's fitting for a kitchen-sink drama,' Kay said, but Beth wasn't amused.

'It's important to be beautiful,' Beth said.

'But surely the role is more important.'

'Certainly not,' Beth said. 'I don't take anything now unless it's going to make me look good.'

Kay was quite shocked by this admission, but she supposed she wasn't really surprised.

'And between you and me, I should have been cast as Anne Elliot, although I do still think that Louisa is the most important role in the story, don't you?'

'At least you're not Henrietta,' Kay said. 'She gets much less screen time than Louisa.'

'Yes,' Beth said. 'I wouldn't have even read for Henrietta. I don't know why Sophie bothered, really, although beggars can't be choosers, I suppose.'

Kay tried to hide her smile at this comment. She was quite sure Sophie was aware of Beth's sniping comments, and she knew Sophie would just laugh them off.

'I wonder where Oli is,' Beth said. 'What's keeping him out so late?'

'I was meant to be drawing Oli this evening,' Kay said.

Beth didn't look too happy with this piece of information. 'He stood you up just like every other woman he's ever been involved with.'

Kay sighed. She could tell she was pouting and tried to stop.

'I hate men,' Beth said, but the expression in her eyes seemed to be saying the very opposite. 'Most of them are wasters, and the others just waste your time.'

The front door opened and a voice called from the hallway. It was Oli.

'We're in here, darling,' Beth called from the sofa, quickly fluffing up her hair and seeming to forget that Oli was a man and that she hated every last one of them.

'Hello, ladies,' he said as he entered the room, a huge smile on his face, his cheeks glowing with an evening of alcoholic consumption and fine conversation. 'You two missed one hell of an evening. Kim's amazing. You should hear the stories she has to tell.'

'You were meant to be with Kay this evening,' Beth said, completely taking Kay by surprise.

'What?' Oli said.

'Kay was going to draw you, but you forgot. You're a pig, Oli.'

Oli looked suitably crestfallen. 'God! I'm so sorry, Kay,' he said, stepping forward and grabbing her hands in his. 'Beth's right—I'm a pig.'

'No, you're not,' Kay said with a little smile.

'I'm a pig,' he said, giving a little oink, which made Kay giggle. 'But there's still time, isn't there?'

'What do you mean?'

Oli looked at his watch. 'It's only ten thirty,' he said. 'Come on!' Still with her hand in his, he led her through to the dining room, where he pulled out a chair and sat down in it, straight-backed and straight-faced.

'Is that you posing for me?' Kay asked with a smile.

Oli nodded. 'Okay?'

She bit her lip. 'Well…'

'Not okay? Where do you want me, then?' Oli asked, turning around.

Kay swallowed hard, desperately biting her tongue lest she answer him honestly.

'It's fine,' she said. 'You're fine there. Let me get my things.'

'Kay!' Beth called from the living room. 'You just left me.'

'I'm going to draw Oli,' Kay said, poking her head around the door.

Beth pulled a sour face. 'And what am I meant to do?'

'Go to bed?'

Beth did not look amused. 'You'd better pass me that bloody book.'

Kay passed her the copy of *Pride and Prejudice*. 'It'll make you feel better, I promise.'

'I doubt that very much,' Beth said, but she opened the book and cast her weary eyes to the printed page.

Chapter 21

K AY RUSHED UP TO HER ROOM TO GET HER PAD AND PENCILS, but she had to stop by the mirror first, grabbing a hairbrush and attacking her tresses.

'Blast!' she said as the fine hair floated out in a static halo. She hurried into her en suite and ran her brush under the tap, doing her best to control the errant strands. She fished in her makeup bag for a lip gloss and mascara. For a moment, she worried about the dress she was wearing, but she didn't have time to get changed.

Oli was still sitting in the chair when she re-entered the room, and she had to take a moment to believe the scene in front of her.

'Okay?' Oli asked, turning to face her.

Kay nodded, holding up the tools of her profession. She was ready to begin.

She had never sketched such a handsome profile. The heroes she had drawn for her books had always been from her imagination or inspired by the heroes from the films she watched. Never had she been presented with a real-life hero. She had to concentrate on the task in hand in order to do a good job, but she knew how easy it would be to just sit and stare at Oli and end up with a blank sheet of paper. But she was working now and had to take things seriously.

She had experience sketching from life at the art classes she attended at her local college, but the college never had the budget for this calibre of model. They were far more likely to be shrivelled up old men who should have known when to keep their clothes on.

But Kay couldn't afford to think of men with their clothes off when she was drawing Oli Wade Owen—it would be far too much of a distraction.

'What are you thinking of?' Oli suddenly asked.

Kay blanched. It was as if he'd read her mind. 'What do you mean?' she asked, stalling for time.

'I mean, what does an artist think of when she's sketching?'

Kay breathed a sigh of relief. It was just a regular question, and he didn't have the powers of telepathy.

'I usually don't think at all,' Kay said. 'I mean, I'm concentrating on what I'm doing.'

Oli nodded. 'Like acting, then.'

'Is it?'

'A lot of my mates ask me what I'm thinking of when I'm kissing some beautiful actress in a love scene, and they don't usually like the answer.'

'And what's the answer?'

'That I'm thinking of getting the job done.'

Kay smiled.

'You don't mind talking whilst you're working?' he asked her.

'No,' she said. 'What do you want to talk about?'

'Oh, I don't know—anything, really. Like what's a pretty girl like you doing running a dreary old bed and breakfast?'

'Do you think it's dreary?'

Oli cast his eyes around at the tatty wallpaper and swirling carpet.

'I know it's not perfect yet, but it will be,' Kay said.

'But what are you doing stuck out in the middle of nowhere?'

'Lyme Regis isn't nowhere!'

'It's a long way from London,' Oli said.

'And why's that such a bad thing?'

He raised his eyebrows in surprise at her question. 'You don't like London?'

'It's okay,' she said, 'in small doses. I actually once thought about moving there.'

'Why didn't you?'

'Oh, it was just an idea. I thought my father might be there. He always talked about going to London.' She looked up and caught Oli's eye. 'He left when I was young,' she explained. 'And I had this crazy idea that I could find him and make things right again, but it was just a silly dream.'

'I'm sorry,' Oli said.

'It's okay,' she said. 'It was all a long time ago, but I still wonder where he is and what he's doing and if he ever thinks of me. Especially now that mum's gone. He probably doesn't even know it.'

'Families can be crazy, can't they?'

'Yes,' Kay said, 'I'm afraid they can.' She sighed. 'But you're happy in London, aren't you?'

'I couldn't live anywhere else,' Oli said.

Kay's pencil hovered over the paper for a moment. That was a shame, she thought, although she could learn to compromise. After all, it would be fun to have a home in London and one by the sea too.

'Where shall we go this weekend, darling?' Oli might ask. 'Down to Lyme, or stay in town for that party?'

Kay could live with that, she supposed, blushing as Oli looked up at her.

'London's the place to be,' he said with a sigh.

She wouldn't mind—not if it made him happy. 'Just sit still a moment.'

'Sorry,' he said. 'I'm a bit of a fidget, aren't I?'

'You're doing fine.'

'I'm not very good at being still. I can't even sit to read a book for more than ten minutes. I usually read my scripts on the treadmill.'

Kay looked up from her paper. 'Really?' She tried to imagine it: a copy of the script for *Persuasion* in one hand whilst his strong, lean legs ran for miles. It was a heart-stopping image. 'And what did you think of *Persuasion*?' she asked, trying to banish the image of Oli in Lycra from her mind.

'The script was okay,' he said.

'I love *Persuasion*,' Kay said. 'It's one of my favourite Austen novels.'

'I wouldn't know about that.'

Kay looked up again. 'You haven't read the others?'

'I haven't read *Persuasion*,' Oli said.

'You haven't read it?' Kay said in alarm.

'You've got to be kidding!' Oli said. 'I tried once, but it bored me to tears. It's so slow! I think you have to be a woman to get that sort of thing. Or gay.'

Kay looked shocked for a moment. Oli wasn't joking, was he? He really hadn't read the novel. Here he was playing one of Austen's greatest heroes, yet he hadn't even read the book.

'For God's sake, don't tell Teresa. She'd skin me alive.'

'I'm not surprised,' Kay said. 'How can you be in the film adaptation of a novel you haven't read?'

'You don't need to read it,' he said. 'What's the point of a script if you have to read a huge book as well?'

'But it's only a small book. It wouldn't take you long. I could lend you a copy, if you want.' Kay was about to go get one, but Oli stopped her.

'Please! I really don't need to read it.'

Kay put down her pencil for a moment. She couldn't concentrate.

'Great,' he said. 'I've upset you, haven't I?'

'Yes,' she said. 'You have.'

He shook his head. 'You women just don't get that Austen is a girl thing. It's not for men.'

'But Adam loves it,' she said.

'That doesn't surprise me.'

'What do you mean?'

'I mean Adam's probably gay.'

Kay gasped. 'He is not!' she said, thinking what a disaster it would be for her plans for him if he turned out to be gay. What would poor Gemma do then? She'd hate to have to break the news to her. She could see the scene in her head.

Gemma, I'm so sorry. I didn't know how to tell you, but you're strong. You'll get over this. You'll see.

I won't! I won't ever get over this. I may as well throw myself from the Cobb right now.

No! Gemma—don't!

God, it would be awful, Kay thought.

'Perhaps you could try an audio book of it,' Kay said, not willing to give up on Oli just yet.

'Tried that,' he said.

'And what happened?'

'I fell asleep in the bath. Nearly drowned.'

'Oh, dear,' she said. 'Maybe I could read it to you.'

Oli looked around at her, his blue eyes wide. 'You'd really do that?'

Kay nodded, thinking of the hours they could spend together.

'That's the sweetest thing anyone's ever offered to do for me.'

Kay smiled. Oli had redeemed himself just a little.

'Can I look now?' Oli asked.

Kay looked up from her sketch. 'I've not finished yet. You keep distracting me.'

'Oh, come on. I'm dying to see.'

'Sit still!' Kay said with a giggle.

But Oli was on his feet and crossed the room in a moment. 'Wow!' he said. 'That's really good.'

'You think so?' Kay said, looking at what she had managed to get down in their brief time as artist and model.

'Of course I think so. You should do this for a living.'

Kay beamed him a smile. 'I'd love to. I really would.'

'Then you should. You absolutely should.' He held her gaze for a moment, his blue eyes mesmeric, and Kay could have sworn something wonderful was about to happen. Just one moment longer and—

Beth's head popped around the door. 'What are you two doing?'

The spell was broken.

'I've been sitting in that front room all by myself,' she said, accusation flooding her voice. 'You've been ages.'

'Kay's just capturing me,' Oli said. 'Take a look.'

Beth hopped into the room and looked at Kay's work. 'Hmmm. Not bad, but then you have a good subject.'

'Shouldn't you be resting?' Kay asked, furious that her special time with Oli had been interrupted.

'I'm bored,' Beth said. 'I've been on that sofa for hours, and I've missed all the fun today. It's not fair.'

'I think it's time we got you to bed,' Oli said. 'Can you make the stairs?'

'I might be able to 'if you help me,' Beth said, her voice becoming all girly again.

''Night, Kay,' Oli said, bending down to kiss her cheek.

Kay felt her skin burst into flame, and she watched as Beth claimed his attention, placing her arm around Oli's shoulders.

'Nice and slowly,' he said, leading her to the stairs. 'One step at a time.'

'That's how I like it too,' Beth said coyly.

Kay rolled her eyes.

Chapter 22

GEMMA COULDN'T BELIEVE HER MOTHER WAS IN LYME REGIS. Well, she could. After all, it wasn't the first time she turned up unannounced. As she lathered her hair with a squirt of her favourite apple shampoo, Gemma remembered the night of her performance as Lady Macbeth at drama school. It was the biggest part she had ever taken on, and she was pacing up and down with nerves backstage when somebody screamed from the auditorium.

'Kim Reilly's here! Kim Reilly's here!'

Everyone flocked to her mother—as they usually did—and she was lost amongst a mass of hysterical drama students. Gemma had been forgotten. Not one person was there to tell her to break a leg that evening, and she remembered spying her mother sitting in the front row, her mouth moving as she whispered advice to her daughter, her hands wringing themselves during the 'out, damned spot' scene as if it were her playing the role of Lady Macbeth and not her daughter.

The party afterwards had been all about Kim Reilly too, and Gemma faded into the background.

'My natural place,' she said to herself as shampoo bubbles rinsed down her shoulders and back. She learned long ago that there was absolutely no point in trying to compete with her mother. She just had to let her mother get on with it and hope that the experience wouldn't be too painful.

Finishing her shower, Gemma pulled on a cotton night dress—the kind her mother would refer to as a 'passion killer.'

'How on earth are you going to get a man when you wear something like that?' her mother had said when she barged into the bedroom of Gemma's flat recently and discovered the knee-length cotton night dress covered in hummingbirds on the edge of her bed, but after a long day on set, nothing was nicer, nothing more snugly, than her beloved cotton night dress, and she didn't care what her mother thought of it.

Sophie had fallen asleep as soon as her head hit the pillow, her breathing deep and calming. Gemma was glad of the privacy, because she knew Sophie would only want to talk about Gemma's mother. That was the curse of being the daughter of a famous actress—everybody wanted to know everything.

What's it like having a famous mother?

Lonely, most of the time.

Aren't you terribly proud of her?

Sometimes, but mostly I just get embarrassed.

I bet you want to be just like her.

That's what I worry about more than anything else in the world.

Gemma closed her eyes and waited to welcome sleep. Perhaps her mother would get bored with everything as early as tomorrow. She had a short attention span and would probably find Lyme Regis dull. A small seaside town with a few bookshops, boutiques, and bakeries wouldn't be enough to occupy her for long, and once everybody had made a big fuss about her and returned to the job in hand, she'd grow restless and go off in search of somebody else to indulge her. Gemma could then stop worrying about being watched all the time. It wasn't as if she wasn't nervous enough about this film already without having her mother's eye roving over every move she made and questioning her delivery.

'She'll get bored soon,' Gemma said to herself and promptly fell asleep, dreaming of missed cues and meddling mothers.

Kay yawned and drew back her bedroom curtains, smiling at the sea view that greeted her. She wondered, would she ever grow bored of it? Would she ever take it for granted and not appreciate its blue beauty? And it really was blue today. After days of slate grey, the sea had changed to the most miraculous blue Kay had ever seen, and it took some of the sting out of the earliness of her wake-up call.

After showering and dressing quickly, Kay stepped out onto the landing. All was quiet, and she guessed the actors were still in bed. She was just descending the stairs when Beth's door creaked open. Kay waited, eager to enquire how she was feeling this morning, but it wasn't Beth who emerged from the room. It was Oli. He was fully dressed, and it didn't take Kay long to realise that he was still wearing his clothes from the previous night. He hadn't gone to bed. At least, he hadn't gone to his own bed, had he?

His blond hair flopped over his forehead, and his blue eyes were bleary, suggesting that he hadn't slept much. Kay stood motionless on the stairs, hoping that the banister rails would hide her, but she didn't have to worry. Oli hadn't spotted her, and he sneaked back into his own room, closing the door behind him.

Breathing a sigh of relief, she fled to the kitchen. Oh, God! How could she have been so stupid as to fall in love with an actor? Hadn't Adam warned her that they always stick to their own? Here was irrefutable evidence that that was exactly what they did. It was the phenomenon that Kay was only too eager to read about in the celebrity magazines—who was having an affair with whom on location. It was one of the oldest clichés in the business; the leading man always had an affair, except this time it wasn't with the leading actress.

'Just as well,' Kay said to herself, seeing as she'd already match-made her.

As she put on her floral pinny and started to get breakfast ready, she tried to console herself.

He never would have looked at you, anyway, she told herself. *You're not in his league at all.* It was true enough, but it still didn't stop a girl from dreaming, did it? Your head might tell you one thing, but your heart can pull in a different direction completely. It was the same old story with Kay; just like her mother before her, she always seemed to fall for the heartbreaker, getting swept up by the romance of everything and eager to overlook the problems that were staring her in the face. And look how it had worked out for her mother.

Kay sighed as she remembered the time her mother swore she was getting married again and the two of them went shopping to celebrate.

'You're going to be the prettiest bridesmaid,' her mother told her, picking out the sweetest pink dress for her to wear whilst buying herself an outrageously expensive tiara. 'Harry is going to be so proud of us.' They smiled and giggled all the way home until they found the badly scrawled note stuffed through the letterbox. Harry, it seemed, had found somebody else.

'Poor Mum,' Kay said to herself, and for a moment, she thought back to the tempestuous relationship between her mother and her father and how badly that had ended too. Was she destined for the same fate? Perhaps that was why she was always trying to matchmake people—it was her way of making up for the doomed relationship of her parents.

Twenty minutes later there was a gentle tap on the door.

'Hello?'

It was Oli. Kay looked up to see his head popping around the kitchen door. Such a wonderful head, Kay thought, despite the fact that he was obviously having an affair with Beth Jenkins.

'How are you this morning?' he asked.

'I'm fine.'

'Something smells good in here.'

'That'll be the bacon,' she said.

He nodded. 'You okay?' he asked, running a hand through his hair, which had obviously been washed since the floppy look he'd been sporting leaving Beth's bedroom.

'I'm fine,' Kay said, smiling brightly.

Oli frowned, obviously not convinced by her answer. 'You seem a little—distant.'

'Do I?'

He nodded. 'Not working you too hard, are we?'

'No, of course not.'

''Cause I know we can be a pain.'

'You're not a pain,' she said. 'I love having you. *Around,*' she added quickly. 'I love having you all around the place. You bring things to life.'

He grinned. 'I've got the morning off. I'm not needed until later this afternoon.'

'Oh,' Kay said, having visions of his hanging around the house all day, forgetting all about Beth Jenkins and slowly falling in love with her—once she'd taken off her pinny and fixed her hair, of course.

'I thought maybe I'd get a bit of lunch somewhere. There's meant to be an amazing pub out near Beaminster. I thought we might have a spin up that way and see what all the fuss is about.'

'We?' Kay said.

'We,' Oli said. 'You and me. How about it?'

Kay nodded enthusiastically.

'Shall we get going then?'

'Right now?'

'I suppose you'd better feed this lot first and do whatever you've got to do.'

'Okay,' she said.

'How's about I see you in the front room at eleven?'

Kay grinned at him, his brief affair with Beth banished from her brain. It wasn't Beth he was interested in at all—it was her!

Chapter 23

Eleven o'clock couldn't come around quickly enough for Kay. She whizzed around Wentworth House, vacuuming, dusting, scrubbing, and tidying like a thing possessed. Finally, at twenty to eleven, she took off her pinny. It was time to get herself ready.

She had the quickest of showers, because she was sure she smelt of bacon and cleaning products, and it wasn't the most romantic of combinations. But then came the problem of what to wear. She had to get this right. Her whole life might depend on it.

'You know when I decided I was going to propose to you?' Oli would tell her in future years. 'The moment you came into the front room for our first date wearing that amazing—'

'*What?*' Kay screamed in the here and now. Amazing *what?* She didn't have anything amazing.

She flung open the wardrobe door in the hope that she had overlooked something and stared gloomily at the contents. It was the usual problem: a packed wardrobe, but absolutely nothing to wear.

'I'll just have to make do,' she said, pulling out a blue cotton dress that was sprigged with tiny pink roses. It wasn't the stuff of sex symbols, but it was sweet. She grabbed the hair dryer to work as much magic into her mop as she could in the time available, hoping her toffee-coloured tresses wouldn't become too flyaway. A quick application of makeup, and she was almost finished. She still needed shoes, and she knew just the pair. The prior summer, she bought a pair of strappy silver shoes that were more like jewellery than shoes. She knew their day would come. She placed her dainty feet into them now and sighed, hoping that sheer stockings and strappy shoes weren't tempting the rain clouds again.

Grabbing her handbag, she took a deep breath and left the room, venturing down the stairs for her date with Oli. There he was, pacing up and down the hallway, his blond hair bright against a sky-blue shirt, the sleeves rolled up to reveal a pair of strong, tanned arms.

'Hello,' she said, her mouth suddenly feeling quite dry.

He turned around, his bright eyes appraising her. 'Oh,' he said. 'You look lovely, really.'

'What's wrong?' Kay asked, dismayed by the look on his face.

'Nothing—nothing's wrong. It's just—well, you look like you.'

Kay's face fell. She knew she'd never be as beautiful as the actresses Oli was used to being seen with, but she thought she'd scrubbed up pretty well, considering the lack of notice he gave her.

'I didn't put that very well,' Oli said. 'I mean—we have to disguise you. There are paps everywhere.'

'Are there?' Kay said, looking around as if a telephoto lens might suddenly poke through the letterbox.

Oli nodded. 'I'm afraid they've got wind I'm here.'

'Oh, dear.'

'Exactly, and if they get a picture of you, it'll be all over the papers.'

Kay didn't think that sounded too bad at all. In fact, the idea rather appealed to her. She could see it now.

Oli's Mystery Girl, the headline would read, and there would be a photo of the two of them driving off together or one of them running into a restaurant together, Oli's arm protectively around her shoulder.

Speculation has arisen over the girl the handsome star is dating, and there are even rumours that the two of them are engaged. Could this be the future Mrs Wade Owen?

'So you see,' Oli said, 'we'll have to disguise you, because we can't possibly have them knowing who you are. It's for your own privacy.'

'Oh,' Kay said reluctantly, her imagined headlines evaporating. 'I see.'

'Leave it to me,' Oli said, and he ran up the stairs two at a time and knocked on Beth's door. Kay followed him, wondering what he was up to. Beth hadn't come downstairs yet that morning and was still resting her ankle. At least she was supposed to be resting, but Kay still didn't know what had gone on in Beth's room the night before. If Oli had spent the night in there, Kay was doubtful that rest would have been much of a priority.

'Beth? It's Oli.'

It was the only password needed, for the door opened almost instantly.

'What is it, Oli?' Beth said with a sweet smile. She was wearing full makeup despite being an invalid, and Kay could see that her hair had been blow-dried.

'We need that wig of yours.'

'Wig?' Beth said. 'I don't wear wigs. Not unless I'm filming.'

'Come on, Beth. I've seen it. It's in your suitcase.'

Beth sighed. 'That's a hairpiece, Oli. Quite a different thing. Everyone's wearing them these days. Some women wouldn't even put out the trash unless they had their hairpiece in.'

'Yeah, yeah. Let's just have it.'

'What for?'

'For Kay. We've got to disguise her.'

Beth frowned. 'Why?'

'We're going out to lunch, and we need to hide her identity from the press.'

'But I'll need to wear it if we're going out to lunch.'

Oli looked uncomfortable for a moment. 'I'm taking Kay out to lunch,' he said slowly, as if testing the waters.

'I see,' Beth said. 'I'm not invited. I'm just the invalid who can be left alone all day with no company.'

'Come on, Beth, don't be like that. We're always having lunch together.'

'Yeah, with about a dozen extras and all the crew.'

'Can we borrow the wig? Please? I'll owe you big time.'

'God, Oli! You're the limit. You really are.'

Beth disappeared into the room and came back brandishing the red hairpiece. 'Be careful with it. It cost me a fortune.'

'We will. Don't worry. Now, help us with it, will you? And that nice blue dress of yours.'

'Not the Versace!'

'The very one.'

'Oli!'

'*Please!*'

Beth gave a gargantuan sigh before going to fetch her things.

Ten minutes later, Kay was transformed. The blue dress was slinky and sexy and skimmed over her figure in a most alluring way. Her own hair had been tied up into a tight bun on the top of her head, the red hairpiece had been carefully pinned around her face, and then everything had been squashed into submission by a hat.

'Sunglasses,' Oli said. 'Those nice big blue-framed ones of yours.'

'Oli, no! They're my Tiffany's.'

Oli's eyes looked up at her pleading. 'You would be doing me such a huge favour. I'd really owe you.'

'You always owe me,' Beth said sulkily, hobbling back into the room on her dodgy ankle and emerging with the prized glasses.

'Just don't lose them or break them.' She handed them to Oli, who gave them to Kay.

'Thanks, Beth,' Kay said, opening the box and eyeing the beautiful glasses. She had never seen anything so lovely, and she was a little afraid to put them on.

'Go on,' Oli encouraged her.

Kay put them on and smiled. 'Okay?'

'Wow!' Oli said. 'You look like Audrey Hepburn.'

'Except with red hair and a squashy hat,' Beth added.

'Do I look okay?'

'You'll do,' Oli said, ushering her down the stairs.

Catching her reflection in the hall mirror, Kay gasped. She looked like a movie star! Versace dress. Tiffany glasses. It was something she could never have imagined. Well, she could have imagined it—after all, she had a fairly wild imagination, but it seemed crazy even by her own ambitious standards. One minute she'd been washing dishes and cleaning bathrooms, and the next she was dressed like a princess and being escorted to dinner by the most handsome man in the world.

She stole a quick glance at him as he opened the door for her.

'How many are there?' she asked.

'How many what?'

'Paparazzi.'

'Oh,' Oli said, 'I don't know. I think they're hiding.'

Kay followed him out and looked eagerly up and down Marine Parade. There were the usual tourists in search of sustenance, but she couldn't see any telephoto lenses. She pouted.

'Come on,' Oli said. 'Let's get to the car before anyone sees us.'

Oli donned a pair of glasses, turned up the collar of his jacket, and held his head down, but he was still unmistakably Oli Wade Owen. Kay rushed along in her strappy shoes, trying to keep up with him. The sky was looking ominously thundery. Some heavy clouds hung over the Cobb, and the sea looked as if it were holding a deep, dark secret.

'Here we are,' Oli said as they reached his car. It was an electric blue Lotus Elise, and Kay got excited at the thought of being a passenger in such a vehicle.

The unknown redhead was seen getting in Oli Wade Owen's infamous Lotus Elise, her shapely legs revealed by her Versace dress.

Kay could imagine the magazine reports as she settled into the smooth leather seat and checked out her reflection in the wing mirror. She was incognito!

'Okay?' he asked.

She nodded, and they both buckled up.

The car sped up Cobb Road and headed out of Lyme Regis and into the countryside. Kay tried to sit back and relax, but it was nigh on impossible. She still couldn't believe he asked her out.

'This is wonderful,' she said, giving him a smile.

Oli's gaze didn't shift from the road, which was comforting as a passenger but disconcerting as a woman.

'It's a real treat,' she said.

'Pardon?'

'I said this is a real treat—to be taken to lunch.'

'Oh,' he said. 'Right.'

He didn't sound too enthusiastic, but perhaps he was tired. He didn't get much free time, did he?

Kay settled back into her seat and adjusted the red hairpiece above her left temple. It felt like it was slipping. She looked in the wing mirror. She wasn't at all sure about herself as a redhead. She'd had visions of being transformed into a beautiful Pre-Raphaelite nymph, but she believed she looked more like a slightly baffled red Irish setter. The hat wasn't helping either, and the glasses—which she'd thought were beautiful at first—were far too big for her face.

'Can I take it all off now?' she asked.

'What?'

'The disguise?'

'No,' Oli said abruptly. 'We don't want anyone recognising you.'

'But I don't think anyone's followed us,' she said, looking behind them at the empty country lane.

'You can never be too sure.'

Kay pursed her lips. Wasn't he being a little bit paranoid? They hadn't seen another vehicle since that mucky tractor, and nobody could keep up with Oli anyway, not at the speed he was driving. In fact, Kay was starting to get a bit nervous. The lanes were narrowing, and the hedgerows were flashing by at an inhuman speed.

'Oli?'

'Yes?'

'Can we slow down?'

'You want to get there in time, don't you? I've got to be back by three, or Teresa will kill me.'

Of course she wanted to get there in time, but she also wanted to get there in one piece.

As they took a corner, Oli slammed on the brakes. The

torrential rain of the past few days had turned the little roads around the Marshwood Vale into rivers, and the way ahead of them was flooded.

'Will your car be all right?'

''Course it will,' Oli said. 'This baby can cope with anything.' He revved the engine, and Kay watched as he slowly built up a bit of speed before plunging the car through the water. A huge spray cascaded over the wheels, and Kay giggled.

'Told you!' he said. 'Wasn't that fun? Like one of those theme park rides, only faster.'

Kay nodded. She felt rather like a teenager on a first date.

She looked over her shoulder as the flooded lane vanished behind them, but it wasn't long before they reached the next. This time, the water stretched as far as they could see, and there was no telling how deep it was.

'Perhaps we should go back,' Kay said.

'You're joking!' Oli said. 'We can't go back now. We're nearly there.'

'Yes, but this looks deep to me.'

'Nonsense,' Oli said. It's just a big puddle.'

Once again, he revved the engine.

'Oli, I really think we should go back.'

He took his sunglasses off and smiled at her, and she could see that there was absolutely no way he was going to do anything other than drive full speed ahead through the flood.

'Hold on to your hat!' he said, but Kay's hands were firmly gripping the edge of her seat as the Lotus gained speed.

This isn't a good idea. This isn't a good idea, she chanted as the water approached.

'Slow down!' she shouted, but Oli didn't seem to be listening. He was locked in complete concentration, as if he were playing some addictive computer game and the rest of the world didn't exist. He and the flood was all there was.

The Lotus hit the water, and Kay closed her eyes as the windows and bonnet were drenched.

'Wow!' Oli shouted. 'Did you see that?'

The sound of water filled Kay's ears, and she sat perfectly still for a moment before she dared to open her eyes.

'Is it over?' she asked. They were completely surrounded by water, but the car didn't seem to be moving. 'Oli? What's happened?'

'I don't know,' he said, frowning. 'I think I might have just wrecked the car.'

Chapter 24

MUCH TO GEMMA'S HORROR, KIM REILLY WAS STILL HANGING around Lyme Regis and insisted on accompanying everyone in the minibus to shoot that morning's Uppercross scenes.

'You won't even know I'm there,' she'd told Gemma, clutching her arm and laughing, but of course it was an empty promise. Kim Reilly could go nowhere without making her presence felt. Even a simple trip to the local newsagent's to get the morning paper was a scene of great theatricality, with makeup and hair in place and a thousand anecdotes to tell any passerby who might be interested. It couldn't be helped—it was just the sort of person she was. Gemma remembered once looking through an old photo album at her grandmother's. Virtually all the photos had been of her mother—not because they'd been taken of her, but because she'd run into them when they were being taken. Every photo of her Aunt Christie's tenth birthday party had Kim in the foreground. Even the blowing out of the candles had Kim leaning into the frame to get in on the action. At Great Uncle Henry's wedding, Kim had cartwheeled down the aisle, showing off her pink knickers to the entire congregation. Gemma was therefore understandably nervous about the chaos her mother might cause on set.

Sitting in makeup, Gemma wondered how long it would be before her mother became bored.

'Oh, my God!' her mother said, popping her head around the door. 'Teresa just asked me if I'd like to have a walk-on role. Isn't that marvellous?'

The colour drained from Gemma's face. 'What walk-on role?'

'That card-playing scene when Captain Wentworth walks in. You know the one.'

Gemma did. It was a scene of great subtlety, and if there was one thing Kim Reilly wasn't good at, it was subtlety.

'I'll be walking into the room before Captain Wentworth arrives and flirting with a gentleman over a game of cards. Isn't it exciting? I've never done a period piece before. It could be a whole new direction for me.'

Gemma didn't know what to say. The thought of her mother in a Jane Austen adaptation was just too much. What was Teresa thinking? But perhaps it was her way of appeasing Kim. She knew what her mother could be like when she got an idea into her head, and Gemma was quite sure it hadn't been Teresa's doing at all. Kim would have chipped away at her until she gave in.

'I thought I might stay on here for a bit. There's nothing for me to rush home for.'

'Oh,' Gemma said.

'Well, you might sound a bit more enthusiastic,' her mother said. 'This could be my big relaunch. I haven't had a decent part in years.'

'But you played Queen Elizabeth for the BBC last year.'

'Oh, tosh! That was a mere walk-on role. I had less screen time than the wolfhound. It was ridiculous,' she said. 'No, you mark my words, this could be the beginning of great things for me.'

'But I thought you were going to concentrate on your charity work now,' Gemma said, hopelessly grabbing onto anything she could think of.

Kim Reilly sighed. 'Charity work's all very well, but it's so *boring*! Honestly, the speeches one has to sit through. And the publicity is appalling. Nobody's interested, because everybody's doing it.'

Gemma grimaced. That wasn't what charity work was about, she thought, but she didn't dare say anything. 'And you're meant to be taking it easy—after that breakdown last year, remember?'

'That wasn't a breakdown,' her mother told her. 'I was just a bit tired, and who can blame me, after that dreadful man?'

Gemma sighed as she remembered Lance Carlson, the Texan with the twinkle who had swept her mother off her feet in Paris, married her in Vegas, and robbed her in New York. The marriage had been swiftly annulled, and Carlson had been arrested a week later at The Chapel of Undying Love in Vegas on the verge of committing bigamy.

'At least it got me some column inches,' Kim said. 'Anyway, one just can't retire from acting. It's not like other professions— it's a part of who you are,' she said, squinting at her reflection in the mirror from behind Gemma's shoulder. Gemma gazed at her own reflection, wishing she had the courage to retire. With immediate effect.

☙

Kay took the Tiffany sunglasses off and put them carefully away in their case before looking out the window. It was obvious that the Lotus was not going anywhere.

'The engine's stopped,' she said.

'I know,' Oli said, turning the key in the ignition. Nothing happened.

'I think you've flooded her,' Kay said.

'I think you're right,' he said. '*Shit!*' He hit his hand against the steering wheel.

Kay bit her lip. This wasn't what she had in mind for her date with a movie star.

'What are we going to do?' she asked.

'We'll have to ring a garage.' Oli patted his jacket and pulled out his mobile, but his face soon fell. 'There's no bloody service. Can you believe it?'

'Yes,' Kay said. 'We're at the bottom of a valley here.'

'We're at the bottom of the sea!' Oli said.

Kay wasn't the sort of person to say, 'I told you so,' especially not to a handsome movie star, but she did wish he had listened to her. Instead, she looked out the windows at the deep water surrounding them and the high hedges and trees. There were sheep in a field, and she could barely make out their bleats as the young lambs raced each other under the shelter of an enormous oak tree.

'Oli?'

'What?'

'I've been here before.'

'What, stuck in the middle of a lake in the middle of nowhere?'

'No, here. I know where we are. There's a village just around the corner. I know someone who lives there. We can use her phone.'

His eyebrows rose. 'Really?'

'Yes, but we'll have to wade through this first.'

'You're not wading anywhere,' Oli said. She watched as he opened his car door, a wave of freezing water sloshing inside.

'Shit!' Oli exclaimed. 'I guess it's good-bye to these shoes,' he said, and his feet disappeared into the cold depths. He waded around the back of the car and finally reached Kay's door, opening it slowly before bending double and scooping Kay from the passenger seat. She just had time to grab her handbag before it washed away, and she quickly secured her arms around Oli's neck. It was her moment as a heroine, she thought. She was Tess being carried along the flooded lane by Angel Clare. She was Marianne Dashwood in the arms of Willoughby. No, she thought. For once, her life was better than fiction. She was Kay gazing up into the blue eyes of Oli Wade Owen. It was like a scene from one of her wild imaginings, and she was enjoying every single second of it.

'Comfy?' he asked with a smile.

She nodded up at him as he sploshed through the water, his strong legs seeming to part it with ease. Kay's own legs felt cold and vulnerable and very on display, the slinky blue dress having ridden halfway up them when Oli picked her up. Her hat was still in place, though, which she was glad of, when it began to rain.

The drops were light at first, and the view of the lane ahead looked half hidden in a romantic pearl curtain, but then it began to pour in earnest, and they were both soon soaked through.

Finally making it to the other side of the flood, Oli placed Kay on the ground, and there was no avoiding the rest of the puddles in the lane. Kay's strappy sandals and pale stockings were soon soaked through, along with everything else.

'Where's this house?' Oli said, his hair plastered to his face and his blue shirt three shades darker than it had been when they left Lyme Regis.

'Just around the corner,' Kay said, leading the way. Unfortunately, it wasn't just around the corner. Nor the next. Or the next. That was the trouble with the country lanes. Each bend looked similar to a dozen others, and Kay was beginning to panic in fear that they would never reach Nana Craig's at all but be walking the wet lanes forever more.

At last they turned a corner and the cottage came into view, its chocolate-coloured thatched roof a most welcome sight, especially when Kay spied a thin trickle of wood smoke coming from its chimney.

'There!' she declared, pointing at the pretty house.

Oli laughed as they approached and he opened the gate. 'Who lives here, Hansel and Gretel?'

They ran up the brick path and sheltered under the porch, knocking on the door and hoping that somebody would be inside to welcome them in.

'Who is it?' a voice came from behind the yellow wooden door.

'Nana Craig? It's Kay—Adam's friend.'

'Kay?'

'Yes! Our car's broken down in the lane, and we need to make a call.'

The door opened, and the sweet face of Nana Craig appeared. 'Kay?' she said. 'Is that really you?'

Kay suddenly remembered she was still wearing the hairpiece and hat and quickly took them off, hoping her own hair wasn't too much of a fright.

'Oh! Your hair's fallen out!' Nana Craig said in horror.

'It's a hairpiece. I'm incognito,' Kay explained.

'And you're soaked through. Get inside before you catch your death.'

Kay walked into the hallway. 'Nana Craig, this is Oli.'

'Hello,' Oli said, ducking his head so as not to hit it on the low door frame.

Nana Craig narrowed her eyes at him. 'I've seen you,' she said in an accusatory sort of tone.

'You might well have done,' Oli said, nodding and sending a shower of water over Nana Craig. 'God, I'm sorry!'

'Don't blaspheme!' Nana Craig said. 'I won't have blasphemers in my house.'

'Oli's an actor,' Kay explained.

'Is he?' Nana Craig didn't sound impressed. 'Well, that doesn't excuse blaspheming. And shouldn't he be acting somewhere now instead of—instead of being with you?'

'I've got some time off,' Oli said. 'Thought I'd take Kay out for lunch, but we kind of got stuck in the flood.'

'Oli's got an amazing car,' Kay said. 'But we've got to ring for a garage.'

'Yes,' Oli said. 'We were wondering if we could use your phone. There's no mobile service out here.'

Nana Craig nodded towards the telephone.

'And a cup of tea would be great,' Oli said. 'And maybe a towel?'

Nana Craig gasped. 'Of course. You're both soaked.' She bustled off in search of towels, leaving Kay and Oli dripping in the hallway.

'I don't think she likes me,' Oli said. 'Why doesn't she like me?' He sounded genuinely perplexed. He'd obviously never met a woman yet who hadn't swooned at the mere sight of him.

'Don't take it personally,' Kay said. 'She just doesn't like actors.'

'Why not?'

'She was once married to an actor who ran off with a girl who promised to get him a part in a movie.'

'My God!'

'Yes. Isn't that dreadful?'

'And did he?' Oli asked.

'What?'

'Get the part in the movie?'

'I don't think so.'

'I hope he got the girl at least,' Oli whispered.

Nana Craig appeared before anything else could be discussed, carrying one primrose towel and one candyfloss pink one. 'I'll leave you two to dry off,' she said. 'Kay, there's a cloakroom down there on the right. I'll lend you a dress and cardigan.'

Kay thanked her and headed for the cloakroom, peeling off the sodden dress and hoping it wasn't ruined. She'd have to face the wrath of Beth if it was.

She towel dried her body and hair, doing her best to restore some order and smiling as she looked around the bathroom. The toilet and sink were dark pink and the walls were covered in a peony-festooned paper.

There was a polite knock on the door. 'Kay?'

Kay opened it, the pink towel covering her body.

'I brought you these. Your figure's a little more slight than mine, but at least these are dry and warm.'

'Thanks so much,' Kay said. 'And I'm so sorry to just turn up like this.'

'What else could you do?' Nana Craig said. 'I'll go and make the tea.'

Kay looked at the dress Nana Craig had given her. She liked blue and pink and yellow and purple, but usually not all together at once. Still, as Nana Craig said, it was dry. There was also a voluminous cardigan in acid green. Kay didn't dare look at her reflection in the gilded cloakroom mirror, for it was probably not the look she was after for a first date with Oli Wade Owen.

Daring to leave the cloakroom, she heard Nana Craig in the kitchen.

'May I give you a hand?' Kay asked, entering the tiny room at the back of the cottage and spying the candy-striped mugs and polka-dotted teapot.

'I can manage,' the woman said, and Kay thought Nana Craig sounded a little bit put out. 'You seen Adam?'

'No,' Kay said. 'Not today. I expect he's working.'

Nana Craig nodded. 'He works hard, you know. Not like these actor types. He doesn't have time to go swanning off at a moment's notice. But I expect you'll see him later,' Nana Craig continued, placing a scarlet sugar bowl on an orange tea tray.

'He might be coming over,' Kay said. 'He's seeing Gemma.'

'Gemma?' Nana Craig looked startled. 'Who's Gemma?'

'She's playing Anne Elliot—the heroine in *Persuasion*.'

'She's an actress?'

Kay nodded.

'I see,' Nana Craig said, pouring hot water from the kettle into the polka-dotted teapot.

'She's lovely—*really* lovely,' Kay said, pulling the acid green cardigan around herself nervously.

'Actors and actresses are not to be trusted,' Nana Craig said, her lips a thin line across her face. 'They're only ever out for themselves.' Nana Craig's hands clutched the edges of the orange tea tray. 'I expect Adam's told you my story,' she said.

'Yes,' Kay said. 'And I was so sorry to hear about your husband. How he treated you was unforgivable, but Gemma's not like that. And Oli isn't either. They're different people.'

Nana Craig shook her head. 'I think you'll find they're all the same.'

Kay watched as she moved through to the living room with the tray of tea things, bringing the conversation to a halt. Kay followed the woman through. Oli was standing by the window and had taken his shirt and trousers off and was wearing the primrose towel around his waist like a funny kind of kilt. Nana Craig almost dropped the tray when she saw him, and Kay came rushing forward to relieve her of it.

'Just trying to dry off,' he said, his wet clothes in a pile on the colourful carpet.

'I'll hang them up in the kitchen,' Nana Craig said, a blush creeping over her face as she hurried out of the room with the wet clothes.

'Oli!' Kay said.

'Sorry,' he said, 'but what was I meant to do?'

'She probably hasn't seen a naked man for over fifty years!'

'I had to get dry,' Oli said.

'I know, but couldn't you—'

'What?'

'I don't know—not be so naked?'

'This isn't how I imagined today would pan out,' Oli said, shaking his head.

'No,' Kay said, 'me either.' Their eyes met.

'How did you think it would pan out?' he asked.

Kay didn't know what to say, but he held her gaze, and something seemed to soften in his eyes, as if he wanted to say something to her.

Kay didn't get a chance to find out what it might be, though, because Nana Craig came bustling into the room with a T-shirt and a raincoat. 'I found these,' she said, breaking the spell between them. 'They're Adam's, so he'll want them returned.'

'Thank you,' Oli said taking them from her. 'No trousers?'

Nana Craig shook her head. 'We weren't expecting a naked man to call by, or we might have had a pair for you.'

Nana Craig and Kay turned their backs to allow Oli to get changed.

'I hope nobody sees me like this,' he said a moment later.

The women turned around and stared at the vision before them, and Kay burst into laughter. 'Oh, Oli, if the tabloids could see you now!'

'I hope they don't,' he said. 'And you'd better get that hairpiece back on.'

'I can't—it's soaked,' she said. 'You don't have a hat I could borrow, do you, Nana Craig?'

'I'll see what I've got,' she said and left the room.

'I rather like this cardigan of yours,' Oli said, taking a step towards her and placing his hand on the bobbly green sleeve.

'Oh, don't tease!'

Oli grinned, and his hand travelled down the length of the sleeve until his fingers caressed hers.

'I've only got this,' Nana Craig said, entering the room and causing Kay to spring apart from Oli.

Kay's eyes widened as she saw the canary yellow rain hat, and she silently prayed that Oli wasn't going to make her wear it.

'Perfect,' Oli said, taking it from Nana Craig and squashing it onto her head. 'Glasses,' he said.

Kay retrieved the glasses from her handbag. 'I'm going to look hideous,' she said.

'You look fine,' Oli said. 'Nobody will guess who you are under all this.'

Kay sighed. This wasn't the date she'd imagined at all.

'Shit! I've got to get back,' Oli said as he saw the clock on the mantelpiece. 'I'd better ring for a taxi.'

Nana Craig's mouth dropped open. 'Your language is diabolical, young man!'

Oli smiled, and his blue eyes crinkled at the edges. 'I know,' he said. 'I'm so sorry.' His adorable expression was enough to win over ninety-nine percent of the women in the UK but it didn't seem to be working with Nana Craig.

'The phone's through there,' she said. 'You'd better be on your way.'

He nodded and left the room, and a frosty silence descended. Kay bit her lip and tried to think of something to say, but her mind went blank.

Oli returned a moment later. 'I've rung for a taxi. It'll be here in twenty minutes. They have to come the long way round, to avoid the flooding.'

'As any sensible driver would,' Nana Craig said, picking up the tea tray and taking it back through to the kitchen.

'Oh, dear,' Kay said. 'I don't think it was such a good idea coming here after all. Poor Nana Craig! I think we've really upset her.'

Oli grinned. 'She loves me, really.'

'Yes, you've really managed to work your charm on her, haven't you?'

'Oh, I could if I wanted to,' he said, the light gleaming in his eyes. 'Except I don't want to. At least not with her.' He held her gaze again, and Kay felt something alarming in the pit of her stomach that had nothing to do with the length of time since breakfast. 'Kay, there's something I've been wanting to ask you.' He took a step closer to her. 'You're so lovely,' he said, and she felt his hand caress her cheek. 'And I really like you, Kay.'

'I like you too, Oli.'

'I know you do,' he said. 'But we shouldn't really be doing this.'

Kay's eyes widened a fraction. 'Doing what? Not having lunch?'

He smiled. 'It's—I don't want to use this word, because it's become such a cliché but it's *complicated*.'

'What is?'

'Me.'

Kay nodded. 'I know.'

'You do?' he asked, looking surprised. 'What do you know?'

'I know that actors can't tie themselves to the people they meet when they're filming.'

Oli nodded, looking relieved. 'We live strange lives,' he said. 'Never in one place for long.'

Kay bit her lip, wondering if she dare say what she wanted to say. 'But,' she began, 'that doesn't mean you can't have fun whilst you're around, does it?'

Oli stared at her for a moment. 'No, it doesn't mean that.'

Kay smiled at him, her heart thumping wildly. 'Good,' she said.

Nana Craig came into the room. 'Your taxi's here,' she said, frowning at the pair of them.

'Right,' Kay said, turning around and doing her best to hide her blushing face under the enormous yellow hat. 'Thanks so much for taking care of us.'

Nana Craig nodded. 'I'll be wanting those clothes back,' she said.

'Of course,' Kay said.

'I was talking to him,' the older woman said, nodding to Oli.

'I'll get them back to you as soon as possible,' Oli said, walking towards Nana Craig and bending to kiss her cheek. She batted him away.

Kay grinned. He hadn't won Nana Craig over at all, had he? But he'd certainly won Kay.

Chapter 25

GEMMA'S SCENE WITH THE ACTRESS PLAYING LADY RUSSELL was cut short several times by the heavy showers. They'd been shooting in the beautiful knot garden behind Marlcombe Manor, and Teresa—for once—had been pleased with how the scene was progressing. Gemma, too, had thought it was going well. She got on well with the older actress, and they found that they could portray Anne Elliot's and Lady Russell's intimacy easily.

But not everybody was as pleased with their performances. Sheltering in the orangery, which was stuffed with extraordinary palms, Kim Reilly sidled up to her daughter.

'She's not very good, is she?' Kim said in a sort of stage whisper.

'Shush!' Gemma hushed. 'She'll hear you.'

'I don't care if she does,' Kim said, sniffing unrepentantly. 'That sort of acting shouldn't be tolerated.'

'She used to act with the Royal Shakespeare Company,' Gemma pointed out. 'And they think very highly of her.'

'The Royal Shakespeare Company!' Kim made a tutting sound. 'Call that acting? That's just standing on stage spouting poetry.'

Gemma rolled her eyes. 'And she's very well respected as a television actress. You should see her CV.'

'I don't need to,' Kim said. 'I bet she's ruined every role she ever touched. I don't know what Teresa's thinking. I would have done a much better job, and I'm your mother, too.'

'What's that got to do with anything?'

'That scene you were shooting—it's between mother and daughter.'

'Lady Russell isn't Anne's mother.'

'Isn't she?'

'No,' Gemma said. 'You really should read the book, Mum.'

'The only things I read these days are the glossies and *Vive!* I can't be doing with any Austen or Shakespeare.'

Gemma knew she wasn't joking. Even when she was growing up, there had been a shocking dearth of books in their house.

'I'll wait for the script, my dear,' she'd told her agent.

Gemma wished she could operate like her mother, but she always had to read the source material and anything else she could get her hands on, anything to help. It was exhausting, but worth it, she hoped.

'So many interruptions,' Kim said, looking out of the orangery as the rain slowly waned. It had been drumming on the glass roof like a thousand tiny tap dancers when the actors rushed inside, but now it was a gentle patter.

'I expect we'll be back to it soon,' Gemma said, tidying a stray strand of hair.

Kim nodded. 'Yes,' she said thoughtfully, dragging the single syllable out.

Gemma was on immediate alert. 'What?' she said.

Kim's mouth narrowed into a nasty little line, and Gemma knew what was coming: criticism.

'No,' Kim said, shaking her head. 'You won't want to hear. You never do. You know what you're like when I have some advice to give you—you get all upset and uptight.'

'No, I don't,' Gemma said.

'Yes, you do. You know you do.'

'Just tell me, Mum!' she said, knowing she wouldn't get any peace until she had her say.

'You want my advice?'

'Yes.'

'You're sure?'

'Mum! Just tell me.'

'Okay,' Kim said, taking in a deep breath before sighing out slowly and dramatically, as if she were about to give a long-awaited speech on the world's stage. 'That scene you were doing with that woman who wasn't your mother.'

'What about it?'

'There are just a couple of things I would've done differently.'

'Like what?'

'Like the dialogue and the actions.'

Gemma closed her eyes for a moment, refusing to respond. Instead, she walked towards the door at the end of the orangery and headed back outside, not caring if it was still raining. Anywhere—even the middle of a storm—was preferable to being in her mother's company.

Rain didn't affect you much when you were a screenwriter, and Adam was in screenwriting mode that afternoon, his laptop open on his knee in his study up in the eaves of his nineteenth-century cottage. He was going to join the film crew later that day, but there was no point heading out to Marlcombe Manor now. He stopped writing for a moment and stood up, stretching his arms above his head and cricking his neck. He wished it would stop raining. The garden was glad of it, but any more and he would be worried the whole plot would be washed away.

The garden was the main reason that Adam had bought Willow Cottage. It had come up for sale three years ago, and he'd driven by it on a balmy autumn day when everything was golden and glowing. He had been renting a small flat above a shop in Lyme Regis before that, splitting his time between there and a nasty little flat in Shepherd's Bush whilst he decided where he wanted to base himself permanently.

Nana Craig had then taken a nasty fall and had been laid up for weeks, and Adam knew he had to spend more time in Dorset. Besides, that's where he was happiest, and the train service to London wasn't bad. There was nothing really stopping him from putting down some roots.

The evening he saw Willow Cottage, he pulled over at the side of the road and opened the little gate into an overgrown front garden. It looked as if the place was empty, and looking across at one of the downstairs windows, he noticed there was more cobweb than curtain.

A side gate led around the old house to a back garden, and it was that which sold the place to him, although it had really been more of a plot of land when he first saw it and had been in no state to be called a garden for some time. It was just a very long stretch of overgrown grass interspersed with nettles, brambles, and thistles, but it was surrounded by peaceful fields and backed onto a tiny stream flanked by willows, and Adam could see its potential immediately, planning out the borders and vegetable patches in his mind's eye.

He made an offer the very next day, not batting an eyelid at the state of the old place. He would get around to sorting it all out.

The rotting kitchen cupboards could be ripped out and replaced, as could the carpets. Wallpaper could be stripped, and the damp problem wasn't insurmountable.

For the first few months, he concentrated on the garden, cutting, clearing, and digging until his limbs were tanned, toned, and exhausted. Growing up with Nana Craig, he had always been encouraged to garden, but with flats in Lyme Regis and London, he hadn't had much of a chance over the years. Willow Cottage was his very first garden.

Nana Craig had been very impressed when she visited him. 'What are you going to grow?' she asked.

'Happy,' he said. 'I'm going to grow happy.'

She chuckled at that. 'As long as there are a few tomatoes and courgettes too.'

Looking out of the upstairs window now, he surveyed his little kingdom with pride. There was still a lot to do. He wanted to create some new borders and plant an orchard too. A garden was never static, but he liked it that way. He had grown lazy living in town, but the garden got him away from his desk and kept him fit.

A sudden flash of ginger caught his eye, and a very hairy cat leapt up onto the windowsill, purring noisily.

'Hello, Sir Walter,' Adam said, his hand stroking the downy fur, sending a little ginger cloud into the air. 'Don't fancy the garden today, then?'

Sir Walter stuck his little pink nose up in the air as if such things as wet gardens shouldn't even be discussed. Adam grinned.

He met Sir Walter the first week he moved into Willow Cottage. The back door had been open, and the scrawny ginger tom stalked into the place as if he owned it, meowing loudly. Adam gave him a saucer of milk and a share of his fish and chip supper, which seemed to go down well. The poor thing was all skin and bone and seemed happy to bed down on an old cushion in the front room. They had been housemates ever since.

None of the residents in the tiny village seemed to know anything about the cat, and the notice Adam put up in the local shop went unanswered. They were stuck with each other. Adam had never owned a pet before. His lifestyle hadn't permitted it, but if he really was putting down roots, a pet seemed as good an idea as any. And Nana Craig loved taking care of Sir Walter whenever Adam had to be away from home, although his habit of sleeping on her favourite candy-striped cardigan and adding a thick layer of ginger to it didn't go down too well.

He had been writing the first draft of his screenplay for *Persuasion* when he moved into Willow Cottage and met the cat, and the name Sir Walter seemed to fit perfectly. He had such an air about him, as if the whole world was quite beneath him, but Adam loved him to bits.

Perhaps one of his favourite things about Sir Walter was the way he followed Adam whenever he set out to walk to Nana Craig's. That had been another deal clincher for Adam—Willow Cottage was just two miles from his nana's cottage, and he could get to it by way of a lacework of footpaths that crisscrossed the Marshwood Vale.

'Maybe I'll saunter over there as soon as this rain stops,' he said to Sir Walter. 'What do you think?'

Sir Walter didn't think much of the suggestion, choosing to lick a front paw instead.

Adam was about to return to his laptop when the phone rang.

'Hello?'

'Adam!'

'Nana! Are you okay?' She sounded breathless.

'I've just seen Kay.'

'Where?'

'She was round here,' Nana Craig said, 'with that actor bloke.'

'What actor bloke?'

'That tall one. Great strapping fellow with too much blond hair.'

'Oli? Oli Wade Owen?'

'That's the one.'

'What were they doing at yours?'

'He was taking her to lunch. That was his story, anyway.'

'Lunch at yours?'

'No!' Nana Craig said. 'He'd driven his flash car through some flooded lane. Probably racing it around like an idiot. Anyway, it's stuck there, and he and Kay walked to mine to dry off. He's got your T-shirt and raincoat, by the way. I told him you'd be wanting them back.'

Adam shook his head in confusion. 'Where are they now?'

'Oh, they've gone. Got a taxi back to Lyme Regis. And what's all this about some Gemma woman?' Nana Craig asked. 'Kay seemed to think you're going out with her.'

Adam sighed. 'That's just some misunderstanding.'

'Are you sure? She seemed quite convinced.'

'Nana, believe me, nothing is going on with Gemma and me.'

'Because you know what these actor types are like, don't you? I don't need to tell you again.'

'No, you don't need to tell me again,' Adam said, rolling his eyes at Sir Walter, who had left the windowsill for the comfort of Adam's armchair.

'So you've not made a move on Kay, I take it?'

'Nana!'

'Don't *Nana* me! If you like this girl, you should tell her. I don't know why you haven't yet.'

'I've only just met her.'

'Yes, and she's only just met this actor too, but she's having lunch and flirting with him all over Dorset already.'

'She was flirting with him?' Adam said.

'In my front room. Disgusting! And he didn't even have his trousers on.'

'What?'

'That actor bloke —his trousers were soaked. He had to take them off, and I didn't have any spare to lend him.'

'Right,' Adam said, thankful, at least, that Oli hadn't been making a move on Kay in his nana's front room.

'You've got to tell her, Adam,' Nana Craig said. 'You do like her, don't you?'

Adam raked a hand through his hair. 'Yes, I do like her.'

'Well, then?'

Adam groaned. He knew his nana meant well, but he did often wish she would let him do things in his own time.

'You're not still put off by what happened with Heidi, are you?'

There was a moment's silence.

'Adam? That was just one unlucky—'

'I know,' he interrupted.

'And you can't let it stop you from meeting other women.'

'Nana, I've got to get back to my work,' he said, hoping she'd take the hint.

'All I'm saying is that you'd better make your move if you want to stand a chance with that girl. I saw the way she was looking at that Oli, and believe me, I know that look.'

'All right!' Adam said. 'I'll tell her.'

'You will?'

'I will,' he said, knowing it was the only way he was going to get any peace.

'When?'

'What do you mean, *when*? You want written notification?'

'I know you, Adam Craig. You're a procrastinator.'

'No I'm not.'

'You jolly well are, but let me tell you, this one isn't going to hang around and wait. You've got to make your move.'

'I've said I will.'

There was a pause. 'Adam?'

'Yes?'

'Give me a call as soon as you tell her.'   .

'Good-bye, Nana.'

Chapter 26

THE TAXI RIDE BACK TO LYME REGIS WAS ONE OF THE STRANGEST journeys of Kay's life. Oli was silent at first, his head bent down and his blue eyes hidden behind his dark glasses. Kay felt horribly conspicuous in her bright green cardigan and yellow hat and had seen the double take the taxi driver had given as they got into the car.

'Where's the fancy dress party, then?' he quipped. 'Dreadful floods at the moment,' he said, peering at them through the rear-view mirror. 'Would avoid driving round here if I were you.'

'It's a bit late for that, I'm afraid,' Kay said and then received a nudge in the ribs from Oli.

'Shush,' he said.

So this was the life of a movie star's girlfriend, was it? Being made to dress incognito and being told to shush all the time? Kay wasn't impressed. In fact, she was just about to tell Oli, when he did something quite unexpected.

He picked up her hand and gave it a squeeze. 'I'm sorry today turned out like this,' he said, leaning in towards her and whispering in her ear.

'It's okay,' Kay found herself saying.

'No, it's not,' Oli whispered. 'I wanted it to be—you know—special.'

'Did you?'

He nodded, and his fingers traced a tiny circle in the palm of her hand, which gave her the most delicious goose bumps. 'Of course I did.'

Kay felt her body heat up and was quite sure her face was too, as she looked into his eyes.

'We were sitting in the back of a taxi when he proposed to me,' she would tell journalists in the years to come. 'He was wearing only a T-shirt and an old raincoat,' she would say with a giggle. 'It's a long story.'

'Oh, tell us, Kay!' they'd beg.

'All I'm going to tell you is that I said yes.'

Gazing into his eyes now, she wondered what he had planned for their lunch together. 'Oli?' she said, but she didn't get a chance to ask him anything, because a phone rang with a blast of Wagner. Kay recognised 'The Ride of the Valkyries' and grinned.

'Ah! We're back in civilisation,' Oli said, finding his phone. 'Hello? Yes. I'm heading back to Lyme.' There was a pause. 'Nowhere. Just out to lunch. I don't know where—we didn't get that far. What?' he said. 'Kay. I was with Kay. In the car. No, I'm in a taxi now. The car flooded.' There was another pause, and Kay could see a frown on Oli's face. 'I don't know. About an hour? I've got to get back to Lyme and get changed. Okay. Yes. I said I will. All right, then.'

'Everything okay?' Kay asked after he put his phone away.

'That was Teresa,' he said.

'She didn't sound happy,' Kay said.

'You heard her?' Oli looked anxious.

'Only her tone of voice,' Kay said.

Oli looked relieved. 'It's a good job I didn't tell her I didn't have any trousers on.'

'Have you got to get to the set?'

'I'm afraid so. Teresa's panicking. They've moved a lot faster than she thought, and she needs me to get out there as soon as I can.'

'But you've not had any lunch.'

'Neither have you.'

'But I can get some at home.'

'I'll grab something somewhere,' he said. 'Don't worry about me. Hey, mate,' Oli said, leaning forward in the taxi as they took the road into Lyme Regis. 'Can you hang around for me? I have to get to Marlcombe Manor.'

'No problem,' the taxi driver said, looking at him through the rear-view mirror. 'You're that actor, aren't you? I've seen you on the TV.'

Oli gave a little nod.

'I thought it was you. You can't fool these old eyes. You were in that—what was it called?' He took a hand off the wheel and clicked his fingers as if he might summon the title. '*Parisian Nights*. Am I right?'

Again Oli nodded.

'Bit saucy, that, wasn't it? I was watching it with my wife and mother-in-law. Now *that* was embarrassing!'

Kay grinned as she remembered the scene the taxi driver was referring to.

'Still, must all be in a day's work for you, eh? All that rumpy pumpy! Now ain't that something—getting paid for that. I tell you, I'm in the wrong job!'

The taxi dropped them off and the driver promised to wait for Oli.

The two wet travelers walked along Marine Parade towards the bed and breakfast.

'I guess that happens to you a lot,' Kay said.

'Now and again,' he said.

'So the disguise didn't work.'

'I'm afraid not,' he said. 'But at least he'll never recognise you.'

'Oh, nobody would ever recognise me,' Kay said.

Oli stopped. 'Well, they should.'

Kay turned around to face him, and he took off his sunglasses.

'The whole world should recognise you,' he said.

Kay wasn't sure what to say, and so she said nothing at all. She was so glad that she didn't when he moved towards her, closing the brief space between them and leaning down to kiss her. It was what she'd dreamed of, but she never expected it to really happen. Now it was. She felt suspended, as if she were dreaming, and if she opened her eyes, Oli would evaporate and she'd be staring into space like a fool. When he took a step back and she opened her eyes, though, he was really there, all six foot four of him, and he was looking at her with such intensity that she couldn't speak.

'You okay?' he asked.

She nodded, and he laughed.

'What?' she asked.

'You! You're so funny!'

'Why am I funny?' she asked, not at all sure he was paying her a compliment.

'Because your head is full of fluffy clouds.'

'What do you mean?'

'You're a romantic, aren't you? You believe in princes on white horses and happy-ever-afters.'

'How do you know that?'

'It's written all over that face of yours,' he said. 'That gorgeous, dreamy face.' He grinned and reached out to stroke her cheek. 'I've never met anyone like you,' he said. 'I'm afraid the acting business usually knocks out any romantic notions I may have about the world.'

'That's awful!' Kay said. 'Especially when you're playing some of the great heroes.'

Oli shrugged. 'You mustn't think we're all like the heroes we portray. I'm not Captain Wentworth, you know.'

'I know that,' Kay said, secretly dismissing his protestation, because she knew that the man standing before her was the perfect hero.

'It's just a job like any other.'

Kay shook her head. 'But you need sensitivity and passion to play a part, don't you?'

'I guess,' Oli said.

'When you played Sydney Carton in *A Tale of Two Cities*, I cried myself to sleep that night.'

Oli laughed. 'But I'm not Sydney. I wouldn't have given up my life like him. I'd have left Paris at the first opportunity and put that silly woman, Lucy, out of my mind.'

'No!' Kay said. 'I don't believe that.'

They walked towards the bed and breakfast, the sound of the sea in their ears.

'I'm a no-good, selfish actor,' he said. 'I'd be wary of getting involved with me if I were you.'

Kay's heart skipped a beat. So he wanted to get involved with her? Was that what he was saying? 'Are you challenging me?' she dared to ask.

He smiled and held her gaze. 'Perhaps I am.'

Kay was about to reply when she looked ahead to Wentworth House and saw two figures sheltering in the doorway of the bed and breakfast. 'Who are they?' she asked. One was a young woman with short-cropped hair. She was wearing a white cap and skinny jeans and looked as if she'd be more at home in Kensington High Street than Lyme Regis. Standing next to her, holding her hand, was a girl no more than five years old. She had bright rosy cheeks and the longest, blondest ponytail Kay had ever seen.

'Annabel?' Oli shouted.

'Oli!' The little girl dropped the woman's hand and came running towards Oli, and Kay watched as he caught her up in his arms and spun her around. Who on earth was she? Kay wondered.

Oh my goodness! She suddenly thought. *It's his daughter.* She had the same butter-coloured hair; that much was evident. *He has a secret love child! If I marry him, I'll be a stepmother!*

'Come on, Bel, I want to introduce you to a very good friend of mine,' Oli said, bringing the girl safely back down to earth.

A very good friend. Kay didn't like the sound of that, but what else could he say in the circumstances? *This is your new mother, and you are going to love her as much as I do?*

'Kay, this is Annabel,' Oli said. 'Annabel, this is Kay.'

The little girl's face flushed the colour of pink roses, and she gave a hesitant smile. 'Hello,' she said.

'Hello,' Kay said, thinking that she was the prettiest little girl she'd ever seen. But why hadn't she heard of her existence before? How had Oli kept her hidden for so long?

'Annabel's Teresa's daughter,' Oli said.

'What?' Kay said, looking startled.

'Teresa's daughter,' Oli repeated.

'But I thought…'

'What?'

'I thought she was yours,' Kay said in a whisper.

Oli grinned. 'She's an angel, isn't she?'

Kay nodded in relief, but she was surprised too, because the girl bore so little resemblance to the harsh mother Kay had got to know over the last few days.

'Where's Mummy?' Annabel asked.

'She's busy filming,' Oli said.

'She's always busy filming,' Annabel said.

'I'm sorry to turn up unannounced,' a voice said, and Kay suddenly became aware of the woman standing in the doorway.

'That's okay,' Oli said. 'Always good to see you both. Oh, let me introduce you both—Kay, this is Clare, Annabel's nanny. Kay runs the bed and breakfast.'

'I hope it's all right, me turning up like this,' Clare said. 'Teresa said it would be okay.'

'It's no problem,' Kay said, liking Clare immediately. She had a lovely round face and smiling eyes.

'Here, come on in, and let's get some lunch. I'm starving,' Kay said.

'Me too,' Annabel said with a giggle.

'You've just had lunch,' Clare said.

'But I want to have lunch with Oli,' the little girl said.

'I'm afraid I've got to get over to the film set.'

Annabel gasped. 'You've got no trousers on!'

Clare's eyes darted down to Oli's legs, and her mouth dropped open.

'You're right,' Oli said, 'and I really should do something about that.'

They all entered the hallway, and Oli disappeared up the stairs in a half-naked streak.

Kay stood looking a little awkward. 'I'm afraid we're all booked up here,' she said.

Clare nodded. 'That's okay,' she said. 'Teresa said she got us a room somewhere up Cobb Road.'

'Oh, good.'

'We've booked in, but I wanted to call here on the off chance of her being around.'

'I don't think she'll be back until the evening,' Kay said. 'Do you have a car? Maybe you could drive out to the set.'

'Can we, Clare?' Annabel asked excitedly.

'We'll have to see,' Clare said. 'Now, why don't you go and sit over there?'

Annabel did as she was told, entering the sitting room and walking straight over to the window. 'We can't see the sea from our flat, can we?'

'No,' Clare said. 'But we've got a very fine view of Primrose Hill.'

Kay went through to the kitchen and made two cups of tea. 'Are you sure I can't get you anything to eat? I'm going to make myself some pasta so it's no trouble.'

'No, really, we've just eaten.'

A sudden thudding was heard on the stairs, and Oli appeared in the kitchen doorway. 'All dressed,' he said.

'Are you sure you haven't got time for something to eat?' Kay asked, rather sorry to have lost the half-naked Oli from her life. Perhaps—once they were married—they'd walk half-naked all day around their plush London apartment together.

'I really haven't time,' Oli said. 'I'll see you later, all right? Maybe we'll have time for that meal together then.'

Kay smiled, hoping he was right and already planning the outfit she'd wear. She'd have to make time to go shopping and surprise him with something beautiful that actually belonged to her this time.

'Oh!' Kay said, suddenly realising she was still wearing the soggy hairpiece and had a bag of wet clothes to sort out before Beth saw them. 'I must get this dress dry.'

'Can I help with anything?' Clare asked. 'I could start lunch for you.'

'Oh, thank you!' Kay said. 'That's so kind. I'm absolutely starving.'

Kay left the kitchen and went up to her bedroom, placing the wet hairpiece and dress above her bath to drip dry. She felt terrible about the dress. It would be the first and last time a film star would lend her any clothes; that was for sure.

After hanging up the soggy items, Kay slipped out of Nana Craig's stripy dress and cardigan and placed them on a Lloyd Loom chair next to her bed. She would wash the dress and return it with a big bunch of flowers to thank her. When she slipped into a cotton shirt and a pair of jeans, Kay's tummy rumbled, reminding her that she left Clare downstairs in the kitchen.

As soon as she was on the landing, Kay heard Clare's voice. She was calling for Annabel—over and over again.

'Is everything okay?' Kay asked as she reached the hallway.

Clare didn't answer.

'Annabel!' she called, moving from room to room.

'What's the matter?' Kay asked as they almost crashed into each other outside the dining room.

'Annabel's missing! Is she upstairs?'

Kay shook her head.

'I don't understand. She was here a minute ago. Where could she have gone?'

'She wouldn't have gone up on the Cobb, would she?' Kay asked.

'What?'

'She wouldn't have gone up onto the Cobb?'

'She shouldn't have left the house,' Clare said, her pretty round face white with anxiety.

'But I think she must have,' Kay said.

They looked at each other, and a second later, they were both out of the door.

Chapter 27

'Tell her,' Adam said to himself as he took a bend in the road a little quicker than usual. 'I have to tell her.'

It was the only way. He knew it. His nana knew it. Soon everybody in Dorset would know it, except Kay. But *how* would he tell her? She was under some crazy illusion that he was in love with Gemma, and he was pretty sure that Kay had fallen under the spell of Oli Wade Owen. Where did that leave things? It was like some Shakespearean comedy where each member of the cast is in love with the wrong person.

Turning into a narrow lane, he startled a pheasant and splashed through a long puddle that hadn't drained away yet. Some of the roads in the valley were still impassable, but Adam had taken the long way around to avoid the worst of the flooding.

'Kay,' he said as the car reached dry land again, 'I know I'm not cut from the same cloth as Oli Wade Owen. I'll never be a leading man. I'll never play the great roles that you love. All I can do is write them.'

Adam shook his head. That was too negative. He was doing nothing but showing his own shortcomings, and that would never do.

'Kay!' he began again. 'I'm in love with you.'

That was certainly to the point, but would he be able to pull it off? For a moment, he thought of her sweet rosy face and her bright eyes that were always darting about and shining with curiosity. He had never met anyone like her. She was so fresh and funny and—

'What am I going to say to her?' he said, sighing as he reached Lyme Regis. More importantly, what would she say to him? He dreaded to think. But he had to say something, or he would burst.

～♡

Kay was running up and down Marine Parade and dodging the tourists in her panic. 'Annabel!' she called into the wind. '*Annabel!*' Her heart was racing in time with the pounding of her feet, but there was no sign of the little girl anywhere.

The arcades! Maybe she was in there. The bright lights and beeping machines might have lured her in. Kay ran towards them, hoping that she'd spot the girl with the long blond ponytail, but when she went in, there were only a couple of teenage boys at the slot machines.

Clare seemed to have had the same idea, because they met outside.

'She isn't anywhere,' Clare said, her eyes filled with tears. 'I've been all the way to the Cobb and asked everyone.'

'Let's get back to the B and B,' Kay said, trying to remain calm. 'Maybe she's waiting for us there.'

The walk back was a short one, but it seemed to take an age, and when they were in view of the front door, they could see that there was no little girl there waiting for them.

'Maybe we should call Teresa,' Kay said.

Clare's face crumpled. 'Oh, God. She'll kill me.'

'It's not your fault,' Kay said, placing a hand on her shoulder.

'But I should've been looking after her.'

'You were.'

Clare shook her head. 'I wasn't. I'm a terrible nanny.'

'No, you're not,' Kay said. 'Come on. Let's get inside and think this through.'

Clare had already thought it through and was on her phone. 'Teresa? Yes. We're here in Lyme. I don't know. About an hour ago. Yes, we've met Kay. Listen,' she said and then took a deep breath, 'I can't find Annabel.'

Gemma was sitting in a patch of sunlight on some steps leading down into the sunken garden at Marlcombe Manor.

A voice greeted her. 'Hello.'

She looked up, shielding her eyes from the sun, which was getting quite bright, and saw Rob's face smiling down at her.

'Hello,' she said. 'What do you suppose is going on with Teresa?' she asked. 'She's been pacing up and down like a caged lion.'

Rob shrugged. 'You've got more chance of finding out than I do.'

'I doubt it,' Gemma said. 'I don't like to bother her unless it's absolutely necessary.'

'But you're the lead actress. You *should* be bothering the director,' Rob said.

Gemma gave a little smile. 'I'm not that sort of actress.'

'No, you're not, are you?' he said. 'But I've seen actresses who never leave the director alone for a second. *What should I do here? Is this right? What if I do it like that?* They can't make a single decision for themselves. But you're so sure of yourself.'

'Am I?' Gemma said, sounding genuinely surprised.

'I mean, you seem to know what you're doing. There's no nonsense about you. You just get on with the job.'

Gemma's eyes widened. This was a whole new Gemma she was hearing about, and it had nothing to do with the one *she* knew.

'Take that last scene, for instance,' Rob said. 'It was pretty good, and you got it in one take. Well, you did, but the sound guy managed to wreck it, and then that black cloud passed over.'

'You were watching it?'

'Of course.'

'I didn't realise,' Gemma said, suddenly feeling self-conscious. 'I thought you guys just got on with your job.'

'I sometimes do,' Rob said, 'but there's something about you that is very distracting.'

Now Gemma really was feeling self-conscious, especially when he sat down on the steps next to her, his long jeans-clad legs stretching out in front of him as he made himself comfortable. She looked away into the shrubbery at the far end of the garden.

'You're a wonderful actress,' he said.

She sighed. 'Don't,' she said.

'Don't what?'

'You don't have to do this.'

He frowned. 'I don't understand.'

'Did Teresa put you up to this? Or Sophie?'

'Put me up to what?' he asked.

'Flattering me,' Gemma said. 'Boosting my confidence.'

'What *are* you talking about? Can't a chap come up and tell you he thinks you're doing a great job?'

'It's never happened before.'

He looked surprised. 'Well, it should have.' He cocked his head to one side. 'You don't believe me, do you? You don't know how wonderful you are.'

'I'm not wonderful,' Gemma said, tucking a stray strand of hair behind her ear.

'It sounds as if somebody's told you that,' he said in a low voice. 'Somebody called Kim. Am I right?'

Gemma's eyes shot up to meet his, and she could feel the colouring drain from her face. 'What gives you the right to say such things?' she said, her voice quiet and guarded.

'Nothing,' he says. 'I'm just trying to work things out here.'

'Why?'

He gave her a smile that unsettled her. 'Because there's something extraordinary about you.'

'You don't know me,' Gemma said, and she stood up.

Rob stood up too. 'Maybe I don't know you all that well,' he said, 'but I'd like to.'

Gemma shook her head. 'I've got to get back.'

'But they don't need you for at least another hour,' he said.

She started to walk away, feeling flustered. Nobody had ever talked to her in that way before. It was as if he could see into her very soul, and it was a very unsettling feeling.

'Ah! There you are,' Kim Reilly said as Gemma rounded a corner and nearly crashed into her. 'Good gracious, girl! What *are* you doing?'

'Nothing. I was just going back—'

Her mother didn't give her time to explain. 'You really shouldn't be flirting with the crew, Gemma. I saw you with that man, sitting on the steps all cosy together.'

'I wasn't flirting with him.'

Kim's mouth, which had been recently plumped up with

collagen, almost disappeared in a thin line. 'You have to remember, you're an actress. It isn't right that you should be milling around with such people. They're no more than labourers.'

Gemma's mouth dropped open. 'Mum—'

'It's a good job I was here to rescue you.'

'I don't need rescuing.'

'Of course you don't. You always make such sensible decisions about men, don't you? Like the time you went out with that doctor who turned out to be married with four children.'

'He didn't tell me,' Gemma said with a sigh, wishing her mother wouldn't drag out all her mistakes every time Gemma even thought to look at a man.

'As long as you're my daughter, you'll always need rescuing,' Kim Reilly continued. Luckily for Gemma, one of the girls from wardrobe waved over to Kim.

'Ah, there's Sherry,' Kim said. 'What a darling—she's going to do my colour chart for me before we start thinking about costumes. I want to look my very best.'

Gemma groaned as her mother flitted across the lawn, waving to everyone she passed. What had she done to deserve this? she wondered. It was like being ten years old again when her mother used to turn up early at the end of her drama class and holler advice to her from the auditorium. This was much worse, though, because not only was her mother advising her about her performance as an actress, but she was also dispensing advice about her love life, which was incredibly unjust, because when did she have time for a love life? All she had was a big love muddle. Whilst she was harbouring some sort of mad crush on Oli Wade Owen, she was being haplessly matchmade to Adam, and now there was this Rob guy on the scene. Goodness only knew where it would all end!

Chapter 28

C LARE WAS CRYING IN EARNEST, AND KAY WAS DOING HER BEST
to comfort her.

'She'll turn up. I'm sure she will.'

'But where could she be?' Clare asked. 'She never runs off. It's not in her nature to.'

Kay pursed her lips. She'd never been in a situation like this before. Well, not since Andy Edwards had gone missing in the Natural History Museum on a school trip when she was nine and had been found cowering under the blue whale crying his eyes out.

'You don't think she went after Oli, do you?'

Clare stopped crying. 'She adores Oli.'

'Yes,' Kay said, having seen the evidence for herself.

'But she wouldn't have left the house, not without saying something.'

'Are you sure?' Kay said. 'Are you absolutely sure?'

Gemma was having her hair tidied away by a girl from the makeup department when a screech of tires sounded on the gravel driveway.

'Captain Wentworth's arrived,' the girl from makeup said, her eyes sparkling. It was the usual effect of Oli turning up anywhere. Eyes would sparkle, lips would pout, and hearts would race.

'Yes,' Gemma said, 'and Teresa looks ready to pounce on him. He must be horribly late.'

Gemma and the makeup girl had been watching Teresa pacing up and down for the previous twenty minutes. They had never seen her looking so worried. Had something gone wrong? Was the film about to be shut down? Had the money run out?

'What's it like?' the makeup girl said.

'What's what like?'

She giggled and looked away. 'You know—kissing Oli.'

'I haven't kissed him,' Gemma said, suddenly wondering what sort of rumours were flying around about her.

'I mean, in the film,' the girl said.

'Oh!' Gemma said in relief. 'Well, we've not done that scene yet.'

'But it's coming up soon, isn't it?'

Gemma nodded.

'And you'll tell me all about it, won't you?'

'If you like.'

The girl giggled again. 'I bet he's a good kisser,' she said. 'I mean, I've heard he is.'

Gemma wished she'd stop talking about kissing. She had a scene to do with Oli later that evening, and all this talk of kissing was bound to put her off.

'I heard that he has an affair with every actress he kisses,' the girl went on.

'Who told you that?' Gemma said, spinning around to face her.

'It's just what I've heard.'

'Well, it's probably just a silly rumour, and you shouldn't go around spreading it.'

'But he isn't involved with anyone, is he?' the girl said. 'It's not like he shouldn't be allowed to have some fun.'

That was true enough, Gemma thought. Oli was one of those types who wouldn't settle down until he was at least forty-five, and then he'd probably have about a dozen kids and live on a vineyard in the South of France, telling the press how he turned his back on the bright lights of fame and had found the simple pleasure of farming and family. And Gemma would play no part in it, because he wasn't interested in women like her at the moment. He wanted them young, stunning, and fun. He wanted the kind of woman who could stay up partying with him all night. He wouldn't want somebody whose perfect evening was to sit down with a new ball of wool to dream up a new design for a waistcoat. Gemma would never be exciting enough for someone like Oli, so why did she have to go and fall for him? It really was perverse.

'Who's that girl?' the makeup artist asked, breaking into Gemma's thoughts about how unfair love could be.

Gemma looked across the lawn expecting to see Oli arm in arm with a skinny model, but he was holding the hand of a little girl with a blond ponytail.

'I don't know,' Gemma said.

At that exact moment Teresa saw him, and Gemma and the makeup artist watched as she launched herself towards Oli with the speed of a cheetah.

'Annabel!' she cried.

'Mummy!'

'Mummy?' Gemma said. 'That's Teresa's daughter?' She suddenly remembered Teresa mentioning her daughter on the minibus and how she'd love one of Gemma's knitted outfits for her.

Gemma and the makeup artist watched as Teresa spun the little girl around, hugging her close.

'Where have you been?' Teresa cried.

'She's been with me, silly,' Oli said, coming forward with a big smile.

'What were you thinking?' Teresa shouted at Oli, causing everyone on the film set to stop what they were doing and watch.

'What are you on about?'

'Everyone's been worried sick!'

'What's the problem?' Oli asked. 'She wanted to see her mother, and I thought it would be fun.'

'Clare's been in tears, Oli,' Teresa said.

Oli frowned. 'I don't understand.'

'You can't just run off with a child like that.'

'But I didn't run off. I told Clare,' Oli protested.

'You told her to her face?' Teresa said.

'What do you mean? Bel went through to ask Clare's permission, didn't you, Bel?'

Bel hid her head in her mother's skirt and didn't say anything.

'Annabel—did you go and ask Clare permission to leave with Oli?' Teresa asked.

Oli raked a hand through his hair as he waited for her answer.

'I didn't think she'd let me come,' Annabel said in a quiet voice, 'and I wanted to see you.'

Teresa sighed. 'For God's sake, Oli—you can't believe the word of a child. You should have told Clare yourself what you were doing.'

'But I did,' he said. 'I shouted through before I left with Bel.'

'But Clare's partially deaf, Oli! She needs to be able to read your lips.'

'What?' Oli's face fell. 'I had no idea! God. I'm sorry.'

'You should be,' Teresa yelled. 'Don't *ever* do anything like that again!'

'I won't,' Oli said, his face pale.

Everyone watched as Teresa stalked towards Marlcombe Manor's front door, Annabel's hand tightly held in hers. 'Five minutes, everyone,' she yelled. 'We've wasted enough time today.'

When Clare's mobile rang at the bed and breakfast, both she and Kay jumped.

Clare answered it, holding the phone to her left ear. 'Teresa?'

Kay's heart hammered in her chest as she waited to hear more.

'Really? Oh, thank goodness!' Clare said, her eyes closing. 'No, he didn't tell me. And she's okay?' There was a pause. 'All right. No, that's fine. I'll see you later on. Thanks, Teresa.'

'She's safe?' Kay asked.

'She's with Teresa. Oli took her with him.'

'What? He just took her?'

'Apparently he told her to check with me, and she told him she had, and then Oli yelled through to us before he left. Did you hear him?'

'No,' Kay said. 'I mean, I heard the door close and knew he'd gone, but I didn't know he'd taken Annabel with him.'

Clare shook her head. 'He didn't know I'm partially deaf,' she said. 'I usually get by with this rather poor excuse for a left ear and lip reading, and I think Annabel's taken advantage of that.'

'Oh, dear,' Kay said.

Clare sank down into a seat. 'I guess she really wanted to see her mum.'

'I guess so.'

There was a knock at the door. Kay got up, wondering what on earth could possibly happen next.

'Adam,' she said a moment later.

'Hello,' he said, a tiny smile lighting his face. 'May I come in? There's something I'd like to talk to you about.'

Chapter 29

K AY USHERED ADAM THROUGH TO THE LIVING ROOM.
'You won't believe what's been going on here,' she said.
'We've been absolutely beside ourselves.'

'*We've?*' Adam questioned, wondering who else was at Wentworth House.

'Come and meet Clare.'

'Ah,' Adam said, realising that his declaration of undying love was being put on hold for a little while longer.

'Clare,' Kay said, entering the living room, 'this is Adam. Adam, meet Clare.'

'Hello, Adam,' Clare said, and the pair of them shook hands.

'Clare's Teresa's nanny,' Kay said.

'I was nearly her ex-nanny,' Clare said, flopping down into the armchair by the window.

Kay sighed. 'We've just been startled out of our wits. Teresa's daughter went missing.'

'Annabel?' Adam said.

Kay nodded. 'She just disappeared.'

'But she's okay?'

'Oh, yes. Turned out Oli had taken her out to Marlcombe Manor.'

'Without telling anyone?'

'It was a misunderstanding,' Clare explained. 'One never to be repeated, I hope.'

'I thought Teresa sounded stressed when I called her,' Adam said.

'She didn't say anything to you, then?' Kay asked.

'No. But she never really talks about her private life. Her whole family could be kidnapped and held to ransom, but Teresa would still want to get on with the day's scenes.'

'That sounds like Teresa,' Clare said. 'Listen, I'm going to get going to our bed and breakfast.' She stood up. 'I can't thank you enough, Kay. I don't know what I'd have done without you.'

'I'm afraid I wasn't much help.'

'I hope we'll see each other again soon.'

'You and Annabel must come and have dinner with us when the gang's all here.'

'I'd like that.'

Adam watched as Clare left the room and listened to them saying good-bye at the door. He was alone with Kay. Now was his chance.

She came back into the living room. 'I expect you'll be heading up to Marlcombe too,' she said.

'No, actually, I was wondering if you'd like to go out somewhere.'

'You're not working?' Kay asked him.

'The mobile's on, so I'm officially available for work,' he said with a little smile. 'And I've already dealt with at least a dozen calls today, so I'm hoping things will quieten down now.'

'But I'm afraid I've got to work here.'

'Then I can't tempt you to come fossil hunting with me?'

Kay smiled. 'Oh, Adam, I have so much to do.'

'Like what?'

She looked at him. 'You can't keep helping me out with the chores.'

'But I don't mind. If it means I have the pleasure of your company, I don't mind helping out with a few tasks first.'

'But there's a huge meal to prepare for tonight.'

'Teresa said they're going to eat out tonight,' Adam said. 'She didn't tell you?'

'No,' Kay said. 'Are you sure?'

He nodded. 'Said there'd been so many delays that they weren't going to be back until late.'

'Oh.'

'So that leaves you free, doesn't it?'

'I suppose,' Kay said. 'Although I really wanted to make a cake.'

'A cake?'

'Yes,' she said. 'Something nourishing and luxurious. I've got to practise.'

'And you'll come with me if I help you with the cake?'

'You don't have to help me.'

'But I want to,' Adam said. 'Come on. Lead me to the nearest apron.'

The two of them headed into the kitchen, and Kay giggled as Adam reached for a floral apron that hung on the back of the kitchen door.

'It actually suits you,' she said with a grin.

'I hope you're joking.' He washed his hands at the sink as Kay donned an apron of her own. 'So what were you thinking of?' Adam said. 'Nourishing *and* luxurious?'

'Aha!' Kay's eyes misted over, making Adam wonder what she was thinking, and then it hit him. She was making the cake for Oli, wasn't she? It was he she wanted to impress.

'Okay,' he continued, undeterred. 'What ingredients do you have?'

'I'm not sure,' Kay said, opening and closing cupboards. 'Just a bit of flour and some eggs and sugar. Nothing exciting.'

'No cocoa powder?'

'I'm afraid not.'

'So chocolate's out.'

'I guess.' Kay looked disappointed.

Something caught Adam's eyes. On the worktop by the sink, two bright lemons sat side by side. 'Can we use one of those?' he asked.

'Sure,' Kay said. 'What do you have in mind?'

'Wait and see.'

There then followed a flurry of activity as sieves, spoons, and bowls were brought together in the pursuit of deliciousness. Kay measured and Adam mixed, the two of them working in harmony.

'I've never made a lemon sponge before,' Kay said.

'This is a very special lemon cake,' Adam said. 'Nana Craig used to make it for me. It was a cure-all cake, and I could tell she'd made one as soon as I opened the front door. The whole house smelled lemony.'

Kay smiled, and Adam watched as she poured the gooey yellow mixture into the loaf tin and put it into the oven.

'So the lemon juice and sugar are in here?' Adam said.

'Aye-aye, Captain!' Kay said.

It was Adam's turn to smile. He might sound like a captain, but he very much doubted that Kay viewed him in the same way as she did Captain Wentworth.

'Good,' he said, removing his apron.

'You'll make someone a very good wife one day,' Kay said.

Adam looked at her disapprovingly. 'Very funny.'

'Oh, I didn't mean to make fun of you,' Kay said quickly. 'I'm just impressed. All the men I've been out with couldn't even open a can of beans, let alone make a cake.'

'That's what happens when you're brought up by your grand-mother,' Adam said. 'You can make cakes, sew on buttons, and tell your delphiniums from your hollyhocks. Only don't go spreading such news around. I do have a reputation to keep up.'

'You mean you wouldn't want Gemma finding out about such things?'

Adam sighed. She was still fixating on him and Gemma, wasn't she? 'It's just that I might be taken advantage of,' he said, 'by women who want to use my culinary skills to impress others.'

Kay looked at him. 'You know who this cake's for, don't you?'

'I have a hunch.' He watched as Kay's face flushed pink.

'I don't suppose I'm very good at keeping secrets, am I?' She untied her apron and hung it up on the back of the kitchen door.

Adam wondered if she was going to say any more, but she didn't. He didn't press her, because he wasn't sure he wanted to hear what she might say.

'So,' he said, 'are you up for some fossil hunting?'

Kay smiled. 'Really?'

'You bet,' Adam said. 'You've got to see Charmouth.'

'Okay. I'll go and get ready,' Kay said. 'Will you keep an eye on the cake?'

'Aye-aye, Captain.' He watched as she left the room and listened as her light feet padded up the stairs. He raked his hand through his hair. God! What was he going to do?

Tell her, a little voice said to him—the voice that had hurried him on to Lyme.

'But she's not interested in me. It's Oli she's in love with,' he told himself.

And you don't stand a chance of her being interested in you if you won't even put yourself in the picture.

That's true, he thought. If he just brooded and remained silent, he would get nowhere. He had to take action and let her know.

He paced around the kitchen for twenty minutes, thinking about how things might turn out and then panicking that everything would go wrong—just as it had in the past.

Don't think about that, he told himself. *The fact that it happened once doesn't mean it will happen again.*

'No, it just *feels* as if it will,' he whispered. Why was that? How could one knock affect a person so much? Nana Craig was always telling him to put it behind him, which was ironic, as she'd never been able to put her husband's infamous misdemeanours with an actress behind her.

'You're not living your life properly,' she told him on numerous occasions. 'You can't let that one incident shadow the rest of your life.'

It made sense to him; it really did, but nevertheless, he lived in horror of it happening again.

'Okay,' a voice said, bringing him back to the present. He looked up and saw Kay standing in the doorway. Her hair was loose and had been brushed, and she was wearing a pretty floral Alice band. 'I'm not sure what to wear for fossil hunting,' she said, smoothing down her sky-blue dress, which dazzled Adam's eyes.

'Something sturdy on the feet,' he said.

'Oh,' Kay said. 'Not sandals?'

'It's not that kind of beach, I'm afraid.'

Kay wrinkled her nose, and at first he thought it was because she was changing her mind about the whole idea of the beach trip, but then he realised it was the cake she could smell. He watched as she grabbed the oven gloves and opened the door, an aromatic waft of lemony heat escaping.

'Wow!' Kay pulled out the cake tin and examined it. She tested it with a skewer and pronounced it cooked.

'I have to say that is the cutest cake I've seen in a long time,' Adam said.

'Do you really like it?'

'I think it looks gorgeous, but there's one thing more to do.' He handed Kay the bowl with the lemon and sugar mix, giving it one last stir. He then lightly pricked over the cake with a fork and nodded to Kay.

'I'm a bit nervous,' she said, and he watched as she poured the sugary mixture over the warm cake and then stood back to admire it. 'Gosh.'

Adam smiled. 'It looks great.'

She nodded. 'I can't thank you enough, Adam.' She turned and smiled at him.

He shrugged.

'I mean, I would have ended up with a bowl full of gunk if I'd been left on my own.'

'I'm sure you'd have done fine.'

'No, really—the last cake I made shrivelled and burnt. It was a complete disaster. Even my neighbour's dog didn't want it.'

'Well, I'm sure everyone will want a piece of this.'

Kay nodded. 'They will, won't they?'

Adam smiled.

'Shall we get going, then?'

Adam blanched slightly. She wasn't going to offer him a piece, was she? Of course she wasn't. His suspicions were confirmed. She had made it for another man, and he had helped her. What an idiot he was!

Chapter 30

OLI WASN'T PAYING ANY ATTENTION TO GEMMA, AND SHE WAS getting annoyed.

'You'd think I'd deliberately done something to make her miserable, wouldn't you?' he said, his face slightly less handsome than usual because of his furrowed brow and the thunderous expression in his eyes. 'You'd think I never do anything right.'

'Oli—'

'I don't know why I put up with it,' he said. 'Why do I keep putting up with it?'

'Because she's a great director.'

'Director!' Oli said, the word exiting his mouth like a poison he was trying to rid himself of. 'More like dictator!'

Gemma had never seen him so worked up before. She hadn't realised there was such tension between Oli and Teresa. She knew they had worked together on several projects over the years—she could tell from the way they interacted on set. Either they were screaming at each other or working to the very best of their ability, because of a kind of shorthand they used. It was quite common between actors and directors, and it was always fascinating to watch.

'I think she was just worried about her daughter,' Gemma said.

'But I brought Bel here to see her mum. You'd think Teresa would have liked the surprise.'

'I'm sure she did,' Gemma said, 'but you probably scared her witless. She didn't know where Annabel was. Honestly, I've never seen her look so anxious.'

Oli sighed. 'This is the last time I work with her—the very last.'

'Oli—'

'She treats me like a child, and I'm not going to put up with it.'

Gemma watched as Oli stormed off across the lawn. 'Oli?' she called, but he had vanished.

∽

Adam and Kay were walking the length of Marine Parade towards the parking lot by the harbour. The sea was the colour of slate, and the sandy beach was quiet and newly swept.

Adam's gaze drifted to the Cobb, and he smiled. 'When I first saw that when I was a little boy, I thought it was a sleeping dragon.'

'Were you afraid of it?'

He shook his head. 'No,' he said. 'I kept wanting to visit it to see if it had woken up. Drove Nana crazy.'

'You're very close to Nana Craig, aren't you?'

'She's my family. She's like parents, siblings, and best friends all rolled into one.'

'That's nice,' Kay said.

'What about you?'

'What about me?'

'Whom are you close to?'

Kay stopped walking for a moment. 'I don't know.'

Adam looked surprised. 'You don't know?'

Kay sighed. 'My mother died recently,' she said, 'and I lost a good friend too.'

'I'm sorry,' he said. 'Is that what made you move here?'

She nodded. 'I had to get away, and I wanted a complete change. There were too many sad memories for me in Hertfordshire.'

'What about your father?' Adam asked.

Kay looked up at him. 'He left when I was little.'

'And never came back?'

'Oh, he came back, all right,' Kay said, 'but only to leave again.' She shook her head. 'I think he was one of the reasons I became obsessed with fictional heroes. They're so much more reliable, aren't they?'

For a moment, Kay thought about all the times she had been hurt in love and remembered Harry Golden, the man who stole and then broke her heart when she was twenty-one. They had been dating for just over a year when he dropped the bombshell about being married.

No, she didn't miss Hertfordshire.

'But didn't you worry about being lonely?' Adam asked. 'I mean, you don't know anyone here.'

'I know you,' she said.

He grinned. 'And I'm very honoured to be your friend.' He winced at the word that now lay between them as heavy and cumbersome as a slab of cement. He didn't want to be her friend. Well, he *did*—of course he did, but he wanted to be more than that. 'I'll always be around if you ever need to talk to anyone. You know that, don't you?'

'You're so sweet, Adam,' she said. 'Gemma's a lucky girl.' She began to walk again, leaving Adam to cringe.

Shortly before they reached the parking lot, they passed a secondhand bookshop, its windows crammed with gems.

'I can never resist the lure of books,' Adam said.

'Neither can I,' Kay said. 'You know, Oli told me he hasn't read *Persuasion*.'

'Really?'

'He doesn't like reading at all. Well, other than scripts.'

'But that's terrible,' Adam said, aware that it was bad practice to slander one's rival, but nevertheless, it was tempting to do just that.

They entered the shop together and marvelled at the shelves and the magical musty smell of old books. As if of one mind, they both ventured towards the fiction section, and it wasn't long before Adam made a discovery, pulling out an old copy of *Pride and Prejudice* from the shelves.

'Look at this,' he said, handing it to Kay.

'It's illustrated,' she said in delight as she flicked through the pages. 'They're wonderful. Look at them!'

Adam looked at the pages she held open for him and nodded. 'I'm betting they're not as lovely as your illustrations,' he said.

'Oh, you flatterer!'

'And you must let me have a look at them some time.'

'Really?'

'I've said so before. Perhaps I could help you find an agent for them—get you on the road to publication.'

'Oh, I don't know about that,' Kay said.

'Why not? Isn't that what you're aiming for?'

'Well, yes. In the long run.'

'Why not now?'

Kay bit her lip, and Adam hoped he hadn't pushed things too far. 'I—I'm just a bit busy with the bed and breakfast.'

He gave her a little smile. 'It's rejection, isn't it? You're scared of rejection.'

Kay didn't answer at first, but then she nodded. 'Of course I'm scared of rejection. Who isn't? You see, at the moment, the paintings are mine and they're—well—perfect, because nobody's told me otherwise. But what if somebody does? What if somebody doesn't like them and says they're no good?'

Adam scratched his chin. 'If you're going to try to get published, you're going to have to accept that someone's going to say that at some stage—that is, unless you get incredibly lucky first time. But you shouldn't let it put you off. My goodness, if I'd given up after my first rejections—'

'You've been rejected?' Kay asked in surprise.

'Countless times!' he said. 'There was one really awful year when I got nothing *but* rejections, and yes, it knocks you back a bit and you feel like your work's worth nothing, but then you dust yourself down and start again.'

Kay's face looked pale with anxiety. 'I don't know if I could survive it. It sounds brutal.'

'It is, but you get over it. At least, you do if you want to have your work out there and you love doing what you do. Truly love it.'

'Oh, I do!'

'That's what will get you through the rough times.'

Kay puffed out her cheeks in a sigh. 'I'm not sure I like the sound of *rough times.*'

'They're not easy—I won't paint an unfair picture for you—but when you have a piece of work accepted…'

'What?' Kay asked.

Adam smiled. 'It's the best feeling in the world.'

'I wonder how Jane Austen felt,' Kay said, 'when she first saw her book in print.'

'*Sense and Sensibility*, wasn't it?'

Kay nodded. 'In 1811.'

'She was in her midthirties,' Adam said.

'Yes.'

'So there's plenty of time for you!'

Kay laughed and flicked through the illustrated copy of *Pride and Prejudice* again. 'This is lovely,' she said.

'Let me buy it for you.'

'Oh, you don't need to do that.'

'But I want to,' he said, plucking it from her hand and taking it to the till.

How very sweet Adam was, Kay thought. It was rather a pity that she'd matchmaded him to Gemma; otherwise she might be starting to have ideas about him for herself. He was certainly cute with his dark hair and bright eyes.

She shook her head. He was Gemma's. Anyway, wasn't she in love with Oli?

Once he purchased the book, Adam handed it back to her.

'Thank you,' she said. 'What a lovely gift.'

'My pleasure. But now you're beholden to me.'

'I am?'

'Yes. You have to promise me that you'll send your work out to agents and publishers.'

'Oh.'

'I'll help.'

Kay was still looking anxious, but she finally nodded. 'Okay,' she said. 'I will.'

On the way out, they passed a great shelf full of well-loved Enid Blytons.

'I used to adore *The Famous Five*. First-class escapism for children,' Kay said with a happy sigh. 'But I always wanted Anne to fall in love on one of the holidays.'

'So you've always been a romantic?' Adam said with a grin.

'Oh, yes!'

'And when did you graduate from Miss Blyton to Miss Austen?'

'Very early,' Kay said as they finally managed to leave the shop and head towards the parking lot. 'One of my cousins was staying during the holidays, and she was meant to be reading *Pride and Prejudice* for school, but she hated it. I don't think it had anything to do with Jane Austen, because my cousin was going through a phase when she hated everything. Anyway, she left the book in the garden one day, and I ran outside to get it when the rain started. I couldn't resist taking a look to find out more about the dreadful book, and I was hooked. I had to buy my own copy after that. How about you?'

'How did I discover Jane?'

Kay nodded.

'Nana Craig sat me down one Saturday afternoon to watch the old Laurence Olivier and Greer Garson adaptation of *Pride and Prejudice*.'

'And you didn't run out of the room screaming?'

'No. I'd been in a terrible mood. My team had lost a big football match at school, and she thought I needed cheering up.'

'Nobody can do cheering up quite like Jane Austen.'

'You're not wrong there,' Adam said. 'All the same, I didn't let my mates know. I don't think it would have done my reputation any good on the pitch.'

Kay laughed. 'I guess not, but—' she stopped.

'What?'

A frown creased her forehead. 'Do you think it gave you unrealistic expectations?' she asked slowly.

Adam was surprised by her question. 'You mean of love?'

Kay nodded. 'I mean, I'm always being told I'm—that I have—that Jane Austen has given me—'

'A horribly warped view of the world?' Adam suggested.

'A *wonderfully* warped view of the world,' Kay corrected him.

'How?'

'Oh, you know—the usual stuff about happy endings and expecting to fall in love with the perfect hero.'

'And you haven't?' he dared to ask her.

Kay's bright eyes misted over. 'I'm afraid I have, but it seems to happen an awful lot.'

'You mean the heroes don't turn out to be heroes?'

'That's *exactly* it!' she said, thinking of her own sorry history with various ex-boyfriends who let her down—like Charlie Russell, whom she dated for six months before receiving a postcard from him from Barcelona where he decided to move without telling her.

'And you're blaming Jane Austen?'

'I have to blame somebody, and I don't like the idea of it being my fault.' A small smile spread across her face. 'How about you? Any failed relationships you can blame on dear Jane?'

Adam cleared his throat. 'One or two,' he said. 'One or two.'

Chapter 31

HALF AN HOUR WENT BY AT MARLCOMBE MANOR, AND OLI Wade Owen was still a missing person. Teresa had paced up and down for ten minutes, wondering what to do.

'He just stormed off,' Gemma said when Teresa asked where her leading man was.

'Where? Where did he storm off?'

Gemma pointed across the lawn where the garden sloped and was lost in a group of trees.

'Bloody hell!' Teresa said, and Gemma watched as the director followed the path that Oli had taken earlier.

'What did he say to you?' Sophie asked as she approached from behind.

'Oli?' Gemma said. 'Not much. Just that he was fed up with the way Teresa was treating him.'

'The usual, then?' Sophie said.

'What's going on?' a voice suddenly cried from behind them. 'What have I missed?'

Gemma and Sophie turned around to see Beth emerging from the back of a taxi, wincing as her sprained ankle hit the ground.

'Shouldn't you be resting?' Gemma asked.

'I couldn't stay in that bed and breakfast a minute longer,' Beth groaned. 'I was so bored!' The taxi pulled away and Beth hobbled over towards them. 'What's going on?'

'Oli stomped off in a huff after upsetting Teresa.'

'Her daughter turned up at the bed and breakfast with her nanny and then promptly disappeared,' Beth said.

'Yes,' Gemma said. 'She turned up here with Oli.'

'I was trying to hear what was going on from my room, but it was no use, and then Kay seemed to forget I was there at all. She's gone off with Adam.'

'Now we've lost our director on top of everything else,' Sophie said. 'I thought we were trying to make a period drama here, but it's turning into more of a farce.'

'I don't think Oli and Teresa should be working together,' Gemma said. 'They constantly wind each other up.'

'But have you seen their films?' Sophie said. 'She always gets the best out of Oli.'

'I don't think he should be acting at all,' Beth said.

'What?' Sophie all but screamed.

'What makes you say that?' Gemma asked. 'He's a brilliant actor.'

'I know,' Beth said.

'What, you think he should give it all up and make babies with you?' Sophie teased. 'Because that's not going to happen.'

Beth scowled at her. 'And how do you know?'

'Because he's got his eye on someone, and it's not you,' Sophie declared.

'Who?' Beth asked.

'I think it might be our little hostess,' Sophie said with a smile, delighting in taunting Beth.

'But she's off out somewhere with Adam,' Beth said.

'So?' Sophie asked.

'Oh, for goodness sake, you two!' Gemma cried out. 'Can't you talk about anything else?'

Sophie and Beth exchanged puzzled expressions.

'What else is there to talk about except love?' Sophie asked.

⁓

As Adam and Kay crossed the parking lot, he thought about her question about Jane Austen. Did Jane Austen ruin lives by giving people false expectations about love? Were her heroes just too good to be true? Could a real man of flesh and blood ever hope to live up to such paragons? And were books with happy endings cruel? Did they give their readers a warped view of the world and what they could expect from it?

For a moment he thought of his own view of the world. Had it been coloured by the literature he read? He wouldn't be surprised if it had, and now here he was adding to the sum total of happy endings in the world with his own writing. Was he perpetuating the myth?

Adam sighed. As long as he could remember, he had been an optimist. He always looked on the bright side of life. He always thought things would turn out for the best and never had anything but the highest expectation of things. Until Heidi Clegg, that was. Before Heidi, Adam believed that love was a pure and simple thing and that being honest and open was a sure way to find a happy ending of his own. He was wrong.

⁓

Adam met Heidi Clegg at a wrap party for the first film he produced. She came as a friend of one of the actresses but was not an actress herself, much to the relief of Nana Craig.

Heidi was tall with short blond hair cut elfin-like around a beautiful face, and she had the most hypnotic eyes Adam had ever seen. They were like polished jade and gave her face a feline appearance. Adam had fallen in love in the space of a moment.

There followed a few blissful months of wonderful dates and romantic nights when he felt that the city of London had been made for them alone. They did many funny, silly things together. He took her to London Zoo, where they ate ice cream and laughed at the penguins. They took a boat out on the Serpentine in Hyde Park and picnicked on Primrose Hill. It had been the most perfect summer of Adam's life, and he knew that she was the one.

He bought the ring—a beautiful square-cut diamond set in platinum—from a jeweller's he walked by a dozen times on his way to the studio where he worked. That morning, it had stopped him in his tracks, winking at him as strongly as a lighthouse beam. It had been a sign. Well, that's what Adam thought at the time.

He chose a restaurant by the river, the sun setting behind the city, and then he waited for her to arrive. This, he thought, is going to be the most perfect night of our lives. He felt excitement bubble up inside him and then wondered if he should order a bottle of champagne to get some real bubbles in on the action. He motioned to the waiter and tried not to splutter into his tie when he saw the prices.

'Thank you,' he said, 'I'll have this.' He chose a bottle that cost more than he received for the first short story he sold. *It's a special occasion*, he told himself. *A very special occasion, and if one can't have champagne on such an occasion, then it was a poor do.*

He looked out into the darkening night and wondered where Heidi was and if she had any idea what he was going to ask her. Didn't women have a sixth sense for these sorts of things? Maybe she was panicking about what to wear or was fixing her hair so that everything would be perfect. He tried to imagine her arriving—walking in through the restaurant door. She was a woman who made heads turn, and he was quite sure it would happen that night. How proud he would be to see her! He'd catch her eye and she'd beam him one of her bright smiles, and the other diners in the restaurant would turn to see who she was meeting.

'That's my future wife you're admiring,' he'd want to tell them.

He checked his watch again. She was fifty minutes late, which was perfectly normal for Heidi. He had come to expect her to be late, and she always had a good excuse. Take the time when she was late for the theatre because she broke a nail. It must have been horribly painful, and of course she had to fix it, and he didn't mind not being let in to the show until the interval. After all, you couldn't expect to ruin the enjoyment for everyone else—not when you were sitting in the front row. It would have been disruptive. Then there was his hour-long wait for her outside the Victoria and Albert Museum for the exhibition he wanted to see. Heidi hadn't been able to decide what shoes to wear and so went shopping on the way. He had to admit that she did look fabulous, and he hadn't minded missing the exhibition. Who wanted a timed ticket entry anyway? Wouldn't it be more fun to just look around the permanent collection at one's own leisure?

A fifty-minute—make that fifty-five minute—delay, then, wasn't anything to worry about. It also gave him a chance to practise things in his mind.

'Heidi,' he could say, 'you know how much I care about you?'

Hmmm. Did that make him sound too overbearing? He didn't want to smother her and scare her away. She was a modern, independent woman who would laugh in his face if she thought he had visions of hiding her away from the world and mollycoddling her.

'Heidi—what can I say but I love—'

'Oh, Adam!' her voice called across the restaurant, and sure enough, a dozen pairs of eyes flashed in her direction as she waltzed towards him wearing the sort of dress that Nana Craig would have sworn should be classed as underwear. 'Have you been waiting ages for me, darling?' She leaned across the table, flashing an ample of bosom and leaving a red smear across his mouth.

'No,' Adam lied. 'Not at all.'

'I just couldn't get away on time.' That was as much of an excuse as she was going to give this time, but Adam didn't mind.

'That's okay,' he said, watching as Heidi arranged herself, flicking her hair back and fluffing out her dress around her knees. Because he couldn't bear to delay it another moment, he reached across the table and took her hand in his. She looked at him with her huge cat-like eyes, and he cleared his throat.

'Heidi,' he said.

'What is it? Are we going to order?'

Adam smiled. 'Yes, of course we are, but I wanted to ask you something first.'

'Oh?'

'You know how I feel about you, don't you?'

Heidi's eyes narrowed. 'I guess,' she said.

'I've never met anyone like you before.'

'No,' she said. 'I don't expect you have.'

'And I want to ask you to marry me.'

Heidi's pretty mouth opened in a perfect circle. 'Really?'

'Yes, really,' Adam said with a little laugh. And then an awful silence fell between them.

'Oh, dear,' Heidi said at last.

'What?' Adam said, panic rising in him.

'I didn't see this coming,' she said. 'I mean, we've been having fun, haven't we?'

'Yes,' Adam said. 'We have.'

'What we have—it's a lovely, summery thing, isn't it?'

Adam swallowed hard. A lovely, summery thing? What the hell was that supposed to mean? 'Heidi—I love—'

'Don't say that,' she said, removing her hand from his.

'Why not? Why shouldn't I say it? It's what I feel.'

Heidi took a deep breath and then dropped her bombshell. 'But I'm already married.'

Adam's face froze, and he was unable to speak, anger and confusion boiling inside him as he thought about the time they had spent together—the *nights* they spent together, and the weekends away, the parties they attended together *as a couple*. Everything had been pointing to a future together, hadn't it?

'I'm sorry, Adam. I just wanted a bit of fun, you know?' Heidi said. 'My marriage has been stale for years and—well—this has been fun, hasn't it? You don't regret it, do you?'

Adam could feel himself heating up as he looked at the stranger before him—the stranger he'd fallen in love with.

'I don't know,' she said. 'You men are strange. You get so worked up about a few dates and a little bit of sex. Why can't you just enjoy things for what they are?'

Adam closed his eyes, willing the scene to be some dreadful nightmare from which he was about to wake, but when he opened his eyes, Heidi was still sitting across from him with a taunting expression on her face.

After a pause, the waiter came to the table. 'Ready to order?'

'Adam?' Heidi said. 'Are we ready to order?'

He shook his head. 'I've suddenly lost my appetite.'

Heidi sighed. 'I guess that's it then, is it?' She looked across at him; her eyes narrowed and looked like little chips of ice.

'I guess it is.'

She pushed her chair back, and he watched as she stormed out of the restaurant, causing heads to turn once again.

'That's not my future wife,' Adam said.

'Excuse me?' the waiter said.

Adam laughed. 'I'll just finish this bottle of champagne,' he said. The waiter nodded and left him to it.

It took Adam a full hour to pull himself together, but pull himself together he did. He was furious with himself. How could he have not known?

Leaving the restaurant, he walked along the river, his eyes gazing out across the city. London was a great place to be when you were in love and a horrible prison when you weren't.

That evening he decided to go back to Lyme Regis—for good—and it was not just to run away from his doomed relationship. He wanted to smell the sea air. He wanted to stride across the fields and breathe in lungfuls of fresh air.

He left within a fortnight, determined that he was going to focus on his work. He was through with women. Well, until he met Kay.

Now, driving out of Lyme Regis with Kay beside him, he wondered if she was right. Maybe Jane Austen fans were destined to be disappointed by love because nothing could ever live up to the happy endings created in fiction, and yet here he was in love again. Even though he had told himself that it would never happen again and that he would be better off single, he found himself falling for Kay.

Chapter 32

A VOICE CAME OUT OF THE SHRUBBERY, AND IT DIDN'T SOUND too happy.

'I have enough to worry about with schedules and the weather and a million other things without having to worry about my lead actor as well.'

'Stop bloody worrying about me then!'

'How can I, when you kidnap my daughter and then go stomping off?'

'I did not kidnap Annabel.'

'No, you just went off with her without telling anybody.'

'I'm not going through all this again,' Oli's voice shouted. 'I told Clare, okay?'

Gemma bit her lip. She hated arguments, but she couldn't help listening in on that one. Not that she had much choice. The whole cast and crew had downed tools and were listening too.

'I'm not going to discuss it anymore!' Teresa's voice yelled. 'That's an end of it.'

The voices quietened.

'I don't think we're going to get that other scene done today, are we?' someone said.

Gemma turned around and saw Rob. He was grinning, and his eyes sparkled with mischief.

'I wonder what's going on with those two, anyway?' Rob said when it was clear Gemma wasn't going to answer his question.

'What do you mean?'

'I mean it's like they can't live with each other or without each other.'

'I wish they could just get on with things until we finish shooting.'

Rob walked towards her. 'You okay?' he asked.

'I'm fine,' she said.

'Want a cup of coffee?'

'No, thank you,' Gemma said, her mind still on Oli and Teresa.

'Tea?'

'No.'

'How about—'

'Look,' Gemma interrupted, 'I'd just rather be on my own—if you don't mind.'

'Oh.'

Gemma started to walk back to the trailer. Filming was hard enough without all this business with Oli, and now Rob kept popping up every time she turned around. What was it with men?

As she climbed the steps into the trailer, she dared to glance back, and sure enough, he was staring right back at her, his smile bright and undiminished.

⁓

The drive from Lyme Regis to Charmouth was short, and the sweep of sea that greeted Kay from the parking lot at the bottom of the lane took her breath away.

Jane Austen had written about this countryside, and Kay had

read that passage in *Persuasion* over and over since moving to Lyme Regis.

'You'll love it here,' Adam said. 'It's such a special place.'

Charmouth might not be the first destination for those with a bucket and spade; the visitors were far more likely to be wielding metal hammers.

'This is the best place ever for fossils,' Adam explained. 'People come from all over the world to find them. We'll have a quick tour of the heritage centre and shop before hitting the beach; then you'll be an expert and know exactly what we're looking for.'

Twenty minutes later, and with a tiny guidebook to help her, Kay was ready to attack the beach. They crossed a little wooden bridge over a river and headed towards the main beach. There was a good stretch of shiny sand but the beach was predominately stony with great grey cliffs stretching heavenwards all the way along to Golden Cap. Kay looked back along the coast and saw the sandy beach at Lyme Regis.

'Can you see Wentworth House from here?' she asked, shielding her eyes.

Adam looked. 'There's the row of beach huts, so Wentworth House will be about there,' he said, pointing.

Kay smiled. Her own little piece of the Dorset coast.

Adam's phone rang. 'Blast,' he said.

Kay turned away to give him a moment's privacy.

'No, no, no,' he was saying, 'the budget won't allow for that. There's got to be another way. Yes, but we tried that before, and it doesn't work.'

Kay frowned. There was obviously more to filmmaking than handsome actors and beautiful costumes.

'Sorry about that,' Adam said a moment later. 'I've switched it off now.'

'Are you allowed to do that?'

'I think the film world can manage without me for a couple of hours. Come on,' he said, 'let's get to work.'

At first, progress was slow as they walked along the pebbly beach, but then a rhythm set in, and Kay almost felt as if she were in a trance with her feet moving quite independent of thought and her eyes cast to the ground while she tried to make out certain shapes in the sand. She'd seen the pretty ammonites in the gift shop and was desperate to find one of her own, but it wasn't easy, and she was lazy to begin with, expecting her prize to be quickly won with only a quick shove with her boot to reveal the hidden treasure. Soon her technique frustrated her, and she crouched down to be nearer the ground. Adam was crouching too, which made Kay anxious. What if he found something before her? Competitiveness set in, and a fossil frenzy began with fingers turning over stones quickly but carefully while she shuffled along the beach with her bottom hovering in the most ungainly of fashions. Kay didn't care, as long as she got her fossil. Anyway, everybody else seemed to be doing exactly the same thing, so nobody would be interested in her bottom. Charmouth, she thought, was the most unfriendly beach in the country, because everyone's eyes were fixed on the ground and everybody was a rival.

After about ten minutes, Kay stood and stretched. She couldn't hover any longer and so took to bending down instead.

'You'll get fossiler's stoop if you do it for too long,' Adam said, turning around from his patch on the beach.

'Why can't I find anything?'

'Be patient. It's a case of training the eyes, that's all. There's no secret.'

'But you've found so many,' she said, looking at the collection in his hand crammed full of tiny ammonites.

'Yes, but I've been doing this since I was a kid.'

'I need a fossil hound or something to help me,' Kay said, squatting down to the ground again. Once again, the world became a square metre of concentration, but still, Kay found nothing.

She looked up at the grey cliffs above her. They looked horrendously unstable and almost alive with menace. It was easy to imagine the wonders that they must hide—the prehistoric beasts that were ready to burst free from their muddy tombs. All it would take was one extra storm; just one more landslip, and they'd be free. Adam had warned her not to go too close to the cliff and told her the story about the famous nineteenth-century fossil collector, Mary Anning, who had been trapped by a landslip that nearly killed her, so Kay kept her distance from them.

She took a deep breath and began again.

'Oh, my goodness!' Adam exclaimed. He was leaning over a dark boulder, his chisel in hand and his back to Kay.

Straightening up, Kay stumbled over the beach to reach him. 'What is it? What have you found?'

'I think it's a tyrannosaur.'

'What?' Kay's mouth dropped open. 'Show me!'

Adam turned from the boulder and held out a tiny purple toy dinosaur he'd been hiding in his jacket. 'It's the discovery of a lifetime,' he said, a big grin bisecting his face.

'Adam!' she said with a laugh, 'I thought you were serious.'

'I saw him in the shop and couldn't resist him.'

'And I thought you'd gone back in to get proper equipment,' she said.

'Go on, then,' he said, 'back to it.'

Kay giggled as she put the furry dinosaur in her pocket and returned to a patch of beach of her own.

The sound of hammering rocks vied with the incessant waves as Kay worked her way slowly along the beach once more. While she continued to hunt, she wished Oli were there. Not that this would be his kind of thing. In fact, she couldn't imagine him there at all. She remembered seeing a photograph of him in a celebrity magazine once. He'd been on board a very expensive-looking yacht somewhere in the Mediterranean. That would be the kind of holiday by the sea he'd enjoy, not fossil hunting on a wind-battered bit of Dorset coast.

She looked up and watched Adam for a moment, how patient he was, searching the stones and sand with relentless precision, his thick dark hair flopping over his face. He had his sleeves rolled up, and Kay noticed he had nice strong arms that had obviously caught the sun recently. No wonder Gemma had clapped her eyes on him, she thought. He really was very handsome.

Feeling a little bit disloyal to her dear Oli at having such thoughts, Kay returned to scanning the beach and—suddenly— there it was. Sitting on the shingle as if it had been waiting especially for her was a tiny golden ammonite. It was the size of a thumbnail and seemed to be winking up at her, daring her to pick it up, which Kay was only too happy to do.

'I've got one!' she yelled. 'I've got one!'

Adam stood up and came running towards her. 'Let's see then, Darwin.'

Kay held it up for his inspection. 'Isn't it gorgeous?'

'It's a beauty, all right.' Adam took it from her and examined it closely. 'Well done!'

Kay beamed with pride. 'Gold, too!'

'That's the iron pyrite or fool's gold,' Adam said, handing it back to her.

'It's beautiful. It's like a piece of jewellery.' She held it up so that it caught the light.

'Nothing beats that first fossil,' he said. 'And I think you win the prize for the best today.'

'I'll keep it forever,' Kay said. 'Unless—'

'What?' Adam said.

'Do you think Oli would like it?'

'I thought you said you'd keep it forever.'

'Yes, but Oli might like it, and I can always find another one, can't I?'

'I don't know,' Adam said. 'It's not always that easy. You've got a particularly good one there.'

Kay thought for a moment. Adam was probably right. What would Oli do with a funny old fossil, anyway?

'Well, I'll keep it,' she said at last.

'Good,' Adam answered.

'I've had so much fun,' Kay said, her face warm and pink from the sunshine and the wind.

Adam smiled at her, and his eyes crinkled at the edges.

'What?' she said, having the distinct impression that he was about to say something.

'Kay,' he began.

'Yes?'

He cleared his throat.

'What is it?' she asked encouragingly.

He looked shy, but then he took a deep breath. 'There's something I've been wanting to tell you.'

'Yes?' she said, but she instantly knew what he was going to say.

She could tell from the look on his face that he was a man in love. It was obvious. 'It's about Gemma, isn't it?' she said.

'What?'

'It *is*, isn't it?' Kay's voice rose in excitement. 'Oh, Adam! I think it's wonderful. I just *knew* you two would hit it off.'

'But I—'

'It's all right—you don't have to say anything else. I don't need to be thanked. It was my entire pleasure—it really was. You are two of the nicest people I've ever met, and I could see that you were right for each other.'

'Kay—listen—'

'I have a natural talent for this sort of thing. Maybe I should be running a dating agency instead of a bed and breakfast. What do you think?'

Adam didn't answer. He was walking along the beach in the direction of the parking lot.

Probably thinking about Gemma and the next time he'll see her— that will be it, Kay thought. What a sweet couple they made. Lyme really was turning out to be the most romantic of places.

'Adam!' she called. He'd confided in her, and now she wanted to confide in him. It was the least she could do.

He stopped and turned around.

'Listen!' she said, feeling breathless with excitement. 'I can tell you, can't I? I mean, this is turning into a day of confessions, isn't it?'

Adam nodded. 'I guess it is.'

'I think I'm in love.'

Adam's eyes widened. 'You do?'

Kay nodded again, the wind blowing her hair over her face and half covering the huge smile fixed there.

'I mean, I haven't said anything to him yet, but I'm quite sure. Quite sure.'

'Oli. You mean Oli, don't you?'

Kay sighed. 'I do.'

'And do you know how he feels about you? What's he said? Has he told you how he feels?'

'Oh, Adam. You sound like an anxious parent,' Kay said with a little laugh. 'No, of course he's not said anything, but you don't always need to, do you? I mean, emotions are sometimes bigger than words, don't you think? Anyway, that's how I feel, and it's a wonderful feeling too. I feel like I'm flying—like Louisa Musgrove from the Cobb, only without the unhappy landing.'

They reached the little wooden bridge.

'Adam?'

'Yes?'

'Thanks for today. I always have such a good time with you.'

'Don't sound so surprised.'

Kay laughed, and the two of them walked over the bridge together. He really was a sweet guy, she thought. Gemma was a lucky girl indeed.

Chapter 33

COMING HOME TO A CAT USUALLY MADE ADAM SMILE, BUT THAT day, it just made him sigh. As much as he adored Sir Walter, he wished there was somebody human rather than feline with whom to share his life.

'No offence, buddy,' he said as Sir Walter greeted him and deigned to be stroked. The cat seemed to realise he was being fussed and insulted at the same time.

What a disastrous afternoon it had been! After plucking up his courage to tell Kay how he felt about her, his plans had been dashed by her insane belief that he was in love with Gemma. She looked so thrilled at the thought that he and Gemma were a couple that all the things he was going to tell her—all the pretty little speeches he had tumbling around in his head—evaporated. The words wouldn't come out after that.

Just as well, really, because then had come the big revelation about Oli. He had guessed, of course, but he'd hoped Kay's feelings for him were more of the starstruck onlooker and that they would pass as soon as Oli left town. He hadn't realised they were quite so deep.

'Let's get you some tea,' he said to his feline companion, opening a can of food and filling his Posh Paws red-and-white bowl. Sir Walter stuck his little nose up at the food as if to say, *What do you call this?* He was soon tucking in all the same, though.

'She doesn't love me,' Adam told the cat. 'She loves a movie star, and who can blame her? What have I to offer her? I'm just a saddo who talks to his cat.'

Sir Walter looked up at this statement as if he understood and gave Adam one of his disdainful looks that was so human it was spooky.

Adam watched as the cat ate. How simple life was when you were a cat. One didn't get knotted up by emotions such as love. One ate and slept and occasionally stalked about in the fields. Adam decided there and then that he was going to be reincarnated as a cat. Life would be much easier then.

〜〇

When Kay got back to Wentworth House, she had a quick tidy round, making sure everything was perfect for her guests. She popped out to the shops to get a few necessary items for breakfast and some fresh flowers for the living room and dining room.

Once in her bedroom, she picked up the sketch she had made of Oli and examined it. She really was in love with him, wasn't she? After all the things she'd said about not falling for the hero, here she was falling for the biggest hero of them all—a handsome movie star.

She put the sketch down. She had something to get on with, didn't she? Since being with Adam and hearing him talk about her drawings, she'd been dying to get back and get things moving again. It was one of the promises she'd made to herself when Peggy left her the money—she was going to make something of her life—follow her dreams and achieve something for herself and for Peggy's memory.

'And that's going to start right now.' She got up and opened the blanket box at the bottom of the bed. It was an old stripped pine box, but it didn't contain blankets; it was filled with all her sketches for her new book, *The Illustrated Wentworth*. *The Illustrated Darcy* was in there too, but he was all tidied away neatly into a folder. Poor Wentworth, however, was all over the place, with doodles here and half-finished paintings there. It was a mess that needed to be sorted out, especially if she was ever actually going to submit the thing to a publisher.

Adam thought she should definitely give it a shot.

'But he's never seen your pictures,' she said to herself with a wry smile. 'He was just being supportive, like a good friend would be. It doesn't mean you've got the talent to make it.'

She picked up a drawing from the Darcy folder. It showed the hero sitting at a table writing a letter to his sister, Georgiana. He looked stiff and uncomfortable, because he was being teased by Elizabeth in this scene and probably was still thinking about how fine her eyes were. Kay held the pen sketch up to the light. She liked it, but then again, she liked everything she did, because it was from her favourite books, and you couldn't go wrong with Jane Austen, could you? She therefore was not necessarily the best judge of the merit of the work.

There was only one way to find out if it was really any good, and that was to send it out into the world. Adam was right about that.

'I'm going to do it,' she said to herself, and she got to work sorting the sketches into neat piles.

She was still sorting through everything when she heard the door opening downstairs. Looking up, she saw it was after seven o'clock. Was everyone back from filming already? She had expected them to be later.

She popped the sketches and paintings back into the safety of the blanket box and headed downstairs.

'Hello?' she called.

'Just me,' Sophie's voice came back.

'Nobody else with you?'

'Not yet,' Sophie said. 'They all disappeared into the pub. Well, Gemma didn't. She said she was going for a walk, and Teresa's off with Annabel.'

'Everything okay?'

Sophie flopped into a sofa in the living room and ruffled her hair with her hand. 'Teresa and Oli let rip.'

'What?'

'A big fight.'

'Oh, no! What happened?'

'Teresa was furious with him for taking Annabel, and they wouldn't stop shouting at each other. It was awful. Filming stopped completely for hours.'

Kay sat down next to her. 'She doesn't like Oli, does she?'

Sophie laughed. 'He winds her up like nobody else. I've never seen anything like it.'

'And was Annabel there when this was going on?'

Sophie shook her head.

'Someone took her into Marlbury for lemonade. I don't think she heard anything.'

'It must be tough having a mother like Teresa,' Kay said. 'I mean, I know she's a brilliant director but—'

'She must be the strictest mother ever.'

Kay nodded.

'I don't think it's all her fault, though,' Sophie said.

'What do you mean?'

'I think he's hiding something,' she said.

'Oli?'

'Yes.'

'What's he hiding?' Kay asked, leaning forward on the sofa.

'I don't know, but it's something he's keeping hidden from everyone.'

They were silent for a few moments.

'You don't think he's gay, do you?' Kay blurted.

'Oli—gay? You've *got* to be kidding.'

'Gosh, imagine that—a gay Captain Wentworth.'

Sophie giggled. 'As bad as a gay Mr Darcy?'

'Oh, don't even joke about it,' Kay said, horrified by the idea.

'Just imagine Pemberley if Mr Darcy was gay. It would be all pink drapes and floral cushions.'

'And he'd probably end up proposing to Mr Collins instead of Elizabeth,' Kay said, getting into the swing of the alternate Austen world.

'Yes!' Sophie said. 'My dear Mr Collins. In vain have I struggled. It will not do. My feelings will not be repressed. You must allow me to tell you how ardently I admire and love you.' She laughed. 'It's hard to think of the Regency period as being anything but perfect, isn't it? I don't think it was perfect, but it was pretty damn close. Apart from the mortality rate and lack of medicine and the hygiene issues.'

'And the lack of chocolate,' Kay added. 'And jeans.'

'And job opportunities for women.'

'Yes. Apart from all that.'

They stopped laughing, and Sophie looked at Kay. 'You mustn't fall in love with him,' she said.

'What do you mean?' Kay asked in surprise. 'Everyone's in love with Mr Darcy, aren't they?'

'I didn't mean Mr Darcy.'

Kay sighed. 'I know.'

'I expect it's too late for me to warn you, isn't it?'

Kay bit her lip and didn't answer at first, but then she said, 'Probably.'

Sophie grimaced. 'Oh, Kay! You know these things never last, don't you? They're like holiday romances. It's all heady and heat of the moment stuff. It's unsustainable. What happens on the set stays on the set.'

'But I'm not on the set,' Kay said.

'But Oli is, and he'll be moving on.' Sophie's face was gentle and sympathetic. 'Look, I don't want to be the voice of doom—Oli's a great guy, and I can absolutely see why you've fallen for him, but this happens wherever he goes, and he's not settled down yet.'

Kay pouted. She wanted to tell Sophie that she was wrong and that *this* was the film-set romance to prove everyone wrong.

Sophie got up from the sofa. 'Take care of yourself; that's all I'm saying. You're sweet, and I'd hate to see you get hurt.'

Kay watched as Sophie left the room. Why did nobody believe this could work? Why had Adam sounded so worried? And why did Sophie have so little faith in Oli? Why couldn't she be the girl to change Oli Wade Owen? Even the wildest of film stars settled down sooner or later, didn't they? Why shouldn't it be her that he chose to settle down with?

Kay knew there was only one thing left to do, and that was to prove everyone wrong.

Chapter 34

WHEN THE MINIBUS GOT BACK TO LYME REGIS, EVERYONE made a run for The Harbour Inn for food and a drink, but Gemma wasn't in the mood. She didn't want to chat and have a laugh, and neither, it seemed, did Oli. She watched him as he crossed the road and headed towards the Cobb, but he didn't climb the steps and walk along the grey length that stretched out to sea. He turned right onto a beach strewn with white pebbles.

Gemma wondered where he was going. His head was down, and he didn't seem to notice the tourists around him with their trays of chips and ice creams, and before she had time to realise that she was following him, he turned around and caught her.

'Gemma?' he said. 'You after me?'

The question made her want to laugh and shy away at the same time, but she did neither. 'I… er… just wanted a walk.'

He waited for her to catch up to him. 'Me too,' he said, his blue eyes staring out to a sea that matched them perfectly.

They walked along together for a bit, Gemma carefully watching her step as she walked across the fist-sized pebbles. It was a bright evening, and the air sparkled with light, but there was a chilly wind around the harbour, and she was glad she brought her denim jacket with her.

They walked by a line of white wooden beach huts, and she wondered what Oli was thinking about and if she should ask him, but she didn't have to, because he surprised her by volunteering something.

'I've been thinking of giving it up,' he said.

'What do you mean?' Gemma said.

'Acting.'

Gemma's eyes sprung wide open. She'd expected him to say alcohol or women or—well, *anything* but acting.

'You're not serious.'

'I'm deadly serious.'

She stared at him and realised that he did, indeed, look serious. 'What's brought this on?' she asked. 'The argument with Teresa?'

He took a deep breath of salty sea air and sighed it back out again. 'Maybe,' he said. 'She said some things.'

'What things?'

'Just things. It's not important. But it makes you take a step back, you know? Makes you look around you for a bit and assess things.'

'And what are you assessing?' Gemma asked.

'Everything,' he said, his voice low and serious.

They continued walking for a bit, passing a row of holiday chalets. The pebbly beach continued out towards tree-covered cliffs that followed the coast all the way into Devon. It was a beautiful spot and far too lovely to be sad and thoughtful in.

'Oli?' Gemma said.

He turned to look at her.

'You're not really thinking of giving up acting, are you?'

He smiled at her. 'I did four films last year. Four. Two

full-blown movies and two for television. It barely left me time to breathe. Don't get me wrong—I love my work, and I certainly love the lifestyle it's allowed me, but there's got to be more to life.'

Gemma nodded and smiled at the uncanny resonance of his words. 'I was thinking exactly the same thing.'

He looked at her and chuckled. 'You were?'

She nodded.

'Then you should do something about it.'

They began to walk again, their feet stumbling over the white stones on the beach.

'Acting's all I've ever known,' Gemma said.

Oli nodded. 'Me too. Although I did that modelling stuff as a teenager.'

'Yes,' Gemma said, remembering seeing the pictures that had been recently rediscovered and splashed all over the papers. 'I did that too.'

'God!' Oli suddenly said, coming to a standstill and raking a hand through his hair. 'I mean—*God!*'

Gemma watched him in silence for a moment. He appeared to be wrestling some inner demons.

'I need to do something different,' he said at last. 'I need a change, because this just isn't working out. I mean—I'm a mess. My life's a bloody mess, and I've got to sort it out.'

Gemma wondered what he was talking about. Did he mean the endless stream of girlfriends he was photographed with? The empty relationships and the never-ending line of airports and hotels where hours were wasted so that a two-hour film could be made?

'I've been thinking—for a while now—is it all worth it—what we do? Does it make us happy? And I'm not just talking about that momentary happiness that comes from a good day's work but real, satisfying happiness that comes from knowing you've made a difference.'

Gemma was a little surprised to hear all this from Oli. 'Well,' she said, 'films can make a difference to people. They're powerful things sometimes. It's one of the reasons I wanted to be an actress. I remember watching *Terms of Endearment* when I was a kid and crying for weeks after, and I couldn't help wondering what it must feel like to be an actress and have such an effect on your audience.'

Oli nodded. 'It was Indiana Jones for me. I wanted to be a hero and make the girls swoon.'

'And you are—you do,' Gemma said, sure a little blush was colouring her face.

'But I'm just not connected to it like I was before, you know? It doesn't give me that same buzz.'

They both stood for a moment, gazing out to sea.

'You've met someone, haven't you?' Gemma said, looking at Oli. 'That's what this is all about, isn't it?'

He didn't answer for a moment. He looked down at the pebbly ground and kicked one boot against the other like a schoolboy.

'You're right,' he said, 'there is somebody.' A tiny smile played around the corners of his mouth. 'And I'm not being fair to her. In fact, I've been an absolute bastard, because my work takes up pretty much all of who I am. If I'm not reading scripts, I'm acting them out or promoting them or travelling from location to location or in meetings with agents and directors. It never ends, and I know I'm sounding like a spoilt kid, and I know this was exactly the life I'd dreamed of all those years ago, watching those Indiana Jones movies, but it's not the same now.' He took a deep breath and held it for a moment before exhaling.

Gemma wondered if she dared to push for more. 'You've been seeing her for a while?'

Oli looked at her and grinned. 'Long enough to know,' he said.

Hm, Gemma thought. That could mean anything. It could be a long-term relationship or a whirlwind romance, and it was more likely to be the latter with Oli.

'That's brilliant, Oli,' she said. 'I'm really happy for you.'

'Thanks,' he said. He gazed at her with his big blue eyes, and Gemma felt a little bit jealous that it wasn't her that his feelings were being channelled towards.

Pull yourself together, she told herself. *Oli Wade Owen is nothing more than a crush. You're not in love with him—not really.*

She looked at him again as they began to walk back towards the town. For years she'd thought he was the perfect hero—the perfect man. With his tall, lean figure, handsome face, and roguish ways, he made for many a happy fantasy, but having worked with him over the last few weeks, Gemma had slowly come to realise that she wasn't in love with him at all. She still found him attractive, which was just as well, because it was much easier to get into the character of Anne Elliot if she actually fancied the man playing Captain Wentworth, but as Gemma Reilly, she was realising that she was looking for more than a handsome face. She wanted somebody she could talk to—really talk to—and somebody who was interested in her. Like Rob.

She frowned. Why had his name popped into her head? The fact that they'd had a couple of conversations didn't mean she was interested in him, but at least he seemed interested in her, whereas Oli clearly had somebody else on his mind.

As they walked back towards Wentworth House, moving through the evening crowds in search of seaside food, Gemma wondered who Oli's girl was. He'd certainly been flirting with Kay at the bed and breakfast. Was she the girl who was about to change his life around?

Something else about what Oli said resonated with her, though. She wasn't happy, was she? Whereas Oli had slowly felt himself moving away from acting as a profession, Gemma was realising that she'd never totally engaged with it. It wasn't right for her, and something had to change.

'And I'm the only person who can change it,' she said to herself.

Chapter 35

KAY WAS IN THE KITCHEN WHEN SHE HEARD THE FRONT DOOR again. She put down the cookery book. The black forest gateaux was far beyond her capabilities anyway, but the lemon drizzle cake had come out a treat.

'Just wait there,' she told the cake before venturing through to the hallway. 'Hello?' she called.

'Hello, my lovely,' a voice said.

'Oli!' she said. 'Come through to the kitchen. 'I've got something for you.'

His eyebrows rose, and he followed her through. 'What's all this, then?'

Kay pulled the rose-festooned tin towards her and prised off the lid to reveal the cake.

'For me?'

'I made it this afternoon,' Kay said, thinking it was probably wise not to mention the help she'd had. 'Would you like some?' She rushed forward to open a cupboard. She reached in for two pretty yellow plates, which she deemed perfect for lemon cake. 'Oli?'

When she turned around, she saw that his eyes were closed and his face looked as pale as the moon.

'You look absolutely drained,' she said, placing the plates on the worktop.

'I *am* absolutely drained.'

'Is there anything I can get you?'

He opened one eye and looked at her. 'What are you offering?'

Kay blushed. 'I was thinking of a drink—maybe a mug of hot chocolate?'

His other eye opened, and he grinned. 'What a sweetheart you are.'

'Is that a yes, then?'

'Don't you have any whisky?'

She shook her head.

'Okay—hot chocolate it is, then.'

'Why don't you go and sit down in the living room? Here,' she said, quickly cutting a thick slice of cake, 'take this with you. Keep up your strength.'

Oli eyed the plate proffered to him and nodded before leaving the kitchen. He hadn't looked at all enthusiastic about the cake. Maybe it wasn't as good as she first thought. *No, he's just tired*, she thought. *He puts all his energy into his work. You can't expect boundless enthusiasm after hours*, she told herself as she got a milk pan out from the cupboard.

As she stirred a generous heap of cocoa powder into the milk and added sugar, she checked her reflection in a metal spatula and decided that a touch of lip gloss wouldn't go amiss. She'd hidden one in the tea towel drawer for such occasions and brought it out. Then, placing the yellow mugs on a tray, she went to find Oli.

He didn't look up when she entered the living room. His eyes were closed, and Kay wondered if he'd fallen asleep on the sofa. It was easy for her to think that he was there as her boyfriend and not as a paying guest. That was the trouble with living in one's workplace, she thought; lines were easily blurred.

'Oli?' she whispered, putting the tray on the coffee table in front of him.

'Tibs?'

Kay frowned. 'It's Kay.'

He opened his eyes and smiled and was instantly forgiven.

'Who's Tibs? A cat?'

Oli didn't answer. 'I forgot where I was there.'

'I've got your chocolate,' she said, handing him a mug. 'It's hot. Be careful.'

'Thanks,' he said.

'Oh, you haven't eaten your cake,' she said, her disappointment undisguised.

Oli cleared his throat and leant forward. 'Was just about to,' he said.

Kay smiled and did her best not to watch him like a hawk as he took his first bite.

'Okay?'

'Delicious,' he said, wolfing down the rest of it.

'I made it for you,' she said and then blushed. She hadn't meant to blurt it out.

'Did you? What a doll you are!'

'So, how was your day?' she asked.

'Do you mind if we don't talk about it?' he said.

'Of course I don't mind,' Kay lied; she'd have loved to have heard all about his day on the set. Instead, she watched as he downed his hot chocolate in one long gulp. The door opened, and Les Miserable came in followed by Teresa and a hobbling Beth.

Kay got up to greet them. 'Can I get you anything?'

Teresa didn't answer, and Beth shook her head and almost crashed into the hallway table. Only Les answered.

'Don't worry about us,' he said. 'We've all eaten.'

'There's some cake if you want it,' Kay said and watched everyone file upstairs. 'Guess not.'

Oli appeared in the doorway. He watched the retreating figures.

'Good night,' he called up after them.

''Night,' Les called.

''Night, Oli, sweetheart,' Beth said, turning around and flashing a scarlet-painted smile at him.

Teresa didn't say anything.

'I need some air,' Oli said. 'You want to come with me?'

Kay nodded. It was an easy decision to make.

⁓

Gemma did not go back to the bed and breakfast after she and Oli left Monmouth Beach. She hung back somewhere along Marine Parade and then doubled back to buy herself an ice cream from a nearby shop that was still open. She knew she should eat something proper, but she couldn't face a crowded pub that evening—not when her mother might make her presence felt at any given moment—so Gemma took her strawberry cornet and sat down on the low wall that overlooked the beach, kicking her shoes off and feeling the sand beneath her toes.

It almost felt as if she were on holiday, a feeling she hadn't had for a number of years now. Not since—when? That terrible trip to Spain with a friend who abandoned her as soon as she clapped eyes on that handsome DJ. Why did so much of a woman's life revolve around men? It was the same in Jane Austen's time, but surely things had moved on since then. After all, a woman didn't need a man anymore. She could make her own way in the world now, so why did modern-day heroines insist on finding a hero? Couldn't a girl be happy on her own?

No, a little voice said. *Life would be pretty dull without them.*

No, it wouldn't, Gemma thought. It would be calm and contented. It would be a place free from impossible crushes and gut-wrenching heartache, and it would allow you to focus on other things, like your work.

But you don't like your work, the little voice said.

Then I'd have more time to find out what it is I really want.

'Hello,' another voice said—one from outside her private thoughts. She looked up, and there stood Rob, a great fat ice cream in his hand. 'Great minds and all that,' he said. 'Is this wall taken?'

Gemma shrugged, and he took it as invitation enough.

'Mint chocolate chip,' he said with a wink. 'Best flavour in the world. What's yours?'

'Strawberry.'

'And I had you down as a double chocolate sort of a girl.'

'Did you?'

He nodded, and Gemma didn't like to ask what made him draw such a conclusion about her taste buds.

'You didn't want to join the others in the pub?' he said, motioning to The Harbour Inn behind them.

Gemma shook her head. 'Too much noise.'

'And it's been a noisy day too, hasn't it? I mean on the set.'

Gemma nodded.

Rob gave a long, low whistle. 'I don't think we'll ever get this film finished,' he said.

'Oh, don't say that!'

His eyebrows rose at her exclamation. 'You know, you're the least likely actress I've ever met.'

'What do you mean?' Gemma said, immediately on the defensive.

He shook his head. 'Don't get me wrong, because I didn't mean you couldn't act—I think you're one of the best actresses we have in this country, and I'd be very surprised if Hollywood didn't snap you up and whisk you away, but—well—it doesn't seem to suit you.'

Gemma frowned. 'I don't know what you're talking about.'

'Yes, you do,' Rob said, completely undeterred by her unwillingness to engage with him on the subject. 'I've been watching you, and—' he held his hand up as he tried to deflect the glare directed at him by such an admission, 'I can't help noticing how unhappy you look. Don't deny it! I've seen you.'

Gemma didn't answer. She didn't know what to say. Acting was nerve-wracking enough without knowing that people were watching you off set as well as on.

'Watch it!' Rob pointed to her ice cream. 'You've got a drip— right there!'

'Where?'

Rob laughed. 'The other side,' he said, pointing to her cone.

Gemma twisted it around, but not before the drip travelled the length of her arm, leaving a brilliant pink squiggle behind.

'Can't take you anywhere, can we?' Rob said, his eyes crinkling in delight.

Gemma opened her handbag, reached in to retrieve a clean tissue, and dabbed at the strawberry trail. 'What a mess!' she said.

'All part of the seaside experience,' Rob said.

Gemma finished tidying herself up and then thought it best that she ate the rest of her ice cream as quickly as possible before there were any further strawberry-related incidents.

'How's the knitting going?' Rob asked, eyeing the contents of her bag. Gemma reached down and closed it. Had he been secretly watching her knitting as well?

He frowned. 'Can't I take a look?'

'It's—it's not finished.'

'Doesn't matter,' he said. 'Let's have a look.'

'No, really, it's not—'

He reached down and opened her bag, reaching inside and lifting out the little pink jacket. 'Well, I never!' he said. 'This is good. Better than my mum's, and she was the best. I had four sisters and two brothers, and my mum knitted all our clothes until we went to college. Actually, she insisted we still wore her clothes then too. I think she would have knitted my sisters' wedding dresses if she thought she could get away with it.'

Gemma laughed.

'You could probably make a living from this, you know,' he said.

Gemma almost choked. She'd been wondering the very same thing herself for ages. She knew it didn't sound very glamorous, and it certainly wasn't on a par with acting, as far as public recognition was concerned, but all Gemma wanted to do was sit at home and knit. She had constant daydreams of the garments she could create and drew little designs on the back of her script. She thought of all the luxurious wools and the glorious colours she could bring together, but could she really make a living from it? 'Teresa likes it too,' she said.

'I'm not surprised,' Rob said. 'It's wonderful. You really should pursue it. Maybe create a website and sell on the Internet. I think it would be great.'

Gemma found that she was smiling. She had never talked to anyone about her secret dreams.

'You should give it a go—if you're serious about it.'

'Oh, I am,' Gemma said.

'I can tell,' he said. 'And I believe you can make a go of anything, if you put your mind to it. It's like your acting. You're really good, Gemma, but I can see your heart isn't in it.'

She stared at him for a moment. He had the most intense eyes she'd ever seen, and they seemed to be staring right into her very soul. Who was this man who seemed to know more about knitting than the *Northanger Abbey* Henry Tilney knew about muslin?

'Look what you've achieved in your acting career so far,' Rob said.

'But this is only my first film,' Gemma protested.

'But you did the TV film too.'

'I know that, but it wasn't very—'

'You're always putting yourself down,' he interrupted, 'but you've achieved so much. What I'm trying to say is that you've done all that without having your heart in it. Just imagine what you could do if you really put your mind to it.'

Gemma realised that she was smiling. 'You really think I could do it?'

'I really do.'

'You're funny,' she said.

'Why?'

'Because you could be getting the pints in with the lads, but you're sitting on a wall eating ice cream and talking about knitted jumpers.'

He leaned towards her a little and smiled. 'I'm with you,' he said. 'And that's all that matters.' Before Gemma could say anything, he leaned forward and kissed her. Gemma was taken completely by surprise, but she didn't pull away. Instead she closed her eyes and kissed him back, the harsh shriek of the gulls filling the air around them.

She could taste the faintest trace of mint chocolate chip, and she wondered if he was enjoying her strawberry-flavoured lips as much.

Chapter 36

THE LIGHT WAS FADING AS KAY AND OLI LEFT WENTWORTH
House and an inky night was creeping in from the sea and
sky. The harbour looked magical at night. The water looked
almost violet. Not for the first time, Kay felt thankful that she
could call Lyme Regis her home. It was a bittersweet feeling,
though, because her good fortune had come at a cost—her
dear friend Peggy's life. She missed Peggy. There were so many
moments in every day that she thought about her dear friend.
How Kay wished she could tell her about Oli! Peggy would love
Oli; Kay knew she would. For a moment, Kay wondered what it
would be like introducing Oli to her. She would have been able
to tell he was the perfect hero, even though her eyesight had been
appalling at the end.

'What are you thinking about?' Oli asked, breaking into her
thoughts.

'A friend of mine,' she said. 'She would have loved you.'

Oli smiled. 'Would have?'

'She died.'

'I'm sorry,' Oli said.

'So am I,' Kay said. 'She was a sweetheart.'

'And so are you,' Oli said, picking up Kay's hand and bringing it to his lips. Kay gasped.

'I'm not in disguise,' she said, realising that they'd come out without a single wig or pair of dark glasses between them. For a moment, Kay thought Oli was going to say that he didn't want their love disguised anymore and he didn't care how many paparazzi might be hiding behind the Cobb wall—he was going to flaunt his love for her in front of the whole world. But he didn't.

'It's pretty dark now,' he said. 'I'd be very surprised if anyone recognised me.'

Kay blinked. He still wasn't happy about being seen with her, was he? But could she really blame him? Imagine what would happen if their relationship were discovered. Kay would be swept up in chaos. It would be a media frenzy in Lyme Regis with journalists camping out on the doorstep of Wentworth House and photographers snapping her when she tried to go shopping. She'd hate that, wouldn't she? That's what Oli was trying to protect her from, wasn't it? He had nothing but her best interests at heart.

As they walked along the front, a magical moon shone high in the sky above the sea and was reflected in it perfectly. The warm night had brought out the crowds, and happy voices were heard wafting from the pubs and the restaurants along the front, but Oli was right—nobody seemed to be paying them much attention. They were just another couple enjoying the night air.

Like with most people, the pull of the Cobb was inevitable, and they soon found themselves climbing the steps onto its stone bulk. Kay sighed with pleasure. In her short time as a resident, she had climbed onto the Cobb many times and always got a thrill. She loved looking back across the harbour from its height and spying the yellow walls of her beloved home. She adored the almost Mediterranean view across the bay to Golden Cap and the equally magnificent view of the Undercliff, which stretched into verdant Devon. There also was the uninterrupted view of the sea ahead of them, but all this was muted in deep blues, for the sun was long gone.

Oli had his hands in the back pockets of his jeans, and Kay wished he were holding her hand again. Still, it was amazing being there right then, walking along the Cobb with Captain Wentworth.

You must stop thinking of him like that! her inner voice said.

But I can't help it, Kay thought. *Persuasion* was one of her favourite novels, and here she was with its hero.

But he isn't the hero. He's just an actor.

I know. I know! Let me fantasise for a moment, won't you? Kay glanced at Oli. He was staring out to sea. She wished she could read his thoughts, but she didn't interrupt him by asking him questions.

It was just amazing to be walking along Jane Austen's Cobb. It wasn't really Jane Austen's Cobb—it was an ancient monument, after all, but wouldn't Austen fans always think of it as being Jane's? A few literary traitors might think of the Cobb as belonging to John Fowles, but Jane got there first, and nobody would ever be able to rival her portrayal of it in fiction.

Kay loved that she was following the same curve of stone and seeing the same views that Jane Austen would have seen. What had she thought when she was walking here? Kay wondered. Had she known she would write about it one day and set one of her most moving love stories here? Had Captain Wentworth swept by her on her visit to Lyme? Kay remembered that Jane had visited in 1803 and 1804 but hadn't written *Persuasion* until 1816, which meant a gap of twelve or thirteen years. The place had obviously stayed with her during those years of absence, weaving a wondrous spell in her memory until she was ready to write her story.

Before Kay knew it, they had walked right to the end of the Cobb.

'It's a beautiful evening, isn't it?' she said as they looked out across the rocks into the flat expanse of endless sea.

'What's that?' Oli said, turning around.

'I said it's a beautiful night.'

Oli looked up at the moon and nodded, as if he were seeing it for the first time.

'You've been miles away,' she said. 'What are you thinking about?'

He frowned. 'Women always ask that, don't they?'

'I don't know,' Kay said. 'No woman's ever asked me that.'

He grinned. 'You're lovely,' he said. 'Shall we head back? You must be cold.'

'I'm not,' Kay said, trying not to betray herself with a shiver. There was a little bit of a breeze coming from the sea, but she couldn't bear the thought of heading back already.

'Come on,' he said. 'Can't have my girl turning into a block of ice.'

The phrase *my girl* was enough to heat any girl up—even a half-frozen one—and she turned around for the walk back without a single word of protestation.

When they reached the famous steps, which were thought to be those that Jane Austen's characters had descended, Oli led the way and held his hand out to her to follow.

'You're not going to jump me down?' Kay teased.

'I will if you want me to.'

Kay paused and giggled. 'Go on, then!'

Oli reached the bottom and held his arms open wide for her.

'No running back up them, though,' he said. 'We don't want you doing a Louisa Musgrove.'

'Or a Beth Jenkins!'

'Indeed,' Oli said.

Kay could feel her heart thud-thudding as she launched herself into the air, her hair flying out behind her. It took only the space of a second, but for Kay, the moment lasted a lifetime, and she almost regretted the moment that Oli caught her in his arms, wishing that she could suspend time and be forever travelling through the air towards him.

'Was that good enough for you?' he asked when she finally came down to earth.

'It was wonderful!' Kay said, laughing.

'You're a lot lighter than Beth,' he said.

'Oh! Don't let her hear you say such a thing!'

Oli laughed. 'You really are lovely,' he said.

'You keep saying that,' Kay said.

'Because it's true.'

Kay wondered if he really was telling the truth. After all, he was used to dating the world's most beautiful women. How could she hope to compete with them? She wanted to believe him, though, so she gave in to the moment as he moved closer to her, his lips descending towards her own.

Kay couldn't remember the last time she had been kissed like that. She knew that no kiss in the history of kisses—whether real or fictional—could compare to it, because she had been thinking about it for so long and was already in love with the idea of being kissed by Oli. He couldn't go wrong. Not that he would go wrong, of course.

The old stone wall of the Cobb was cold behind Kay, but Oli was warm. The pressure of his body pushed firmly against hers, but alas, the moment couldn't last forever, and Kay's eyes slowly opened as his mouth left hers.

'Well,' Oli said, 'I wasn't expecting that.'

'I hope you mean that in a good way,' Kay said.

'I do!' he said. 'I mean, I hadn't banked on this happening at all.'

'Oh, you must have a girl in every port,' Kay said. 'Isn't that what they say about actors?'

'I think that's what they say about sailors.'

'That's right,' Kay said with a laugh. 'Actors have a girl in every town. They don't like to limit themselves to seaside locations.'

'You seem to have a low opinion of actors,' he said.

'No,' she said. 'I'm just being realistic about what this is.'

'And what is it?' he asked.

Kay fell silent. She didn't like to speculate about what this was. They'd shared only a single kiss, but she was already planning their honeymoon and had named half of their four children. Wasn't that always the way with women? Wasn't there a wonderful quote from *Pride and Prejudice*? 'A lady's imagination is very rapid; it jumps from admiration to love, from love to matrimony in a moment.' Kay knew it was certainly true of herself.

'This,' Oli continued when Kay didn't answer him, 'is a wonderful surprise.'

Kay smiled, but she wondered if wonderful surprises ended as soon the film was finished shooting.

Surely not, she thought. Not after a kiss like that.

They walked back along the harbour, and Kay felt as if she were floating as they passed the kiosks and beach huts. A light breeze tickled her skin and her hair flew back behind her. She gazed up at the moon. She would never be able to look at it again without thinking of this moment—this precious moment with Oli. Would he think of it too? she wondered.

They climbed the steps up to the higher level of Marine Parade, and Kay looked up at Wentworth House.

'I think we've been spotted,' Kay said when she saw a curtain twitch. 'That's Teresa's room.'

'Is it, indeed?' Oli said. 'Then she shouldn't be spying on people.'

'She won't mind, will she?'

'Why would she mind?' Oli asked.

'I just thought—well—you always seem to be getting into trouble with her.'

'What I do on my own time is my business.'

'Oh, I'm business, am I?'

He grinned. 'Of course not,' he said. 'You're pure pleasure.' He took her hand in his, brought it to his lips, and kissed it.

They entered the bed and breakfast. It was quiet. The little lamp glowed warmly on the hallway table, but nobody was about.

'Come here,' Oli said, closing the space between them and kissing her again. 'Kay, Kay, Kay,' he whispered, and for a dizzying moment, Kay wondered if he was going to invite her to his room. He didn't. A part of her felt disappointed, but she knew it would have been oh, so wrong—unprofessional was the word. She was sure there was some unwritten rule about bed and breakfast owners not sleeping with guests.

'Good night, Kay,' he whispered at last.

'Good night,' she whispered back, watching him as he walked up the stairs. Her heart was still thudding, and she knew no amount of hot chocolate would be able to calm her. At least she knew that she'd be likely to dream the sweetest of dreams that night.

Chapter 37

'He's been messing around with Kay, I'm sure of it,' Sophie said.

'Come away from the window,' Gemma said, promptly walking over to it herself and peering out into the night. 'Where are they?'

As soon as the words were out, they heard the front door open downstairs.

'They've just arrived back,' Sophie said, 'but I bet you anything they've been to the Cobb, and I'm sure they were holding hands.'

Gemma returned to the bed and picked up her knitting. 'I don't think it's any of our business what they're doing.'

'Not even if it's wrong?'

'Why's it wrong?' Gemma asked.

'Because there's no way that relationship can work out.'

'Why not? I think you're giving Oli really bad press. You know, he was just talking to me before—'

'What about?' Sophie interrupted, leaving the window and flinging herself down on the bed opposite Gemma.

'You mustn't say anything to anyone.'

Sophie nodded.

'But he's thinking of giving up acting.'

'Really?'

'There's someone he wants to spend more time with,' Gemma said.

'Kay? He's giving up acting for Kay?'

'Well, he didn't mention her by name.'

Sophie frowned. 'But he's only known her for a few days.'

'That doesn't matter, does it? Some people know really quickly when they fall in love.'

'I suppose,' Sophie said. 'And it did happen for me once. We'd only known each other for six hours, but I knew he was the right man for me.'

Gemma smiled. 'I didn't know you were in a relationship.'

'Oh, I'm not,' Sophie said. 'And it lasted only three weeks, but they were the most wonderful three weeks of my life.'

There was a squeak in the floorboard of the landing.

'It's Oli,' Sophie said, springing up off the bed and tearing across the room to the door. Gemma watched, horrified, as Sophie removed the key and peered out onto the landing. 'He's alone,' she said, her voice full of disappointment.

Gemma tutted. 'What did you expect?'

'I thought they might come upstairs together,' she said.

Gemma returned to her knitting pattern. 'I doubt that will happen. They wouldn't want to risk being caught.'

∾⭗

At shortly after eleven o'clock, there was a knock on Kay's bedroom door.

She'd been rereading one of her favourite scenes towards the end of *Persuasion* when Captain Wentworth and Anne meet and 'the evening seemed to be made up of exquisite moments.' She loved that scene and couldn't wait to see how it would be played out in the new film version with Oli and Gemma.

She put the book on her bedside table and swung her legs off the bed. She was wearing a white knee-length nightgown in *broderie anglaise*, and her hair was loose and newly washed and smelled of strawberry shampoo. Since becoming the owner of a bed and breakfast, she'd thought it better to ditch her manly nightshirt and invest in something a bit more seemly to wear in case she was called on in the middle of the night. It was just as well that she had.

It's probably Beth wanting something for that ankle of hers, Kay thought as she opened her door. But it wasn't Beth.

'Oli?' Kay said when she saw his handsome face. 'Is everything okay? Do you need anything?'

'Yes,' he said, a boyish smile spreading over his face. 'There is something I need.'

Chapter 38

K AY WOKE UP TO THE SHRIEK OF SEAGULLS AND LAY DAZED FOR a moment, staring up at the ceiling. The light in the room was dazzling, coming straight in from the sea. She turned over in bed and faced the other pillow—the pillow that Oli had slept on last night. He was gone.

'Mustn't give the gossips any fuel,' he'd said, taking her in his arms one last time and kissing her before leaving, and Kay knew he was right. She could just imagine how awkward it would be if Beth or Teresa found out. No, no. She mustn't interrupt Oli's work. She could wait. He'd be finished filming soon, and then they could tell the whole world that they were in love.

Getting up, she drew back the curtains and gazed across the pebbled beach out to sea. The sun was bright and the sea was almost turquoise. How she loved seeing its ever-changing colours. It was never the same for long—one minute it could be a stormy grey, and the next a perfect cerulean, but Kay would always remember the exact shade it was that day, and it would be her favourite.

After washing and dressing and applying a quick hint of makeup, Kay went downstairs and made a start on breakfast for the hungry actors.

I bet you won't be doing this for much longer.

Cooking breakfast—running a B&B. It's not the sort of life for the wife of a famous actor, is it?

Kay shook her head. She knew she mustn't think such thoughts. It was dangerous. It was too early in their relationship, yet she couldn't help hoping. She couldn't help dreaming—it was her default setting for coping with a cruel world. If she wasn't dreaming of Mr Darcy, she was dreaming of some appalling man who would be sure to break her heart. But Oli wasn't going to break her heart. He'd told her how lovely she was last night—over and over again.

But he didn't say he loved you.

Kay stopped cracking eggs for a moment. He hadn't said he loved her.

'But I didn't expect him to,' she whispered.

Didn't you? Didn't you really? But you told him you loved him.

I know, she thought, and I shouldn't have done that. 'Men get spooked by such things.'

'By what things?' a voice behind her asked.

Kay turned and saw Teresa. 'Morning,' she said, blushing at having been observed talking to herself.

'Morning,' Teresa said, although the word might well have been *mourning*, for the mood she seemed to be in.

'All ready for another day's filming?' Kay asked, doing her best to be cheerful in the face of such misery.

Teresa shook her head. 'We're doing something different today. Some publicity shots along the Cobb and a few little pieces here and there for the DVD extras. Those sorts of things are expected nowadays,' she said as if she took no pleasure in it herself. 'But we're done with filming now. In Dorset, anyway. Got to get to Bath next.'

'You're done?'

Teresa nodded. 'I didn't think we were going to be on schedule, but I'm actually quite happy with the last few days' shooting.'

'Who's happy?' another voice said, and Beth hobbled into view. 'You're happy, Teresa? I never thought I'd hear you admit to such a thing,' Beth teased.

'And neither did I,' Teresa said.

'So we're off to Bath?' Beth asked.

'First thing tomorrow—if we get today right.'

'Tomorrow?' Kay said. 'But you're all booked in for three more nights.'

'That's okay—you'll still be paid,' Teresa said.

Kay watched, unable to speak, as Teresa and Beth left for the dining room. They were leaving tomorrow. Did Oli know? Kay was just about to drop everything and run up to Oli's room, but Teresa called through.

'Breakfast nearly ready, Kay?'

'Yes,' Kay replied with a frown. Was it her imagination, or did Teresa sound particularly abrupt with her?

'I need to get out of here as soon as possible,' Teresa added.

'No problem,' Kay shouted back, and then a thought occurred to her. Perhaps Teresa really had seen her and Oli outside the B&B the previous night. Or—worse—what if she'd heard them together later on? Kay's face blanched at the thought. Not only was it unprofessional of her, but also Teresa was well-known for keeping business and pleasure totally separate. The last thing she'd want was an on-set romance with her leading man.

Kay sighed and decided to get back to work in the kitchen, although she longed to join the cast in the dining room and hear their plans for the day ahead. Still, she did her best to eavesdrop and heard the occasional snippet.

'Yes, of course we'll need you, Beth.'

'Because my ankle is much better today. I feel I could even take Louisa's jump again.'

'Oh, no you don't! We'll just set you up in a nice deck chair, and you can talk about your role.'

Kay took the pots of tea and coffee through and saw that Gemma, Sophie, and Les Miserable had joined them. Sophie was looking as buoyant as ever, but Gemma looked tired—as if she'd been up half the night too. Or maybe she was looking wearisome because her mother was still in town. Kay had heard what a nightmare Kim Reilly could be. But where was Oli? There was no sign of him yet.

'Kay?' Teresa said, making the name sound like a poison-tipped arrow.

'Yes?'

'Eggs?'

'Coming,' Kay said.

She dashed back through to the kitchen, quickly heating some butter in a pan.

She served breakfast in record-breaking time and received a curt nod from Teresa when Oli entered the dining room.

'Good morning!' he said. Kay turned to see him, smiling as she took in his big blue eyes and his mass of blond hair, which hadn't been combed through since his shower.

'Sort your hair out, Oli,' Teresa barked as he sat at the table opposite her. 'You're on first this morning.'

'And a very good morning to you too,' he replied, making Kay smile. Honestly, how could anyone bark at dear Oli when he looked so cute? Kay cleared a couple of empty glasses from the table, doing her best to catch Oli's eye, but he didn't seem to notice her as he buttered a piece of toast.

'My tea's cold,' Les Miserable said, shoving his cup at Kay.

'I'll get some more,' Kay said, willing Oli to look up before she left the room, but he didn't.

The next twenty minutes flew by in a flurry of activity. Breakfast was finished and bodies tore up and down the stairs in preparation for the day ahead. Kay bustled in and out of the kitchen, trying to catch Oli, but she wasn't having much luck, until he stood in the hallway—the last to leave.

'Oli!' she cried.

'Kay. You all right?'

'You didn't talk to me at breakfast,' she said. She hadn't meant to sound accusatory, but her words had blurted out.

'How could I, with Teresa—with everyone sitting there?'

'I know,' Kay said. 'But I wanted to talk to you.'

'What about?' he asked.

She looked at him. 'You're leaving.'

'Yes,' he said. 'Teresa just told me. It's brilliant, isn't it?'

Kay frowned. She couldn't see anything brilliant about it. 'But I thought yesterday had gone badly. You said—'

'I thought it had too, but evidently Teresa got what she wanted. That's the way of the film business. You never really know what you're going to get day to day.'

'So this is your last day in Lyme?'

'Looks like it,' Oli said with a big grin. 'And I must say, I'm looking forward to Bath.'

Kay felt wounded by his response. 'It's all happened so quickly.'

He nodded. 'We might finish the whole thing on time at this rate, and heaven knows I could use a break after all this.'

A break! Kay heard the phrase and interpreted it. 'So you'll be back?'

'Back where?' he asked.

'Oli? Where the hell are you?' It was Teresa's voice, and she soon appeared in the hallway. 'We need you—*now!*'

'My lord and master calls,' he said. Neither Teresa nor Kay smiled. 'Gotta go,' he said to Kay.

'But Oli—'

He didn't stop. He turned around and threw a quick wink in her direction before following Teresa down Marine Parade towards the Cobb.

Chapter 39

ADAM HAD DONE HIS BEST TO PUT KAY OUT OF HIS MIND. What was the point of declaring oneself to a woman when her heart belonged to another man? It was useless, and he had to persuade Nana Craig that it was useless too. He and Kay were never meant to be, and the sooner he put the whole thing behind him, the better.

He busied himself with his role as producer as well as writer of a new screenplay—a lesser-known Thomas Hardy novel that would make a beautiful adaptation and be absolutely perfect for another Dorset-based production. He tried not to think about Kay. He did fairly well too and had been sleeping soundly later that night after a solid day's work, when the phone rang.

It was Tony Glass, a producer friend in California who was looking for an English actress for a film he was involved in.

'It's going to be huge,' he told the bleary-eyed Adam. 'Think *Dr Zhivago* set in New England.'

Adam became instantly awake. It sounded like an interesting concept, and he was intrigued.

'But we can't find anyone for the lead. We need someone English—proper English—not one of these American girls with a fake Oxbridge accent. But she can't be too well-known, you know?'

'Tony, I may have just the girl for you,' Adam told him.

He hadn't been able to sleep after that. He'd tossed and turned until his bedding was tied up in knots, and he finally got up and flung his bedroom windows open, breathing in the soft spring air. He was anxious for Gemma, because he knew a little something about her personality. She was one of the few actresses he knew who wouldn't automatically jump at a chance of appearing in a Hollywood film.

'What will she say?' he whispered into the night, but only a distant owl replied. He'd have to wait until the next day to find out the real answer, so he got up as soon as he could, driving into Lyme Regis and parking as close as possible to Wentworth House. It was early, and he thought everyone would still be in the bed and breakfast, so he made his way along the seafront, gazing up into a perfect blue sky and listening to the ear-piercing shrieks of the seagulls.

Not only was Adam anxious about Gemma's reaction to his proposal, he was also anxious about seeing Kay again. He might have persuaded his head that she was in love with another man, but he couldn't persuade his heart to listen.

Reaching the bright blue door, Adam took a deep breath and knocked. He didn't have to wait long before it was answered.

'Oh, it's you,' Kay said in greeting, her face glum and gloomy.

Adam's eyebrows rose. He hadn't been expecting a warm embrace, but he'd hoped for a slightly kinder reception.

'All right if I come in?' he asked.

'I suppose,' Kay said.

'Are you okay?' he asked. He had promised himself that he

wouldn't get involved with this woman, when it was so clear that he meant nothing to her, but seeing her sad eyes and sorrowful face, he had to know if she was all right.

'I'm fine,' she said.

'You look upset,' he said. 'Is something worrying you?'

'Adam, what are you doing here?' she snapped. 'You're always hanging around.'

Adam looked stunned for a moment, not quite knowing how to respond. 'I've come to see Gemma,' he said.

'She left with others ages ago.'

'I didn't know that.'

'She's probably at the Cobb. They've all gone there, okay?' she said sharply.

'Okay,' he said, turning to go. She'd managed to put him in such a bad mood that he almost slammed the door behind him, but instead, he turned to take one last look at her and saw that she was running up the stairs. He took a step back into the hallway.

'Don't be a fool,' he said to himself. 'She doesn't want you here. She doesn't want you at all.'

And so he left.

'My head is throbbing!' Kim Reilly told her daughter as they sat at a table outside The Harbour Inn. Gemma had been waiting on the Cobb until she was needed for her DVD extra piece, 'A Day in the Life of a Heroine,' when her mother grabbed her and frog-marched her to breakfast.

'I've already eaten,' Gemma said.

'You'll keep me company,' her mother told her, so they were sitting together looking out over the stretch of sandy beach as the first day-trippers set up with towels and windbreaks. 'I'd forgotten about these early mornings on set.'

'It's not the early morning,' Gemma said. 'It was the late night filled with too much alcohol.'

'Don't shout at me.'

'I'm not shouting,' Gemma said. 'Anyway, what are you doing getting up so early? You're not needed today, are you?'

'Teresa wants me to be in the extras—talking about the acting life.'

Gemma tried not to react. When was her mother going home? She'd follow them to Bath too, wouldn't she? Oh, why on earth had Teresa encouraged her?

'I know what you're thinking,' Kim said.

'What? I'm not thinking anything,' Gemma said, terrified, lest her mother had somehow read her mind.

'You're thinking you wish you could be more like me.'

Gemma frowned. 'What do you mean?'

'I'm not past it yet, you know.'

'I didn't say you were.'

'And you're jealous,' Kim said. 'I can see it in your face. I know the way your mind works. You've always been jealous of me.'

'Mother, I haven't! How can you say such a thing?'

'You've always wanted my confidence—my *je ne sais quois*, and that's a fact.'

'I'm not going to argue,' Gemma said.

Kim nodded, taking it as a sign that she was right.

Gemma gazed out towards the sandy beach and the sea. She watched as a gull swooped down and landed near a day-tripper who was sitting on a wall eating a bacon butty. The gull looked far more comfortable than the day-tripper.

Gemma saw a familiar figure walking towards The Harbour Inn. 'Adam?' she said. 'Adam!'

He stopped and turned to look at her. 'Just the very person I was after.' He joined them on the terrace, pulled up a chair, and sat down. 'Good morning, Kim. How lovely to see you.'

Kim's face brightened at Adam's attention, and Gemma noticed that her mother's bosom suddenly swelled up and out and her eyelashes batted for England.

'I was wondering if I could talk to you, Gemma. I've got some news.'

Gemma looked at her mother in the hope that she might remember she had to be somewhere else.

'Oh, don't worry about me,' Kim said. 'We don't have any secrets, do we, Gemma?'

Gemma sighed. 'Of course not,' she said politely, and Adam cleared his throat to begin.

'I've been talking to someone,' he began. 'Someone in Hollywood. He's a producer friend, and we've worked on a couple of projects in the past. Anyway, he's looking for an actress—a good one. She's got to be English, and he wanted someone yet to make the big time.'

'Ha! That's our Gemma,' Kim chipped in.

'What's his name?' Gemma asked.

'Tony Glass.'

Gemma nodded. The name certainly rang a bell.

'I think it's going to be big. A huge summer hit,' Adam continued. 'This could really open some doors for you, Gemma. Hollywood isn't an easy one to crack, but this sounds like just the sort of production to do it for you.'

Kim's mouth was hanging open in wonder, but Gemma's was a thin line across her face.

'Auditions are next month in LA. You'll be finished with *Persuasion* then. You could fly straight out there. He's dying to see you. I hope you don't mind, but I sang your praises a little bit.' Adam grinned.

There was a moment's silence before Gemma spoke. 'Gosh, Adam—I don't know what to say.'

'Say *yes!* That's all you have to say,' Adam told her.

'I didn't expect this.'

'Well, you should have. You've done such a brilliant job here, and word gets around quickly, you know.'

'It's so kind that you put me forward for this.'

'It has nothing to do with kindness,' Adam said. 'It's simply about knowing talent when I see it. So what do you say?'

Gemma took a deep breath. 'What do I say? Gosh.'

'Yes, but *after* gosh?'

'After gosh,' Gemma said, 'comes... sorry.'

Adam frowned. 'What do you mean?'

'I can't, Adam. I really can't.'

He didn't look happy. 'Is this some crisis of confidence here? Because if it is, I can help you get over that.'

'It's not that,' she said.

'Then what?'

'I'm giving it up,' she said, and as soon as the words were out of her mouth, she felt wonderfully light. 'I'm giving up acting.'

'You can't be serious?' he said.

'I've never been more serious about anything in my life.'

Kim Reilly's mouth dropped open and her eyes saucered in absolute horror at her daughter's words. 'Are you crazy?' she blurted across the table.

'No,' Gemma said. 'I'm perfectly sane—maybe for the first

time in my life. I'm giving up acting. There—I've said it.' She gave a funny little laugh. 'Wow! That was so easy. I can't think why I haven't done it before.'

'What do you mean, *before*? Before what? You've only done two films!' Kim said.

'Mother, I've been acting since you took me to ballet class when I was four years old. I had to pretend I liked it to please you, and I've been acting ever since—all the way through drama school and beyond.'

'Of course you were acting at drama school,' Kim said. 'That's what they were teaching you to do.'

'But I also had to pretend that I was happy, when I wasn't.' Gemma looked at the appalled expression on her mother's face and felt a little sorry for her. 'Please try to understand,' she said. 'Acting was more your dream than mine. I just went along with it to please you.'

'That's rubbish!' Kim said, spitting the word out in anger.

Gemma calmly shook her head. 'No,' she said. 'I just didn't know what other options were available.'

'Oh, and now you do, I suppose.'

'No,' Gemma said, 'but I'm going to find out.'

'You're making a huge mistake,' Kim said. 'And don't expect me to pick up the pieces when you realise what you've done.'

'I'm not expecting you to pick up any pieces. I can take care of myself,' Gemma said. 'You might not have noticed, but I'm a grown woman now, I have a mind of my own, and I'm not going to be bullied by you any longer.'

'Bullied?' Kim's tight eyes narrowed even tighter.

'Yes, you're a terrible bully.'

'Gemma! How dare—'

'You've *always* been a bully, but I'm not going to put up with it any longer. It stops now, Mum. Right now!'

Kim stood, her chair scraping harshly behind her. 'I'm not staying to listen to any more of this stupidity. Name-calling your own mother and turning down the best offer you could possibly receive as an actress! You've gone mad. But you'll have changed your mind by the end of the day, no doubt. You always were fickle, Gemma.'

Gemma's mouth dropped open at the blatant lie, and she watched as her mother stormed off towards the Cobb. She turned to look at Adam. His face was frozen in shock.

'Did that really just happen?' he asked.

Gemma nodded. 'I think it did.'

'And you're the same girl I saw shaking with nerves just a few days ago?'

She nodded again. 'It was time,' she said. 'Time I stood up to my mother and time I found out what I really want to do with my life.'

Adam's face broke into a smile. He leaned across the table and took her hands in his. 'Good for you, Gemma,' he said. 'Although I shall miss you. There aren't many like you in this business.'

She smiled back at him, and then, sensing someone behind her, turned to see Rob standing there.

'Rob!' she said.

He didn't reply, although it was quite clear that he was looking at her. Gemma realised that Adam was still holding her hands.

Chapter 40

KAY IMMEDIATELY FELT ROTTEN ABOUT THE WAY SHE HAD treated Adam. He hadn't deserved it, and she ran back down the stairs and tried to call him back, but he didn't hear her.

'Men!' she cried. 'Bloody, bloody men!' She returned to the B&B and slammed the blue door behind her, stomping up the stairs to the privacy of her bedroom. The dishes could wait. The bedrooms could wait. Sitting down on her window seat, she looked out across the sea towards the Cobb. Oli would be down there, charming everybody as usual, everyone except Teresa.

'And then he'll be gone,' she said, pulling out the sketch she had made of him.

Kay's head was still spinning at the thought. Was Oli really going to leave Lyme Regis? Would he ever come back or ask her to go with him? He had said nothing to her. He had made love to her, but he hadn't talked about the future; he hadn't talked about *them*.

Kay stood up suddenly, knowing that she had to take action. She couldn't wait a moment longer. If she did, Oli would be gone, and she would be nothing more than a distant memory. She had to find out if he had any feelings for her at all, and if so, did they have a future together?

When Gemma rejoined the film set, Rob had disappeared. She looked everywhere for him but couldn't see him, and then it was time to do her piece to camera.

Someone had positioned a stripy deck chair in front of the Cobb, and Gemma was asked a series of questions about her experience playing a Jane Austen heroine. It was all fairly straightforward, and she didn't have time to get nervous, because she kept thinking about Rob and the look on his face when he saw her with Adam. What must he be thinking?

Finally, her piece was finished and she was free to go. She should have been walking on air at having made her decision to leave acting and at finding the courage to stand up to her mother at long last, but she wasn't thinking about those things. All that mattered was that she found Rob.

She walked along the seafront by the kiosks that were filling the air with the scent of hot vinegary chips, and her tummy gave a rumble. She realised how long ago breakfast had been. As an actress, she had been wary of what she'd eaten over the years, but she smiled at the thought of being able to eat anything she wanted to now. She didn't have to worry constantly about her waistline and could enjoy a bag of chips when she felt like it, but not just yet. She still had the last few scenes to film in Bath, and she couldn't have Anne Elliot piling on the pounds, could she?

Leaving the tempting smells behind her, she walked on, and then she saw him sitting on the low wall overlooking the sandy beach. He was holding a polystyrene cup and sipping from it slowly.

'Rob?' she said quietly before sitting on the wall beside him.

Rob looked up from his coffee. 'Hello,' he said.

'You ran away from me,' Gemma said. 'And I couldn't find you.'

'I didn't run away,' he said.

'Didn't you?'

'I just didn't want to interrupt you and Adam.'

'But you wouldn't have been interrupting anything,' Gemma assured him. 'We were just talking.'

'Were you?'

'Yes!'

'Because you looked very much like a couple to me.'

Gemma shook her head. 'Why does everybody keep thinking that?'

'Maybe everybody's right.'

'But they're not right. Not at all! Can I tell you something? Adam's wonderful, and we made friends immediately. I guess we're quite similar characters. He's as shy as I am, and we find life on a film set hard at times. But we're not a couple, even though Kay at the bed and breakfast has been trying to push us together.' Gemma gave a little laugh, but Rob didn't join in. She sighed. 'You want to know the truth? It's strange but I feel as if I want to tell you everything.'

Rob looked at her and didn't try to stop her from continuing.

'When I found out I was doing this film, I was really nervous, because I knew I would be acting opposite Oli. It's not very original of me—I'm not the first and I certainly won't be the last actress to have a crush on her leading man, but my crush on Oli began at drama school, and this whole experience of filming with him has been strange.'

'You're in love with Oli?' Rob said.

'Listen to me,' Gemma said. 'I thought I was for a while. I mean, most men would look good dressed as Captain Wentworth, and Oli quite took my breath away, but I soon realised that although he's a wonderful hero, he's not the right man for me.'

'No?'

'No,' she said. 'Not at all. I was just dazzled by him, that's all. But then I got to know him and—don't get me wrong—he's a great guy, but I was beginning to realise that I was falling for somebody quite different.'

Rob frowned, his forehead puckering like an adorable puppy's. 'Adam?'

'No!' Gemma cried in frustration. 'You!'

For a moment, Rob looked at her as if he hadn't heard her properly.

'Say something,' Gemma said. 'I don't want to be the only one sitting on this wall baring my soul.'

Rob's eyes widened and he laughed. 'You know how I feel about you. I fell head over heels the first time I saw you shaking with nerves in rehearsals.'

'Oh, don't!'

'Before that, even. I think I was in love with you in that film *Into the Night*, although you didn't notice me at all.'

'I can't think how I overlooked you.'

'Neither can I,' Rob said, his eyes sparkling. 'I mean, I'm witty and charming, handsome and—'

Gemma gave him a playful punch, and they both laughed.

'So what were you and Adam talking about?' Rob asked.

'We were talking about Hollywood,' Gemma said, suddenly serious. 'Adam wanted me to audition for a film, but I said no.'

Rob's eyes narrowed. 'You said no?'

'Yes, and I told him that I wouldn't be acting anymore. I told my mother, too. I told her a lot of things, actually.'

'Really?'

Gemma nodded.

'I would have loved to have seen that,' he said with a tiny smile.

'I wish you had. I still can't quite believe I did it.'

'Wow,' Rob said. 'So there's no going back now?'

'I don't think so,' Gemma said. 'At least, I hope not.'

'What are you going to do?'

'I don't know,' Gemma said. 'I might open a knitting shop somewhere in Dorset. I might get married and have hundreds of children.'

Rob's eyebrows rose at her declaration.

Gemma laughed at the expression on his face. 'I don't know what I'm going to do. I think I might work it out as I go along.'

Rob nodded and picked up her hand. 'That sounds great,' he said. 'And may I keep you company whilst you're working things out?'

Gemma smiled a big, broad smile. 'I'm counting on it,' she said.

~~⌒~~

Kay didn't see Anne Elliot on a wall overlooking the beach and kissing a member of the crew. Kay's eyes focussed straight ahead to where she could see filming taking place along the Cobb. She was going to miss the little village that the cast and crew had created in Lyme Regis. Life was bound to feel a little dull once they departed, and she'd never be able to walk along the seafront without expecting to see them all filming around the harbour. Wentworth House would seem empty without them. How could any other guests possibly fill the gap that the actors would leave?

As she reached the Lower Cobb, she caught the eye of Sophie, who looked stunning in her Henrietta Musgrove costume. She ushered Kay through the security rope and gave her shoulder a squeeze.

'Gosh, it's chaos here,' Sophie said. 'Nobody seems to know what they're doing.'

'What are they meant to be doing?'

'We're meant to be doing all these DVD extras and publicity photos, but everything's going wrong. Some mad tourist just ran on to the set and attacked Oli.'

'Oh, God! Is he all right?'

'Oh, yes! He loved it,' Sophie said. 'Although the pair of them almost toppled into the sea. She was quite determined to kiss him. Teresa went mad, of course, and now Gemma's disappeared. Seems she's got something going on with one of the guys from the lighting department.'

'Really?'

'I can't think what's going on there,' Sophie said shaking her head. 'And rumour has it that she's giving up acting.'

'What?'

'Kim Reilly turned up ranting and raving and said that Gemma had gone mad and that she was having nothing more to do with her.'

'Gosh,' Kay said.

'Exactly,' Sophie agreed. 'Then that nanny turned up with Teresa's daughter.'

'Annabel?'

Sophie nodded. 'And Oli disappeared with the child and came back with ice cream all down Captain Wentworth's jacket. Teresa was furious—*again!* Oli had to have a costume change, which held everything up, and now they can't decide what they're doing. He's been marching up and down the Cobb for ages.'

Kay looked up at him from the Lower Cobb, willing him to look in her direction, but he didn't seem to be aware of anything around him.

'What's the matter with Oli?' Beth said, pushing in between

Kay and Sophie and gazing up at Oli, who continued to prowl along the Cobb.

'He's got on the wrong side of Teresa again,' Sophie said.

'Has he ever been on the right side?' Beth asked. 'Teresa's got no respect for him. She treats him appallingly.'

'No she doesn't,' Sophie said. 'He's the kind of guy you've got to keep in check.'

Beth tutted. 'Everyone's so mean to Oli.'

'Oh, dear,' Sophie said, looking up at Oli on the Cobb. 'Something's brewing.'

The three of them watched as Teresa stalked towards Oli. Her face was full of thunder, and her eyes looked small and stony.

'What's he done now?' Sophie asked.

'Poor Oli,' Beth said.

'Shush!' Sophie said, 'I want to hear this.'

Kay did too, except she was a little afraid. There was something in Oli's face that she couldn't quite read. He looked anxious and furious, but there was something else too, something that looked as if it were about to leap out and make itself known to the world.

'Why do you do it?' Teresa shouted. 'Why do you always do that to me?'

'What are you talking about?'

'You *know* what I'm talking about. It's always the same when we're on location. You always go and—'

'Don't be so melodramatic.'

'I'm not being dramatic. I'm being honest, which is more than you're being.'

Oli ran a hand through his hair. 'You don't get it, do you?'

'What's there to get, Oli? You are who you are, and you'll never change, and there's nothing I can say that will make a difference, is there?'

'Oh, you think I can't change, do you? Is that what you think? Well, you're wrong. I can't tell you how wrong you are!'

Teresa turned and half-walked, half-ran along the Cobb.

Oli watched her go, a look of anguish on his pale face. 'Tibs!' he suddenly cried.

'Tibs?' Sophie repeated incredulously.

'Tibs,' Kay said. She'd heard that name before, hadn't she? When Oli had woken up in the living room, he'd said that name. He'd been dreaming about someone called Tibs or else had expected or wished that Tibs were there when he woke up. And now Tibs was here in Lyme Regis, because Tibs was Teresa.

Teresa stopped, and everyone watched as Oli ran the length of the Cobb to where she was standing.

'What's going on?' Beth asked.

'I think we're about to find out,' Sophie said, and Kay had a horrible feeling that she was right.

For a moment, it felt as if the whole of Lyme Regis was holding its breath as Oli grasped Teresa's face in his hands and bent his head to kiss her. There was a collective gasp from all who stood watching as the kiss deepened.

'Oli and Teresa?' Beth said in horror. 'You've got to be kidding me!'

'Doesn't look like they're kidding, does it?' Sophie said.

'Oh, my God! Look at the way they're kissing! I've never seen anyone kiss like that before,' Beth said.

'It's totally wasted too,' Sophie said. 'I mean, it's not even going to make the film. It'd make a pretty good DVD extra, though, wouldn't it?'

Kay could watch and listen to no more. She closed her eyes,

trying to put a stop to the image, but it was burned into her brain. She ran as fast as she could along the seafront, knowing she had to get far away from Oli.

Chapter 41

KAY HAD TO GET THROUGH THE REST OF THE DAY WITHOUT having a nervous breakdown in front of her guests, but as she closed the door of Wentworth House behind her, she couldn't stop the tears from falling.

Her head was filled with so many questions that it throbbed and it took her a moment to realise that she wasn't alone in the house. The sound of laughter was coming from the living room. Kay quickly found a tissue in her pocket and dried her eyes. What a state she must look, she thought, quickly checking her reflection in the hallway mirror. Sure enough, her normally creamy complexion was red and blotchy. She couldn't face anybody. Whoever was in her front room—even if it was a couple of burglars—could be dealt with later.

She was sneaking up the stairs when a voice stopped her.

'Kay!'

She turned around to see Gemma standing at the foot of the stairs, a handsome man beside her.

'Are you all right?'

Kay nodded hopelessly.

'What a silly question—you're not all right at all, are you?'

The handsome man touched Gemma on the shoulder. 'I'll be getting back. I'll see you later, okay?'

Gemma nodded and leaned forward to kiss him.

Kay blinked in surprise. Could the day possibly get any stranger? What had been going on in her front room? she wondered. Wasn't Gemma supposed to be seeing Adam?

Both women watched as the handsome man left the bed and breakfast.

'I didn't mean to interrupt you,' Kay said.

'You weren't interrupting anything,' Gemma assured her. 'Now tell me what's wrong. Has something happened?'

Kay didn't know where to look or how to begin, so after moving through to the living room and sitting on the sofa with Gemma, Kay began at the beginning and told Gemma the whole story right up until what had just happened on the Cobb.

'Teresa and Oli!' Gemma said. 'I can't believe it. I thought they hated each other.'

'That's what everyone else is saying.'

'And he didn't tell you anything.'

Kay shook her head.

'God! He's such a rat!' Gemma said. 'Oh, my goodness!'

'What?'

'I was just talking to him yesterday. He said he was thinking of giving up acting. There's a lot of that going around at the moment. Anyway, I got the impression he was thinking of settling down, and I just assumed...'

'What?'

'I assumed he was talking about you or someone he'd managed to keep well hidden from the press until now. Gosh, I'm so sorry, Kay.'

Kay simply shook her head.

'I'm going to kill him when I next see him,' Gemma continued.

'No, don't!' Kay said in alarm. 'Please don't say anything.'

'But he hurt you, Kay.'

Kay took a deep breath. 'It was my fault. I let myself fall for him. I let myself think that he was someone he wasn't. He never led me on.'

'But he slept with you!'

'I know. But he never made me any promises,' Kay said.

They sat in silence for a moment.

'I hate men,' Gemma said at last. 'Apart from Rob.'

Kay frowned. 'Is he the man who was here?'

Gemma smiled.

'But I thought you and Adam were together.'

Gemma looked uneasy for a moment. 'I'm afraid there never was a me and Adam.'

Kay looked confused. 'I don't understand.'

Gemma took a deep breath. 'I like Adam, but we're nothing more than good friends.'

'But I thought Adam was really in love with you.'

Gemma shook her head. 'No.'

'That's so strange,' Kay said. 'I was so sure—on the beach, he said—' Kay paused.

'What?'

'He was going to tell me something, but I didn't give him the chance,' she said, realising that she'd never had a full confession from Adam at all when it came to Gemma. 'What on earth was he going to say?' she asked. 'Oh, goodness! This is all so confusing. And I thought I was a natural matchmaker.'

'Like Emma Woodhouse?' Gemma asked.

Kay nodded. 'And I've ended up making as big a mess as Emma, haven't I?'

'But your intentions were the very best,' Gemma said, squeezing her hand. 'Look, I've got to get back to the set before I'm missed. Will you be okay?'

'I've been thinking of chucking myself off the top of Golden Cap, but I'll try to let the feeling pass.'

Kay accompanied Gemma to the front door, where they gave each other a hug.

'You know,' Gemma said, 'I can't help thinking that you were right about Adam.'

'What do you mean? That he really is in love with you?'

'Oh, no,' Gemma said quickly, 'not me, but maybe there's somebody else he's got his eye on.' She gave a little smile, and Kay watched as she left. What on earth had Gemma meant?

She closed the front door, and the image of Adam was instantly banished from her mind, because all she could think about was Oli. And that kiss. How long had he and Teresa been in love? Kay was guessing that it predated her brief affair with him by a good, long time. What did that make Kay, a mere distraction? Was she just some sort of stopgap whilst Oli sorted himself out? That's what it felt like.

'I mustn't think about it,' she whispered to herself. 'I must keep busy. I must keep sane.'

She walked to the kitchen where a sink of dishes awaited her, but all she could see was Oli's beautiful golden face staring up at her from out of the greasy plates. She turned to face the door and saw him standing there, his lopsided grin tormenting her, and then a thought crossed her mind. She had to tidy his room before he got back. She'd done it before, of course, but not since they spent the night together. Not since he kissed Teresa.

Without a moment's pause, Kay bolted up the stairs and into his bedroom. She saw the unmade bed in the middle of the room and felt a stab in her heart, because she knew he slept in it for only half the night. She felt anxious. She had every right to be there, of course, but it felt strange nevertheless. She felt like an intruder.

Curiosity soon got the better of her, and she began to hunt around the room, opening the drawers in the bedside table, peering into the wardrobe, and patting the pockets of the jackets hanging in there. There must be something here—*something* that would tell her that he was in love with Teresa—something linking them together.

When she saw his large suitcase in the corner of the room, she bit her lip. It was shut, but not locked, and when she knelt down next to it, her hand shook. This was wrong, she told herself, but she knew she couldn't leave the room until she did it, and so she unzipped it and opened it up.

Why was she surprised to see just a regular suitcase? There were a couple of neatly folded T-shirts, an ancient pair of jeans, and a couple of rugby shirts. She closed her eyes for a moment. What had she expected? What did she think she could find that was going to make the slightest bit of difference to her relationship with Oli? Closing the suitcase up again, she sank to the carpet and sighed.

She noticed a notebook she'd previously overlooked. It was on the window seat and was half hidden by the curtain, but from her sitting position on the floor, Kay had a perfect view of it.

'It won't be anything,' she said, getting up off the floor and dusting herself down. Still, it would be silly not to take a peep now that she was here. It was a small notebook—just a cheap spiral-bound one that a person could pick up in any stationery shop, and it was scuffed at the edges as though it has been endlessly put in and taken out of pockets and suitcases. Kay flipped it open and

311

saw Oli's scrawling handwriting. The first page was a to-do list, and Kay smiled as she read through it. *Laundry. Order takeaway. Pack script!!! Ring Mum. Tell neighbour not to overfeed the fish. Ring Teresa.*

Ring Teresa. It could've been a professional call he had to make, but Kay got the feeling that it wasn't. She flipped over to the next page and read the name Captain Wentworth. What had gone through his mind when he'd written that? she wondered. Was he thinking about the character he was going to portray? She flipped to another page, and as she did so, something fluttered to the floor. Kay bent down to retrieve it and saw that it was a photograph of a little girl on a swing. She looked no more than four years old and she had bright blond pigtails. There was only one girl it could be.

'Annabel,' Kay said, sinking down onto the window seat.

And there was only one reason he'd keep a photograph of Annabel in his possession, and that was because she was his daughter.

Chapter 42

ADAM MADE A QUICK VISIT TO THE COBB AFTER HE PARTED from Gemma but left before the excitement with Oli and Teresa and headed home. As he pulled up in his driveway, a familiar head popped around the gate.

'Nana!' Adam cried, getting out of the car quickly. 'What on earth are you doing here?'

'I wanted to see you,' she said, sounding horribly out of breath. 'You didn't return my phone call.'

'Yes, I did.'

'Well, not to my satisfaction,' she said. 'Now what's been going on with you and that bed-and-breakfast girl?'

'Kay.'

'Yes, Kay.'

'Come and sit down first. How did you get here, anyway? I hope you didn't walk.'

'I didn't fly, did I?'

'But you're not meant to walk so far.' He gave her attire the once-over. She was wearing a scarlet jumper, a pair of floral trousers in blue and white, and bright pink wellington boots.

'Not walk so far? I used to walk miles and miles in my

time—farther than any of you youngsters nowadays. Anyway, I had my stick with me and had a nice little rest by that stream.'

'Where's your stick now?' Adam asked, wanting proof.

Nana Craig nodded towards the hedge, and Adam saw the candy-striped aid.

'Come on,' he said, shaking his head and ushering his nan into the house. He put the kettle on and reached into a cupboard for biscuits. 'Here,' he said. 'You must be starving.'

Nana Craig peered inside the Charles and Diana tin with a frown.

'I think you have some specimens in here from about the time of their wedding,' she said.

'Nonsense,' Adam said, 'I replenish that tin every week. Or so.'

Cautiously, Nana Craig chose a fruit shrewsbury, giving it a sniff before eating it.

'So what is so urgent that you have to walk halfway across Dorset?' Adam asked, placing two mugs of tea on the old kitchen table and pulling out chairs for them both.

'A walk can't kill me. I need to keep moving at my age, or I'll seize up and solidify.'

'But you shouldn't take risks when you don't have to you. I worry about you,' Adam said, placing a hand on hers.

'And I worry about you too, which is why I came over here. Anyway, it's nice to get out and talk to somebody, even if it is only Sir Walter,' she said as the cat waltzed into the kitchen in case he was missing out on anything. 'Now, what on earth is going on?'

Adam sighed. 'I told you—Kay's in love with that actor.'

'Yes, but I didn't like him,' Nana Craig said, dipping her hand into the biscuit tin and chancing another fruit shrewsbury.

'I'm afraid it doesn't matter who *you* like. It's who Kay likes that matters.'

'So you've said nothing,' Nana Craig said, biscuit crumbs cascading down her chin.

'I told you, there was nothing to say. She's in love with Oli Wade Owen.'

'She *thinks* she's in love with Oli Wade Owen, and she probably thinks that only because she hasn't been given a choice.'

Adam shook his head at his nan's logic.

'She doesn't know what's on offer,' Nana Craig continued. 'It's rather like the contents of this biscuit tin. If there was more on offer than these rather soft fruit shrewsburys, I might have made a different choice.'

'I don't think it's that simple,' Adam said.

Nana Craig shook her head. 'You've got to tell her, Adam. It's the only way.'

There was really nothing more Adam could say to convince his nan, and luckily, he didn't have to, because his phone rang.

'Hello?'

'Adam? It's Gemma.'

'Gemma!' Adam said. 'Don't tell me, you've changed your mind about the Hollywood film?'

'I'm afraid not,' she said. 'It's Kay.'

'What about her?' Adam interrupted quickly.

'Something awful's happened. I think you should make sure she's all right.'

Somehow Kay managed to get through the rest of the day. After replacing the photograph of Annabel in Oli's notebook, she got on with her chores, moving through the bed and breakfast like a domestic whirlwind. She vacuumed and mopped, scrubbed and polished, and tucked and folded until there wasn't a single square inch that had been neglected. She then went shopping, replenishing her cupboards with everything that a guest could possibly request and a few other items she knew she might use to console herself, once the guests had gone. She filled every second with activity, because that way, she didn't have to think.

Before she knew it, it was evening, and the cast returned to the bed and breakfast. Well, most of them did. Oli and Teresa were noticeable by their absence, and it was soon assumed that they found a room together elsewhere. It was a little after seven o'clock when a tall man in a suit turned up to pack and collect their belongings.

Kay followed him up the stairs to show him to their bedrooms. 'Did they send any message?' she dared to ask him.

'Not by me,' he told her. 'I'm just the runner and was only told to collect their things.'

'Where are they staying?'

'Just outside Bath, I believe,' he said politely.

So he'd gone. And without even saying good-bye.

Kay watched as the man did a thorough job of emptying the wardrobes and drawers, packing everything neatly away.

'I think that's about it,' he said at last.

'Yes,' Kay said quietly. 'It really is.'

She followed him back downstairs, and he nodded politely to her as he left. That was it. No message, no forwarding address; she didn't even have his mobile phone number. Captain Wentworth wouldn't have behaved in such a manner; Kay felt sure of it, and Mr Darcy's good opinion would have been lost forever at such behaviour.

Kay walked through to the living room where Sophie and Beth

were sitting with Les Miserable and offered everyone dinner. It was eagerly accepted, because everybody was too tired to bother changing and going out to dinner that evening. Kay was relieved, because it meant she'd be kept busy and have company too.

She was walking back to the kitchen when she heard Beth groan loudly.

'God! Can you believe that today?' she said. 'Oli and Teresa! I'd never have guessed that in a million years.'

'Well, you'd better start believing,' Sophie said. 'I hear they're getting married.'

Kay's hand flew to her mouth to stifle a scream.

'All I can say is it's about bloody time,' Les Miserable said.

'You knew they were a couple?' Beth said.

'Of course I bleedin' knew.'

'How?'

'I've been working with Teresa for years. It's been a well-kept secret from the media, I warrant you, but industry insiders have known what's going on for ages.'

'Blimey,' Sophie said.

'I wish someone had told me,' Beth said. 'It might have saved me hours of flirting.'

'I reckon you would have flirted anyway,' Sophie said.

'And who could blame me? They're not married, and what sort of relationship is it anyway, if they don't want anyone to know about it?'

'A private one,' Sophie said. 'Not everybody wants their love lives to be fodder for the national press.'

'I think it's really weird. Besides, Oli's been messing around for years.'

'Not anymore,' Les said. 'Not if Teresa has anything to do with it.'

There was a pause for a moment before Beth spoke again. 'Oh, my God! Do you think Annabel is his daughter?'

'Of course she is,' Sophie said.

'But she called him Oli all the time,' Beth said.

'Maybe she doesn't know,' Sophie said, 'or maybe she's under strict instructions *not* to call him "Daddy". If I were Teresa's daughter, I'd do *exactly* what I was told, wouldn't you?'

'God!' Beth said. 'How can Oli be in love with Teresa, of all people?'

'There's nothing stranger than love, and I've never seen such a passionate kiss in my whole life,' Sophie said.

'Don't!' Beth said. 'It was disgusting.'

'You're just jealous that he wasn't kissing you.'

Kay couldn't bear to hear any more and hid in the kitchen to prepare dinner and then spent the rest of the evening cleaning pots that didn't need cleaning before going to bed and crying herself to sleep, putting a merciful end to what was probably the worst day of her life.

When she drew her curtains the next morning, she wished she could go straight back to bed. She didn't want to face the day ahead, because it was the day that everyone was leaving. This was the last breakfast she would prepare for the actors, and then they would be gone. If she wanted to see them again, she'd have to hire their films or watch them on television, but they'd never again sit on her sofa or pop their heads around the kitchen door asking for more coffee.

Breakfast was a quiet affair that morning. Les Miserable looked as glum as ever, and Beth looked pouty and petulant.

'I don't want to go to Bath,' she complained, pushing the remains of her toast away from her.

'I thought you'd like the shops,' Gemma said. She'd come in late the night before, and Kay guessed she'd been with Rob.

'I suppose there is that consolation. But why can't we film it in London?'

Sophie looked at her as though she were quite mad. 'You have read *Persuasion*, haven't you? You can't make a film version of *Persuasion* and not shoot in Bath.'

'Oh, don't be so exact. It doesn't have to be Bath, does it, Les?'

'Of course it has to be bloody Bath, you idiot. Jane Austen *is* Bath. You don't hear of bloody Jane Austen's London, do you? It's Jane Austen's Bath, isn't it?' he said.

Sophie and Gemma giggled.

Beth tutted in annoyance.

Kay left them to their debate.

'Kay?' a voice said about half an hour later. She turned around to see Gemma standing in the kitchen doorway, and she knew it would be for the last time. 'We're ready.'

Kay nodded and joined everyone in the hallway.

'You've been the best host ever,' Sophie said. 'I wish we could take you with us to Bath.'

Kay smiled weakly. She'd wanted to go with them as well, until the day before. Now the thought of seeing Oli again was too much.

'I'll miss you, Sophie,' Kay said. 'Come back and visit, won't you?'

Sophie nodded and gave her a big hug.

'Bye, then,' Beth said, giving Kay the briefest of hugs.

'Take care of that ankle, won't you?' Kay said.

'There's nothing wrong with my ankle,' Beth said.

Les Miserable moved forward and extended a hand. 'Thanks for putting us up and putting up with us,' he said without a glimmer of a grin.

'You're very welcome,' Kay said.

And then there was Gemma.

'I feel like Dorothy in the *Wizard of Oz* when she has to say good-bye to her new friends,' Kay said with a sad smile.

'Oh, don't,' Gemma said, 'or you'll start me off!'

The two hugged, and Kay felt tears threatening to spill.

'Come on, come on,' Les said. 'Got to get a move on, or we'll all be in trouble with you know who.'

'Take care of yourself,' Gemma said.

'You too,' Kay said. 'And keep in touch, won't you? Come and visit if you're ever in Lyme Regis.'

'I will,' Gemma said.

Sophie, Beth, and Les were already out of the door, and when Gemma was quite sure she had a moment's privacy, she doubled back.

'Kay,' she said, 'Oli gave me this to give you, the rat!' She handed her a little envelope. 'I told him the least he could do was to give it to you himself, but he refused. Do you want me to stay whilst you open it? I could give him your reply, if you want.'

Kay shook her head, knowing that whatever was in there would probably make her cry, and Gemma had already seen enough of her tears.

Gemma gave her shoulder a quick squeeze. 'If it's any consolation, I told Oli exactly what I think of him.'

'*Gemma!*' Les's voice bellowed from outside. 'Get a bloomin' move on!'

'Got to go,' Gemma said, and Kay gave a little smile and watched as her friend left. Kay then looked at the envelope with her name scrawled across it in blue ink and felt that there was something inside it—something round. Her heart skipped a beat for a moment and her imagination whirled in a direction she could hardly hope was real. Oli had left her a ring and a note of explanation. The whole scene on the Cobb with Teresa had been only an elaborate cover to fool the press. It *wasn't* Teresa he loved. How could it be, when he was in love with Kay?

With shaking hands, Kay opened the envelope. Sure enough, there was a note, but there was no ring. She frowned as a shiny gold button fell into the palm of her hand. She examined it for a moment, not quite knowing what to make of it, and then she unfolded the sheet of paper, quickly reading the brief message.

Dear Kay—I hate leaving without saying a proper good-bye, but all this has happened so fast. I hope you will understand, and I know you will, because you are such a lovely girl.

I thought you might like the enclosed. It's one of Captain Wentworth's buttons, and it fell off during filming. I told the girl from costume it had rolled off the Cobb into the sea, so it won't be missed. I had a feeling you might like it.

Love,
Oli x

Kay stared at the letter in disbelief and then read it through again. Was that it? Was that all she meant to him?

'He *knows* I'll understand!' she shouted into the hallway. 'It was okay to use me like that because I'd understand!'

She looked down at the little gold button in her hand.

'I gave him my heart, and he gave me a bloody button!'

Chapter 43

AFTER ADAM RECEIVED GEMMA'S PHONE CALL, HE WONDERED whether he should return to Lyme Regis straightaway and check on Kay, but he decided against it. The cast weren't due to leave until the next day, and he guessed that Kay would be far too busy looking after them to need him barging in and offering a shoulder to cry on. He would wait; he would do his best to wait until the next day.

Nana Craig looked at him quietly as he sat down again.

'That was Gemma from the film. She thinks I should go and see Kay. It seems Oli's left without even saying good-bye.'

'I told you!' Nana Craig said, finishing her tea with an almighty slurp. 'Didn't I tell you he was no good?'

'Nana, you think all actors are no good.'

'Because it's true! And especially him. The minute he walked up my garden path, I knew he was no good. A woman can tell that sort of thing. Well, *I* can, but it sounds like that poor dear girl can't. But at least that makes things simple.'

'How do you mean?'

'I mean you can tell her how you feel about her now.'

'Nana, I'm going to see if she's okay—that's all. She doesn't want a big confession from me at the moment.'

'Don't you go blowing your opportunity a second time,' Nana Craig said, wagging a warning finger at him. 'This could be your last chance.'

Adam rolled his eyes. 'Do you want another cup of tea?'

'I want some great-grandchildren—that's what I want.'

'Yes, but I'm offering you a cup of tea,' Adam said.

Nana Craig sighed. 'If that's all that's on offer, I guess I'd better say yes.'

Half an hour later, Adam drove his nan home.

'And don't do that again, Nana. I don't want to get home and find you on my doorstep again.'

'What a fuss!' she said, getting out of the car in a brilliant flash of red, blue, and pink. 'Don't you forget to go and see that girl now,' she said, tapping the passenger door with her candy-striped walking stick.

'I won't forget. I'm going to see her first thing tomorrow.'

Nana Craig nodded. 'Adam,' she said.

'Yes, Nana?'

'I know I go on, and I know you don't like me interfering, but I just want to see you happy, that's all.' She gave a little smile and her cheeks dimpled.

'I know,' Adam said. 'I know you do.'

The rest of Adam's day seemed to drag interminably, despite filling it with the endless phone calls he had to make. At one stage, Adam could no longer concentrate, so he got up, stuffed his feet into a pair of boots, and went out into the garden. Sir Walter followed him, his little pink nose high in the air.

'I'm afraid you can't come with me, old man. Back in the house with you.' He scooped up the cat and took him into the house, locking the cat flap, and making his escape before Sir Walter could follow. What he was going to do was far too dangerous to risk a cat being around.

Somewhere in the tangle at the bottom of the garden stood a brick wall. It was crumbling and teetering, and Adam had been meaning to knock it down for weeks, but he had spent all his spare time renovating the cottage, and the garden had been shamefully neglected.

Finding the patch of ground where the wall stood, he cleared away the long grasses, grazing his arm on a bramble. Finally, the bricks were clear. They were a rather beautiful rosy red, and he was going to lay a path using them, but first the wall had to come down, and he was in just the right mood to do it. Opening the tiny shed, he picked up his sledgehammer, and walked across the garden to the wall. He took a deep breath and began.

It was hot work, and he was soon sweating. Pausing for a moment, he rolled up the sleeves of his shirt and undid a few buttons at the throat. It felt good to feel the air on his body. He needed to spend more time out of doors, for although his arms were far from pale, his job meant that he spent a lot of time in an airless, sunless office, which was good for neither mind nor body. Hard, physical work was what he needed right now, and although he knew he was benefiting from the workout, he also realised his motivation.

It was Oli Wade Owen.

Since Adam received the phone call from Gemma, he had been boiling with rage, because Oli's actions had been totally unacceptable. From what he understood from Gemma, Oli's behaviour had been abominable, and dear, sweet Kay had been heartbroken. How could somebody behave so callously towards somebody like Kay? Adam couldn't get his head around it. What had Oli thought he was doing? He was obviously involved with Teresa, so what was he doing messing around with Kay?

It wouldn't be seemly for the screenwriter/producer to slug the leading man, and Adam was certainly no avenging angel, so here he was taking his anger out on an innocent brick wall. It was also an excellent way to fill in the time before he could see Kay and find out exactly what happened.

If she'll talk to me, he thought. She might not want to see anyone. She might have denounced all men and barred the windows and doors of Wentworth House against them.

He stopped work for a moment, fear flooding his veins. What would he do if she wouldn't see him?

'Persist,' he said. It's what every good hero did, from Mr Darcy to Captain Wentworth. They waited and they persisted.

He hoped he wouldn't have to wait too long, though. He was barely certain that he would be able to make it until the next day.

Chapter 44

Not long after Adam's resident blackbird pierced the early morning with its radiant song, he awoke from a restless night's sleep, and the first thought in his mind was that he would see Kay that day. If only he could be sure of it every day. How amazing his life would be with her in it—waking up in the morning to see her beautiful face on the pillow beside his, spending day after day with her fossil hunting on the beach, eating ice cream along the seafront, and cooking together in the evenings. But was life really meant to be that sweet? He'd had a tiny glimpse of what it might be with Kay, but life often had its own ideas, and Adam knew that he couldn't let himself hope again. He'd made that mistake once before.

Still, as he drove into town, the sea sparkling with diamonds, he couldn't help hoping. He was a writer, the sort of writer inclined to believe in happy endings.

Walking towards Wentworth House, he realised that he could barely remember a time when Kay hadn't lived in Lyme Regis.

How dull and empty the seaside town must have been before she arrived. He remembered the first day he had seen her, walking into the estate agents, her face lit with a little smile and her toffee-coloured hair blowing in the breeze. He couldn't have imagined how quickly he would fall in love with her, and the thought of his feelings not being returned was almost too much to bear.

His heart beat wildly when he reached Wentworth House, and his hand shook as he reached up to knock on the door. He was quite sure that the cast and crew had left by then and Kay would be on her own.

'Please let her be in,' he said to himself. 'Please let her answer the door!' He noticed the sign in the front window: No Vacancies. That was odd, he thought. He was sure that she didn't have any bookings. Hadn't she told him that day at Charmouth that there were no bookings yet? The cast and crew of *Persuasion* had been her first and had surprised her, because she hadn't officially opened.

A thought occurred to Adam—what if she'd decided not to run the bed and breakfast anymore? What if her brief time in Lyme Regis had been more than enough for her, and she was returning to Hertfordshire?

Adam knocked on the door again. 'Come on,' he whispered. 'Open the door.'

His wish was granted a moment later, and he couldn't hide his shock at the sight that greeted him.

'Kay!' he said as he saw her tear-drenched face. 'What's happened to you?'

She took a moment to register who was standing on her doorstep. 'Adam?'

'Yes!' he said. She didn't invite him in but turned away from the door and half shuffled along the hallway. Adam followed. 'Are you all right?'

She stopped suddenly just ahead of him, and he almost crashed into the back of her.

'You want to know what's happened to me? I'll tell you what's happened to me. It's what *always* happens to me. I fall in love, I give my heart away, and it gets broken. That's what's happened to me.'

Adam blanched at her grief-laden words. 'Gemma told me,' he said quietly. 'She was worried about you. Come and sit down,' Adam said, aware that she was teetering slightly.

'I need another drink,' she said, making her way towards the kitchen.

'It's all right,' Adam said. 'I'll get you a glass of water.'

'No, Adam. I mean a proper drink.'

'It's a bit early, isn't it?' he said, looking at the hallway clock and seeing that it wasn't even eleven.

'Not today it isn't,' Kay said. 'I'm going to get pickled, sizzled, and sloshed.'

'I believe you,' Adam said.

'So don't try to stop me.'

'Okay,' he said, thinking the best thing he could do would be to supervise her. He watched as she entered the kitchen and opened the fridge, reaching in for a bottle of white wine.

'I had some whisky before,' she said. 'I bought it in case some of the cast might want it. It was disgusting.'

'How much did you drink?'

Kay shrugged. 'About this much?' she said, lifting her 'I Love Darcy' mug in the air.

Adam winced and watched in horror as she poured a large measure of wine.

'Come and sit down now,' he said, and she meekly followed him through to the living room. He sat down next to her on the sofa, and it was all he could do to restrain himself from putting an arm around her shoulder.

He watched her as she drank the wine from her mug. Well, that wasn't quite the right word for what Kay was doing; guzzling seemed to be more appropriate.

'I don't think you should drink any more, Kay,' he said, quietly taking the mug from her before she could protest. 'You mustn't let this get the better of you.'

She nodded slowly, as if half recognising his words. 'When everybody left yesterday, I realised that I was alone,' she said. 'For the first time since moving here, I was really alone. When I first came here, I was surrounded by builders and plumbers and decorators, and then the cast and crew of *Persuasion* arrived. But now I'm alone, and this house feels empty and quiet, and I hate it, and I don't know anyone here.'

'You know me, Kay.'

She gave a little laugh. 'But what am I doing here?'

'You're running a marvellous bed and breakfast,' he said, 'and making a living in one of the most beautiful towns in the country.'

Kay didn't seem to hear him, and he could see tears swimming in her eyes once more.

'But I feel so—so alone.' She shook her head and stared at the swirling pattern of the carpet that had yet to be replaced. 'Why can't I get things right? Just once—that's all it takes. Even Jane Austen wasn't as cruel as this. Marianne Dashwood had her heart broken only once, but mine gets broken over and over again.' A tear escaped and rolled down her reddened cheek. 'Just like my mother's did.'

'Kay—'

'And he's just forgotten me, hasn't he?' she said. 'Hasn't he read *Persuasion* properly? Or maybe that line didn't make it into the script.'

'Which line?'

Kay flapped her hand in the air. 'That bit where Anne's talking about the difference between men and women and says, "We certainly do not forget you as soon as you forget us".'

'That's certainly in the script,' Adam said.

Kay sniffed. 'And I bet it won't mean anything to him when he reads it.'

'I wouldn't be so sure.'

She looked at him, desperation in her eyes. 'What do you mean?'

'I don't think you're the sort of woman men forget.'

'Ha!' she scoffed. 'You think that? You *really* think that? Because I seem to have been forgotten by more men than there are pebbles on that beach out there.' She flapped her hand and knocked Adam's, and the contents of the mug slopped onto his trousers. 'Oh, God! I'm *so* sorry.' Kay leapt up off the sofa. 'I'll get a cloth.'

'It's okay,' Adam said, but she'd already dashed to the kitchen, returning a moment later with a tea towel with which she rubbed Adam's leg ineffectually. Adam let out an involuntary laugh and took the towel from her. 'Perhaps it's best if I do it,' he said.

Kay sat back down on the sofa, a scowl of gigantic proportions on her face.

'You will get over this, Kay.'

She nodded. 'Yes, they'll clean up okay in the wash, won't they?'

'I wasn't talking about my trousers,' Adam said.

'I know.'

'Listen to me,' Adam said. 'You're very special, Kay.'

'Special K!' She laughed.

Adam frowned. 'You're also very drunk.'

'I'm not,' she said. 'I need to get drunker. I need to be the drunkest I've ever been, because everything is going wrong. *Everything!* I couldn't even get you and Gemma right! Why didn't you tell me you weren't in love with each other? You should have told me, Adam.'

'I don't think you'd have believed us.'

Kay swayed slightly, even though she was sitting down. 'You're probably right. But how could I have misread the signals? How could I have got everything so spectacularly wrong?' Her eyes went wide and wild. 'I've made such a fool of myself, haven't I?'

'No, you haven't.'

'And here I am. I'm doing it again, right now.'

'You're not making a fool of yourself.'

Kay gave a gigantic sniff. 'He didn't love me. He didn't even have the decency to explain things to me. He only left me a stupid note that didn't say anything. He just left me, Adam. Just like my dad left me, and my mum and Peggy too. Everyone leaves me.'

'I won't leave you.'

Kay looked at Adam. The space between them had closed imperceptibly.

'Oh, you've cut yourself,' Kay said, pulling his arm up for inspection.

'It's nothing.'

'Have you bathed it? You must take care of yourself.'

'Yes, I bathed it.'

'Do you want a bandage? I should get you a bandage,' Kay said, looking around her as if a bandage might be hanging around in the air somewhere.

'It's fine,' Adam said. 'It really doesn't need a bandage.'

She let go of his arm, patting it tenderly and then looking up at him. 'Why can't all men be as nice as you, Adam? You're so nice.'

Adam swallowed hard. He could feel Kay's warm breath on his face, and his skin still tingled from her touch.

'Kay, I—' He didn't get a chance to finish what he was going to say, because she shushed him, pressing a finger to his lips, and before he could react, she leaned forward and kissed him. It was the sweetest, saddest kiss, but Adam couldn't help responding to it, moving his body forward and folding his arms around her.

'Adam!' Kay said, her voice breathy.

Adam kissed her, his fingers running through her beautiful hair and touching the soft skin of her cheek. He had dreamt of such a moment, although this wasn't how he'd imagined it. This was wrong, and however much Kay thought she wanted him to kiss her, he knew that now wasn't the right time.

'Kay,' he said, moving away from her and holding her hands in his.

'What?' she asked, startled.

'This isn't right.'

'What do you mean? Don't you want to kiss me?'

He gave a little smile. 'Of course I want to kiss you. I've been wanting to kiss you ever since I saw you that first day in Lyme Regis. You don't remember, do you? I saw you outside the estate agents, and you turned and smiled at me.'

Kay looked confused. 'I saw you?'

He nodded. 'I think I fell in love with you that day.'

'Oh, Adam!'

'And that's why we can't do this.'

'But that doesn't make any sense.'

'You're a little bit drunk, Kay, and if anything is going to happen between us, then call me old fashioned, but I'd rather that you be completely sober.'

'I am sober!' Kay cried. 'I'm totally sober.'

Adam stood up, and Kay followed his lead, swaying alarmingly.

'I'm just a bit—unstable, that's all.'

Adam took her hand in his and slowly led her upstairs. 'Which is your room?'

Kay nodded to the door that was hers. He opened it, and they entered the bedroom together.

'Now,' he said, 'you're going to bed. You're going to sleep all that whisky off.' He watched as she sat down on the bed, and then he knelt beside her, gently easing her feet out of her ballet-style shoes. 'You need to sleep.'

'But I'm not at all sleepy,' Kay protested. Nevertheless, she swung her legs up onto the bed and rested her head on her pillow, looking up at Adam with big soulful eyes.

'God, Kay!' he said, wishing she wasn't quite so beautiful and vulnerable. It was a potent, irresistible, and dangerous mix. 'I have to go. You'll give me a call if you need anything, won't you?'

'I need *you*,' she said quietly. 'Stay with me.'

Adam sighed. 'I'll stay downstairs for a while—just to make sure you're okay, all right?'

She nodded and closed her eyes, and despite her earlier protestations, she fell fast asleep.

Chapter 45

By the time Kay awoke, the sky was beginning to darken. She stretched out an arm to reach her alarm clock and grimaced at the throbbing pain in her head. She had a hangover, and she hadn't had one of those for years.

Sitting upright in bed, she winced as she remembered the whisky. As somebody who didn't normally drink much, her alcoholic abuse earlier that day was taking its toll. At least nobody had been there to witness it.

She frowned. Fragments of the morning started to reassemble themselves. She hadn't been alone, had she?

'Adam!' she said, the name filling the silence in the bedroom. Adam had been in her bedroom, hadn't he? She tried desperately to remember what happened, and swinging her legs over the side of her bed, she recalled that he took off her shoes.

So he'd helped her upstairs. He'd seen her at her most hopeless and helpless. She covered her face with her hands and groaned. Why had he turned up? Why was he always popping up when she least wanted to see him? And then she remembered something else.

'I kissed him!' Her eyes flew open at the recollection. What on earth must he think of her now? She'd been mourning one man and had flung herself at another. But then she remembered something else. Adam had kissed her right back!

I've been wanting to kiss you ever since I saw you that first day in Lyme Regis.

That's what he'd said, wasn't it? His words were clear in her mind. Adam Craig was in love with her, and she hadn't known it. She'd been smart enough to realise that he was a man in love, but she'd had no idea that his feelings were directed towards *her*.

'The rose!' she said, remembering the beautiful flower he had brought with him to dinner. Kay had convinced herself that it was for Gemma, but Adam hadn't even known that Gemma was joining him for dinner. But what about that day on the beach at Charmouth? Hadn't he been about to tell her that he was in love with Gemma?

'But I stopped him,' Kay said, realising that she'd interrupted him. So what had he been about to say? That it was her he was in love with? Dear, sweet, kind Adam, who'd been such a good friend to her; she had barely noticed him, not with Oli Wade Owen around. She'd noticed he was attractive, of course, but she hadn't been thinking of her own attraction to him, because she'd been too busy matchmaking him to somebody else.

But then he'd kissed her and something happened. Kay felt something approaching happiness, and it was a totally different feeling from kissing Oli. When Oli kissed her, she'd been panicking about what she looked like, panicking about whether they were being watched and if she was doing things right. But none of those thoughts, none of those insecurities had mattered when she kissed Adam. She hadn't been thinking at all. She realised part of it might have had to do with the alcohol, but she felt there was more to it than that.

More than anything, Kay wanted to see him again, but she was in no condition to be seen. She had to do it the right way, and that began with a shower.

The next hour was spent trying to make herself look half decent. Her hair had been tangled and knotted from a restless sleep, but a shower soon sorted that out, and as she battled with the comb, she remembered the feeling of Adam's fingers as he stroked her hair. He'd been so tender with her, and there was nothing but love in his eyes. How hadn't she seen it before?

'Because you've been looking at another man,' she told her reflection, which was beginning to look a little more human. She'd had eyes for only one man, and it hadn't mattered that he'd been looking in a totally different direction; she'd been besotted, and nothing and nobody else existed.

Pulling on a cream cotton dress sprigged with tiny lilac flowers, Kay at last felt ready to leave the house, but first she went into the kitchen and ate a couple of slices of toast. She hadn't eaten anything all day, and the last thing she wanted was to swoon at Adam's feet, after she'd practically collapsed at them already.

She was just about to leave when it dawned on her that she had no idea where he lived. It was somewhere in the Marshwood Vale, but she didn't have his address, and she'd never made it to his home, even though he'd been hoping to show it to her and introduce her to his cat, Sir Walter. She smiled at the memory. She should have gone to Adam's house that day, but her head had been full of Oli, hadn't it? Things seemed clearer. Her head was still throbbing, but her mind felt sharp and focused.

Adam's number. She had to find Adam's number. He'd given her a card. Where was it? She searched through the kitchen drawer where all manner of things, from appliance instruction guides to colour charts for the bedrooms were housed, and there it was: a simple cream business card with a name and phone number embossed in black. She went through to the hall, picked up the phone, and dialed, but his mobile went straight to voice mail.

'Damn!' she said, hanging up. She noticed somebody had left a message on her answering machine. She pressed Play.

'Kay?' a voice said a little hesitantly. 'It's Adam. I wanted to make sure you were all right, but I guess you're still sleeping. Give me a call when you have a moment. All right? Bye.'

Kay bit her lip and thought about trying to ring his number again, but she didn't know what she wanted to say and felt quite certain that she couldn't say it to a recording. She then remembered someone who knew where he lived, and without further delay, she grabbed her car keys and left Lyme Regis.

Her head was still throbbing as she drove through the Marshwood Vale to Nana Craig's. She hoped she could remember the way. It was the first time she'd driven around the little country lanes in the dark, and despite wanting to do things as quickly as possible, she kept her speed down, taking the bends in the road slowly and carefully and thanking her lucky stars that the worst of the flooding had drained away.

Finally she recognized where she was, spotting the perfect little thatched cottage up ahead. It looked even sweeter in the evening with its windows all lit up. Kay parked her car at the side of the road and opened the little gate, walking up the little pathway before knocking on the door.

It took a couple of minutes before there was a response.

'Who is it?' Nana Craig asked from the other side of the door.

'It's Kay. Adam's friend. I'm sorry to call so late,' she said. 'May I talk to you? It's important.'

A key scraped in the lock and the door opened slowly. The face of Nana Craig appeared in the narrow gap. Intent on her mission, Kay barely noticed the fuchsia jumper and electric-blue slacks Nana Craig was wearing.

'You'd better come in,' Nana Craig said.

Kay followed her into the living room and sat down on the red sofa.

'I've got to speak to Adam,' Kay said without any preamble.

Nana Craig nodded as if she'd been expecting her to say it.

'But I don't know where he lives, and he isn't answering his phone.'

'No,' Nana Craig said.

'No—what?' Kay asked, confused.

'I don't expect he's answering his phone.'

Kay frowned. 'He's told you, hasn't he?'

Nana Craig sighed. 'He wouldn't have volunteered the information, but I managed to winkle it out of him.'

'*Please*, Nana Craig—you have to tell me where he lives.'

'Why?'

The question surprised Kay. 'Because I have to speak to him. I have to tell him how I feel.'

'And how do you feel?'

'What?' As much as Kay adored Nana Craig, she felt uneasy with the way the conversation was going and wasn't at all sure she wanted to share the feelings of her heart with her.

'How do you feel about my grandson?'

'I… well, I… look!' Kay sat forward slightly. 'That's for me to discuss with him. No disrespect—I mean, I know you two are very close, but I'd rather talk to him about all this.'

'But he doesn't want to see you,' Nana Craig said.

'What do you mean? He asked me to call him. He told me he—he loved me. How can he not want to see me?'

'Because it doesn't matter how he feels; it's how *you* feel that matters here.'

'But I love him,' she said, realising it for the first time. 'I love him.'

Nana Craig shook her head. 'I thought you'd say that, but it's more than likely just a knee-jerk reaction to what's happened with that awful actor.'

'No! It isn't—I promise you!' Kay was beginning to feel fractious. 'I know what you think of me. I know I've made a huge mistake, but I want to put it right, and the only way I can do that is if I see Adam.'

Nana Craig stood up, her face tender but immovable. 'Go home, Kay. Go and think things through. You're not being fair to Adam.'

'Doesn't he love me anymore? What did he say?'

Nana Craig sighed. 'He didn't say much, but then again, he never does, but he's hurting. I could tell he's hurting.'

Tears pricked at Kay's eyes. '*Please*—let me know where he is.'

Nana Craig's bottom lip wobbled, and Kay felt sure she was about to relent, but she just shook her head. 'Look, Kay, if you want my advice, you'll leave this be for a while. Go home. Make that business of yours work. Have some time to yourself, and when you're ready, when you're *really* ready, speak to him.'

Kay didn't say anything for a moment. She bit her lip, knowing she wanted to push this further. She also knew that Nana Craig wasn't going to be pushed, so she left the little cottage.

As she walked down the pathway through the garden, she turned back and saw Nana Craig standing in the doorway, her face as pale and anxious as she was sure her own was. Kay didn't like to admit it, but she knew there was some sense in what Nana Craig had said. She wasn't being fair to Adam. She *had* just been thinking about herself, but it didn't mean that her feelings were muddled and confused. She'd never felt more sure of anything in her life, and the thought of waiting to see Adam was unbearable. As she returned home, though, she had an idea. There was one way she was sure Adam would see her—and sooner rather than later, too. He'd promised to help her with her book, and he was a man of his word.

All she had to do was finish it.

Chapter 46

K AY WASN'T SURE HOW MANY HOURS SHE SPENT FINISHING HER paintings, but by the end of June, she had something she was happy with. Sitting at the dining room table, she surveyed her work. Adam was going to be surprised, wasn't he?

Kay sat back in her chair for a moment. It was quite an achievement, and even if nobody else in the world so much as glanced at them, she could feel proud.

Now the question was what to do with them.

During the prior few weeks, Kay had followed Nana Craig's advice and thrown herself into her work. Not only had she been working on her paintings, but she also made progress with the B&B, advertising it locally and nationally and creating her own website too. The bookings had come flooding in, and three of the rooms were booked now and the summer holidays looked as if the place was going to be very busy indeed. Her future in Lyme Regis seemed assured.

Other than leaving a message for Adam telling him that she was okay, though, she hadn't spoken to Adam. Not that she hadn't wanted to, but she respected Nana Craig's advice and had given both him and herself time to think. She'd half expected to bump

into him around town and was always disappointed when she
didn't. She'd spent hours walking around the harbour and the
Cobb and on Monmouth Beach at low tide. She even drove to
the beach at Charmouth a couple of times, hoping to see his figure
bent double in search of fossils, but it was as if he disappeared from
the world.

'Like Oli,' she said to herself. She hadn't heard from him either,
which didn't come as a surprise. Since he'd gone, she hadn't been
able to look at her sketches of Captain Wentworth, because they
all resembled Oli. She hid them all away in the chest at the end of
her bed. She hadn't been able to read *Persuasion* either, until the
previous night.

This is ridiculous, she thought. How dare she let a man who
obviously didn't care a jot for her ruin one of her favourite reading
pleasures, so she spent the entire evening reading her beloved book
again, trying desperately not to picture Oli as Captain Wentworth.
Instead, she imagined someone with dark hair and kind eyes.
Someone who looked a lot like Adam.

Now, scraping her chair back, she raced to the phone in the
hall. It was time to ring him. She picked up the phone and swallowed hard. She put the phone down again. Her throat had gone
horribly dry. She ran through to the kitchen and quickly filled a
glass of water, downing its contents, and then she returned to the
phone. Why was this so difficult? Adam was her friend, wasn't he?
No, she thought, he wasn't. They passed the barrier of friendship,
and things were different.

'But I can make this work,' she said, picking up the phone
again. 'I have to make this work.'

She heard the phone ring and willed it not to go to voice mail.
It didn't.

'Hello?' a voice said. Adam's voice.

'Hello?' Kay croaked.

'Kay?'

'Yes!'

'How are you? I've been thinking about you.'

'You have?'

'Of course I have. I've been worried. You never called again,' he said.

'You never called again either!' she said.

'I thought you needed some time—you know,' he said.

'Yes, I guess I did.'

'Is everything okay?'

'It's fine,' she said. 'I just wondered if I could see you.'

There was a lengthy pause, and Kay felt the full weight of it. He didn't want to see her, did he?

'Don't worry,' she said. 'I understand.' She was about to put the phone down when he interrupted her.

'No, Kay! It's just, I can't get away from home. It's Sir Walter. He's on medication at the moment and is a bit groggy. I don't want to leave him.'

Kay sighed in relief. 'I can come out to you, if you like.'

'Really?'

'Except I don't know where you live.'

Adam quickly told her the address, giving her some obscure directions involving wooded tracks she wasn't to mistake for roads as well as cattle grids she wasn't to drive over.

'Are you sure I'll find the place?' she asked.

'I hope you will,' he said and it was encouragement enough.

'Right,' Kay said once she put the phone down. Her paintings were in tip-top order, but was she? She looked at herself in the hallway mirror, grimaced, and ran upstairs to run a brush through her hair, sending it into flyaway chaos. Next to go were the paint-splattered jeans and the shirt she'd put on once her bed and break-fast guests left for the day. She opened the wardrobe and had the usual dilemma of having absolutely nothing to wear. Making the best of a bad lot, she reached in and pulled out a white cotton dress printed with sepia flowers and butterflies. Placing her feet in a pair of pale gold sandals, she went back downstairs and put her paint-ings into a neat portfolio. She was ready.

Driving through the Marshwood Vale was far preferable a task in the day than it was at night. The woods were bright, and Kay looked in wonder at the acid-green beech trees that lined the lanes.

She was glad that she had Adam's directions; otherwise she might have taken one or two wrong turns. The endless lanes were labyrinthine, and it would be easy to end up going around in circles, but finally spotting the cattle grid, she knew she'd reached her destination, Willow Cottage.

It was the sweetest house she'd ever seen. Okay, so it wasn't picture perfect like Nana Craig's thatched cottage, but it had a strength of character that was appealing with its rosy red bricks, sweet chimney pots, and tiny windows.

She parked the car behind Adam's in the driveway and got out, straightening her dress and flattening her hair, which had no doubt gone flyaway again, as she'd been driving with her window open. Going around to the boot of the car, she opened it and retrieved her portfolio.

Adam had told her to go around to the back door, and she did, finding it open.

'Hello?' she called, popping her head into a tiny but bright kitchen. It had a terra-cotta tiled floor and pale wood cabinets, and Kay smiled as she saw a beautiful royal blue Aga iron stove. She could easily imagine early mornings in this kitchen, warming her bottom against the Aga whilst nursing a cup of tea in her hands and looking out across the garden to the fields.

I'm not to do this anymore, she told herself. *I'm not to daydream! It's real life for me from now on.*

She took a deep breath and called again. 'Adam?'

She heard the sound of footsteps on stairs somewhere in the heart of the cottage.

'Kay?' He appeared in the kitchen wearing an indigo shirt that made his eyes dark and intense behind his glasses. His hair looked damp.

'I've just had a shower,' he said. 'Been digging in the garden.' He nodded to a patch of bare earth. 'There's a lot of work to do.'

Kay turned around. 'It's a lovely garden,' she said. 'That's one of the downsides of living in town—I have only a small courtyard with room for a washing line and a pot of geraniums.'

'Come in!' he said, staring at her portfolio. 'What's that?'

'Some paintings,' Kay said. 'You said you'd take a look at them for me when they were ready.'

'Oh, right,' Adam said. 'Of course.' He led the way toward the dining room, but Kay didn't get quite that far.

'Oh, is this Sir Walter?' she asked as a very furry animal wound its way around her legs.

'Ah, yes—this is he.'

Kay bent down to tickle his head. 'He's gorgeous. How's he feeling?'

'Still a bit groggy, but he's just had something to eat, which is a good sign.'

'He's not at all snooty like Sir Walter in *Persuasion*,' Kay said.

'That's because he's charming you,' Adam told her. 'But he does a very fine line in snooty, believe me.'

She followed Adam to the dining room, and Sir Walter decided that he would join them.

Adam motioned to the table, and Kay placed her portfolio on it, opening it up for his inspection. She twisted her fingers together as he flipped through the paintings. What would he think of them? Had she been fooling herself all these years with her dream of becoming an artist?

Adam's forehead furrowed in concentration, and Kay bit her lip. His eyes looked intense, and she was anxious that it meant her work was no good, and he was trying to form the right words to tell her. Oh, God, she thought. I've made an absolute fool of myself. These silly watercolours should be no more than a hobby—a secret hobby I shouldn't inflict on innocent people.

Finally Adam looked up. 'These are lovely,' he said. 'All of them. They're beautiful.'

'You think so? You *really* think so? You're not just saying that to be polite?'

'No!' he said. 'Why would I do that? But what happened to the illustrations you were doing? I expected to see your book, *The Illustrated Darcy*.'

Kay waved her hand. 'I put those away.'

Adam frowned. 'I don't understand.'

'I'm afraid I got a bit disillusioned with fictional heroes. I think it's time I stopped daydreaming about Mr Darcy and Captain Wentworth. I want to paint something real now, you know? I felt it was time to move on and explore something new.'

Adam nodded. 'And they're wonderful. Look how you've

caught the Cobb here. The early morning light is perfect. And Monmouth Beach too. And this one of Charmouth. They're all lovely, Kay.'

'I've sold some too.'

'Really?'

'Just to guests,' she said. 'But I was wondering if you knew of any galleries around here that might be interested. That's why I'm here.' She stopped and looked down at the floor.

'What is it?' Adam asked her.

Taking a deep breath, Kay looked up at him. 'That's not why I'm here,' she said. 'Not really. I mean, I do want your advice, and I'd love to have your help with this, because I really don't know what I'm doing, but it's kind of an excuse to see you.'

'Did you need an excuse?' he asked. 'I told you to call me whenever you wanted. You don't need an excuse, Kay.'

'But Nana Craig told me you need some space—you know—after the film crew left.'

'Did she?'

Kay nodded. 'And I guessed that was true when you didn't call me again.'

'But I thought *you* needed some space.'

'I guess I did, but I really wanted to see you too.'

'And I wanted to see you.' He smiled a beautiful shy smile. 'Look,' he said after a pause, 'I've been wanting to say sorry about— well, I shouldn't have—you know—made a move on you.'

'You didn't!' Kay said. 'I made a move on you. I'm so sorry. I shouldn't have done that. I mean, I *should* have, because you're wonderful and—' She covered her face with her hands. 'Oh, I'm making such a mess of this!'

Adam took a step towards her. 'No, you're not.'

'It's just that I don't know what to say to you. I feel so embarrassed about the way I've behaved.'

'You don't need to be embarrassed,' he said, 'and you don't need to keep apologising either.'

'But I do! I've been rude to you, Adam, and blind too! And you've been nothing but kind to me. I don't know how I didn't see it before. I guess I was so busy trying to fix you up with Gemma that I didn't see how perfect you were for me.'

They stared at each other for a long moment, and Kay abruptly felt very shy. Adam was the first one to speak.

'I know I'm not a hero,' he said. 'I know I'm not in the same mould as the Oli Wade Owens of the world.'

'But that's a good thing,' Kay interrupted. 'I don't think I was ever really in love with Oli. I think it was Captain Wentworth I fell for.' She sighed. 'Anyway, I fictionalised Oli. I turned him into a hero that he clearly wasn't. Or at least, he wasn't *my* hero. I don't know—I seem to have spent my life fantasising about fictional men. But I want something real now. I want something—' She paused, but she never got the chance to finish her sentence, because Adam stepped forward and took her face in his hands and kissed her.

Kay felt herself sway; not because she was tipsy this time, but because she was deliriously happy.

'Was that real enough for you?' Adam asked a moment later.

Kay laughed in surprise. 'I'm—I'm not sure. I think you might have to run that by me again.'

And so he did.

Chapter 47

Three months later

KAY AND ADAM WALKED ALONG THE COBB HAND IN HAND. IT was a cool September morning, and Kay stuffed her other hand in the pocket of her jacket. Her fingers found a small round metal object, and she instantly knew what it was. It was Captain Wentworth's button. She took it out and glanced at it briefly before throwing her arm back and flinging it into the sea below them.

'What was that?' Adam asked.

'My past,' Kay said, and she rested her head on his shoulder for a moment.

She felt him kiss the top of her head, and she pictured them walking along the Cobb together in the years to come. She could just imagine two little children—miniature images of themselves with their tiny hands clasped in theirs. Maybe they would even bring grandchildren here one day with her and Adam shuffling along the length of the Cobb behind their Zimmer frames.

Kay shook her head. She was daydreaming again, and she'd said she wouldn't do it anymore, because it had got her into far too much trouble in the past. But it's different this time, she told herself, because—and she was quite sure about this—she had got things right at last.

'Ready to go back?' Adam asked her. 'There's a bit of a breeze picking up.'

'Let's just walk to the end first,' she said. 'And then you can jump me down the steps.'

Adam's eyebrows rose. 'Are you sure you want to do that? I mean, aren't you tempting fate a little bit?'

Kay shook her head. 'No,' she said. 'I know you'll catch me.'

READ ON FOR AN EXCERPT FROM

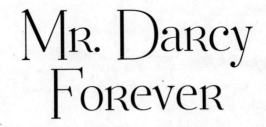

Mr. Darcy Forever

Coming Spring 2012
from Sourcebooks Casablanca

Chapter 1

SARAH CASTLE WASN'T IN THE HABIT OF BLINDFOLDING PEOPLE, but her sister's twenty-first birthday was a delightful exception. As she drove through the winding lanes of Devon, she glanced quickly at Mia. She did look funny with the red polka-dotted scarf tied around her eyes and her curly dark hair flattened into submission.

Slowing down to take a bend in the road, Sarah tried to think how she'd spent her own twenty-first birthday. With a nine-year gap between them, Mia would have been just twelve and had probably been at school.

I would have just finished university, Sarah thought, remembering that summer. It had been the summer their mother had walked out on them and the summer Sarah's role had changed. There had been no note of explanation and no telephone call to check up on them. It was as if Monica Castle had decided she'd completed her role as a mother and moved on to other things somewhere else. Of course, neither of their fathers wanted to know, although the occasional check arrived to pay the rent and assuage some guilt.

From the wide-eyed graduate who was going to conquer the world, Sarah became a surrogate mother, tidying up after her little sister and making sure she always had clean clothes and was eating properly. Her own life had taken a back seat and, whilst working part-time at a restaurant, she'd studied to become an accountant.

No wonder she hadn't had time to celebrate her twenty-first birthday, but this weekend was going to make up for it.

She glanced quickly at Mia and smiled. Some sisters might not have survived the kind of relationship that was forced on them, but it brought Sarah and Mia closer together, and now that Mia had also graduated, she was about to leave home and start leading her own life. She'd already been talking about sharing a flat in Ealing with her friend Shelley, and Sarah was desperately trying not to act like a mother hen, fussing around Mia and making life impossible with endless questions. Mia was a grown woman, and Sarah had to remember that, although, looking at Mia now, she still seemed young and naive. She'd always reminded Sarah of Marianne from Jane Austen's *Sense and Sensibility*. She had the same drive and passion, teamed with inexperience. A lethal combination, Sarah thought.

Oh, stop worrying. Stop worrying, she told herself. This week was about pure unadulterated pleasure. She wasn't going to think about Mia living in an appalling flat, unable to pay her bills, and getting into all sorts of trouble because she wouldn't have her big sister to keep an eye on her. Oh, no. It was going to be a week of 'busy nothings.' They would walk. They would talk. They would eat and read and watch films. Sarah had a suitcase that was almost completely full of films, from the 2005 adaptation of *Pride and Prejudice* to the BBC version of *Persuasion*. She had been forced to take out some of her clothes, because they wouldn't all fit in. Of course she could have put the films in a separate case, but that would never have done. Sarah was very particular about such things. You took *one* suitcase away on holiday, and that was all. She only hoped that the warm weather would continue and that she wouldn't have need of the big woolly sweater she pulled out at the last minute.

Banishing thoughts of a freak May snowstorm, Sarah thought about the week that lay ahead. No doubt there would be the usual arguments about who was the best Elizabeth Bennet and who made the most dashing Mr Darcy. This disagreement was when their difference in age became most pronounced, as Sarah would be singing the praises of Colin Firth as Mr Darcy and Ciaran Hinds as Captain Wentworth, whereas Mia would be swooning over Matthew Macfadyen and Rupert Penry-Jones.

'But he's *far* too pale to be a convincing Captain Wentworth,' Sarah would say. 'He doesn't even look as if he knows where the sea is!'

'Well *your* Captain Wentworth looks like a grandfather,' Mia would retort.

Sarah grinned. There were some things about which they would never agree, but one thing they agreed on was that this week was going to be free from men. Sarah had just ended a relationship that had been a complete disaster from start to finish, and Mia was still nursing a broken heart after her latest boyfriend, Guido, had gone back to his mama in Italy. Sarah sincerely hoped there were no men in Devon or, at least, not in their little corner of it. She was fed up with living in a city where there was a rogue around every corner. The only men she wanted to think about were the fictional heroes in her Jane Austen novels. They were the only perfect men in the universe, weren't they? They never broke your heart. Living safely within the confines of a novel, they were the very best kind of lover.

'Are we nearly there yet?' Mia asked, breaking into Sarah's thoughts.

Sarah laughed at the childlike question. 'Nearly,' she said. 'You're not feeling dizzy, are you?'

'No, I'm fine,' Mia said.

'Because we can take the scarf off, if you'd like.'

'Oh, no! I like surprises,' Mia said.

'And you've no idea where we are?'

Mia shook her head. 'Somewhere complicated,' she said. 'All these twists and turns.'

It had certainly been a complicated journey, with Mia coming from London and Sarah from Winchester. They'd finally managed to meet up in Exeter and had driven through the rolling Devon countryside together, both glorying in being released from their city lives for a few days. Sarah couldn't wait to get out of the car and stretch her legs and stride across a few fields like Elizabeth Bennet or Marianne Dashwood.

It was then that she saw the track that she'd been looking out for and turned off the main road onto the private one. Mia swayed in the seat beside her.

'We're getting close, aren't we?'

'Not long now,' Sarah said, although she had never been there before herself, so had no real idea of where they were going. Still, she could feel a bubble of excitement inside her. It had been such a hard secret to keep from Mia. Sarah didn't like secrets. She liked openness and honesty, but, she told herself, this was different. This was a secret to beat all secrets, and she couldn't wait for it to be revealed.

The turnoff came quickly, and Sarah slowed the car, parked it, and turned off the engine.

'Can I take the scarf off?'

'No!' Sarah said. 'Stay right there.' She got out of the car and ran around to open Mia's door, releasing her seat belt and taking her arm.

'I feel like an invalid,' Mia said.

'Come on,' Sarah said.

'It's steep,' Mia said.

'It's all right. I've got you.' Sarah led the way down a path and then up a grassy bank until she reached a small wooden gate. She placed Mia's hands on top of the gate, and only then did she untie the scarf.

'Happy birthday,' she said, leaning forward and kissing her sister's pink cheek.

For a moment, Mia just stood blinking, as if getting used to seeing again, but then she gasped and her mouth dropped open.

'Oh, my goodness! It's Barton Cottage! You found Barton Cottage!' Mia jumped up and down on the spot like a little girl, which, Sarah knew, she would always seem to her. She would always be her little sister. She smiled as Mia's eyes widened in delight at the sight that greeted her. It was truly beautiful—the perfect Georgian country manor, its pale walls and large sash windows so open and friendly. But it was more than just a beautiful house—it was the house used in the 1995 film adaptation of *Sense and Sensibility*—the one to which the Dashwood sisters have to move after their father dies.

'It's so beautiful,' Mia said. 'This really is it, isn't it?'

'It really is.'

Mia turned to face Sarah, her dark eyes brimming with tears. 'I can't believe you found it, and I can't believe we're really staying here.' She opened her arms wide and then wrapped them around Sarah, squeezing her until she begged for mercy.

'Don't you want to see inside?' Sarah asked, extricating herself from Mia's embrace.

Mia nodded, her smile reaching gigantic proportions.

They opened the little wooden gate and walked up through the garden. Everything was lush and lovely. Frothy cow parsley grew in abundance, and bright red campion blazed in the hedgerows. To the left of the house lay a field of bright bluebells, and a beautiful lawn stretched out in front of the house in green splendour. It was as if spring had danced over everything, leaving no surface untouched.

As they reached the front door, Sarah turned around to admire the view down to the estuary. It was flanked with pale blond reed beds, and a little lane ran alongside it.

Mia gasped. 'That's the lane Willoughby rode along, isn't it?'

'And Colonel Brandon too,' Sarah said, wistfully glancing along it in the hopes that Alan Rickman might show up on horseback at any moment.

'We're going to have the best week ever here!' Mia said.

'Of course we are,' Sarah said. 'A perfect week.'

But perfection is hard to come by, even in Devon, and Sarah had been wishfully thinking when she'd hoped there were no men in their little corner of the English countryside.

Chapter 2

Three years later

S ARAH CASTLE WOKE UP AND COULDN'T BELIEVE WHAT SHE was seeing. What on earth had she been thinking? How had she let it happen? She felt absolutely mortified and tried to shut her eyes, banishing the image from her brain, but it was no good— it had to be faced head on.

Sitting upright, she flattened down her hair with her hands and then swung her legs out of bed. She placed her left foot into its slipper and then the right one, careful not to touch the carpet.

It wasn't the first time this had happened, and she swore silently to herself that it would never ever happen again. Taking a deep breath, she stood up and straightened the offending curtain, shaking her head at the kink that had somehow been left in it overnight, and then she sighed in relief. That was better. Now the morning could begin properly.

There followed a strict routine of bed making, washing, and tidying before Sarah allowed herself to have breakfast. Not for her was the slatternly slippered shuffle into the kitchen for that morning cup of coffee. Oh, no. Sarah had to be immaculately dressed before she graced the kitchen. There she would take break-fast whilst writing her first list of the day, which was actually a list of lists. She would need to make a list of jobs for the week ahead, a list of all of jobs that needed doing that day, and a list of things that needed doing around the house.

Today was different, however, because she was going away. Work could be forgotten for the next few days. Well, not completely forgotten—she wasn't the type of person who could wholly switch off from work—but being a self-employed accountant, she found it easy to take time off when she needed, and the Jane Austen Festival in Bath each September was an annual treat.

People would come from all over the world for the festival, taking part in the great costumed promenade through the beautiful Georgian streets and going to talks, dance lessons, and classes in etiquette and costume. It was an event that no true Janeite could miss.

The only thing that could make her forget her OCD was Jane Austen. When she immersed herself in Austen, her lists were forgotten, and she managed to stop thinking about the dust that might be accumulating behind her wardrobe and the fact that the vacuum marks in the carpet were no longer visible. Whenever she picked up one of the six perfect books or switched on the television to watch one of the wonderful adaptations, she could truly relax and become a person that she barely recognized. That was the power of Austen.

She first discovered Jane Austen when she was at school. Her English teacher was meant to be teaching them Charles Dickens's *Hard Times* but had rebelled and given each pupil a copy of *Pride and Prejudice* instead, and thus began a lifetime of romance for Sarah. Whenever she was feeling stressed, whenever life got too much for her and even she couldn't organise or control it to her liking, she could lose herself in the magical world of heroes and heroines, where love and laughter were guaranteed, and where a happy ending was absolutely essential.

Then, a few years ago, she discovered the Jane Austen Festival in Bath. It had been a complete revelation to her that, all over the world, there were fans who were as obsessed as she was of the Austen books and films. She made many new friends, and they were the loveliest people in the world. Well, you couldn't imagine a mean, nasty person adoring Jane Austen, could you?

And here she was packing her suitcase once again, except she was a little nervous this time; she hadn't been for the past two years. She and Mia usually attended together, dressing up in Regency costume and giggling their way around Bath together, eyeing up any young man who might be a contender for Mr Darcy, but that was before things had gone wrong, wasn't it?

She sighed and picked up a tiny silver photo frame that sat on a highly polished table by the side of her bed. It was a picture of her and Mia at Barton Cottage in Devon three years earlier. They were both squinting into the sun and laughing. How happy they both looked, and how long ago that all seemed now!

'Three long years,' Sarah said.

And not a single word spoken between them in all that time.

Acknowledgments

Many thanks to my lovely agent, Annette Green, who has been hidden under a pile of manuscripts since taking me on!

To Kate Bradley, Helen Bolton, Charlotte Allen, and the rest of the marvellous team at Avon. And to Deb Werksman and the team at Sourcebooks. I love working with you all.

Thanks to Clive and Sheila Anstey for their peaceful cottage, where it's always a pleasure to write, and to Tracey Marler for her perfect place in Lyme Regis.

To Natalie Manifold at the marvellous Literary Lyme Walking Tours, which I highly recommend.

To Teresa Flavin and Lynne Garner for their expertise on illustrations, and to Kath Eastman—an expert quotation finder.

To my dear friend, Gael, who is such an inspiration.

To Jo Terry for introducing me to lemon drizzle cake.

To Ann Channon and the team at the Jane Austen's House Museum in Chawton for their enthusiasm and support.

And to my wonderful friends on Twitter and Facebook—especially Heather Zerfahs and Emma Dye, who helped me choose Oli's car. And to my lovely friends at Austenauthors.com—a wonderful website for Janeites.

And, as ever, huge thanks to my husband, Roy. I'm so lucky that he loves Lyme Regis as much as I do.

About the Author

Victoria Connelly was brought up in Norfolk and studied English literature at Worcester University before becoming a teacher in North Yorkshire. After getting married in a medieval castle in the Yorkshire Dales, she moved to London, where she lives with her artist husband and a mad Springer spaniel.

She has three novels published in Germany, and the first, *Flights of Angels*, was made into a film. Victoria and her husband flew out to Berlin to see it being filmed and got to be extras in it. Her first novel in the UK, *Molly's Millions*, is a romantic comedy about a lottery winner who gives it all away.

Dreaming of Mr. Darcy is second in a trilogy about Jane Austen addicts, which is a wonderful excuse to read all the books and watch all the gorgeous film and TV adaptations again. First in the trilogy is *A Weekend with Mr. Darcy*.